Carlucci's Edge
PHILIP K. DICK SPECIAL AWARD-WINNER

''Multiply everything sad, sordid, and hopelessly romantic about the City by a factor of ten, and you've got Richard Russo's San Francisco of the mid-21st century. Serial murders, cyborgs, foxy ladies, wise street kids, and a tough ex-cop with a good heart and bad karma—Russo is mining a classic American vein.''
— Ursula K. Le Guin

''Russo's latest SF crime novel is mean streets, callous mega-corps, venal politicians, and ordinary lowlifes in a jam . . . Russo's characters succeed in stirring our empathy, but their strangeness is what holds our attention.'' —*Analog*

''Russo has an excellent eye for the urban landscape [and] the crime writer's well-tuned ear for vernacular . . . from street punks right up to the high-level officials.''
—*Asimov's Science Fiction*

''Russo's people and their obsessions are delightfully real.''
—*Analog*

''The characters are well-crafted, the setting interesting and vivid, and the pacing is brisk.''   —*Uncle Hugo's Newsletter*

continued . . .

"As in the Carlucci books, Russo uses the extremes of human experience to explore central moral issues. The result is a strong novel by a writer who has been doing fine work for years. Russo is overdue for a breakout book; maybe *Ship of Fools* will give him the larger audience his work certainly deserves."
—*Asimov's Science Fiction*

"Relentlessly suspenseful, full of mystery, and with a very exciting ending. Russo just keeps on getting better from book to book."
—*Science Fiction Chronicle*

"At one level, this is the best piece of hard SF I have read for a long time. But the book is much more than that: it has subtexts below subtexts below subtexts. It's the kind of book that people pin you to the bar about at parties; it's the kind of book that academics will argue over; it's the kind of book you'll start off reading with the expectation of the Sense of Wonder and discover you never before fully understood what the expression 'Sense of Wonder' actually meant; it's the kind of book that would make a marvellous movie but a movie after the watching of which the cognoscenti would say: 'You thought *that* was good? Wait'll you read the novel . . .' Oh, go and read this book. It'll save me having to explain any further why you should."
—*Infinity Plus*

"*Ship of Fools* is a highly successful fusion of SF and the macabre, perhaps best construed as *Alien* with an intellect . . . [I]t will be remembered . . . for its powerfully iconic scenes and settings—stained glass windows shining upon the void, charnel houses in space, colloquies in artificial deserts, chambers of treacherous gravity. Russo has added to the ranks of the fine metaphysical thrillers, no mean achievement."
—*Interzone*

Ship OF Fools

RICHARD PAUL RUSSO

ACE BOOKS, NEW YORK

This is a work of fiction. Names, characters, places, and incidents either
are the product of the author's imagination or are used fictitiously,
and any resemblance to actual persons, living or dead, business
establishments, events, or locales is entirely coincidental.

SHIP OF FOOLS

An Ace Book / published by arrangement with the author

PRINTING HISTORY
Ace mass-market edition / January 2002

All rights reserved
Copyright © 2001 by Richard Paul Russo.
Cover art by Bruce Jensen.
Cover design by Finn Winterson.
Text design by Tiffany Kukec.

Visit our website at
www.penguinputnam.com
Check out the ACE Science Fiction & Fantasy newsletter!

ISBN: 0-441-00893-3

ACE®
Ace Books are published by The Berkley Publishing Group,
a division of Penguin Putnam Inc., 375 Hudson Street,
New York, New York 10014.
ACE and the "A" design are trademarks belonging to Penguin Putnam Inc.

PRINTED IN THE UNITED STATES OF AMERICA

10 9 8 7 6 5 4 3 2 1

Acknowledgments

I can't adequately thank my wife, Candace, who read the entire manuscript several times and made numerous suggestions and corrections, large and small, gently persisting even when I got defensive. This is a better book because of her.

I'd also like to thank Karen Fowler for her many invaluable suggestions on an early draft of this novel, and, once again, for her friendship and encouragement over the years.

My thanks, too, go to my editor, Susan Allison, who helped me bring this book into focus.

Finally, a belated thanks to my long-time friends Patricia Miranda and Paul Katz for their medical expertise and help with my previous book, *Carlucci's Heart*. I inexcusably neglected to acknowledge their contributions then, but do so now with apologies. Thank you both.

For Candace
All my love

Ship OF Fools

PART ONE

Insurrection

1

WE had not made landfall in more than fourteen years. One disastrous choice of a star after another. The captain viewed this string of failures as absurdly bad luck; the bishop, as divine intervention. Either way, I saw it as prelude to the captain's downfall, which would almost certainly mean my own downfall as well.

When we detected a transmission from the world that would later be called Antioch, I sensed opportunity. But opportunity for whom? The captain, or his enemies? It was impossible to say. The captain's position was tenuous at best, and everything was uncertain aboard the *Argonos*.

I was exploring one of the dark, abandoned vaults of disabled machinery deep in the core of the ship, studying a length of cable scorched and fused at one end, neatly severed at the other. Shiny blackened metal sparkled in the light of my hand torch. The air was warm and stuffy and smelled faintly of burnt plastic and old lubricants. There were dozens of such rooms on the *Argonos*, some quite small, others like this one—large vaulted chambers that had become dumping grounds for machinery that had ceased to function and which could no longer be repaired or salvaged. I loved those rooms and spent hours in them, hoping to find some engine or device I could rebuild and bring back to life.

I swung the hand torch around, widened the beam, and aimed it upward. Great, massive chains hung from the ceiling far above, shiny silver-blue stars of reflection glittering down at me as if the metal were wet and dripping. Entwined in one of them was a longer section of cable much like the one I held in my hand; it, too, appeared to be severed, near the point where it emerged from the bottom link. I was mystified.

A winged creature flapped through the beam, an amorphous shadow that seemed to flicker in and out of existence as it flew. It swerved abruptly and dove. Eyes gleamed at me for a moment; then the creature canted away and out of the light with a hushed flutter of air.

A terrible grinding vibrated through the chamber and I instinctively snapped off the hand torch. The grinding slowly faded, but was followed by scraping noises and the clanging of metal against metal. I stood motionless, listening, waiting for my eyes to adjust to the darkness. Dull red glowed in the distance, a glow that seemed to gradually brighten.

The scraping and clanging ceased, replaced by a low, deep rumble. Then I heard a voice. Too faint, too distant to make out, yet familiar.

I wanted to get closer, but trying to move blindly through all that broken and rusted machinery would be dangerous as well as noisy. I adjusted the hand torch to its dimmest setting, aimed it down at the floor, and turned it back on. There was just enough light to see my footing; I decided the risk of detection was low, and moved forward.

Progress was slow: the way was rarely clear, I was trying to be quiet, and my club foot was a minor hindrance. As I got closer, I felt even warmer; sweat trickled down my sides, itching. Sometimes I heard the voice, sometimes more scraping or banging, sometimes grunting. The red glow intensified as I neared it, and soon it was bright enough to light my way.

A horrendous metallic squealing tore at my eardrums and brought me to a halt. It ceased abruptly, and I was just about to take another step when I heard the voice again; this time I recognized it: Bishop Soldano. His deep, resonant baritone was unmistakable, though I still could not make out any words. Who was he talking to? Himself?

My exoskeleton vibrated twice in succession, and I silently cursed. It was a signal from the captain. I felt a nagging irritation, more at myself than at Nikos; the signaling system had been my idea, and this wasn't the first time I'd regretted it. I ignored it and crept forward, pulled myself across a tangle of wire mesh between two huge rusting cylinders, then through a corroded structure of bent and twisted metal rods.

I was seven or eight meters above the floor of a large, hollowed-out bay. Below me were the bishop, three shirtless men, and two enormous pieces of machinery that dwarfed the men beside them. One machine was dark and lifeless, resting on a crude, wheeled platform. The other shook and rumbled and glowed a deep red from rings of crimson-tinted lights circling the upper cylindrical section; pipe and cable snaked up from the floor, feeding into the base, and heat radiated from it in waves. The three men strained at the platform, pushing it closer and struggling to align the massive couplings of the two machines.

The bishop watched, frowning and silent now. In the red glow, his large, shaved head glistened with beads of sweat. He was a big man, nearly two full meters in height and a hundred and twenty-five kilos or more in weight. He wore a plain black cassock and heavy black boots.

The wheeled platform stopped moving, less than a meter from the rumbling engine, and the three men fell back, exhausted. They were drenched in sweat and breathing heavily. The bishop stepped forward, and I thought he was going to shout at them, but he only nodded.

"Good," he said. "Once more, men. Once more and we'll be there."

The three men looked up at him, then rose together and leaned into the platform, grunting and straining again. The platform barely moved, the wheels turning almost imperceptibly, scraping the floor; then it lurched forward, and the two machines united with a loud and satisfying crash.

The bishop smiled; when he did, the three men smiled with him, and the expression on their faces was one of admiration . . . and worship. The bishop stepped forward, attached cables and plugs, worked some levers and wheels; then the second machine came to life.

Everything about the machines changed now. The rumble quieted, overcome by a steady thrum, an electric vibration that seemed to penetrate muscle, even bone. The bishop's smile broadened, and he gazed at the great engines as he might upon his congregation, his skin glowing and his eyes shining. He put his hand on the shoulder of the nearest man and nodded.

"Good work, men. Good work."

The bishop watched for another minute or two, as if lost in a trance. Then he nodded to himself, still smiling, and shut down both machines, bringing silence and darkness to the chamber.

A few moments later a lantern came to life. Stark shadows fluttered all around them, and I pulled back farther within the metal cage.

"Let us go," the bishop said. "A good day's work, and we will have many more. Our day is coming."

The man with the lantern led the way, the bishop followed, and the two other men came last, walking side by side. They walked up a wide, gently sloping ramp, then out through a large opening in the chamber walls and into a broad corridor. Long after I lost sight of them, I could see the gradually fading light moving up and down, side to side.

The bishop was building a machine. It was not the first, and probably not the last—if anything, the bishop was more fascinated with these old devices and engines than I was. I switched on the hand torch and cast its full beam on the lifeless metal below me. What was it? I had no idea, but with the bishop involved I felt distinctly uncomfortable, even afraid.

The exoskeleton vibrated once again. I'd been able to ignore it all this time, but I couldn't anymore. Whatever the captain wanted me for, it had to be important. I turned away from the bishop's machine, and made my way back.

2

I was the captain's adviser. Bartolomeo Aguilera, counselor to Captain Nikos Costa; his unofficial lieutenant. There were others, of course, who offered their counsel, others in the official chain of command, but I was the one who really mattered. Many were hostile to me for this, many feared me, and a few, I believe, actually respected me. Most of them, as far as I knew, disliked me, sometimes even the captain.

But I was content with that. It suited me.

I am not an ugly man, but I am deformed. I was born with hands attached almost directly to my shoulders, on vestigial arms that are, even now, no more than a dozen centimeters in length, though my hands and fingers are almost normal in size and shape, and function quite well. Several vertebrae are missing, but the spinal cord itself is intact. I have a club foot.

Throughout my infancy and childhood I was fitted with a series of prosthetic arms and hands which I could manipulate from within by my own hands and fingers. I was also fitted with special spinal braces to support my body; synthetic vertebrae were devised to protect the spinal cord.

The limbs were made to look like real flesh, muscle, and

bone, but when I reached adulthood and full growth—slightly taller than average—and was ready for my permanent prosthetics, I chose to have them constructed of shining metal, plastic, and steelglass. I also had the spinal braces augmented with a metal, cage-like exoskeleton which I attach over my clothing each day after I have dressed. For the club foot I did nothing to compensate. My boot was constructed to fit the twisted shape of my foot.

With the augmentation of the exoskeleton, braces, club foot, and my shining arms, I limp swiftly and magnificently along wherever I go. I have never wished to hide my differences. I prefer to celebrate them.

S EVERAL hours after first receiving his signal, I entered the captain's command salon, a steelglass bubble on the forward surface of the *Argonos*, protected from the ravages of space by deflectors and a retractable canopy of anodized metal. The canopy was open when I walked in, and the clear dome revealed thousands of stars shining with a hard and icy light. Surrounded by all those stars, I felt disoriented, afraid I would lose my balance if I moved too quickly.

Nikos sat slumped in the command chair in the center of the room. He was staring at a flat monitor screen mounted on a vertical support that rose from the floor. A steady pulsing light moved slowly and regularly across the screen. He turned and looked at me, but didn't say a word.

Nikos was a strong, dark-haired man with a neatly trimmed beard and deep blue eyes. Gray had begun to appear in his hair despite the re-gen treatments, and more recently dark crescents had become permanent fixtures beneath those blue eyes. He was not sleeping well. He hadn't admitted this to me, but I knew, just as I knew about the hours he spent alone in the Wasteland; the seven-year-old downsider daughter he had with a woman not his wife; and his clandestine meetings with Arne Gronvold, who had been banished to the lower levels nearly six years earlier. I was his shadow, though he was unaware of this.

I had known Nikos nearly all my life, and there was little I did not know about him. On the other hand, though Nikos had known me equally as long, there was much he did not know about me, much he did not understand, and this, I suspect, frightened him at times. He was wary of me and did not trust me completely. Yet I had never betrayed him in any way. I admired him more than he knew.

I felt he was holding back, as if reluctant to inform me of something important.

"What is it?" I finally asked.

"That," he said, and pointed at the pulsing light. "It's a transmission from the fourth planet."

I felt an electric buzzing down my deformed spine. We were approaching a planetary system, and had been traveling under conventional propulsion for several months now. We were still weeks out from the star, the circling planets laid out like a disk in our path. After so many disappointments, everyone was afraid to hope we would find anything this time. A transmission? It had the potential to change *everything* on this ship.

I turned and watched the light on the monitor. "So there's someone there."

"Questionable. It isn't much of a transmission. A steady, unvarying pulse, no change of wavelength, duration, or intensity. There's no content. And nothing else has been picked up."

"But someone *was* there," I said. "At one time, someone must have been there. Maybe an entire colony."

"Probably."

"Then something will remain. There could even be people still alive down there, in trouble, waiting for help."

Nikos gazed up and out at the stars surrounding us, and I realized he was wondering whether this would save him, or accelerate his demise.

"Does the bishop know?"

Nikos shook his head. "Not yet. But I'll have to inform him soon. Today."

"And what will the bishop do?" I asked.

Nikos just shrugged. He had been like this for too long

now—despondent, apathetic, almost lost, as if he had already given up hope of remaining captain of the *Argonos*. It was unlike him, and I had worried about it for some time.

"We need to be careful," Nikos finally said. At last he turned from the stars and looked at me. "I have to call a session of the Executive Council. Make the arrangements."

"Do I tell them about this?" I asked, nodding at the pulsing light.

"Yes. Most will find out before you talk to them anyway." He gave me a halfhearted smile, but it quickly faded. "Make it for tomorrow night. I need time to think."

Yes, I thought, we *all* needed time to think. But he had better not take too long. I nodded, and left.

T I M E. There wasn't much of it left to Nikos because the ship was in crisis—we had not made landfall in all these years, and we had no unified mission. We were traveling almost at random through the galaxy, had been for decades, if not centuries, and there was no consensus of purpose or goal. This had always been the case, at least during my lifetime, but we had never gone quite so many years without landfall of one kind or another. Uncertainty and a deep restlessness, which had spread throughout the ship in recent months, was now intensifying as we approached our newest destination.

Some had suggested we return to the place from which we began this voyage. But to which beginning? To the last place we actually set foot on dry land? Returning to that place was impossible. To the land we came from before that? Much the same story there. There had always been good reasons for leaving our landfalls and continuing on with our voyage.

Why not, then, return to our original home? The ship was our home. Nearly every one of us had been born aboard the *Argonos*, and most of us would die on the ship before our corpses were launched into the cold black reaches of space. No one knew where the ship was first built, or first launched, though there was plenty of speculation. Many suggested Earth, the legendary birthplace of humankind. That, I believed, was the most likely. But returning to Earth was not an option, either. We had already tried that once, years before I was born. All they found was a toxic, irradiated world, in ruins and abandoned.

The bishop, on the other hand, claimed the ship had *always* existed—a "Mystery" that was usually a large part of his conversion sermons, a large part of his basic theology. A large part of his nonsense.

So we went on, searching for land, sailing from star to star through the unending universal night. Because of the vast distances involved, and the complexities and imprecision of the subspace jumps (which I do not pretend to understand), combined with the time spent under conventional propulsion, we had managed to visit only four stars in the last fourteen years. The first three, while orbited by planetary systems, offered up not a single world close to being habitable; certainly no signs of past human visits. The last star was a desolate solo without even a barren ball of rock in orbit. It was after the visit to the fourth star, as great a failure as was possible, that the captain's power and influence began to seriously decline, and the calls for new leadership began in earnest.

An astute and clever politician, Nikos had hung on to his position despite the pressures, but we both knew he could not last much longer. The ship's original mission, whatever it was, had become irrelevant. What mattered now was the ship's current mission, and its future leadership. Both were quite undecided.

3

THE Executive Council met in the dead of shipboard night. I was not an official member of the council, though I attended all council sessions, seated in a corner of the room; it was a perspective I actually preferred. Nikos sat at the head of the long, wooden table, and there were four seats on either side. His table keypad glowed faintly in front of him, but the wall screens were dark. To his left was Aiyana, his wife—a nonvoting member. To his right was the bishop.

To Aiyana's left was Rocco Costino, head of Maintenance; he was the bishop's man, no matter what the circumstances. Beside him sat Susanna Hingen, the ship's quartermaster, an organized but thoroughly unimaginative woman. Next came Margita Cardenas, the chief engineer—she was thoughtful and intelligent, and I had more respect for her than for anyone else on the council.

On the opposite side of the table, to the bishop's right, sat General Marshal Wainwright in full dress uniform emblazoned with medals and ribbons that were purely ceremonial—the man had never participated in an actual military action in his life. His eyes were slightly dilated, he licked his lips repeatedly, and his hands were afflicted with a dis-

cernible palsy; he was a Passion addict in the terminal
stages. Next to the general was Michel Tournier, the ap-
pointed representative of the First Echelon, the ruling circle
of the ship's upper levels; he was a handsome but empty-
headed man. Last was August Toller, the oldest man on the
Argonos at nearly a hundred and forty standard years, and
the ship's official historian (though hardly anyone ever read
his accounts); he walked with the aid of a wooden cane
that he claimed had originally come from Earth.

Maximilian, the chief steward, came in with a tray of
coffee and tea and iced fruit nectars; he served the drinks,
setting cups and glasses before each member of the council
according to their usual requests. He left pots and pitchers
in the middle of the table, and retreated.

Nikos was about to speak when the bishop straightened,
leaned forward, and said, "We will be making landfall soon,
and I shall appoint the exploration team."

Nikos was so stunned he did not know how to respond.
I was just as stunned, as was everyone else on the council.
This was bad. The meeting had hardly begun, and already
Nikos had lost control of it.

"What the hell are you talking about?" Nikos finally
managed to say.

"We all know about the transmission," the bishop said.
"We know we've adjusted our course. We will be making
landfall, and I just wanted to assume some of the burdens.
You are a busy man, Captain. I want to help. It is quite
simple."

"It's *not* that simple," Nikos said. "First, we don't
know what the environmental conditions will be like, and
we won't be making landfall on a world we can't live on."

The bishop sighed. "My understanding is that initial
readings are very favorable. Is my understanding inaccurate?"

After a brief hesitation, Nikos replied. "No, your understanding is not inaccurate, but the data is very preliminary."
He paused, and I knew he was angry, wondering where the
bishop was getting his information. "But even if environmental conditions are favorable, we have no idea what the

social conditions are—who, if anyone, is living there, and what the situation is. We need to discuss the possibilities so we can be prepared for whatever we might find. Our last landfall, if we all remember, was a major disaster. I'm certain *you* remember, Bishop.''

I could barely keep from smiling. That last landfall, nearly fifteen years ago, was the *bishop's* disaster—he tried to convert people who did not want to be converted. We were driven away by angry mobs eager to rend us limb from limb. Several of us *were* killed before we made our escape. But the bishop waved his hand in a gesture of dismissal; he had never accepted, or admitted, that he was in any way responsible for what happened.

''Nothing like that is likely to occur again. Those people were barbarians. I don't think we need to worry about the 'social' circumstances. Certainly we will try to contact anyone who remains, and there will be specific plans, but those are logistical details which will be worked out over the coming days.'' He paused, obviously for effect. ''What we do *not* need at this point, after all these years of failure, is timidity. We need an assertive plan of action—an exploration team ready and waiting, and then landfall. I will take responsibility for it. It's quite straightforward. If there is a problem, say so, and we can have a discussion and vote.''

Time and tension stretched interminably. Nikos was livid, but he knew there wasn't much he could say or do. Finally General Wainwright spoke.

''Yes,'' he said, his voice shaking almost as much as his hands. ''That sounds like a perfectly reasonable approach. My soldiers will provide the necessary protection; yes, I will see that the arrangements are made. Yes, yes . . .'' His voice trailed off as if he were speaking to himself, which he probably was.

The bishop looked around the table, his gaze ending on me, in the corner of the room. ''Any other comments? Objections?'' No one replied. They all saw how it was going. Besides, it was what everyone expected would happen eventually, assuming there were no unexpected surprises, and no one saw any percentage in coming to Nikos's defense. At

least not yet. The bishop turned his attention to Nikos.
"Captain?"

Nikos shook his head. "No, I have nothing else to say
for the moment."

"More at another time?" the bishop suggested.

"Yes," Nikos replied. "Another time. And much more."
But his words sounded hollow.

"Good. One final thing," the bishop said. "Two days
from now is Holy Thursday. I am preparing a special sermon related to our forthcoming landfall. I expect you all to
attend." With that, Bishop Soldano rose to his feet and
walked out, effectively ending the meeting on his own.

The other council members remained seated, waiting for
Nikos to formally close the meeting. Most would not look
at him. Even Aiyana kept her gaze averted, and stared at
the table. He closed the meeting, and we left.

NIKOS, of course, was not happy with the way the
council meeting went, and was especially unhappy with
the way it ended.

He and I and Aiyana went to his personal stateroom
afterward, and when he asked Aiyana to leave, she glared
at me with jealous hatred. She could not bear her regular
exclusion from our private conferences, and I did not blame
her—she had always wanted to consider herself an equal
partner in everything, including the running of the *Argonos*.
This had caused so much friction between Aiyana and Nikos
that their marriage had become as shaky as his position on
the ship.

When she had gone, Nikos sat slumped on the wall
couch and dimmed the stateroom lights. A dozen small orange globes near the ceiling provided the only illumination,
casting moving shadows as they drifted randomly above us.
I sat in the padded chair behind his desk.

"Bishop Soldano is preparing to move against you,"
I said.

"He has been for a while," Nikos replied, as if that
could minimize what was happening.

"Yes, but now he can hardly restrain himself. He is no longer waiting for the opportunity, he is working to *create* the opportunity."

Nikos said nothing, just seemed to sink further into thought, or despair.

For one of the few times I could recall, I had no idea what the captain was thinking. Was he completely aware of what was going on, planning strategy and tactics to deal with the situation? Or was he somehow oblivious to the real dangers? Or, even worse, was he aware but incapable of responding to the threats? Was I seeing the beginning of his end?

Nikos did have strong tradition on his side, and the First Echelon would be extremely reluctant to break with that tradition, if only because doing so might threaten their own security. Though technically an elected position, in practice the captaincy was inherited, and had resided within the Costa-Malvini clan for several generations. Also, though it might not be true any longer, Nikos had been a good captain for many years, as had his father and his great-uncle before him.

But the situation had deteriorated badly. Nikos was losing respect and authority, and tradition would not hold sway much longer. Nikos had no direct heir, his nephew was an idiot, and no one else within the clan displayed either the qualities or the desire to be captain, which meant the captaincy after Nikos would be open to outsiders for the first time in decades. The situation brought out ambition everywhere. Especially in the bishop.

"The bishop wants to be captain," I finally said.

In response, Nikos chuckled.

"I know that, Bartolomeo. At first, I thought he merely wanted to remove me and replace me with a figurehead that he could control. But no, you're right, he wants to be captain himself." He nodded. "The bishop is a fool."

That was the Captain Nikos Costa I had known all my life, and I felt a little better when I heard his words, his confidence.

"I'm preparing for him," Nikos said, looking at me with a sly grin.

"How?" I asked.

But Nikos shook his head. "My plans aren't completely ready yet, Bartolomeo. The bishop will not move until after the landfall, when he will attempt to either take credit for any successes, or place blame for any failures. By then, I will be ready. I will let you know what I have in mind; you will give me your advice, and we will be ready for him."

I had worried about Nikos, but it was as if he needed to be faced with a real threat to stir him, to bring out his cunning and his political strengths. Now that I could see he was prepared, I felt confident again. I thought everything would be all right.

4

THERE was a dwarf who lived in the lower levels of the ship, and I visited him often. His name was Pär. He was less than a meter in height—ninety-two centimeters, to be precise—yet he was strong and powerful. Although he was relatively well-proportioned, his head was slightly too large for his body; his face was heavily wrinkled, and he had always looked like an old man, even when he was young.

We distrusted one another, but this was tempered with mutual respect and admiration—he for my position of influence with the captain, and I for his intelligence and cunning.

I went to see Pär before the bishop's sermon. Dirt and grime and stink all increased the farther you descended through the ship. Poor maintenance and different lifestyles. The downsiders actually cooked most of their meals in their own cabins, adding huge quantities of spices and other enhancers to give flavor and texture to the processed food product which provided the bulk of their diet, and you could smell it; the air circulation systems functioned inefficiently down there. In many ways, the lower levels felt more real.

Pär's quarters consisted of two rooms filled with so much

detritus I was always surprised it didn't spill into the corridors whenever the door was opened. Stacks of shipping crates formed tables and counters which were covered by candles, music modules, hardcopy books and pamphlets, wood and stone carvings, drawing and painting supplies, strange bits of clothing and strings of beads, tiny glass figurines. The walls were almost completely concealed by pictures and drawings, photographs and framed strips of fabric. Some of this had been created by people aboard the ship, but much of it had been collected by earlier generations during landfalls on populated worlds.

Pär served coffee when I arrived—the best coffee anywhere on the ship, and the only time I drank it black. Pär and two other downsiders cultivated a clandestine coffee plantation in one of the ag chambers, kept most of the beans for themselves, and bartered the rest. Another reason I visited frequently. He settled into the cushions of his small bed, and I sat on a thickly padded chair that folded out from the wall.

A furry, elongated snout topped by two tiny black eyes poked out from the jumbled contents of one of the crates. It was Skate, one of a couple hundred stennets that now lived on the *Argonos*, making themselves pets of a sort, adopting people throughout the ship. Someone had brought two mated pairs aboard fourteen years ago, at our last landfall. They were long and thin, about half the size of cats, and were now more numerous.

Skate sniffed once, opened her mouth to reveal small but extremely sharp teeth—she seemed to be smiling at me—then pulled back and disappeared.

"She likes you," Pär said. "Usually she won't even make an appearance, but she always says hello when you come."

"I feel honored." I drank some coffee and sank back in the chair.

Pär sat up and looked intently at me. "There won't be any survivors," he said, referring to our new destination.

I nodded. He was right. No one had said it aloud in the Executive Council session, but we all knew.

"It doesn't take brilliant analysis," Pär went on. "A single, steady signal, no other electromagnetic emissions of any kind." He shook his head, almost smiling. "There's no one alive down there. Either they've all died, or there was never anyone there—maybe it's some emitter left behind by a commercial exploration team that discovered nothing of value, or impossible conditions." Then he shrugged as if the matter did not concern him much, but I knew him better than that. "What does Captain Nikos say?"

Pär was the only one who called him that. To everyone else he was either Nikos, Captain Costa, or simply "the captain."

"Nothing much." I was always reluctant to be too forthcoming with Pär. We traded information—the real key to our relationship—and I didn't like to give away what might later turn out to be valuable. "He is unsure what effect our landfall will have on the ship's dynamics."

"He is in trouble no matter what we find." Pär said this with a nasty, almost gloating smile. "Abandoned colony, *dead* colony, even a surviving outpost or a full-fledged settlement with towns or cities spread out around the planet—though that, of course, is the least likely possibility. All of those would be bad, some worse than others. What your captain should hope for is that we find a planet completely uninhabitable for humans."

Pär was wrong about that. The captain's position was so tenuous that he feared almost any change in the ship's routine, even if it appeared aimless. The captain was wise to be afraid. But if *something* didn't change soon, nothing would help him.

"If the planet *is* habitable, however," Pär resumed, "any number of possibilities present themselves."

"Like what?"

"Colonization. For instance."

I just shook my head. Those in the upper levels, particularly in the First Echelon, had always resisted any moves in that direction, but I didn't want to get into a discussion with him about it.

"Why not?" Pär asked.

"You know why not."

"That's no answer. What are you people afraid of?"

"Just drop it," I told him.

Pär stared at me with that ancient wrinkled face, his expression hard, and I was afraid he was going to push it. Then his face sagged and he slowly shook his head.

We talked some time longer, but about nothing else of import. I stayed long enough for another cup of coffee and a glass of his homemade distilled liquor. He called it whiskey, but it was far less successful than his coffee.

As I was leaving, Pär said, "Things will be changing. Think about that. You and I can work together. We can be of use to one another."

I didn't want to encourage him, however, so I left without giving him a response. I did not trust him. But then I did not trust anyone, not even the captain.

B ISHOP Soldano always managed to make major announcements on holy days. On that Holy Thursday, his voice booming from speakers mounted throughout the cathedral, he announced to an almost full congregation what most people already knew—that a signal had been detected. What *was* surprising, however, was that the bishop had given the planet a name.

"If there are people on this planet who have already christened their world," the bishop began, "then it shall be called by the name they have given it. If, however, they have not given it a name, or if there are no people there, it shall be called Antioch, after one of the great, early centers of Christian learning on Earth. It was in Antioch that many different peoples were brought the word of God. I will read from Acts:

"*Now those who were scattered because of the persecution that arose over Stephen traveled as far as Phoenicia and Cyprus and Antioch, speaking the word to none except Jews. But there were some of them, men of Cyprus and Cyrene, who on coming to Antioch spoke to the Greeks also, preaching the Lord Jesus. And the hand of the Lord was with them, and a great number that believed turned to the Lord. News of this came to the church in Jerusalem, and they sent Barnabas to Antioch. When he came and saw the grace of God, he was glad; and he exhorted them all to remain faithful to the Lord with steadfast purpose; for he was a good man, full of the Holy Spirit and faith. And a large company was added to the Lord."*

I laughed to myself, hearing that, for I couldn't help thinking about what had happened on our last landfall, when the bishop tried to do something similar—convert a city, an entire colony, to the Church—although in his case he attempted to do it by force, not by words. A disaster, as I have already mentioned. He should have read the Bible more carefully.

The bishop paused, and I nearly nodded off. Protocol required me to attend holy day services, but protocol couldn't always keep me awake, especially when the bishop preached. I tipped my head back and stared up into the shadowed reaches of the vaulting high above me, thinking about this vast and solemn place and thinking, as the bishop wanted, about the uncertain mission of the *Argonos*.

The bishop claimed the ship's mission was to spread the word of God throughout the galaxy, even throughout the entire universe, to man and alien alike (there was no recorded contact with intelligent alien life that anyone was aware of, but the bishop continued to hope). The bishop pointed to his unshakable faith and his exalted position in the ship's hierarchy as evidence for the religious nature of the ship's mission, which I found unconvincing. What *was* convincing, however, was the existence of the cathedral.

There could be little doubt that the cathedral had been incorporated into the original design of the ship. The occasional suggestion that the cathedral had been built into the ship at some far later date, after the Church had forced its way into a stronger position within the ship's social structure, was absurd. Structural engineers pointed to the cathedral's size and its central location, as well as the way the ship's infrastructure so perfectly accommodated it. The main section of the cathedral was over 450 meters in length and

125 meters in height, with a set of enormous stained-glass windows behind the apse actually comprising a section of the ship's outer hull. Physical deflectors and an array of energy shields protected the stained-glass from the forces and debris of interstellar travel. There were also extensions from the cathedral and other connected aisles and chapels that ran throughout that level of the *Argonos*, culminating in the galilee, a small, private, and secured chapel which had its own much smaller stained-glass windows lit from an interior light source.

I looked back at the bishop, trying to remain alert, hoping to get some idea of what he planned for Antioch, and for Nikos.

"Bring people the word of God: that is one of the most important things we can do. The exploration and colonization of worlds presents us with one of our greatest opportunities to do just that. Human and alien alike, we all need God, we all need to know His word and His works. It is one of our missions to bring the word of God to those who are ignorant of Him, and to establish outposts on those places where others may come in the future."

I started losing interest again because he was moving on to one of his regular sermons. The bishop's dream was to set up an intergalactic network of missions committed to converting all intelligent beings, "human and alien alike," and bringing them into the Church.

He had visions of grandeur, and he was arrogant. But he had a great deal of power, which was growing day by day as Nikos's power waned. I sat through the rest of his sermon, no longer listening, but watching him, and I grew more and more afraid that I was seeing my future.

5

THE *Argonos* was still seventeen days out from Antioch when I returned to the chamber to check on the bishop's progress with his new machine. I wanted to know what it was; I needed to be prepared.

After stepping inside the chamber and closing the door quietly behind me, I stood motionless in the darkness and listened. I couldn't hear anything except a distant *ticking* sound that could have been metal cooling, or water dripping, or perhaps something else altogether. No light or glow of any color. The air was cooler, with a hint of moisture.

I switched on my hand torch and made my way through the chamber, choosing a path by guesswork; there were no lights or sounds to guide me this time, although I knew the general direction. Twice I thought I heard something, footsteps perhaps, but both times when I stopped to listen I heard only the faint *ticking* and other ambient sounds.

I finally reached familiar territory—the two large cylinders and the corroded metal structure I had crawled through the last time I had been here. Once again I was perched above the open bay. This time, however, there was only a silent, lifeless structure below me; no bishop, no other men.

There was no easy way down, so I worked my way

around the upper edge of the bay to the far end and the ramp leading down into it from a large, open corridor. I walked down the ramp, my footsteps echoing dully, and approached the massive structure. It seemed dead and somehow incomplete. Perhaps the bishop had abandoned it and moved on to other projects.

A metallic scraping noise startled me, followed by a cry of pain. I swung around, sweeping the torch beam across the jungle of broken machinery surrounding the bay. The light caught a pair of eyes that tried to pull back. I steadied the beam and held it on the face of a boy staring down at me from above a mound of twisted wire and metal. The boy tried to shift to the side, then back again, but his foot and leg were caught in the wire, and it seemed that the more he struggled against it, the deeper his leg went.

"Don't be afraid," I said to him. "It's all right, I'm not going to hurt you."

But the boy kept struggling, and there was panic in his eyes. I wondered whether he didn't understand me, or didn't believe me.

I moved the light away from his face and walked back up the ramp, then worked my way toward him. I stopped when I was still several meters away, and aimed the light at the tangle of metal and wire that trapped his leg. I tried talking to him again.

"I won't hurt you. I just want to help you get your leg free. Do you understand me?"

I moved the light up just enough so that its halo faintly illuminated his face. The panic had changed to defiance, but I was certain the fear was still there, camouflaged. He couldn't have been more than thirteen or fourteen years old.

"My name's Bartolomeo," I said. "What's yours?"

The boy finally spoke. "Let me see your face," he demanded.

I swung the torch around and lit up my face from below.

"You look weird," he said. "What's that metal behind your neck?"

"Part of my exoskeleton."

"What's that?"

"A special support for my body, for my back and neck. My spine is . . . defective." I tried again. "What's your name?"

He hesitated, grimaced, then said, "Francis."

"A saint's name." An automatic response, which I immediately regretted. The boy's grimace twisted even more.

"Yeah, that's what my mom told me. But I'm no saint, and I never will be."

I turned the light back onto his trapped leg and started slowly forward. "Let me help you with that. You don't want to get stuck in this place. No one would ever find you in here, and you'd starve to death."

"*You* found me," Francis said. "And that big bald guy would come around pretty soon. I wouldn't starve."

"The big bald guy? You mean the bishop?"

"I don't know." I was right next to the boy now and I could see him shrug. "He comes here and other places, and he builds machines."

Yes . . . he builds machines. I knelt beside the boy and aimed the light down into the chaotic webwork of metal and wire. His leg was buried in it to midthigh.

"Any idea what that machine does?" I asked the boy.

"Not really. Makes a weird sound and it gets real hot. But it doesn't go anywhere. He likes these old machines, he likes to make them work."

"You don't know who the bishop is?"

"No."

"Have you ever been to the cathedral?" I began carefully pulling and pushing at the wire around his thigh, creating a gap around his trouser leg.

"Is that the big church?"

"Yes."

"I've never been there." He paused, and I could almost sense him staring down at me. "Your arms aren't real."

"They're real," I replied. "They're just not flesh and muscle and bone."

"They're not real," he insisted.

I nodded, smiling to myself. "I guess you have a point."

"And there's something wrong with your foot."

"Yes, club foot. I was born that way."

"Your body's pretty messed up."

"Yes. But I get by just fine. No, don't move your leg yet; hold still until I tell you to pull." A twisted metal rod had become wedged against his knee. I couldn't get a good grip on it, but I pulled at it anyway. My fingers slipped; I grabbed the rod again, grip better this time, and managed to pry it a few centimeters away from his leg.

"All right, try pulling your foot out now, slowly."

The leg came up a bit, but his foot was caught almost immediately. It was stuck underneath a bundle of corroded wire.

"Can you straighten your ankle and twist your foot around to the right a little?"

There was some slight movement, but he stopped. "It hurts," he said.

"All right, let me work on it some more." I lay down on my stomach and stretched my arm far down, grabbed the bundled wire, and pulled. There is a lot of strength in my prosthetic fingers and arms; suddenly the wires broke apart and the boy's foot came free. He pulled his leg and foot all the way out and stumbled backwards. He sat down on a metal bench that was attached to a dark blue apparatus littered with broken rubber belts.

"Are you all right?" I asked.

Francis nodded. "Foot still hurts is all."

I sat beside him. "Do you think you can walk?"

He snorted. "I can walk."

"What were you doing in here?"

The boy shrugged. "Looking around."

"Do you come here often?"

"Sometimes. And other places like this. I like them."

"How about school?"

Francis barked out a laugh. "What's the point of *that*?"

"Do your parents know you come here?"

"I don't have any."

I hesitated, feeling a sharp pain of recognition in my chest. "No parents at all?"

Francis didn't answer right away. He looked down at his feet and rubbed his left ankle.

"No father," he finally said. "My mother's sick. They say she's dying and they won't let me see her. I haven't seen her in a long time."

"Who are you living with, then?"

"No one."

"No one?"

"I can take care of myself."

Yes, I thought, he probably could. But that wasn't excuse enough for a thirteen-year-old boy to be living alone. "Don't you have some other family? Sisters or brothers or aunts and uncles? Grandparents?"

"Yeah, but they don't really want me." He shrugged again. "I don't want them, either, so it kind of works out."

I didn't believe him, but I didn't say anything. Then I noticed he had no light.

"Don't you have a hand torch, or some kind of light?" I asked.

"I dropped it back there, when I got stuck."

I climbed across the mound of wire and searched for it with my own light. Far inside I saw what might be another hand torch; I lay down and tried to dig for it. But it was well beyond my reach; I realized there was no way I could ever get to it.

"I can't reach it," I said. "We'll go out together."

The boy didn't respond. When I turned around to ask him where I should take him, he was gone. I swung the light around, among the hulks of old machines, between hanging cables and rusting metal rods, but saw no sign of him. He couldn't have gone far.

"Francis."

I listened carefully, but didn't hear anything.

"Francis." Louder this time. Again no response, no sound of movement.

I knew he was nearby, motionless and silent, cloaked in shadows. I was also fairly certain that if I searched long enough I would find him. But he didn't want to be found, and I felt I should honor his wishes. There was something about the boy that reminded me of myself.

I stood watching and listening, still reluctant to leave him, but his wishes were clear.

"Goodbye, Francis," I finally said. "I hope I'll see you again."

There was still no response, so I headed out on my own.

I have no parents. Certainly there was a woman who gave birth to me (the bishop and the Church forbade all use of artificial wombs), and certainly there was a man who fathered me, in either the "natural" way or as a donor—probably the former, although the use of artificial insemination would have been far easier to conceal than the use of an artificial womb. So I almost certainly had parents of some kind, but I have never known who or what they were.

I was born an orphan, presumably because of my deformities, and was raised communally by a small circle of families high within the social and command structures of the ship, which leads me to suspect that my parents were among that circle, or at least had some influence.

I am almost sure that my deformities were known well before my birth, but for some reason I was not aborted (the Church's strictures against abortion did not seem to stop most convenience terminations). I imagine there are a number of people who later regretted that decision, whatever the reasons for it at the time. This always gave me some degree of satisfaction.

The people who were my parents may still be alive. I doubt that it would have been difficult to discover who they are, or were, but I never tried. They decided to abandon me at birth, so I have returned the favor throughout my life. As far as I am concerned, they no longer exist, and never did.

6

PÄR was talking mutiny.

There was no other word for it. The thought filled me with both excitement and fear.

We met again, this time in the Snow Gardens, which were currently out of season. There was no snow on the ground, and the trees were completely bare, without even a dusting of frost or ice. But the air was cold, burning the nose and biting at the lungs. We walked through a forest of skeletal trees, the dead dry leaves and branches cracking and snapping under our boots.

"There are a lot of people who want to leave the ship," Pär said when we were deep into the woods.

"Where are they going to go?" I asked disingenuously. "Out the air lock?"

Pär scowled up at me. "When we reach Antioch. You know that's what I mean."

"Temporarily, or permanently?"

"Permanently."

"It may not be habitable."

"It probably is, though, isn't it?"

"Yes," I admitted. "But even if it *is* habitable, we don't know what we'll find."

"It doesn't matter. These people will want to leave the ship under any and all circumstances. Join those already living there, in the extremely unlikely event we find anybody, or start their own settlement if the place is deserted. They won't care about hardships. Anything to get off this damned ship. Permanently."

"Downsiders," I said.

Pär nodded.

We walked on in silence for a while, our breaths like disintegrating smoke. The Snow Gardens appeared to go on for kilometers when they were in season and there was snow everywhere, the ground blanketed and the densely leaved trees heavy with snow and ice. But now the boundaries were visible—the gray walls enclosing the gardens, which were in need of basic maintenance; the dark ceiling high above us, pitted and cracked, appearing nothing at all like the vast and open sky it was in season with chaotic cloud images moving across its surface.

We neared a wall and changed direction. Directly ahead of us was a half-burned tree, branches and trunk charred and broken.

"There would need to be a vote," I finally said to him.

Pär snorted. "Yeah, but what kind? None of the downsiders would be voting."

"That's true," I said. "On the other hand, the vote would be taken not by the Executive Council, but by the full Planning Committee."

"Either one, we know how that vote would go."

"It depends on the circumstances."

"Crap," Pär said with disgust. "They'd never agree to let people leave. Especially not downsiders. They need them to do the scut work—cleaning and maintenance, all the manual labor this ship needs, and needing more all the time. Not to mention providing the servants for you all."

He was right, of course. Over the years, the issue had come up several times in Executive Council sessions as well as in other informal discussions. With few exceptions, no one wanted to allow the downsiders to leave, unless the upper-level residents were to also leave the ship, which was as unlikely as finding anyone alive in this solar system. Those in the upper levels were afraid to leave the *Argonos* after all these centuries; they were afraid they would lose the power and control they had over the downsiders. They were right to be afraid.

"We can help each other," Pär eventually said.

"You said that once before."

"And I mean it now as much as I did then."

I wasn't sure what he was after, or what he could offer in return, so I finally asked him.

"You have shipwide access," he said, "full authority over all systems."

"Not all," I corrected. "I cannot launch weapons on my own. I cannot shut down life support. I cannot change or set course—"

Pär shook his head in dismissal. "You have access to everything we need."

He said *we*. So he was with them, which I had already suspected. But I wondered if his *we* was meant to include me as well.

"Landing ships, supplies, all of that," he went on. "We have people who can run the loaders and navigate the shuttles. But we'll need access codes for the shuttles, ship's stores, fuel allocation, launch coordinates . . ." He shook his head. "Too much we can't do on our own." He stopped and leaned against the charred tree trunk; a pair of violet-and-indigo butterflies rose from a scarred branch and fluttered away. Pär looked up at me. "We can't do it without you."

"Why should I?"

Pär stared at me. "Because it's the right thing to do," he finally said. "We all have rights, every person on this ship. Or we *should*. Downsiders have *no* rights. We should have the right to make this decision ourselves, to leave the ship or stay, as we *choose*. But we don't."

"Why should I risk helping you?" I asked.

He snorted then. "You mean, how would it be to your advantage?"

"Something like that." I didn't like it put so crudely, but I couldn't argue his point.

Pär nodded; not in agreement, it seemed to me, but rather as if he'd expected as much.

"Your captain is in trouble. If he goes down, you go down with him. And he is almost certainly going down, no matter what we find. This is your way out."

"How?"

"You go with us."

"And if I don't want to leave?"

"Will you really want to stay when the captain has been deposed? The way everyone on the Planning Committee and Executive Council, in fact nearly everyone in the upper levels, despises you?"

"Despises? Isn't that a little harsh?"

"Harsh?" And here Pär smiled. "Yes. But it's accurate. You must know that. You'll have no power, no influence, and my guess is that all access will be cut off, all authority canceled. You'll be nothing." He pushed off from the tree and walked away. "Think about it," he said without turning back.

I watched him walk deeper into the skeletal woods, watched my own breath form and dissipate over and over. Yes, I would think about his proposal. I had no choice.

T H E downsiders did all the scut work on the ship, just as Pär said. Although most of the ship's systems were automated, and most of the machinery was self-maintaining and self-repairing, nothing was completely trouble-free, and much manual labor was needed to keep everything running. Cleaning, servicing, other kinds of maintenance. Also to run the manufacturing and fabrication equipment, the ag rooms, and countless other jobs. And more needed to be done each year as systems gradually faltered and broke down.

Costino and his staff were in charge of production and schedules, coordinating all the downsider work crews. I'd never been interested in the details, but I knew that much of the labor was exhausting, and some of it dangerous. People were occasionally killed. But someone had to do it. I did not make judgments one way or the other.

According to the ship's history, as recorded by Toller and his predecessors, there had been periodic attempts by downsiders to change the way things were done. I had even heard vague stories of a massive revolt, called the Repudiation, associated with some kind of plague three or four centuries earlier. Such efforts had never been successful. I had been through one attempted insurrection myself, six years earlier. It did not last long.

At that time, the downsiders began negotiations reasonably enough—they asked that all the work be shared equally by those on all levels. This request was of course refused. So the downsiders threatened to cease all work. In response, we (and I'm afraid I must include myself, whether or not I agreed with the actions taken; I *was* a part of the upper-level society, no matter how much of an outsider I was to most of them) simply cut off all the food and water conduits to the lower levels, secured the ag rooms so they could not get at *our* food, and shut down their recycling systems.

They held out for six days. Arne Gronvold tried to restore all the lifelines for them, and when he was unsuccessful he tried to cut off all of ours. That, too, failed. When the insurrection was over, Arne was banished for life to the lower levels.

So I understood why the downsiders would want to leave, and I understood why the upper levels would never agree. And Pär was asking me to risk sharing Arne Gronvold's fate.

He was asking too much.

7

AS we neared Antioch, the exploration party was formed. We numbered thirteen.

I would go as the captain's representative. Nikos had to stay with the ship—there was no question of that; he feared losing all authority if he were to leave, and I was the only one he trusted to provide him with an accurate report of what we would find.

Besides me, there was a science team of three, and an armed military squad of six. A woman named Sari Mandapat was chosen to be the representative for the downsiders, and Andrew Thornton was selected to represent the upper levels after Michel Tournier backed out, claiming illness; Tournier's real illness was fear. The ship's crew would have no representative—they did not need one, nor did they care.

Last, Father Veronica was to go as the Church's representative. I did not know her well, but I had spoken with her on occasion, and had heard some of her sermons. I admired her. She was intelligent, and she was sincere. And she was a believer.

The bishop, I was certain, did not believe. But the three priests *did*, and none more than Father Veronica. The strange thing, though, was that she was not a fanatic. I didn't understand her.

I understand hypocrites, like the bishop, and I understand fanatics, or at least I can more easily predict their behavior, which is much the same thing, as far as I am concerned. But I admit I did not know what to make of true believers like Father Veronica. Her belief, her *faith*, was both profound and real. Her faith disturbed me.

I wanted to talk with her before we made landfall, so I went to the cathedral. When I entered, the cathedral was huge and empty and silent. The only light came from candles burning in clusters along both aisles flanking the main nave, and there were flickering shadows everywhere. I could barely make out the arched vaulting high above me. At the far end, behind the apse, was the enormous stained-glass window that formed a section of the outer hull. With only the darkness of space behind it, the window was lifeless and indistinct. I had never been able to make out the images in the glass, although I felt certain there was something more than abstraction in it.

I'd never spent much time in the cathedral. I had attended a few sermons, services on holy days as required, the occasional wedding, funeral Masses, but at those times all I did was sit on a pew and struggle to stay awake. I registered little of my surroundings, and never paid them much attention. But that day, with the cathedral so empty, I was curious.

I walked slowly along the right aisle. The vaulting, while still quite high, was lower than that looming above the central section of the cathedral. There was a series of stained-glass windows, each illuminated by some diffuse source embedded in the interior walls behind them. Between the windows were tiny alcoves; in each alcove was a kneeling pad and a cluster of candles. The candles, few of which were alight, were in small colored-glass containers, the flames glowing softly within them. The mood created was a strange combination of serenity and disquiet.

I stopped and looked up at one astonishing stained-glass window. It depicted an enormous two-headed monster ripping itself out of the belly of a man, one of the heads in the process of devouring a child with its massive jaws and teeth. I was amazed at how detailed and gruesome it was. The monster's body was that of a muscular scaled reptile with short, thick legs, taloned feet, and a long and powerful tail. The two heads had doglike features and blazing red eyes. Although the monster was ripping its way out of the man, it was more than twice the man's size. The one head held the child in its teeth, and the other stared out and down—with the bright red eyes glowering at me, it looked disturbingly alive.

I was still staring at the images, trying to make sense of them, when a voice broke my concentration.

"Horrifying, isn't it?"

Startled, I turned to see Father Veronica standing at the end of one of the pews. She was looking at me, then turned to gaze up at the stained-glass window.

She was not what I would call a beautiful woman, but I would use the word "handsome." Nearly as tall as I, with dark ash-brown hair that hung halfway down her back, she was wearing a black cassock with white collar, and her hands were hidden within the dark folds of material.

"Yes," I said. "What is it supposed to represent?"

"I can give you the official Church version, or I can give you my own."

"How about both?"

She smiled then, a smile that cut my breath short for a moment, and nodded. "All right." She walked toward me and stood at my side, and we both looked up at the window.

"If you were to ask the bishop," she began, "or the other priests, they would tell you that the two-headed monster represents Satan, the Fallen Angel, cast out of Heaven for defying God. Satan, the manifestation of Evil, will do anything to work his way into the souls and hearts of men and women, only to destroy them from within, as represented by this picture, for no other reason than because we are God's children, and this is Satan's way of seeking his revenge upon God."

"And if I were to ask *you*?"

She shrugged. "It is heresy, perhaps, but I do not believe in Satan as a real being, an external force or manifestation." She held her hand out toward the images above us. "That monster is coming from within. I believe that creature is nothing more than the dark and terrible aspect of our own souls." She paused, gazing steadily at the stained glass. "We all have the potential to be good, to *do* good, and that potential is nearly limitless." She smiled gently. "That potential is rarely fulfilled, but most of us do well enough." Then the smile was gone. "We also have a similar potential for evil, to deliberately do harm to ourselves and others. If we give in to that aspect of our souls, if we let evil rule our minds and our hearts, it will not only destroy us, as it is doing here, it will destroy the innocents around us as well—the child being devoured by the creature's second head."

"You believe that potential is in *all* of us?" I asked.

"For both good and evil, yes."

"Even in you?"

She nodded. "Yes, even in me. I am no less human than you are."

We were silent for a while, and I continued to gaze at the stained glass. Father Veronica's interpretation of the images resonated far more with me than did the Church's. Eventually I turned to face her.

"We'll be making landfall together," I said.

"Yes, and I'm looking forward to it. So many years . . ." Her gaze became unfocused . . . or focused on something distant and unseen. "Open skies, a visible horizon in the distance, the sun or moons or clouds hanging above, maybe a wind blowing through the trees. Free-flowing water, rain pouring from the sky, the black night shattered by electrical discharges . . . I miss all that."

"You can experience rain or snow right here on the ship," I told her. "In the gardens, in the ag fields."

She shook her head. "It's not the same."

"No," I agreed.

"Of course, the last time we made landfall was something of a debacle. I never did completely understand what

went wrong, though regrettably the bishop had something
to do with it.''

I was surprised she was so forthcoming about the role
her superior played in that fiasco.

"The language difficulties were part of the problem,"
she continued. "So strange. We spoke the same language
as those people, that was clear, and yet our individual versions of it had diverged so greatly over time that often it
was like two *different* languages." She paused, lost in her
thoughts. "As I said, the bishop must bear some of the
responsibility for the trouble." She paused again, and I
wondered if she now regretted admitting her feelings about
the bishop. But she went on. "He does not seem to understand that you cannot force belief. You cannot create faith
in others through force of will."

"We're not likely to have a repeat of what happened
there," I said. "Not this time, anyway."

"No. From what I understand, it isn't likely that we will
find anyone, is it?"

"I suppose not. No one alive."

"That's too bad."

"Why?"

She shrugged. "We are too isolated. For a few years at
a time, it may be harmless. But we need contact with other
people—people who do not live on the *Argonos*, people
with different ways of life, different ideas, different ways
of looking at the world."

"Different beliefs?"

"Yes, different beliefs, too. But we *don't* have contact
with other people. We go far too many years without seeing
anyone other than ourselves. In fact, I do not think it is a
good thing that we spend our entire lives on this ship."

"Why not?" I was amazed at how open she was with
me, and I wanted to encourage her to keep talking.

"We stagnate, and we have no history."

"We create our own history."

"But we *don't,* actually. Most people know little or nothing about what occurred on this ship before they were born.
And what little they know has no context."

She may be right, I thought. It was something I would have to think about.

"We might find people down there," I said to her, trying for optimism. "To give us context."

But she just sighed. She put out her hand and I grasped it in mine.

"It's been good talking to you, Bartolomeo. I'm looking forward to making landfall with you, whatever we find." With that she released my hand, turned, and walked away, quickly becoming lost in the shadows.

S HE smelled of honey and cinnamon.

8

"THE transmission has changed," Nikos said.

He stood in the open doorway of my quarters holding a bottle of wine.

"Then there *is* someone alive down there."

Nikos shrugged, then stepped into the first of my two rooms. "Share a bottle with me," he said.

"All right." I stood up and got glasses; then we sat in the two chairs at my small table, bottle and glasses between us. Nikos looked awful. His skin was pale and drawn; the dark crescents under his eyes were deeper and seemed permanent. I could smell alcohol and knew he had already been drinking, but his hands were steady as he opened the bottle and poured a glass for each of us. The wine was dry and good, far better than what was usually available, even in the upper levels. The Costa-Malvini clan had a private vineyard downside, and their own personal master vintner.

"I don't know, Bartolomeo." He glanced up at the overhead lights, squinting. "How about bringing them down a bit?"

I dimmed the lights to half-normal, and he nodded his thanks.

"I don't know," he said again. "It changed frequency,

and the duration shortened, but the damn thing is now as steady and unvarying as it was before. I have a feeling the change doesn't mean a thing.'' He was staring into his glass, tipping it slightly from side to side. ''We've been sending our own transmissions, everything Communications can think of, but we don't get any response.'' He slowly shook his head. ''I don't think anyone's down there.''

''Unless they're scared,'' I suggested. ''Scared and hiding.''

That seemed to pique his interest, and he looked up from his wine. ''That's a possibility. But if that's true, why is there *any* transmission?''

''Good question. Perhaps it's meant as a warning. Or . . . perhaps no one knows about the transmission.'' There was a third possibility, which had just occurred to me, but I was reluctant to bring it up. I hesitated, then said, ''It could be bait.''

''Bait.''

''To lure a ship like ours into some kind of trap.''

Nikos stared long and hard at me, then drank the rest of his wine and refilled his glass. He turned his face to the dimmed light globes above us. ''Traps,'' he said. ''Traps everywhere.'' I wondered if he was thinking about the bishop, and about what trap the bishop might be laying for him.

He stood up, a little unsteady now, and took his glass with him as he wandered about the room, drinking, looking at everything but me. I gradually became unnerved, but I couldn't figure out just why.

''We've known each other a lot of years,'' Nikos said.

''Yes. Since I can remember, really.'' When we were children, he befriended me when no one else would. Something I would never forget.

He finally turned to me. ''I don't know what to hope for down there,'' he said. ''It's all or nothing now—I can feel it—and too damn much can go wrong.''

''You said you have a plan to deal with the bishop. Tell me what it is, Nikos. Let me help you.''

''I can't, Bartolomeo. Not yet.'' He returned to the table

and sat, his eyes locked on mine. "I'm counting on you, Bartolomeo. Whatever happens down there, I'm counting on you to tell me what is really going on, what is really there, to make the right decisions, to give me the best advice." He drained his glass again, refilled it and refilled mine. "I'm counting on you."

PÄR found me in the cathedral the day before we went into orbit around Antioch. We had no meeting scheduled; in fact, we hadn't spoken in several days. I was in the cathedral hoping to find Father Veronica alone, hoping to speak with her again before we made landfall. But there was no one there. I sat on one of the pews to wait; Pär's approach was so quiet, I was startled when he slid in beside me. More disturbing was that he knew where to look for me—I had never been known to frequent that place.

"We'll be there soon," he said.

I nodded. "Tomorrow."

"Have you thought about what I asked you?"

"Yes, I've thought about it."

"And?"

"And nothing. I'm still thinking about it."

"Bartolomeo, Bartolomeo . . ." Then he coughed out a kind of laugh. "You're on the landfall team."

"Yes."

"It would be best if you made a decision before you left."

I didn't like being pressured. The mutiny seemed a reckless and foolhardy undertaking. Even though I understood his arguments for my participation, I refused to be rushed into a decision. There were too many possible outcomes, and almost all of them were bad.

I finally gave him a shrug for an answer, which didn't please him.

"Sari Mandapat is on the landfall team," he said.

"I know."

"If you haven't decided before you leave, let *her* know your decision when you manage to summon enough courage to make a commitment." He stood, and flashed a sly grin at me. "Say hello to the priest for me next time you see her." Then he turned and walked away before I could respond.

But what would I have said? The dwarf knew far too much.

T**HE** next day we went into geosynch orbit around Antioch, directly above the source of the transmission. Satellite probes were launched; final preparations were made. All or nothing, Nikos had said. He was right, and I was ready.

9

THE small ship fell out of the clouds. Came down shaking and shimmying in the wind currents, turbulence that diminished as we dropped farther and then swung around into a more gradual descent. I felt queasy all the way down.

The shuttle was tiny compared to the *Argonos*, of course, but large enough to comfortably hold the landing team of thirteen, two pilots, two armored terrain vehicles, and a smaller, faster, and more maneuverable flyer capable of making further exploratory surveys of the planet.

We watched our descent on video monitors mounted in the ceiling around the cabin, choosing from among several different views of the ground, the sky, even the surface of the shuttle itself. The shuttle's skin was coruscating metal, color and texture changes popping chaotically across its surface. Every so often it all snapped into focus, a perfect camouflage against the terrain below, but then the focus burst apart and the chaos returned. Once, decades or centuries earlier, that metal skin worked perfectly, providing three-dimensional camouflage, making the shuttle almost invisible from any vantage point; but like so many other things on the ship, it functioned sporadically, and no one knew how to repair it.

The terrain below was awash in the orange glow from the rising sun, the sun's rays cutting in under dissipating clouds. A muddy river snaked through densely wooded flatlands, the woods bordered several kilometers to the west by a ragged range of foothills that in turn gave way to higher, stony mountains scarred by swaths of burned trees and vegetation. No signs of smoke rose from the charred stumps, the spikes and spines of blackened wood. A herd of large, mottled beasts moved through the devastation.

Down by the river, a large section of the woods had been cleared, and in that clearing was a town, dozens of low buildings, roads and pathways and other artificial structures. There was no movement in the town except for leaves and bits of flotsam blown about by the wind, a few pieces of cloth flapping from their places of attachment. But no creature moved, unless it was inside a building and out of sight. How likely was that?

We approached the town, descending more slowly now, arcing around it. Finally, over an open space just back from the river—a flat rectangle of dirt partially fenced—the shuttle shifted into a hover. Stationary for several moments, we began a slow vertical descent with loud, wailing noises from the shuttle's engines. The dust below us boiled and swirled until the shuttle touched down. The wailing faded, the engines shut down, and eventually there was silence.

We waited for an hour or so while sensors and probes were dispatched and data was transmitted back to us. When everything checked out as we'd expected, we readied ourselves, masking our faces with breathers. The shuttle's belly opened up and dropped down, a wide ramp leading to the ground. A few minutes later, led by the soldiers, we walked down the ramp, and took our first steps on that alien world.

THERE was no one left alive.

We had not expected to find anyone, but the desolation of the settlement was surprisingly grim, and I could *feel* the emptiness as I stood near the shuttle, looking out at the buildings. A pall rapidly settled over us, worked its way into our bones so that it became impossible to dispel. A discomforting stillness hung over the area, as if there was nothing alive; no humans, no animals, not even tiny creatures like insects.

I noticed the light more than anything else. It was like nothing on the *Argonos*, even in the largest of the nature rooms that tried to re-create natural environments. Not brighter, but more intense somehow, so that everything around us seemed to have the faintest hint of shining outlines. I had forgotten what real sunlight could be like.

The soldiers insisted on leading the way as we left the fenced landing area. Our first task was to find the source of the transmission. Barry Sorrel, the head of the science team, had some instrument that homed in on the signal; we followed him through the buildings, along rutted pathways. I searched each structure we passed for signs of life, but everything was dead and quiet, abandoned or forgotten.

The transmitter was on top of a building near the center of the town, powered by surrounding arrays of solar panels. No way to know how many decades it had been pulsing out its steady, meaningless transmission. Andrew Thornton wanted to destroy the transmitter—out of pique, I think. But the science team wanted to take a closer look at it over the next few days, see if there were codes or messages stored somewhere, anything more meaningful.

We were not a military-minded group, and after we found the transmitter, we began to disperse—the science team members stayed together, though they ignored the soldiers; Sari Mandapat and Father Veronica drifted toward the outer edges of the settlement; Thornton stuck with two of the soldiers; and I went off on my own.

I was the first to find bones. Down near the river was a rectangular building of rotting wood, the sunlight slashing through cracks and jagged holes and broken windows. I stood in the doorway, watching dust luminesce in the beams of light, when the bright white curves of a rib cage caught my eye.

We spent most of the rest of the day making a general search of the settlement, through all the buildings that were easily accessible. We found the remains of at least a few of those who had once lived here. Only bones. No flesh remained. Four skeletons mostly complete and completely bare except for an occasional shred of colored fabric or bands of plastic or metal, oxidized rings circling white finger bones. The scattered pieces of two or three others, perhaps. Once we had gone through the entire settlement, we began collecting all the skeletons, partial or whole, every bone that looked like it might be human. The science team examined the bones as we collected them, particularly the complete skeletons, but it soon became clear there was no way to glean even a clue to the reasons any of them died—there were no obvious signs of trauma, no shattered and strangely disintegrating skulls, no unusual lesions.

In an open area near the woods, the soldiers blew open a small pit with explosives and stone burners; then we carefully laid the skeletons and bones on the bottom.

Father Veronica stood at the edge of the pit, gazing down at bones and earth. She made the sign of the cross, and began to speak.

"*Absolve, Domine, animus omnium fidelium defunctorum ab omni vinculo delictorum. Et gratia tua illis succurrente . . .*"

A dead language spoken for the dead. None of us understood what she was saying, and if the dead could have heard, I'm sure they would not have understood, either; they couldn't hear, so perhaps it didn't matter.

But I was certain Father Veronica understood what she was saying, for there was strong emotion in her voice, a sadness eased by hope, a comfort and acceptance.

"*. . . Dies illa, dies irae, calamitatis et miseriae; dies magna . . .*"

We were all silent, standing along the edge of the pit on either side of her, gazing down along with her on all those bones. She was beautiful, and in a way magnificent, and my admiration for her grew as I watched and listened.

"*. . . Kyrie, eleison . . . Christe, eleison . . . Kyrie, eleison.*"

She once again made the sign of the cross, and this time everyone except me joined her.

That was it for the day. Barry Sorrel and the other science-team members wanted to use the last of daylight to explore the town, but Thornton, Sari Mandapat, and I overruled them, and we all returned to the shuttle. There was no hurry. The dead there had been long dead, and the living had nowhere to go.

Father Veronica remained until dark standing at the edge of the pit, presumably praying; then she, too, returned to the shuttle. I wanted to talk to her about the graveside ritual, but she said she needed to be alone. She gave me a copy of the text she had spoken from (I still have it), then retreated to one of the armored land vehicles and shut herself inside.

There was no translation for the text, no explanation, but I read it over several times, quietly aloud; the sound and rhythm of it gave me an unexpected sense of comfort.

A violent storm blew in during the night, and it only worsened throughout the day. I couldn't see the settlement through the viewing windows or on the monitors, just the vaguest of dark outlines through the torrential rains crashing down from the black clouds above us.

It was odd. Stuck inside the ship for all these years, searching for a habitable world, waiting for the chance to walk on solid ground once again, maybe even breathe open air, and now that we'd landed we were trapped inside a small metal vessel with far less freedom and space than we would have had if we'd still been aboard ship.

The storm raged on. Three days and it never let up. We barely managed to get daily transmissions through to the *Argonos*, apprising them of our status.

Father Veronica went out into the storm the morning of the third day. Sergeant Woolf wanted to take one of her soldiers and go after her, but I persuaded her to stay with the shuttle. I reminded the sergeant of her duty to the ship and the exploration team, arguing that if she or one of her soldiers were lost, she would put us all at greater risk. I didn't believe any of it, but I felt that if Father Veronica needed to go out into the storm, she should be allowed to do so.

She returned several hours later. The shuttle's security/detection system apparently wasn't functioning, for we only knew of her return when we heard her banging on the shuttle's hull. We lowered the embarkation ramp, and had to help her inside; she was so wet and exhausted she could barely walk, but at the same time she looked refreshed and somehow invigorated. She wouldn't answer any questions. She dried off and changed into another cassock, then settled down in silence to read from an old bound book with thin, translucent pages. She appeared content and peaceful, and I thought that maybe we should all make trips out into the storm.

10

T**HE** storm broke during the night, and the sun rose bright and radiant on the fourth day, lighting up stray clouds with red and purple, bringing light and warmth to the silent, empty buildings. Steam rose from the river, from the building rooftops, from the mud, from the trees surrounding the town—antediluvian jungle.

I was the first to leave the shuttle, and stood alone beside it, my face and lungs exposed to the air of this world. I had decided to abandon the breathing apparatus—people had lived here long enough to build a settlement; it probably wasn't anything in the air that killed them, and if it was . . . I'd accept whatever came. For some reason, I felt comfortably reckless.

Without the breather, the smells were intense. Exotic and strange and exhilarating. More than ever, I knew I was on an alien world, my mind trying to identify so many odors that didn't match anything I'd ever experienced.

The air was nearly silent. But as the sun climbed, sounds of life finally emerged from the woods—animals presumably, although the clicks and chitters and rustlings and mewling cries sounded distinctly alien, as they should. This was an alien planet, alien to human beings, alien certainly to those human beings who had landed here just days ago.

Then there was another sound, a low and quiet yowling. Not from the woods, though; this time the sound came from one of the nearest buildings. I turned and stared in the direction of a long, weather-beaten structure, at the open doorway and shattered windows.

A large cat stepped through the doorway and emerged into the sunlight, staring back at me. The cat was larger than any I'd ever seen on the ship. The low yowling became almost a growl, and its tail, fat and puffed, twitched stiffly.

I squatted and reached out a hand.

The cat hissed, then ran off toward the trees.

I was filled with a wonderful sense of peace and content-ment, and wished that none of the others would leave the shuttle.

BUT they did, and the exploration of the settlement resumed. The ground was still muddy, and moving about was tiresome and sloppy. I lost interest before noon. Buildings filled with rotting furniture, broken doors and windows, warped and mildewed floors and walls, unrecog-nizable masses and shafts of rusting metal. I doubted anyone would discover anything useful, anything to tell us what had happened.

Leaving the others to explore, I went down to the river at midday. The remains of a crude dock extended three or four meters into the water, although it was clear that at one time the dock had been much longer. When I took a few steps onto it, the wood was so decayed I sank slightly into it, and the entire structure creaked and swayed, threatening to collapse beneath me. I backed off and sat on a section set into the bank and watched the muddy water flow past.

The water was hypnotic, so that I lost all sense of time, and even a sense of place. This was only the second time in my life that I had seen a real river—it felt so different from the small, artificial streams that flowed in the nature rooms on board the ship. Vast and uncontrolled and somehow alive.

I heard a noise and looked up. Father Veronica stood just a few feet away, watching me.

"Why are you here?" she asked.

"The settlement doesn't interest me," I told her. "Digging through the mud and the rot of the past . . ." I shook my head. "Not when it's so unlikely that any answers will be found."

She didn't reply at first, and it seemed she was bothered by my answer, or made thoughtful by it, I wasn't sure which.

"Then why did you come with us? On this landfall?"

"To be the captain's representative," I said. "He needs eyes and ears down here."

She smiled slyly, and I wondered what she was thinking. But whatever it was, she kept it to herself. "I meant *personally*. If you hadn't wanted to come, you could have found a way to stay on the *Argonos*."

"I'm not sure that's true. But yes, I wanted to come. I wanted to see this place. I wanted to stand on solid ground. I wanted to experience real weather, not the simulated rains and winds of the nature rooms. See a real sun and a real moon."

"We all should be allowed to make landfall," she said, gazing across the river and into the dense undergrowth on the other side. "Everyone on board should be given the opportunity, for at least a few days." It was something Pär might have said, and I wondered if she knew of the plans for mutiny. "It isn't right." Her face was set, and I thought she might actually be angry.

"Why did *you* come with the team?" I asked.

"For the Church. So there would be someone to comfort the living, someone to bury the dead."

"And *your* personal reasons?" I asked.

She turned back to me. "There is no difference," she said. "My life and my faith and my Church are all the same."

I could see that she believed that about herself, but I

wasn't sure that *I* did. I wondered if *her* Church was the same as the bishop's. I doubted it.

"I'm going back now," she said. "I want to be there if I'm needed. I just wanted to see that you were all right."

"I'm fine."

"I can see that," she said. She turned and walked back toward the settlement, leaving me alone with my thoughts and the swirling of the water beneath my feet.

T H E orbiting probe surveys were completed that day. Photos and imaging scans were transmitted both to the *Argonos* and to us on land. The science team spent hours in consultation with the captain, the bishop, and another science team up on the ship, trying to determine what, if anything, needed further exploration.

There was only one obvious site, another large group of buildings, although no electromagnetic emissions whatsoever could be detected from it, and there were no signs of life. It would be several hours to the southeast by flyer.

After that there was much disagreement. Lots of discussion, lots of uncertainty. I retreated to the rear of the shuttle's main cabin, not wanting to get involved. Eventually, though, their uncertainty was overcome, and it was decided that two other sites warranted further exploration. Then it was time to select a two-person team to make the trip. I wondered if anyone would volunteer. This was an alien and unknown world, and any venture would only add to the risks we all currently faced.

"I need to be with the exploration party," Father Veronica said. "In case there are survivors that need help, comfort." She paused. "Or more dead to be buried."

I waited for the objections, but none were forthcoming. There was silence, people in the shuttle looking around at one another. The bishop's voice came through the linkup.

"I approve," he said.

His approval surprised me, until it occurred to me that the bishop might actually *want* Father Veronica put at risk. Just as Nikos saw the bishop as a threat to his captaincy, the bishop might see Father Veronica as a threat to his own position. The fact that Father Veronica had never demonstrated the slightest ambition might only make her more dangerous in his eyes.

I came forward and said, "I'll accompany Father Veronica."

Everyone was surprised, I think.

I had two reasons for wanting to go with her. First, I preferred to be with her rather than with any of the others; and second, I suspected the bishop's motives, and felt protective of her. If he was willing to put her at risk, I was willing to risk myself to provide what protection I could. Absurd, perhaps, but that was what I felt.

"Shouldn't one of the science team go instead of Bartolomeo?" It was Sari Mandapat raising the objection.

But none of the science team wanted to leave. They wanted to remain together; they believed from what they'd seen of the charts and photographs that there was likely nothing of much interest at the other sites; and they had gained renewed excitement there in the settlement with the afternoon discovery of an extensive laboratory which was fairly intact.

"If something is found," said Barry Sorrel, "the flyer can be sent back and one or more of us can go out to the site and investigate further. We don't need to go now."

There were no other objections, and no other volunteers. Andrew Thornton, though not the coward Michel Tournier was, would never take any added risks, and I'm certain Sari Mandapat felt she had to remain with the shuttle in case something needed to be done for the mutiny. And so, by default, I was approved.

Father Veronica and I would go. We would leave at first light the next day, after the harvesters arrived.

11

THE harvesters descended screaming from the sky.
Three great shining metal leviathans dropping almost
directly over the settlement, their descent gradually slowing
even as the screaming sounds intensified.

The entire exploration party had come out to watch. Pre-
dawn, we couldn't yet see the sun from where we stood,
but the harvesters were high enough for the sun's rays to
illuminate their scarred metal bellies, the rims of their enormous gaping maws.

The reprovisioning of the ship was about to begin. The
ship's recycling systems—of air, water, waste—were incredibly efficient, but the ship was not a completely closed system. No matter how efficient, there was always some
leakage, loss, dissipation. . . . Fresh organic matter was
needed.

For the next several days, the harvesters would ravage
this part of the continent. With blazing, churning mouths
they would consume all organic matter in their paths—animal and plant and anything in between. When their holds
were full they would return to the main ship and unload,
and all that organic material would then be broken down
into basic constituents and detoxified, neutralized, then revi-

talized and cycled back into the ship's food and environmental systems.

This was long overdue. Too many years without this
opportunity.

One of the harvesters broke away still howling, slowly
banked around and headed east toward the shore, where it
would begin harvesting from the sea. The other two continued their steady descent, drifting away now from the settlement. Copper and orange and magenta flowers of light
floated around them, and it was impossible to know if that
light came from the sun, the engines, or the burning furnaces within them.

The two finally dropped out of sight, but soon flames
could be seen rising above the jungle in the distance, along
with swirling towers of smoke. The sound changed, became
a deeper, harsher roar tearing the dawn air. The harvesting
had begun.

FATHER Veronica and I, along with Marcus Krisk
and Trude Stimpl—our two soldiers/escorts/pilots—
boarded the flyer and took off, headed south and east. There
were no windows in the flyer except for those in the pilots'
cabin, and our only view of the terrain came from a set of
small video monitors, only half of which functioned—
watching them was like trying to put together a child's
mosaic puzzle with some of the pieces missing. But I could
make out thick forests below us, sectioned off by rivers
carving their way through the dense vegetation. This was
followed by vast marshland, then more forest. The woods
rapidly transitioned to dense jungle, and a torrential rain
began, obscuring visibility.

When we finally reached our destination—a grouping of
perhaps thirty buildings in the middle of the jungle—we
could find no place to land. Trees and vegetation surrounded
the buildings, enclosing them, sometimes overgrowing them
so that their roofs were only partially visible, and there were
no nearby clearings. We circled the area, but the nearest
clearing we could find was twenty kilometers away.

We flew back to the buildings, and after hovering over them for several minutes, Trude picked out what appeared to be the strongest flat roof (based on what, I had no idea), and made a slow, careful descent. As we touched down, the roof buckled, but held.

It was still raining hard. Cloaked in waterproof body coverings, the four of us left the flyer to begin exploring. I was stunned by the heat. Because of the rain, I had expected the air to be cool, but it was hotter and more stifling than anything I could remember experiencing. We had difficulty breathing. Marcus and Trude returned to the flyer for the breathers, but when Father Veronica declined to use one, I decided to do without as well.

We climbed down from the roof using a tangle of trees and lianas; once on the ground, progress became more difficult. Presumably there had once been pathways between the buildings, but if so they had long ago become overgrown, and passage was impossible. Marcus and Trude burned trails through the foliage with their stone burners, the same weapons that had been used to carve out the grave back at our original landing site. The air filled with smoke and the stench of burning, vaporizing plant matter; probably animal flesh as well, for we occasionally heard what sounded like screams.

By mutual consent, we examined the building we'd landed on first. We could not find a way in. It was rectangular, four meters high, about twenty meters in length, and fifteen in width, constructed of a black, plastic-like material; there were no doors or windows, no openings of any kind. There had been no openings on the roof, either. Marcus wanted to use the stone burners to melt our way inside, but Father Veronica and I argued successfully against it. With no way to know what was in those buildings, using the stone burners would be risky—a good way to get ourselves killed in an explosion of some sort. We moved on.

Each building was more of the same, or close enough. Burning our way from one structure to another was slow going, and then we found buildings with no access, or buildings with doors that, when forced open, revealed empty, abandoned rooms.

Halfway through the afternoon, exhaustion growing, Father Veronica and I gave in and began using the breathers. Even with the aid of oxygen, the more we explored this place, the stranger we felt. None of it made sense. The empty buildings were *completely* empty except for thick, oozing mud, tangles of green and purple vines, clumps of rotting vegetation. The emptiness was unsettling. Although some of the buildings had doors, not a single one had any windows or outer openings for ventilation, despite what appeared to be ventilation screens inside some of the buildings.

I have no idea how many buildings we examined by the time the dim light began to fade even further. All of us were dazed, and we knew we had to quit soon.

Then we came across the strangest building of all. It was located in the center of the site, and its walls were all glass, or something *like* glass. The building was star-shaped, seven-pointed. Although darkness was falling, with our hand torches we could see inside. In the points: machinery and cables and padded benches; hanging baskets that seemed to be chairs of some kind; oblong metal containers, shiny reflections of liquid inside them; floor-to-ceiling tubes fluorescing in the light of our torches. In the central area: a broken ring of instrument panels and consoles; amazingly, there were lights glowing in some of the panels—green, amber, and one blinking crimson in the dark.

We found the doorway, then stood facing each other. "Tomorrow would be best," I suggested. We were exhausted, and this would probably take some time. The others agreed. But as they turned away and started back, I thought I saw a silver, ghostlike form drift through the central section. I stood there a long time, studying the interior, but didn't see anything more. I told myself it was exhaustion, but I didn't quite believe it.

12

NOTHING felt right the next day, not from the moment we once again left the flyer. There was the steaming, oppressive heat, everything wet and dripping though it was no longer raining, and there were strange whimpering noises; a long, haunted caw; incredibly loud clicking sounds: the only signs of animal life in this jungle.

We were all wearing breathers, and we climbed down the vine-choked trees to reach ground level, then made our way slowly toward the star-shaped building near the center of this . . . what? Town? Settlement? Industrial complex? Memorial? We still didn't know. Perhaps when we explored the building we would have a better idea.

When we reached the central building, we worked our way to the door we had identified the day before. It was mostly glass, like the walls. Marcus raised his stone burner, but I stopped him before he could fire the weapon.

"Wait," I said, my hand on Marcus's arm. I took hold of the metal door handle, pushed, then pushed harder, but nothing happened. Then I pulled instead, and the door swung easily open. After pausing for a few moments, I stepped inside.

Though stale, the air was cooler and lighter, and we no

longer needed the breathers. I led the way on a cursory inspection of the star sections. We felt obligated to do so, although all of us were anxious to move on to the central area and the still-functioning machinery. We briefly examined the furniture, the tables and desks, and the hanging, cushioned baskets that seemed like strange, hovering chairs; we stepped over massive cables, some of them no longer connected to anything at either end; we peered into half-filled metal vats, wondering at the composition of the liquid and its purpose; we noted shredded fabric hanging from the ceiling and dried tracks of color smeared on some of the glass walls.

Finally we came full circle back to the open door. Once again I took the lead, and we moved toward the central section. There was a broken ring of consoles ten meters across, seven equal sections divided by narrow, shallow steps leading down toward a central circular section slightly lower than ground level. Colored lights glowed and flickered on the consoles—tiny amber squares, rotating green spirals, an occasional blinking red circle. But there were no markings, no words or characters or numbers, no dials or toggles or buttons. What purpose could all this serve?

"Is it real?" I wondered aloud.

"What do you mean?" Marcus asked. He tapped at one of the consoles with his stone burner, producing a loud ringing. "We're not imagining this."

"He's suggesting it might be a mock-up," Father Veronica said; I nodded. "Empty metal casings with some lighted displays. Not connected to anything."

"Why would anyone do that?"

I shrugged. I pointed at a metal handle attached to a circular cap on the floor, by the bottom step nearest me. "Looks like an air-lock handle," I said. "And look." There were six others, one at the bottom of each set of steps.

I walked awkwardly down the steps—they were unnaturally shallow and long, and my club foot was no help. I crouched beside the handle, gripped it, and twisted. It turned easily one quarter revolution, then would go no farther.

We waited, looking around, but nothing happened. "Let's try all of them," I said.

The others descended the steps and fanned out, each to a handle, I to a second. Four more handles turned one quarter revolution each. Still nothing; Trude and I moved to the last two. Looking at each other, we turned them almost in unison.

The floor opened up, dilating. Fortunately none of us had gone farther than the handles so no one dropped through the hole now forming in the center of the building.

No, not a hole exactly, for there was a spiral flight of stairs leading eight or nine meters down to a dimly lit floor.

Father Veronica was closest to the stairs, so she started down first, and we followed. Our steps echoed with a muffled quality which sounded unnatural. The air was musty, as if it had been trapped for decades.

We gathered at the bottom before the outline of a wide door in the wall. There was a simple, metal handle. Father Veronica gripped it, pulled upward, and pushed the door. There was resistance at first, then the door swung inward; at the same time there was a sound like a giant breathing in, and a breeze was drawn past us into whatever rooms lay beyond the door.

A loud and terrible racket erupted, clattering sounds like dozens of hollowed stone wind chimes, and lights were coming on, spitting and flashing into life, nearly blinding us. Then the stench hit us, working its way against the breeze still blowing inward, not quite overwhelming, but strong and invasive, sticky sweet and rotting and musty and acrid burning all at once, driving its way through our nostrils and into our brains.

We stood stunned and unmoving, and now, finally, we were starting to make out with blinking and stinging eyes what it was that filled the vast chamber beyond the wide, open doorway. . . .

Bones.

Hanging bones. Skeletons rattling and clattering in the air currents; tightly woven ropes knotted on large and vicious hooks embedded in the ceiling, then noosed around the nearly fleshless necks of discolored skeletons with skulls grinning and staring at us from shadowed, empty sockets.

No one moved. No one said a word.

How many were there? How many hanging skeletons in this chamber that seemed to stretch on endlessly in all directions? Too many to distinguish, too many to count.

Only gradually did more details become apparent—not because they had been hidden, but because it was all too much to take in at once, and only bit by bit could it be processed; maybe not even then; perhaps there would never be enough time to assimilate everything we saw in this chamber. That, after all, might be best.

The skeletons were not completely stripped clean. On most there still remained dangling strips of leatherlike skin, translucent strings of sinew, the reflection of metallic wrist bands, stray tufts of hair caught in splintered bone.

Looking more closely now, I saw that some of the bones were broken, crushed, particularly the fingers and toes, digits missing or barely hanging on with bits of cartilage or ligament. But there were occasional signs of damage to the larger bones, too, and, more rarely, to a few of the skulls.

The air currents had died down, and the skeletons swung more slowly now; there was less clacking and clattering, quieter now, though just as disturbing. The left wall was fifteen meters and two dozen skeletons away, the right wall the same, but the far wall was beyond view—all we could see were more skeletons, stretching endlessly into the distance . . . literally hundreds, I guessed. Thousands? It was horribly possible.

Father Veronica was the first to move, the first to step farther into the chamber. The skeletons were not lined up in rows, and they were so close to one another that there was no way to move among them without grazing the bones. As Father Veronica worked her way toward the back, she set some of the skeletons swinging and clattering again. I followed, making my own path, making my own terrible music.

There were hundreds of bones scattered about the floor,

strips of decayed flesh, pools and smears of viscous fluid. Just as it was impossible to avoid brushing against the hanging skeletons, so was it impossible to avoid stepping on bone or in thick, sticky liquid as I moved through the room. I pushed through the skeletons in a daze, barely able to maintain my balance, my thoughts frozen in place, my body hardly able to function.

Ragged gouges across a kneecap, more gouges in a cheekbone. Scorch marks on some of the hands and feet, and I could only hope they were postmortem, but I suspected, given everything else I'd seen, that they were not. A caved-in skull; a large patch of dark leathery skin flapping at a clavicle; an entire chest of cracked and broken ribs.

Father Veronica had stopped, frozen in place. I made my way to her side, and my breath caught as I saw what she saw: the broken, cracked, damaged, tortured skeletons of children.

Whatever the reasons, this felt so much more terrible, making breath difficult to draw. I opened my mouth, but I couldn't speak. Something should have been said, something should have been asked, but I couldn't imagine what it would be.

After some time—I had no idea how long—Father Veronica and I pressed on, past the bones of the children.

Glimpses of the far wall could now be seen, which meant, at last, an end to this. If there could be an end. We pushed through the last of the hanging skeletons, desperate and faster now, although it meant violently rattling the bones.

But we were still not prepared for the final sight. We reached the end of the chamber, emerged from the hanging skeletons, and found ourselves staring in horror.

Impaled on hooks projecting from the back wall of the chamber were the ruined skeletons of twenty-five or thirty infants. Bloodstained hooks protruded from the infants' chests and necks, through shattered ribs and throats. Crushed fingers and toes. Charred flesh and bone. Broken teeth and desiccated eye sockets and wisps of torn and delicate hair. Babies.

"No," Father Veronica whispered. She began to weep, shaking her head slowly from side to side, the tears streaming down her cheeks. I could do nothing but stand motionless at her side, unable to move, unable to speak, unable to comfort either her or myself.

13

I reported what we found. As I spoke, my voice transmitting back to the shuttle where it was boosted up to the *Argonos*, I felt detached from myself, standing outside of my own body, even outside of the flyer, watching my lips move, listening to my voice relating everything we had seen. Watching the others watching me.

When I finished, there was only a faint background hissing and occasional crackling from the communications equipment. No questions, no requests for clarification. Finally, after several minutes of uncomfortable quiet, Nikos spoke.

"We need to discuss this further here," he said, his tone tired and unsure. "For now, though, we don't think you should stay there. Proceed to the next site tomorrow. If it is decided that further investigation is needed, you can return."

"We need to bury them," Father Veronica said. Even *her* voice was unsure, lost.

"Impossible," Nikos replied. "The numbers . . . the terrain there . . . it's a logistical nightmare, and it would take you days, if not weeks. No, it's impossible. Continue on to the next site tomorrow."

"But the babies," she said, imploring. "At least let us bury the babies . . . they . . . their faces . . . Please. Let us bury the babies."

There was another long wait, several almost unbearable minutes during which we all sat in silence, none of us looking at any of the others. When our wait finally ended, it was the bishop's voice we heard.

"Yes, Father Veronica. Although the captain is reluctant, I have insisted. You may bury the babies."

"Thank you, Eminence."

There were a few more exchanges, formalities, and then we disconnected the linkup. We were so very much alone, the four of us in the flyer surrounded by jungle and darkness and death.

THE next day we buried the babies' skeletons, a gruesome task. I see no reason to recount it in detail. While clearing an area for the grave, Trude went a little insane. She widened the beam of her stone burner and notched it up to full power, then burned and burned her way through the vegetation all around the area, far more than necessary, sending up clouds of choking black smoke that did not dissipate for hours. No one tried to stop her, no one tried to calm her.

That night I sat with Father Veronica outside the flyer, in front of a contained fire she had started with one of the stone burners. Neither of us spoke. The light from the fire did not penetrate very far into either the jungle or the night, and despite the crackling orange flames, I felt that both were closing in on us, and that there was no escape.

WE left at dawn for the next site. I was glad to be leaving all of that behind us, but now I was afraid of what else we would find.

We flew far to the north of the continent, leaving the steaming jungles behind. Near a high mountain lake we found a single dwelling surrounded by a circular, water-filled ditch. The rotting remains of a crude boat were scattered between the dwelling and the lakeshore.

The air was cold and smelled painfully clean. With fallen logs from the nearby woods, we laid a bridge across the ditch. The dwelling was a single room, with handmade wooden furniture, shelves with plates and cups and utensils, cooking equipment, and an unusual apparatus that we surmised was a stove. On the bed, beneath the tattered remnants of a blanket, was the skeleton of a man who, I would like to think, died quietly in his sleep.

Everything was quiet, peaceful, no signs of violence, no signs of madness. There was a palpable sense of relief, although no one expressed it aloud. We buried his remains beside the dwelling, and returned to the flyer.

AFTER the sun went down and we'd eaten, we got the linkup with the Executive Council. They had finally made their decision.

"Something undeniably strange has happened here," Nikos said, speaking over the linkup as if he were making a speech. "But it is far in the past. In the end, it has no relevance to us or our mission. There is nothing for us here, so it is time that we leave." A politician's speech, with little more substantive content than the transmission that had brought us here.

We were ordered to cancel our trip to the final site and start back for the shuttle at first light the next day; then we would take off the day after that to rejoin the *Argonos*. The ship would remain in orbit for several more days to allow the harvesters to maximize our stores, and then we would set course for some other godforsaken star, some other godforsaken world.

Father Veronica started to protest, but the bishop immediately cut her off, stating that this was the Church's considered position as well, and that there would be no further discussion. I could see she was angry, but she said no more.

When the conversation ended and the linkup was shut

down, Father Veronica and I took a walk along the lake. The evening air was cold, and I could smell moisture slowly rising from the black, still water. There was no moon, but the stars provided plenty of light.

Father Veronica gazed out ahead of us, but I had the feeling she wasn't really looking at anything. I remained silent, waiting for her.

We had been walking for ten or fifteen minutes when she stopped, turned to me, and angrily said, "I can't *believe* we are being ordered back to the *Argonos*. We owe these people more."

"What do you mean?"

"We should stay and make a real effort to learn what happened to them. Something terrible occurred here. There are more dead on this planet, in places we haven't seen yet—I am almost certain of that. To just leave it all behind, as if these people never existed . . . we owe them more than that. We owe them more than just a partial burial."

"It will never happen," I said. "You heard them tonight, the *way* they said it. They don't want to stay any longer than they have to."

"Why? Are we in a hurry to get somewhere? There's nothing out there that can't wait a few weeks, or even months. We've been wandering aimlessly for all these years . . . here we have encountered something *real*. We should be *staying*, not leaving."

"Probably all this scares them. It scares *me*. They don't *want* to know what happened. And with no one left alive here, they'll resist any arguments, any protests."

She sighed heavily. "Oh, I know that," she said. "But what about those people on the ship who would *want* to stay here? Those who would like to make their own settlements, start new lives, perhaps be willing to make the time and effort to give the dead the respect they deserve and try to learn what happened."

"Maybe everyone would be too frightened. Maybe no one would want to stay."

"Don't be disingenuous, Bartolomeo. We both know there are many people on the *Argonos* who would give anything to be able to do just that."

I wondered again what she was telling me. Was she saying she knew about the insurrection? I couldn't tell.

"They can make that request to the Executive Council or Planning Committee if they really want to," I said. "Anyone can."

She shook her head at me. "Everyone knows how that vote would go. The downsiders get no vote themselves. The *Argonos* is run by an oligarchy, and the request would be denied. You know that, Bartolomeo. It is an unjust system, and you know that, too." Her voice grew sad. "Anyone who wants to stay here should be allowed to do so. If God can grant human beings free will, the ability and the freedom and responsibility to make their own decisions with their lives, the least that those in authority on this ship can do is grant the same thing for their fellow humans."

I had my own skeptic's thoughts about God and free will, but that was a discussion for another time. The idea of human beings in power acting out of anything except self-interest, however, was absurd to me. "Are you being naive?" I asked her.

"No, Bartolomeo. I know what the reality is. I am only expressing my belief in what *should* be, my belief in what is right. I know the difference, and it saddens me."

With that, she resumed walking again, and I continued with her. We did not talk, but my thoughts were running madly, and I realized I had begun to rethink my feelings about the mutiny. Father Veronica's words resonated with me, and I couldn't shake the growing feeling that she was right. Not for the first time, I thought to myself that in so many ways she was remarkable.

WHEN we arrived at our original landing site the next day, I stepped out of the flyer, looking for Sari Mandapat. She was standing no more than twenty meters away, staring at me. It was only at that moment that I realized my decision had finally, firmly, been made. I nodded at her, twice to make sure she understood. She did, for she nodded sharply at me in return, and walked back to the shuttle.

Tomorrow, I thought to myself, tomorrow it begins.

14

BACK on board the *Argonos*, there was a strained atmosphere, unresolved conflicts that had only festered during the landfall. The captain seemed to be avoiding me, but I had no objections to that; it made it easier for me to help with the mutiny.

We had so little time to prepare. The harvesters would continue processing for three more days, then the ship would break orbit and leave. Fortunately, Pär and his colleagues had been working nonstop while Sari Mandapat and I were down on Antioch, planning the coordination of more than a thousand people, making lists and schedules and calculations. They had done everything that could be done without me.

My own role was to provide access codes and passwords, to open doors and holds and chambers, to activate the machinery and equipment we would need, to deactivate the alarms. They had planned incredibly well, far more thoroughly and creatively than I would ever have imagined.

I began to believe it might actually work.

BY the second day back I was exhausted, but none of us had much time for sleep. Minor missteps and prob-

lems arose with alarming regularity, but Pär and Alice
Springs and Arturo Morales were unconcerned each time;
they had planned for them, and expected them, and their
calm helped to ease my own anxieties.

I suggested revealing our plans to Father Veronica, trying
to convince them that not only would she be sympathetic
to our cause, she might want to join us. I was emphatically
voted down. For them, the Church was part of the upper
levels, and that meant Father Veronica as well. I pointed
out that I, too, was from the upper levels, but to no avail;
I realized for the first time that, with the exception of Pär,
they, too, despised me, and had only included me because
they had no other choice. I considered withdrawing, even
betraying them. Instead, I continued working.

I tried to find Francis. I wanted him to come with us to
Antioch, have a chance to start a new life; it would be
better, I thought, than what he had on the ship.

I started in the chamber of abandoned machines. It was
empty and quiet, and as I walked through the room, playing
the light of my hand torch across the metal all around me,
I called out his name, over and over. There was no response;
there were no sounds at all except the now familiar *ticking*
noise coming from somewhere in the distance.

When I reached the hollowed-out bay, everything was
silent and deserted. The bishop's machine was dark and
lifeless. Although I was still curious about the bishop's intentions, I had in some important way lost interest. Two
more days, and I would be gone from the ship, and would
never see the bishop or his machine again.

AFTER searching the chamber, I roamed through several of the lower levels, asking people I met if they
knew Francis, or knew of him. I wandered through a smok-
ing club, nearly overwhelmed by the harsh reek of tobacco
and star-leaf smoke, and asked about the boy at each table

I passed. I got shaken heads, a few muttered negative words, but just as often I received silent, hostile glares.

In a barter shop I was given shrugs and several offers for my exoskeleton, but no one admitted to knowing Francis.

On another level I inadvertently interrupted a group of flesh gamblers, close to twenty men and women rolling twelve-sided illuminated dice into shadowed maze boxes. As the scarred and tattooed gamblers looked up at me, scowling, I quickly backed out of the darkened room without a word.

On the same level, I walked into a small chapel, where a Shinto priest was quietly speaking with a dozen men and women. There were a number of smaller chapels like this scattered throughout the ship, mostly on the lower levels, with several unofficial and unsanctioned sects and alternative religious groups holding their services in defiance of the Church. The bishop was always trying to suppress them, but he received no support or cooperation from the captain or the Executive Council, so his efforts were ineffective. I don't think he understood that he was better off that way. I mumbled my apologies to the priest and withdrew.

I recognized a few of the people I saw, but most I had never seen before, something which no longer surprised me. Just as the bishop claimed that the ship had always existed, I sometimes imagined that it folded and twisted in on itself so that there were an infinite number of cabins and levels, and an infinite number of people. It made me feel lost and overwhelmed, and I wanted nothing more than to launch myself from the ship, escape its gravity, and drift out into the silent calm dark of space.

I had almost given up. Two or three levels lower down, I came across the open doors of an ag room, a high-ceilinged hold of growing fields and a grove of fruit trees. A small herd of pygmy goats grazed at the edge of the field. Seven or eight people were working in a shed with planting boxes and soil and starter plants. I entered and walked toward them.

"I'm looking for a boy," I said. "His name is Francis, he's about thirteen or fourteen years old." There was no response, although they were all staring at me, not all of them unfriendly. "No father, and his mother's sick, maybe dying."

A young woman who had been kneeling stood up and brushed dirt from her hands. She observed me for some time from where she stood, then said, "I know Francis." She appeared to be about twenty-five, perhaps a little older, dark hair cut quite short. "Why are you looking for him?"

I took a few steps closer to the group. "I'm concerned about him. He said he was living on his own, no place to go. I was just hoping to find him, find family or friends who could take him in."

"Why do you care?" the woman asked.

She was gazing intently at me, and I felt compelled to answer her honestly. "Because he reminds me of myself."

The young woman broke away from the group and approached me. The others returned to their tasks. She put out her hand, and didn't flinch when I grasped it with my artificial fingers.

"My name is Catherine," she said. "Francis is my brother. Half brother."

"My name's Bartolomeo."

She nodded. "I know who you are."

"Is that good or bad?" I asked, trying to smile.

She ignored the question. "I appreciate your concern, Bartolomeo, but Francis will be all right. He always is."

"That may be so, but I still want to help him."

"He's a downsider. He doesn't need your help." And with that she turned away and rejoined her group.

I stood there for a minute, not wanting to leave. I felt rejected, which confused me. Catherine didn't look back, although a couple of the others glanced briefly in my direction as though afraid I was going to stay. I left.

N I K O S was preoccupied. We spoke rarely, and when we did, neither of us said anything of substance. He did not raise the issue of his plan for dealing with the bishop in their power struggle, and I did not ask him about it, afraid to be drawn into something that would take me away from the work I needed to do with Pär and the others. I even began to wonder if he suspected me of something.

But if he did suspect, there was nothing that could be done. It was far too late for that now. There was no turning back.

And yet, at times I wasn't sure why I was doing this. Why did I want to go back to that world, a world that held the dead, that induced nightmares?

I was not sleeping much, and what little sleep I did get was disturbed by haunted dreams—visions of the dead, strings of bones making ghastly music as they clacked together in an uneasy breeze, rotting corpses floating through the air with eyes staring, tiny babies drowning in sand.

I could only hope that eventually the nightmares would end.

I thought often of Father Veronica. I would miss her.

15

T H I S was mutiny.

It was so quiet at first, I could hardly imagine what was about to occur.

Silence and shadowed darkness filled the vast transport hold. Scattered about the far and upper reaches were dim blue lights that cast little illumination—stationary fireflies, tiny beacons in an endless metal cave. A long, muted hissing sounded from somewhere far off, then slowly faded away. Quiet again.

Soft floor lights came to life, and the silence was broken as I led a small group of eight across the open space of the hold to the shuttles on the far side—heavier, darker shadows within shadow. Behind me, in the darkened holding area, were more than eleven hundred people with all the personal possessions they were allowed; a shifting, anxious mass of humanity, waiting. I did not look back at them.

Timing would be critical. We had rehearsed these procedures repeatedly—everyone knew where they would go, what they would do. My group approached the first shuttle, then moved along its dark form to the rear. I gestured at Amelia Ritter, who took her station at the fuel intake. Then

I hurried with the others to the fueling equipment in the back wall. One step at a time, one step . . .

I keyed in the access codes, then nodded at two men who pulled the fueling hose structure from the wall, hydraulics whispering in the semidarkness—a metallic, massively tusked and wingless dragon. They guided it to the shuttle and, with the help of Amelia, locked it into place. But fueling was not to begin yet; not until the last minute, timed to finish when everyone and everything was loaded and ready to go. The fueling, even with authorized access codes, would almost certainly alert someone, somewhere, resulting in an investigation. It had to be put off as long as possible.

Amelia remained at the rear of the shuttle, ready to perform the disconnect, while the rest of us moved on to the next shuttle, where the process was repeated with someone again stationed at the rear. Four more times, step by step, no hesitations, no mistakes, until all six shuttles were hooked up to their fueling structures, waiting. Everyone, everything, waiting.

All was quiet again except for the hushed, tense hiss of machinery. Coils of evaporation swirled in and out of the dim blue overhead lights. I paused, scanning the hold, mentally reviewing our plans, while everyone continued to wait.

What had been forgotten, if anything? Minimal food stores, shelters, tools, testing equipment, water and food processors, crates of other, miscellaneous supplies—all had been clandestinely loaded aboard the shuttles earlier in the day. Not enough to long sustain all the people that were going, but there was no choice. There was no room; as it was, people were going to be jammed together like overbreeding laboratory animals. We had one shot at this, one trip down—no preliminary supply drops, no return trips for extra supplies. All or nothing, nothing or all.

Where was Pär? I hadn't seen him all day; I had been overseeing the loading with Sari Mandapat and Arturo Morales while Pär was off with Alice Springs, helping people prepare. I had recently seen Alice—she told me everyone was ready to go—but no sign of Pär. Could he have backed out, afraid it wouldn't work?

"Lost your courage?" said a voice behind me. I turned to see the dwarf grinning at me from the shadows.

"No," I said.

"Then it's time. A new life, and a new world."

Yes, it was time. I nodded, then signaled across the transport hold to Sari Mandapat waiting in the holding area.

New lights bathed the hold, reflecting off metal surfaces, illuminating the shuttles, and the stillness was gone. Six groups of people emerged from the darkness and hurried across the metal deck. Scraping sounds, echoes of hundreds of footfalls. Like herds of cattle moving to new feeding grounds; or packs of lemmings rushing to their own destruction.

People were overloaded, which was not surprising, and they dropped things. Someone stopped to retrieve a lost item, and everything jammed up around him. Leave it! I wanted to yell at the man. But he wouldn't. He scrambled around on hands and knees, tripping someone, reaching for his dropped bag. Finally he recovered it and struggled to his feet, then was swept along toward a shuttle.

The people in front were now flooding through the open shuttle doors, and I watched the pushing and shoving on the boarding ramps, the growing tension and fear. Hissed curses broke out. Near the entrance to Shuttle Three a scuffle erupted, and two bundles went flying; one of them burst open when it hit the ground, scattering the contents.

A man in the middle of the crowd tripped and fell, several others fell over him and each other. Panic and chaos erupted. People started running, grabbing and pulling at each other. The shoving worsened; more people stumbled and fell, dropping packets and bundles that slid across the floor. My stomach tightened as all of our plans threatened to fall apart. There was nothing I could do except watch, and hope.

Toward the back, anxiously working his way forward, was Maximilian, the chief steward who served drinks at all of the Executive Council meetings. He carried a large pack strapped across his shoulders and gripped a pair of well-wrapped bundles in each hand. I caught his attention, and we stared at each other; I imagined I could see resentment and distrust in Maximilian's gaze, a resentment that had built up during all those years of servitude. *I'm helping you now,* I wanted him to understand, but I knew that it was hopeless. There are things not easily remedied or forgotten, and this was one of them. He turned and joined the throng pushing toward the shuttles.

Then I saw Catherine, Francis's sister, in the group loading onto Shuttle Two. I looked all around her, then through the other groups, but saw no sign of Francis anywhere. I wanted to run to her, ask her about him, but I could not leave my station. Too much depended on me, and I couldn't risk getting trampled in all the confusion. Maybe Francis was already aboard one of the shuttles. I hoped so.

Pär began pacing in small tight circuits beside me. "It will be a miracle if we pull this off," he said, shaking his head, wiping sweat from his face. He coughed out a nervous laugh.

The noise gradually diminished, and the tension seemed to abate. The six groups had become a single disorganized mob massed up against the shuttle boarding ramps, but the worst of the scuffling had ceased. The majority of people were inside the shuttles now; fueling could finally begin.

"Let's go," I said.

I started forward, Pär at my side. I began with Shuttle One, Pär with Shuttle Six. We each keyed in the fueling codes for rapid emergency fueling, set to stop at one-third full—enough to get them down, with a bit to spare. Then we moved to Two and Five, keyed the codes, and finished up with Three and Four.

"Fifteen minutes, right?" Pär said.

"Twenty at most."

We looked at the crowds pushing into the shuttles, now fewer than forty or fifty people left at each. The timing was right. Get the rest aboard, belongings stowed, everyone secured for flight. . . .

"We're going to make it," Pär said.

I nodded. Yes, we were. I moved quickly to the control panels, and punched in another series of codes. I turned and

watched the huge, massive transport-hold doors slowly slide
apart, gradually revealing the star-filled night sky.

Energy fields maintained the atmospheric integrity of the
transport hold—no air was lost, no pressure. That side of
the ship faced away from Antioch, and Pär and I saw dozens, then hundreds, and finally thousands of bright stars as
the doors continued to open, revealing the cold vastness
of space.

"It's beautiful," Pär said.

"Yes."

A deep, heavy clang sounded as the doors locked into
place, fully open now. The night sky waited out there for
us, and another world waited for us below. My heart was
beating hard and fast; I only now noticed it. I could hardly
believe we were about to do this. This was not mutiny, I
said to myself. This was escape.

I turned away from the stars and stepped out from the
wall to check on the boarding. I watched the last passengers
go through the shuttle doors. All that remained now was to
secure everyone and everything aboard, finish the fueling,
and we would leave.

Then I heard Pär cursing behind me.

"Shit," Pär said. "Shit, shit, shit . . ."

I turned quickly to look at the dwarf. But it wasn't Pär
that I saw.

Rising into view, hovering outside the open transport-
hold doors, gaping maw swirling with nuclear fire, was one
of the harvesters. Silent in the vacuum of space, but even
more terrible and frightening because of that silence.

A second harvester came into view and hovered beside
the first; then the third appeared, all three lined up across
the transport hold, blocking out the stars, interior furnaces
glowing and burning, ravenous and waiting to consume us
all.

I stared transfixed at those three luminescent and monstrous beings of metal and fire; I was unable to move, unable even to breathe.

How could this be? I wondered. Why were they here?
They weren't due back for hours, and they didn't dock here,

they docked in another hold far away on the other side of
the ship. Why were they here?

Then I knew. They were here to stop the mutiny. To
prevent the shuttles from leaving. A blockade.

Security forces emerged from one of the corridors at the
far end of the transport hold, shattering my trance.

"Shit," Pär said once more; then he disappeared into
the shadows.

I watched as more security forces appeared, flooding in
from the other corridors, storming across the transport hold
and converging on the shuttles. I hesitated only briefly,
seeing all of our plans and hopes shattering, then like Pär I
backed further into the shadows, turned, and hurried away.

16

WE were discovered, and all was lost.

I didn't know what had gone wrong. I didn't know how the captain, or the Executive Council, or the bishop, or whoever, had learned of our plans, but somehow, someone had.

Someone betrayed us, that is all I could imagine. They knew in advance. They were prepared for us.

In all the confusion, I was able to escape without detection: through an emergency exit and a series of service passageways. I never saw Pär, and had no idea where he'd gone. I made my way back to my quarters by a circuitous route, taking several hours to make a journey which normally would be a fifteen-minute walk and one tube ride. I was half surprised there was no one waiting for me when I arrived.

I didn't know how much time I had. Did they know of *my* involvement? Unless they were truly incompetent, they must. Were they coming for me right now, an armed squad marching along the ship's corridors, preparing to break into my quarters and take me into custody? It seemed ridiculous, but was it really?

There was a banging at my door. For several long, panicky moments I *did* think they had come for me. But it was a woman named Liko, a downsider who worked as a maid for Michel Tournier. She thought her husband, Osamu, had been arrested, although she couldn't be sure. No one would tell her a thing, but she couldn't find him anywhere, and none of their friends had seen him.

Osamu was going to co-pilot one of the shuttles, but I didn't know if Liko knew that. I promised her I would find out what I could, and I assured her that if Osamu *had* been arrested, I would do everything I could to help him.

Which was probably worse than nothing, though I didn't tell her that. If the captain and the Executive Council knew about me, then the last thing Osamu needed was my help. She left feeling reassured, but I knew that assurance was misplaced.

HOURS passed, and not a word, not a sign of security forces. I was afraid to make contact with anyone. I was afraid to leave my quarters. Where would I go? None of this was rational—I knew that, but I felt paralyzed. If they knew about me, they would come.

THEY came for me, silenced and in silence. The soldiers were masked in metal and glass, eyes hidden by shining silver reflections.

They overrode the door's security system and entered the first room; when they saw I was in the second, they advanced masked and silent upon me. They numbered five, which seemed far more than necessary for one man.

The five soldiers stood before me, and I slowly shook my head. In a strange way, I could not believe what was happening. The lead soldier stepped forward, still silent, and motioned for me to stand. I did, and the soldier grabbed my shoulder, wrenched me around, and pulled my metal and steelglass arms together, then bound my wrists with electronic shackles. This, too, seemed unnecessary. I made no move to resist or struggle—I would go with them willingly, because anything else would be worse than useless; it would be pathetic.

"What are the charges?" I asked. But there was no answer. "Am I under arrest?" No reply. "I want to speak to Captain Costa." Still no reply, and by then I knew there wouldn't be one.

I sighed in resignation; then as the lead soldier shoved me toward the door, my acceptance gave way to a tightening of my mouth and a tensing of my eyes. I tipped my head back, and as the door opened I called out.

"Nikos! Nikos, where are you?"

I was led through the door, flanked by two guards, another in front of me and two more behind. The corridor was empty, but I continued to shout.

"Nikos! Have the courage to face me if you do this! NIKOS!!"

17

THEY could have confined me to my quarters. Recoded the locks, put a guard in the corridor, shut down my computer access, whatever was necessary. Apparently that wasn't enough.

I was locked in a cell.

There was one entire level of cabins specifically designed for disciplinary confinement, located one level beneath the cathedral. I knew from the sounds I heard that a number of nearby cells were also occupied, but I didn't know by whom, nor did I care.

My cell was equipped with a bunk, toilet, shower cubicle, sink, and a wall screen with only the most restricted system access, and even that was incoming only. I was given one change of clothing. Meals were brought twice a day, trays of the processed food the downsiders lived on.

Oddly enough, however, I was reasonably content. Suddenly my life had become calm and quiet, and waiting did not seem so difficult. Although I had no idea what would happen, nor any control over it, I could reflect at my leisure. I felt relaxed and pressure-free.

I ' **D** been locked up for nearly a week when Father Veronica came to visit me. She was wearing an ordinary black cassock rather than the white I might have expected her to wear for an official visit to a prisoner. I asked her about it.

"I thought you would prefer a visit from a friend, rather than from a representative of the Church."

"You consider yourself my friend?" I asked.

"Of course. Don't you consider yourself mine?"

"Yes."

We shared the wall bed, sitting at opposite ends. We were forced to sit somewhat awkwardly in order to face each other.

"No one's come to see me," I told her. "No one has told me whether or not I am officially under arrest, or what the charges are, or how long I am to be here. Nothing."

Father Veronica hesitated for a few moments before replying, and her expression was grave. "You are charged with treason, Bartolomeo."

Not surprising, but still distressing to hear. This meant they probably knew everything.

"But you won't be tried," she added.

"What do you mean?"

"There will be no trials, not for anyone."

"No trials?" I felt stupid, as if I wasn't hearing right. "No."

"Then I'll be released soon."

"No." Her eyes seemed to go heavy. "No," she said again.

I didn't like what I was hearing, the way she was saying it.

"What's going on?" I asked her.

"The Executive Council is distinguishing between those who followed, and those who led. Those who followed are being released with only minor sanctions."

"And those who led?"

"Charged with treason, but not to be tried. No convictions, no finite sentences. You are being imprisoned 'at the pleasure of the court.' That's the phrase Bishop Soldano used.''

"Which means?"

"As long as they wish. Until they decide you have learned whatever lesson it is they wish you to learn. They were not specific."

It didn't matter. They were angry, and they would keep us locked up until that anger was gone. That could be years, or decades, I thought.

"I was not a leader," I said.

Father Veronica gave me a tired smile. "Technically, no. But you were integral to their plans, and you joined the enterprise willingly, without coercion."

With your influence, I wanted to say. But I didn't.

"What you provided for them," she went on, "—they couldn't have done it without you."

"They didn't do it *with* me," I reminded her.

She nodded.

"Indefinite sentences," I said. "I could be here for the rest of my life."

"I know—it's incredibly unfair, and 'unjust. I've expressed my concerns to Bishop Soldano, but that was futile. He is as displeased as anyone about what has happened."

"Why?"

She looked around my cell. Wondering, I am sure, if our visit was being recorded in some way. I wanted to tell her that of course it was, but her expression suggested she already knew that. She shrugged, as if to say that it really didn't matter.

"I won't pretend that I am unaware of the political maneuverings of the bishop, and the captain, and others from the sidelines. I know that Bishop Soldano has for a long time wanted someone else as captain. . . .''

"He wants Bishop Soldano as captain," I broke in.

"Perhaps. It hardly matters now. Captain Costa is now the ship's hero. He learned of a mutiny, and put an end to it with relatively little bloodshed. His position has been greatly strengthened, while conversely the bishop's has been weakened. More than that, the captain has managed to ap-

portion a certain amount of indirect responsibility for the
mutiny to the bishop.''

The first hint, perhaps, of what the captain had been
plotting all that time. ''Really? How did he manage that?''

''Do you remember the sermon Bishop Soldano delivered on Holy Thursday? When he announced our approach
to the star system and the transmission we were receiving?
I believe you were there.''

''Yes, I was there. I had difficulty staying awake, as
always, but I remember his sermon. Naming of Antioch.
Bringing the word of God to all worlds, all people regard-
less of station or history. His usual colonization speech.''

''Yes. Your captain has a transcript of the sermon. And
he has pointed to one particular passage, the one you were
referring to, in which the bishop said that we need to spread
the word of God to as many places as possible, that we need
to *colonize* as many worlds as we can, putting permanent
settlements in place so that when others come, be they
human or alien, there is someone there to present to them
God's word. The captain doesn't claim the bishop was helping to plan the mutiny, or even that he knew of it, although
he suggests that those are certainly possibilities—after all,
recolonizing that world is what the downsiders were trying
to do. However, Captain Costa says, the bishop's sermon
certainly can be seen as condoning such actions if they were
to occur, or, if nothing else, fostering a climate that would
encourage them. Very clever, your captain.''

''Why do you keep calling him 'my' captain?'' I asked
her angrily. ''He's imprisoned me, and apparently has no
intention of releasing me soon.''

She didn't reply. What could she say? I waved my hand,
and said, ''Never mind. Who else has 'my captain' imprisoned?'' I wanted to know what had happened to Pär, but
didn't want to mention him by name. It was just possible,
I thought, that no one knew of his role. He had, after all,
managed to get away before I did.

''Sari Mandapat,'' she said. ''Arturo Morales. Alice
Springs. Conrad Martin. And Samuel Eko.'' She paused,

thinking, and I waited. "Yes," she said. "That's all. Everyone else has been released."

Not Pär, I thought. So they *didn't* know about him. But that small bit of pleasure was short-lived.

"Do you know Pär Lundkvist?" she asked.

I was surprised by the question. Surely she knew of my friendship with him. I'd never made a secret of it.

"The dwarf," I said. "Yes, I know him. Why?"

"He, too, has been identified as one of the leaders. However, although they would like to arrest and imprison him with the rest of you, they cannot find him."

I thought I detected a touch of a smile from her.

"They can't find him?"

"No. They have been searching the ship for days. Speculation is divided between two possibilities. Either he is still aboard and well-hidden, or he somehow managed, in all the confusion, to get down to Antioch before we broke orbit."

"That doesn't seem likely, does it?"

"No. But there is a shuttle missing from the other transport hold. We don't know how, nor do we know if Pär was even capable of piloting it. But we can't find it *or* him."

We sat without speaking for a while. It was good just to have her there in my cell with me. I didn't much mind being imprisoned, but I had missed her.

She said she had to go, then asked me if there was anything she could do or get for me.

"No," I told her. "I have everything I need, everything I could ever want." But then I shook my head, and said more seriously, "No."

She got up from the bed. "I'll go now, but I'll visit again."

"Thanks."

She went to the door, tapped on it, and was let out. As soon as she was out of sight and the door locked shut again, I began to miss her. Once again, I smelled honey and cinnamon.

I hoped Pär was alive out there somewhere. I imagined him, as unlikely as it seemed, piloting the shuttle out of the *Argonos*, perhaps struggling with it even as he guided it out of orbit and into a rough and ragged descent.

Did he try to find one of the deserted settlements to start his new life? Or did he head for unknown territory as mysterious and uncertain as his own future? I didn't know. But in my mind he landed the shuttle safely, and stepped out onto solid ground, alone and free.

THE days continued to pass without change. I saw no one, I talked to no one. Father Veronica did not return to see me again. I tried not to speculate on the reasons.

I thought a lot about our betrayal, and what Father Veronica said, thought a lot about "my captain." I came to believe he knew about the insurrection all along. He may have known about it even before I did. He'd told me he had plans to consolidate his position, to take care of the bishop. I wondered, did he know of *my* involvement all along? Was I just a price he had to pay? Perhaps he never thought it much of a price.

I passed the time sleeping, meditating, exercising infrequently, and thinking. I did not become bored. I was in a kind of trance, as if I'd shifted out of normal time so that I had no sense of its passage. I existed, and I waited. For a time, that was enough.

FATHER Veronica finally came to see me again. She was distraught, and apologized for not coming sooner.

"I was denied access to you," she explained.

"Why?"

"I still don't know. Perhaps because of what we talked about when I was here; I was probably unwisely indiscreet. I have been permitted to visit any of the prisoners except you. It's taken all this time for me to work out permission for one last visit."

One last visit. I felt something hard and heavy sink into my stomach with those words.

"I'm sorry," she said. "I will try to get visitation rights

reinstated. I'll keep at it, but it may take time before I make
any progress. No one has any interest in helping me, and
no one has any sympathy for you. The other leaders were
all downsiders, but you come from the upper levels. They
see your betrayal as greater than the others.' Everyone of
influence is quite adamant about keeping you isolated.''

"Let it go," I told her.

"What do you mean?"

"Let it go. Drop it. It won't do *me* any good, and it
certainly won't do *you* any good." I tried to smile. "Maybe
when things have settled down, when people are not so
angry. But for now . . . don't bother. You're a priest. Save
your energy for those you *can* help."

She didn't say anything in reply. She recognized the
reality as well as I did, although I was beginning to understand some things that she did not.

She approached me and took my hand in both of hers.
"They've only given me five minutes." Then, still holding
my hand, she said, "I am very sorry, Bartolomeo. Please
take care of yourself in here. It won't be forever." She
released my hand, and it became immediately cold. "You
might even want to try praying."

"Yes, I might," I said, smiling.

"Don't trivialize it, Bartolomeo. There can be great comfort in prayer."

Then she turned away from me and left, and for the first
time since I had been imprisoned here, I felt despair.

A strange thing happened the next day. The door was
opened, a guard put a tray on the floor, then quickly
retreated without a word. On the tray was a large thermal
pot and a glass cup.

I sat and stared at the tray for a long time, thinking. Was
I being offered poison? An honorable end? I couldn't imagine what else it would be, but at the same time I couldn't
believe that it really *was* poison.

Eventually I went over to the tray, released the top of

the thermal pot, and poured hot, dark brown liquid into the glass cup. It smelled like coffee.

I let it sit there steaming for a minute or two, then I picked up the cup and raised it to my face. I breathed in deeply, and the coffee aroma was strong, without any other detectable odors. I thought to myself, What does it matter? I brought the cup to my mouth and drank.

It *was* coffee. Hot and strong and so delicious I knew only one person could have made it.

I drank slowly, savoring it, then capped the pot, sealing in the heat. Enough for two or three more cups remained, and I saved it; the thermal pot would keep it warm for another day.

I wondered where he was, and how long he could remain free.

NO changes now. There were no more visits from Father Veronica, nor anyone else. Every five or six days another full pot of coffee would arrive, and each time I rationed it. I relished it greatly, but I wished I could contact him somehow and tell him not to send any more, tell him not to risk his freedom. And yet . . . the coffee was a great comfort to me, and I knew I would miss it if it stopped, just as I missed Father Veronica.

I thought of her often. Prayer, for me, was still impossible. I suspected it always would be.

I had been imprisoned for several weeks, but I was still content; at last I came to understand why: I didn't believe I would be locked up for very long.

I had heard nothing at all from the captain, but his sense of security on this ship would not last forever. He was the "savior" for the moment, but this would pass, and people would realize that little had actually changed; the *Argonos* was still a ship without a mission, and the maneuvering would resume, the probing of weaknesses, the pushing, the stresses. The captain would find himself pressured from all sides; he would find himself alone, with no one he could trust, and he would find himself once again in need of my advice. The day would come when he needed *me*.

If I was any judge of what things were like on this ship, and of what people were like, that day would come soon. And when it did, someone would come to the door, unlock it, then step aside for me, and I would be free.

PART TWO

The Dead Ship

18

MY sense of contentment did not last. The weeks became months—far longer than I had expected. The tedium was mind-numbing. There was simply nothing to do. I asked for writing supplies and tried to work daily on a chronicle of sorts, a recounting of the events that had brought me to my cell; a task to sharpen and focus my mind. But soon after Father Veronica's visits ceased, I had brought the chronicle up to date and had little else to write about— rambling, barely coherent thoughts.

I began exercising vigorously, eating every morsel of tasteless food, trying to pull myself together and clear my mind. I re-read all that I had written. I destroyed much of it (though what I did save serves me well now as a reminder of details surrounding those events), and determined not to write any more.

I had no visitors in all that time. Father Veronica would have come if she had been allowed to, I was certain of that. Pär, of course, could not. When I realized there was no one else who would have wanted to visit me, I was surprisingly depressed.

Then I sensed a change. I didn't know what it was, and I couldn't determine where it was coming from, but I was

certain it was there—in the ship somewhere, something . . .
Something had happened. I could feel it.

The routine did not vary for the next few days—food
and monotony remained the same—but the feeling persisted,
grew stronger.

One morning I received another pot of coffee. When I
poured out a cup, I noticed something flash inside the pot.
I pulled out a strip of plastic on which was printed these
words: SOMETHING'S BEEN FOUND.

What did that mean? It was important, or Pär would not
have risked adding the note.

I felt energized, and my hope for release was rekindled.
Something's been found.

BUT after that, nothing.

Days passed, then weeks. Could I have been wrong?

No, I still sensed a strange tension. Undefined, but palpable. And yet, there were no further messages from Pär; in
fact, even the coffee ceased to arrive. That alone distressed me.

I began to feel out of control. I paced my cell. I fought
the urge to pound on the door and demand my release. My
left eye twitched uncontrollably much of the time, and even
my own skin seemed confining.

Unfulfilled expectations. Each time I heard a sound, I
expected someone to appear at my cell door—Father Veronica, Nikos, Pär, *anyone.* To release or visit me; either one,
I didn't care.

I spoke to the masked and shielded guards who brought
my food, but they did not respond. Even the one who normally brought the coffee from Pär would not acknowledge
me, refused to look at the handwritten questions I held up
before his masked face.

What was happening out there?

I began to dream of Antioch again. Skeletons. Bones and
ravaged skulls and stifling jungle. I dreamed repeatedly

of the failed mutiny. Each time, the actual events were slightly different, strange and distorted from what had happened, but the dreams always ended with the harvesters rising silently outside the open transport-hold doors, blazing mouths waiting to devour me.

MORE time passed, the days interminable. I came to believe that whatever had happened, whatever had been *found*, would have no effect on my confinement. My hopes faded, and I prepared myself again for an indefinite stay.

19

ONE day a man named Geller, who had spent two terms on the Executive Council some years back, entered my cell without warning. I was only half-dressed, lying on the floor working through the daily stretching and exercise routine for my back, the exoskeleton propped against the bed.

Geller stopped, looked down at me, then looked away. "I'll come back later," he said.

"No, don't." I didn't know why he was here, but I didn't want him to leave, not even if he had bad news.

I turned over and pulled myself up onto the edge of the bed, put on my shirt, then worked my upper body into the exoskeleton. As I struggled with it, I glanced at Geller. He kept his eyes turned away from me; he knew I didn't want any help. I remembered him as a quiet man who took his position on the Executive Council seriously. He was intelligent and thoughtful, made reasoned and forceful arguments without being aggressive or obnoxious, and always voted with principle, even in a losing cause. Because he could not be manipulated, he had been replaced by General Wainwright, who *could* be.

When I was finished I offered him a seat, but he declined.

"I won't be long," he said. "I am here to inform you that you are to be released tomorrow."

I sat on the edge of the bed, stunned. I should have been elated, but felt more disoriented than anything else. I don't think I quite believed it, although I could not imagine Geller's being involved in any kind of deception; at least, not knowingly.

"Released," I repeated.

"Yes. Tomorrow morning at 0900."

"Why?"

Geller just shook his head. I didn't know whether that meant he didn't know or he was forbidden to tell me.

"Is this to be temporary, or permanent?"

"Permanent." The corner of his mouth turned up slightly. "Assuming you don't attempt to lead another mutiny," he said.

"My sentence commuted?" I asked.

"I believe you were never tried or sentenced," he replied.

I nodded, remembering my conversation months earlier with Father Veronica. "The charges dropped?"

"I don't know."

"Who requested you do this?"

"Captain Costa."

"If I'm to be released," I said, "why can't I just go now?"

Again Geller just shook his head. "Be ready at nine tomorrow. That's all I can tell you."

He turned and started to leave, but I stopped him.

"Wait."

He looked back at me.

"What's going on out there?"

Geller didn't answer. His expression didn't even change.

"What's been found?"

Still no answer, but this time his face visibly tightened. "Be ready," he repeated, then walked out.

THE next morning, upon my release, I was not allowed to return to my own rooms. Instead, I was escorted directly to the captain's quarters by a contingent of six masked and armed security soldiers. I did not feel like a free man.

It had been less than a year, but already the captain's quarters seemed unfamiliar. The six soldiers didn't help, but even after Nikos had dismissed them I still felt like a stranger in those rooms.

Nikos sat behind his desk, saying nothing. I stood in front of him, my hands clasped behind my back as if they were bound and I was still a prisoner.

"It's been a long and difficult time, Bartolomeo."

I gave him a half-smile and said, "For whom?"

Nikos nodded in acknowledgment. "More difficult for you, yes. But difficult for me as well." He waved at the chairs across the desk from him. "Please, Bartolomeo, make yourself at home."

"Like old times?"

"Yes, like old times. We can try, can't we?"

I sat in one of the chairs, which felt unusually soft and comfortable after all the months in my cell. The orange glowglobes were stationary above us, distributed in a patterned matrix. The faint aroma of mood incense lingered in the air, almost cloying.

"I had no choice," Nikos finally said to me.

"Imprisoning me?" I asked. "Or releasing me?"

He sighed heavily. "Is our entire conversation going to be like this? I understand how you feel, but I don't want to do it this way. I don't have the time or the energy for it."

I just shook my head.

"Why don't we have a drink?" Nikos suggested.

"All right."

He seemed greatly relieved. He got up and poured two glasses of whiskey. I remembered the last time we drank together—just before landfall, when he kept emphasizing how much he was depending on me. Apparently he had been depending on me to keep the mutiny going so he could be the hero and save the ship. Now, months later, he brought a glass of whiskey to me, and I could not help but wonder in what new way he was about to deceive me again. He sat back down, and we both drank.

"You were saying you had no choice."

He nodded. "That's correct. No choice. I could not let you remain free while we incarcerated the others. Too many people knew you were involved."

"How long had you known of our plans?"

"Some time," Nikos replied. That was vague enough.

"That was your plan all along to fend off the bishop. You knew about the mutiny all that time, and let it proceed so you could stop it at the last minute and be the hero."

His silence was all the response I needed.

"And how long had you known of *my* involvement?"

"I only found out at the very end, just before they started boarding the shuttles, when it was too late to warn you. By then I had no choice—I had to let it happen."

I didn't believe him, but I let it go.

"I did what I could," he went on. "I managed to convince the Executive Council not to proceed with the charges, no trials, no sentences. I kept things as open-ended as possible."

"Why have I been released now?"

Nikos hesitated a long time before answering, and I began to sense how difficult this was for him. "I've risked everything to have you released. I had to release all of the other conspirators as well."

"Why?" I asked again.

He pulled at his beard, always a sign of distress. "I need you," he finally said.

I almost smiled, but managed to keep my expression under control.

"Does the bishop know?"

"By now, probably. He'll be furious. I've bypassed the entire Executive Council doing this."

"All right," I said. "Tell me what's happened."

"Better if I show you," he replied.

W E walked through the ship corridors to the command salon, a half-hour of tense silence—more uncomfortable for Nikos than for me, I was certain. He carried the whiskey bottle and glasses, which showed me the depth of his distress. The few people we passed pointedly ignored us, although some did appear surprised to see me.

Once inside the salon, Nikos sank into the command chair, setting bottle and glasses on the floor. He did not look much in command of anything. He moved his hands to the control consoles and tapped out a series of key sequences.

There was a faint vibration, a barely audible hum, and the canopy began to retract—robotic iris, a giant eye to us, but a tiny eye to the ship, opening to the vastness of space. Stars came into view, only a handful at first, then more as the canopy continued to retract, a dense and growing expanse of radiant dust.

As almost always happened in that room, I became disoriented once the canopy had fully retracted. I felt unmoored, adrift in a glass bubble.

Nikos raised a hand and pointed out through the clear steelglass. "There," he said.

I followed the direction of his trembling finger, studied the unending night. Nearly lost in all the stars was a tiny smudge of bluish light against a small dark occlusion.

"What is it?"

Nikos handed one of the glasses to me, which I took. He filled it along with his own, then drank most of his down at once, eyes clamped tightly shut. He shuddered, then opened his eyes and stared at the bluish light.

"An alien starship," he said.

Something's been found, Pär's note had said. Oh, yes, something had been found. I stared at the azure light, the dark area within and around it. An alien starship.

"How do we know it's alien?" I asked. "Are we communicating with them?"

Nikos shook his head. "There's no one there. It's a dead ship. Abandoned or deserted, who knows?" He drank again, refilled his glass. "Maybe just empty and dead because everyone aboard has perished. We haven't found any bodies yet."

"How do we know it's alien?" I asked again.

"Because there's not a damn thing recognizably human on that ship, inside or out."

"So we've been inside."

"Yes. We've explored the smallest piece of the thing." He turned to look at me. "That ship is huge, Bartolomeo. A lot bigger than the *Argonos*."

"How far are we from it?" It seemed so small.

"About three thousand kilometers. I wasn't going to bring the *Argonos* any closer until we had a better idea what it was. And now that we do, I still don't want to." He turned his attention back to the alien vessel. "We picked it up three months ago. Spent a week on our approach and deceleration, another week of observation—scanning, listening, probing. No response, so signs of life."

Nikos worked the console, and the monitor screen rose from the floor, three meters square and already coming to life. A black shape flickered into focus, somewhat ovoid, and so dark, its surface features were almost impossible to make out; it seemed to be covered with smaller half-ovoids, like bubbles. Bluish light beacons hovered above the surface of the vessel.

"The lights belong to the ship, or are they ours?"

"Ours," Nikos answered. "Navigational guidance, they help provide orientation and perspective, as well as some illumination. The ship's surface has almost no reflectivity. We don't pick up anything from it. No lights, no heat radiation, no drive disturbances or engine exhaust, nothing. Dead ship. But deadly."

"What does that mean?"

Nikos made a huffing sound. "Nine weeks ago, the first exploration team flew over in one of the maintenance modules and made contact. They spent three days just locating an entrance. It took two more teams and another day and a half to finally figure out how to work the air lock system. We call it an air lock, but there's no atmosphere inside. Cold and black as space . . ." His voice and attention drifted. "Sent in a couple of remotes, but they aren't sophisticated, and they're not very dexterous. Couldn't get any further than the air lock itself, couldn't manipulate the doors. There was another day of discussion and argument on the Executive Council, which won't surprise you, but we finally reached a consensus, and a team went in. A few hours later we had the first casualty.''

I waited for him to continue, but he just stared at the image on the screen, eyes glazed.

"What happened?" I asked.

Nikos breathed in deeply and slowly let it out. "An accident. See for yourself."

More finger movements on the console, and the image on the monitor shifted, flickered, went through a series of changes before finally resolving into shaky video of a pressure-suited figure crisscrossed with light and shadow, drifting weightlessly near a curved, dark metal wall. The figure's left hand reached out and took hold of a bar on the wall, anchoring itself; the right hand held a large hand torch whose beam swept unevenly across the wall.

"That's Santiago," Nikos said. "On point. Every member of the team has a camera and light mounted on their helmet, so we have a pretty thorough record of everything that happens during each excursion. We try to have the video transmitted live back to the *Argonos* so we can follow along and communicate with them, but the transmissions break up fairly quickly, and the teams don't get far inside before we lose them altogether. But everything is recorded, so we can always review it later."

He touched another control, and the team's audio was added to the video images. I could hear someone laughing, then a woman's voice.

"Oh, man, Santiago, you're a crude bastard." Then more laughter, some of it stifled.

"That was Winton," Nikos explained. "That's her video we're watching now. It shows the best view of what happened."

For a time, we could hear only breathing. As Winton looked around, her camera revealed an enormous spherical room twenty-five or thirty meters in diameter. The walls were nearly featureless, broken only by regularly spaced bars that projected out half a meter—the bars served as handholds for the exploration team, but it seemed unlikely that that was their original purpose.

A third suited figure drifted into view, then just as quickly drifted out of sight.

"Marx," Nikos said. "There were three in the first team."

I knew Marx well. He was a very serious and quiet man, did not dislike me, and we got along. He was married and had two children, and I remember hoping as I watched that he wasn't the casualty.

"Over here." Santiago's voice.

Winton turned her head and Santiago came back into view. He was next to a large opening or doorway, a hand on one bar, a boot resting against another. His hand torch was aimed into the opening, the beam cutting its way into darkness.

Winton pushed off the wall and floated toward him. *"What have you got?"* she asked.

"Not much. A huge room of some kind."

She landed on the other side of the doorway as Santiago worked his way closer to the opening, shifting his grip from the bar to the frame. *"I can barely make out the other end."*

Winton turned to look at Marx, who was watching from several meters away, holding onto a bar, his legs drifting about.

"Well, let's check it out," Santiago said.

Winton turned back to him. With one hand on the door frame, he swung himself out into the opening and began floating through it into the next room. Winton's helmet light and hand torch crossed him and cast irregular beams into the darkness.

"What the . . . ?"

He suddenly began moving more quickly, lost his grip on the door frame; then both hands reached out frantically as he picked up speed. But it was too late, the door frame was out of reach and Santiago plummeted into the room.

"Oh, shit!"

"Santiago!"

Winton was at the opening now, but holding back. The beams from her helmet light and hand torch caught Santiago's reeling figure falling rapidly, his own helmet light flashing about in all directions.

No more words from Santiago, but now there was a drawn-out cry as he fell, his shrinking figure tumbling in and out of the light.

The cry ceased with a terrible but brief explosion of a scream. Then nothing.

"Santiago!"

"Winton! What happened?" Marx's voice, rising in pitch.

"Santiago! Jesus, Santiago, answer me!"

Winton had her hand torch aimed down at the far end of the room, and I could see her hand and the beam shaking. Santiago's unmoving body was illuminated by the dim light, sprawled on a flat surface. His helmet light had apparently been knocked out by the impact, but his hand torch was still functional. It lay nearby, its light reflecting off the shiny top surface of his helmet.

"SANTIAGO!"

Then there were no sounds except for rapid breathing from Winton and Marx. No one moved, no one said a word.

The video froze for a moment; then the image flickered and the screen went dark.

"You can watch the whole thing from Santiago's camera if you like, but I recommend against it."

"What happened?" I asked.

"Up to that point, every room and passage was zero g. But that cabin has gravity," Nikos said. "Unfortunately for Santiago, it was twice Earth-normal, and in the wrong direction."

Gravity in one room, none in the adjacent cabins and passages—which meant the aliens had been able to control gravity in a far more sophisticated way than we could. It was incredible. What else might be found in that extraordinary vessel?

"And Santiago?"

"Dead. There was no helmet or suit rupture, but he broke

his neck." Nikos paused, polishing off another drink. "His body was there for hours before we could get the people and equipment in to pull him out."

By that time, we had gone through more than half the bottle of whiskey, and I was feeling it; I'd had no alcohol in months, and wasn't accustomed to it. More than anything, though, it made me tired. I wanted to forget about the alien ship, forget about Santiago, forget about Nikos and his betrayals. I wanted to go back to my own quarters and reacquaint myself with them, go to sleep in my own bed. As if sensing that, or recognizing his own drunkenness, Nikos capped the bottle and ordered coffee brought in.

I was surprised to see Maximilian bring the coffee. We stared at each other, neither of us quite sure what to think. He set up a small table and tray with pot and cups, poured, then left. The coffee was strong but terribly bitter, and I had to dilute it with cream. I resisted the urge to complain that the coffee I'd had in prison was better than this.

I drank one cup quickly, then poured another. Nikos was just sipping his, and I suspected he wanted to add whiskey to it, maintain his blood alcohol level.

"What's happened since?" I asked.

"We've continued to explore the ship," he said. "Much more carefully, of course. We make a little progress each time. Sometimes the access is hard to work out, and the absence of gravity makes things more difficult—it's been all zero g since that one room. And now the teams take the time to inventory and record everything they see."

"Any more casualties?" I knew the answer had to be yes.

Nikos nodded. "Four more dead, seven others with severe injuries. All accidents, each one unforeseen. Ruptured pressure suits, broken limbs, concussions. And stranger things. Barry Sorrel returned from an excursion inside, went to sleep for sixteen hours. Could hardly wake him. Physically, he checked out fine with the doctors. But he refuses to go back into the alien ship, and won't say why. Actually, what he says is that he just doesn't feel like it. And do you know Nazia Abouti?"

I told him the name sounded familiar, but I couldn't picture her.

"She's been inside the alien ship several times, and lately *she's* been behaving strangely. A few days ago, her husband brought her in to see a physician. She didn't want to be examined; she said she was feeling fine, but her husband insisted. Primary symptoms: sleeping more than usual, and periodically going into a kind of fugue state—she'll be unresponsive for hours, but doesn't remember anything when she comes out of it. In fact, she insists the fugue states aren't occurring at all, that her husband is fabricating them. Another major symptom is what her husband describes as an overwhelming apathy." He paused. "You understand why I'm worried?"

"Let me guess," I said. "The physician found nothing wrong with her, either."

"That's right. Three different physicians have examined her, and they spent two days running tests. Nothing. But her husband insists she isn't the same."

"You continued to send teams in," I said.

"Yes. Two weeks ago I temporarily suspended all exploration, but we're going to start up again soon. What else are we going to do? An *alien* starship, Bartolomeo. As far as we know, this is the first and only time in human history that we have had any contact, any evidence of an intelligent alien civilization. We can't just stop now, leave it all behind as if it didn't exist."

That was Father Veronica's argument for staying on Antioch, but I didn't remind the captain of that. I was sure he would say, perhaps with some justification, that this was very different, and far more important.

"I'm sure some people have argued we do just that," I said. "That whatever might be discovered isn't worth the loss of lives."

"Yes, some have."

"The bishop?"

"No. Actually, the bishop has a different agenda."

"And what's that?"

Nikos smiled ruefully. "The same old agenda." But he

didn't say any more, his gaze unfocused, as if lost in his thoughts. Or simply lost.

"Why do you need me?" I asked.

"I'm in trouble again, Bartolomeo."

"Because of the casualties."

"Yes. I am being blamed for them, like everything else."

There was something about the way he said that . . .

"What else are you being blamed for?"

"There's more trouble with the downsiders. After we put down the mutiny, I expected the downsiders would become more docile, at least for a few years. Instead of fear, the quelling of the mutiny has stirred up only more resentment. We have rebellion, now. Nothing major, but dozens of small rebellions, subtle bits of sabotage, disgruntlement, resistance. They are making life on the ship difficult without going far enough to warrant arrests or reprisals or other punishments." He gave a grudging smile. "We often can't identify who is causing the difficulty, or what exactly has been done. Occasionally, I imagine, nothing at all has been done, and some piece of equipment breaks down simply because of age, as has always happened on this ship. Now, however, we question everything."

"You've engendered resentment in them, and they have in turn engendered paranoia in you."

"Yes, that is an apt assessment."

"What do you want from me, Nikos?"

"The bishop wants to take over the exploration of the alien ship."

"Let him. Let him take all the risks."

Nikos shook his head. "I can't, Bartolomeo. I can't trust him, you know that." He paused. "And he's up to something. He thinks he's been sly, that no one's on to him, but . . . He's made an excursion over to the alien ship on his own. I don't know what he's looking for, or what he has in mind, but I do *not* want to put him in charge. If I let him take over now, I might just as well hand the captaincy to him. Even if he failed, I would never become captain again. Never."

"What do you *want*?" I was exasperated. More than that, I was angry, although I wasn't sure at what.

Nikos finally looked directly at me. "I want *you* to take charge of the exploration of the alien ship. I want you to bring me success."

I felt I was being set up as scapegoat and distraction. If by some chance I *could* achieve success, all the better. If not, I gained time for the captain. I didn't like it.

"If I refuse?"

"Your cell remains empty."

"You would imprison us all again?"

Nikos cocked his head and stared at me, and his true state of mind showed itself—in the intensity of his eyes, the tightness of his lips as they formed a mirthless smile.

"I would not hesitate," he said.

20

I slept long and hard and without dreaming, or at least without any memory of dreams. When I woke, I thought I was still in my cell. The room was dark, and as I sat up I became confused, sensing something vaguely unfamiliar about my surroundings. I stumbled out of bed—its height was not the same as the bunk in my cell—and bumped into a wall where one shouldn't have been. Yet some unconscious part of me apparently realized where I was, for my hand reached out involuntarily to the correct place on the wall and brought up dim lights. I saw I was in my own quarters, and finally remembered my release.

I sat in a chair, surveying my quarters, trying to decide what to do, what to think, struggling against the urge to return to bed and go back to sleep. My rooms were so quiet and lifeless, as if the inorganic matter which composed the furniture and all of my few possessions had dropped into an even lower level of existence while I was gone, and now needed to be resurrected to its former state. The same for me, I thought.

I should have been elated to be free of my cell, but I was strangely depressed, and did not understand why. Everything was changed; perhaps that was it. The captain was still fighting with the bishop over the captaincy, but even that had changed, and my place within the struggles, my relationships to the key participants, were not the same. I saw everyone differently now, and I was sure their perceptions of me, too, had changed.

And Nikos? We had been friends for years, since we were children, but that time was gone, and I began to fully understand that there was no regaining that friendship. Out of necessity we could work together, each of us distrusting the other, but there would never again be more, and that realization depressed me as well. An enormous sense of loss threatened to overwhelm me.

I got up from the chair, showered and dressed, then tried to get something to eat. The room's food system had been shut down while I was in prison, and no one had yet restored its function. I would have to go to one of the common halls.

Fortunately it was between regular meal times—late morning—and there were few people in the common hall nearest my quarters. None of them knew how to react to my presence, though I detected less surprise than when Nikos and I had walked along the ship's corridors to the command salon. Word of my release had obviously spread through the upper levels.

I selected simple fare, not much different from what I had been served while imprisoned, and ate quickly. While in my cell, I would often imagine that upon my release I would gorge myself on the widest variety of rich food and drink. Now that I had the opportunity, I felt almost ill at the prospect; eating like that seemed so unnecessary, indulgent, almost immoral.

Nikos was expecting me early that morning. I had agreed to take over the alien ship's exploration, and he wanted me to help select the new exploration teams and begin as soon as possible, but I needed to see Father Veronica first.

I went to the cathedral, but she wasn't there. Only Father George was.

I found him at the far end of the cathedral, kneeling at one of the side altars, his head bowed in prayer. The candles flickered, and their dim light fluttered gently about his head. I sat quietly in a pew some distance away and waited for him to finish.

Father George was an old man, stooped and frail. He rose awkwardly to his feet and lit several more of the candles; then he turned to me, and I realized he had heard me come in. He smiled and walked toward me.

"Hello, Bartolomeo."

"Hello, Father."

"Prison does not appear to have harmed you much."

"Mostly my ego," I said.

Father George chuckled. "Then perhaps you have even benefited from your incarceration." He tugged at his long white hair with bony fingers, as if his thoughts and vision were in another world, which they probably were.

"In some ways," I agreed.

"What can I do for you, my son?"

"I'm looking for Father Veronica."

He nodded to himself as if that was exactly what he had expected. "She's not here. She hasn't been here for several days."

"Where is she?"

"I don't know. Nobody knows." He hesitated, studying me. "But when she does return, I will tell her you came to see her."

"Thank you, Father."

He looked as if he wanted to say something else, but changed his mind. Instead he just nodded.

I had started down the aisle when he called to me. I turned back to him, and he was standing straighter than I had seen him in years, and his expression was grave.

"What is it, Father?"

"Be careful, Bartolomeo."

"Of what?"

"Everything." He paused, then repeated himself. "Everything. But especially of the alien ship." He shook his head. "It is an evil thing, and it should be left alone. Perhaps it even comes from the Fallen One."

"Satan?"

"Why not? Is that any more incredible than the notion that the ship is an artifact of an alien civilization?"

I wanted to tell him that I didn't believe in Satan, or the Fallen One, or whatever he might want to call it, but I didn't see the purpose. It would be an attack on his faith, and he probably knew how I felt, anyway.

"I'll be careful," I told him. "Thanks." I turned to leave, and saw Nikos waiting for me near the cathedral's main doors.

"We might have a problem," he said when I reached him.

He was sweating and smelled faintly of alcohol; I wondered if he had developed a drinking problem while I was imprisoned. If so, I was in more trouble than I had thought.

"What is it?" I asked.

"The bishop has called an emergency session of the Executive Council."

"The reason?"

Nikos gave me a rueful smile. "You, of course."

21

EVERYONE else was already in the council room when we arrived; conversation died immediately, and the tension level rose like a sudden flush of heat. I noticed one change: Geller sat in General Wainwright's place.

Nikos and I stood together just inside the door. The bishop watched us, his expression composed, but he could not hide the edge in his voice as he spoke.

"Bartolomeo should not be here. He is the subject of this emergency session."

"That is exactly why he *is* here," Nikos replied. "I'm not certain what the issue is with Bartolomeo, or what suggestions will be made concerning his fate, but he should be here to argue his side."

"No," the bishop insisted. "We need to be able to speak frankly and openly. His presence makes that more difficult."

"I agree with Captain Costa," Geller said. "Bartolomeo should be allowed to stay, and should be allowed to speak for himself when necessary."

"If that is a motion," added Margita Cardenas, "I will second it."

Everyone waited for Nikos to confirm the motion from

Geller, then call for discussion and a vote. But Nikos remained silent, staring back at the bishop.

Bishop Soldano nodded once, and this time when he spoke the edge was gone from his voice; however, it was replaced not by resignation but by the patience of a predator biding its time. "I don't think a vote is necessary. I defer to my fellow council members. Let the man stay." He paused. "But I will insist that he sits at the foot of the table, and not in his customary position as Captain Costa's adviser."

Nikos took his seat at the head of the table, and I sat at the foot. He formally opened the meeting, but no one spoke for a long time. I felt surprisingly calm. What could they do to me? Imprison me again? That was unlikely, and I knew it.

Finally Nikos turned to the bishop. "Bishop, you called this emergency session. You should begin."

"I will. That man," the bishop said as he gestured at me, "has been summarily released along with the other leaders of the mutiny. This was done without any discussion in the council, and without notice."

"As captain of the *Argonos*," Nikos broke in, "I have the authority to do so."

"You have the authority to commute sentences, and to issue pardons. Since there were no trials, and no convictions or sentences, there was nothing to commute, and there is some question about whether or not you can pardon someone for offenses they have not yet been convicted of. We have seen no formal records or proceedings, Captain. I ask now that you tell us what you have done, and why."

Nikos appeared to be self-assured and relaxed. "I have neither commuted any nonexistent sentences, nor have I issued any pardons. The ship registrar has a record of the orders. I simply released Aguilera and the others with Captain's Directives, pending further proceedings. The charges remain."

The bishop shrugged, as if he wasn't completely surprised by the captain's remarks. "I do not dispute their release," he said. "I merely wanted to note that I had concerns about the legalities. My *primary* objection is that you did not consult the council. Assuming you had the authority to take the actions you did, you were not required to consult us. However, I believe that you have an ethical, if not legal, obligation to do so on matters of this importance. We deserve the opportunity to advise, to register objections, to understand your reasoning. And I would like a sense of the council's thoughts on the matter. I think *you* should have a sense of the council's thoughts."

"You called an emergency session for this?" Nikos asked. "This is not a matter of urgency. It could have waited until our next session, which is only three days from today."

"There is more," the bishop said. "A more *urgent* matter. I understand Bartolomeo is to head a new team on further excursions to the alien vessel."

There was a long silence. The council members were trying to figure out what, if anything, was to follow. Susanna Hingen was the first to speak, glancing first at me, then turning to Nikos.

"Is that true, Captain?"

"Yes," Nikos answered. "I don't see the problem. I have decided to put Bartolomeo in charge. We need a fresh approach, and I believe Bartolomeo is the best person to do that."

"The problem is obvious," said the bishop. "Bartolomeo Aguilera is, as you have just stated for the record, still charged with treason. To place him in such a position of authority is a serious breach of responsibility."

Nikos didn't have an answer to that. It was clear to me that he had not thought through the various consequences of his actions.

"I would like to speak," I said. Everyone turned to look at me, and the expressions were a mix of annoyance (the bishop, Costino, even the captain), puzzlement (Michel Tournier, Susanna Hingen), and interest (Toller, Cardenas, Aiyana, and Geller). When no one objected, I went on.

"This entire matter can be simply resolved," I said. "Until now, I was not aware that the charge of treason is

still outstanding. Frankly, I don't wish to be set free with
that charge unresolved, knowing that at any time I can be
thrown back into a cell. I formally request, as a matter of
due process, that the charges of treason against me, and
against the others who were imprisoned, be dropped, or that
you proceed immediately with a trial or other proceeding.''
I paused for a moment, glancing around me; before anyone
could reply, I resumed. ''I'd like to make my own case
right now for the charges being dropped.''

Attention turned to the bishop and the captain, who
glanced at each other. Nikos was trapped; he had not expected anything like this, and I know he did not want his
hold over me taken away, but he would be forced to advo-
cate my position.

''Bishop?'' Nikos asked.

The bishop appeared to be weighing the consequences,
and eventually said, ''I have no objections. I doubt that this
can be resolved as simply as Bartolomeo suggests, but I am
certainly willing to hear him present his case.''

There were no objections from anyone else—a lot of
nodding and shrugging, still some puzzlement. Michel Tournier, in particular, appeared bewildered by what was happening.

''Go ahead,'' Nikos said to me.

''It wasn't treason,'' I began.

''Then what was it?'' Costino asked.

''A bid for freedom.''

Costino snorted and Susanna Hingen shook her head,
smiling.

''Why do you think it is that the downsiders want to
leave the *Argonos*? With what we found on Antioch, did
that world look like a new Paradise? A new Garden of
Eden?'' I looked at the bishop. ''Which would be your area
of expertise.'' I paused, but he didn't respond except to
narrow his eyes.

''They want freedom,'' I resumed. ''They want the same
freedom you or I have and which we deny them.''

Tournier started to protest, but I cut him off with a look,
as surprised by the power of it to quiet him as he was.

"We deny them freedom. They are servants to us, to this ship. They are little more than slaves."

"You're being melodramatic," said the bishop. "You exaggerate their situation."

"Perhaps. But not much, and you can't argue the general proposition. You can leave the ship any time you want. They cannot. And why not? Because it is convenient for us to have them serve us, do the scut work on this ship, work the ag rooms and the fabrication plants, toil in the detox tunnels, and grind away in the drive engines. To do whatever we do not wish to do ourselves.

"Are we better people than they are? Are we superior beings? No, though some of you may think so. We are only more fortunate. We are fortunate to have been born topside, while they were born downside.

"Treason? No. And this is the important thing: they did nothing to threaten the *Argonos,* nor any one of you. They would have gone quietly, without fuss, without harming anyone.

"*That* is why I chose to help them. They deserved the chance we would not give them."

When I was finished, half of the council members were no longer looking at me. I had no idea how things would go. The captain sat at the head of the table, his chin resting on his fists, staring at me with partially closed eyes.

Margita Cardenas was the first to speak. "Bartolomeo is right. We probably bear a certain amount of responsibility for what happened. I move that the charges against Bartolomeo Aguilera, and the others involved in the attempted mutiny, be dropped."

Most of the council members were silently trying to gauge which way the dynamics were flowing. Then the bishop surprised us all.

"I would second the Cardenas motion. I find, surprisingly, that I am somewhat persuaded by Bartolomeo's argument. More than that, however, there are practical reasons." He glanced sidelong at Nikos. "The downsiders are causing trouble, they're in a state of permanent, quiet rebellion.

Dropping the charges could help defuse the situation, since nothing our captain has done has been effective.''

Nikos seemed stunned, but he gathered himself and finally asked, ''Is there discussion of the motion?''

Heads turned, council members looking at one another, but no one said a thing.

''Call the question,'' the bishop said.

Nikos did. They all voted in favor except for Michel Tournier and Costino. Tournier did not concern me, but I would remember Costino's vote; I took it as a warning. There were others, I knew, who were dead set against me, but they were too smart to tip their hands.

''This does not resolve the second issue,'' the bishop said once the vote was recorded. ''Just because the charges have been dropped does not mean that putting Bartolomeo in charge of the exploration team is wise.'' He turned to the captain. ''I would like to know why *you* think it's a good move. I fail to see Bartolomeo's expertise here.''

''Who *does* have the expertise for exploring an alien starship?'' Nikos asked. ''Has anyone on this entire ship been trained for it? No. Does anyone have any experience? No. Bartolomeo Aguilera is a man who has provided wise counsel over the years, has demonstrated an acute mind and an ability to view things from a perspective different from that of most people. And I think that a different perspective is exactly what we need in this situation.''

''I believe the captain is right.'' It was August Toller, who was usually silent during council sessions. The old man coughed once and cleared his throat. Although he was nearly a hundred and forty years old, moved slowly, and rarely spoke, his voice still had strength. ''I have known Bartolomeo all his life. I was already old when he was born. He is a strange man, as any of us would be had we been born with his deformities, then been raised and treated by others as he has been. He can be unpleasant. But that strangeness may be just what is called for now.'' Toller paused, looking about the table. ''Our forays into that mysterious ship are like the probings of a man newly blind. Because we do not know what we are looking for, or what we hope to find, we do not know *how* to make our search. Bartolomeo may be able to discover an approach unlike what any one of us could envision. If he does, it might not be more successful than what we've tried thus far. But I think we would be foolish not to try something different, and I believe putting Bartolomeo in charge of the exploration is a worthwhile change in direction.''

Michel Tournier had been squirming in his seat, waiting for the opportunity to speak, and he took it as soon as Toller finished. "We are foolish to keep going into that ship at all," he said, his voice rising. "Five people are dead, a number of others have been injured, and some are becoming unbalanced. And we've learned *nothing*. We've accomplished nothing. Even if it *is* an alien ship, what does that matter? It's a death ship to us. We should leave it, leave this part of space, go to the next star. Better yet, we should launch warheads and destroy it before we leave."

"You are a coward, Michel." The bishop's voice was laced with contempt. "We are not leaving that ship. We are certainly not going to destroy it. I doubt we could." He turned away from Michel, who was obviously stung by the bishop's words. "I understand Toller's reasoning," the bishop continued, "and I concur. However, I would offer an alternative. I have suggested this before, and I suggest it again. I propose the Church take over the exploration of the alien starship. Divine guidance would indeed be a different approach, and wouldn't necessitate putting an accused traitor in charge."

This time the vote was much closer—Toller, Cardenas, Geller, and Nikos all voting to formally put me in charge; the bishop, Costino, and Hingen all voting against. Michel Tournier abstained in protest. The bishop did, however, succeed in attaching an eight-week time limit to my authority. The Executive Council would then vote again.

I watched the bishop, trying to gauge his feelings, but he managed to keep his demeanor composed. I decided to make a peace offering of sorts, although I wasn't sure he would see it that way.

"Do you want a church representative on the exploration

team?'' I asked him. "I would gladly accept such an arrangement.''

The bishop hesitated before replying; I could sense the whirring of his thoughts. "I suppose you would want Father Veronica.''

"After our experiences together on Antioch, I would welcome her assistance. But I would welcome anyone you would like to accompany the team, as long as he or she is willing.''

The bishop nodded. "Unfortunately, Father Veronica is unavailable. However, one of our clerics, Eric Casterman, has expressed an interest in the alien vessel. *He* will accompany you.''

I couldn't object, so I let it go and moved on. "One last thing,'' I said. "The earlier vote, to drop the charges against me and the others. No exceptions were noted, so I assume that includes Pär Lundkvist as well.''

From the long silence, I could see I had raised an awkward subject. I was glad.

"Pär was not arrested with you and the others,'' Aiyana finally said. "He couldn't be found. From your question, I presume you already know that.''

"Yes.''

"We don't believe he is on the ship anymore. We believe he took one of the shuttles and escaped to Antioch.''

"But if he *is* on the ship?'' I asked.

"Do you have such knowledge?'' the bishop asked.

I shook my head. There were glances and shrugs; the bishop continued to study me, probably not believing my denial. Finally Nikos spoke.

"As you said, no exceptions were mentioned during the vote. As distasteful as I would find it, I would say the agreement applied to Pär Lundkvist as well.'' He paused. "Unless there are objections, if he *is* on the *Argonos*, he will remain a free man.''

There were no objections, at least none were raised, and with that the emergency session concluded. Afterwards, Nikos did not say a word to me.

22

PÄR was waiting for me in my quarters. He was sitting in a chair in the front room, rubbing at his eyes; my entrance had awakened him.

"How did you get in?" I asked.

He grinned. "I learned a lot about this ship during my exile. I've been waiting a long time."

I was annoyed with him. I had been more than grateful for the regular deliveries of his coffee all those months I was imprisoned, but that seemed washed away by his violating the privacy of my quarters. I stood unmoving, staring at him. As though reading my thoughts, he got to his feet and said, "I shouldn't have done it this way. Sorry. I'll go."

I shook my head, my annoyance already fading, overwhelmed by exhaustion and the fear of losing one of the few friends I had.

"Forget it," I said. "It doesn't matter." I gave him a tired smile. "I'm glad to see you. Unfortunately, I can't offer you anything to eat or drink. The food system isn't working, and the shelves are empty."

"That's all right," he said, reaching behind the chair he'd been sitting in when I first entered. "I came prepared."

He held up a thermal pot. "All you have to provide are cups."

We sat with the pot between us, and I sipped the coffee; just as good as always.

"That meant a lot to me," I said, holding up my cup. "I was surprised you were willing to take the risk."

Pär shrugged. "So was I, to be honest." He shrugged again. "Extreme circumstances . . . I don't know."

I cocked my head at him, his presence finally sinking in. I felt stupid for not realizing it earlier. "Have you already heard?" I asked.

"About the charges being dropped?" he replied, grinning.

"Yes."

He nodded.

"Who the hell is your source of information?"

Still grinning, Pär shook his head. "Not even for you, Bartolomeo." He paused, and breathed deeply. "I also hear you're in charge of exploring the alien starship."

"Yes."

"I want to be a part of it."

I stared hard at him. He was serious, as serious as I had ever seen him. "Why?" I asked.

"I did a lot of thinking while I was in hiding. Lots of time for it. I am sick to death of life on this ship. Look at us. You and I are a couple of freaks. But the reality is, this entire ship is *filled* with freaks. We don't know how to live normal human lives anymore. Living from birth to death inside this hunk of metal is unnatural, and I think it's done unnatural things to us."

I was reminded of my first extended conversation with Father Veronica, during which she'd said something very similar.

"And how is the alien ship going to help that?"

"Hell, I don't know. But it's something different, and I mean *really* different. Whatever happens out there, good or bad or something in between, it doesn't matter, it's got to do something for us, got to *change* us. We had a chance for something on Antioch. It didn't work out. All right. Now we've got another chance. An alien starship or whatever it is. *Truly* alien. I don't think people understand the enormity of what we've found, of what we have ahead of us, of the possibilities. I've been thinking about it a lot during the last few weeks, and sometimes I feel like my mind is going to explode. But the Executive Committee seems to be treating it like . . . I don't know, like we're exploring the ruins of some small abandoned colony on a nice risk-free, habitable world somewhere." He shook his head in disbelief. "That ship could swallow us whole, and it might just do that for all we know. We could find the answers to cosmological mysteries, we could find out what our place is in the universe, we could find the way to eternal life."

"We could find our deaths," I said.

"That, too," he replied, nodding. "And I don't think we have a sense of that on this ship anymore. I suspect that's something we would all benefit from."

My exoskeleton vibrated, and I wanted to scream. Damn Nikos. I decided I would have to see one of the neuro-techs to have the system disabled.

"I want on that ship, Bartolomeo. I need it."

I nodded. "I don't know how much authority I'll have, but I'll do what I can. If I can get you on, I will."

"Thanks."

He poured us fresh coffee, leaned back in the chair, and let out a sigh.

"What was it like?" I asked him.

"What? Hiding out?" When I nodded, he smiled and said, "Enlightening. What was prison like?"

"Boring."

Pär laughed.

The exoskeleton vibrated again, and I cursed.

"What?" Pär asked.

I explained.

"How the hell did Captain Nikos talk you into that?" he asked.

I grimaced. "He didn't," I admitted. "It was my own idea. And it was a bad one."

Pär laughed again.

"Glad you're so amused," I said. "I've got to get the thing disabled."

Pär finally stopped laughing. "I know someone who can take care of it."

"Soon," I said.

He nodded. "Tonight, or first thing tomorrow. I'll arrange it."

I thanked him, then got up to look for a small bottle of whiskey I had been saving for years, waiting for just the right occasion. This seemed as good as any; I suspected the kind of special occasion I had hoped for when I was younger was never going to occur. I found the bottle, a couple of glasses, then poured some for each of us.

"That's good," Pär said.

"A lot better than that stuff you usually have." I sipped at the whiskey, relishing the smooth burn licking down my throat and into my gut. I thought again about Nikos and his drinking.

"I think the captain's developed a drinking problem," I said to Pär.

He nodded. "That's what my sources tell me. If he's not careful, he'll go the way of General Wainwright."

"How *did* General Wainwright go?"

"You haven't heard yet?"

"Too much going on in too short a time. All I know is he's been replaced by Geller."

"He came into a council session so far out on Passion that he couldn't speak. He'd finally gone too far. They voted him off the council, and confined him in the psychiatric ward for a hard withdrawal. He's still there, and I don't think he's ever going to get out." Pär leaned forward. "One more thing of interest," he said. "Arne Gronvold's banishment has been rescinded. Not only that, he's been reinstated on the Planning Committee."

I was reminded of Nikos's clandestine meetings with Arne; I don't know why it hadn't occurred to me that Arne was betraying the insurrection. Probably because Nikos had been meeting with Arne for months before I was even aware of the plans myself; even so, I'd thought Arne's sympathies were with the downsiders. I'd obviously thought wrong.

"I guess we know what happened, then," I said.

Pär nodded. "I guess we do. That bastard."

"Which one?" I asked. "Arne or Nikos?"

Pär just grinned.

There was a banging at the door. Nikos called out my name, his voice only partly muted.

"Bartolomeo, I know you're there! Open the door!"

I thought about ignoring him, but that would only be putting off the inevitable. I put down my glass, got up, and went to the door.

"Damn you, Bartolomeo, what the hell was . . . ?" His voice trailed off when he saw Pär behind me. Nikos was at a loss for words, something I had rarely seen.

Pär stood and said, "I'll go."

I shook my head. "No, don't." Then, to Nikos: "What did you want?"

Anger flushed his face, and his eyes went hard. He stared at Pär. "So you are still aboard, little man. I'd hoped you'd taken that damn shuttle."

"I'm still here."

Nikos turned to me, furious. "We have to talk, Bartolomeo. We need to move before anyone has second thoughts. We've got to select the exploration team, and you and I need to talk before we start choosing people. I got you out, remember? Now it's your turn."

"Fair enough," I said. "Schedule the selection meeting for three hours from now, or a little later if you have to. And I'll meet you in your quarters in an hour."

"No, not there."

"Where, then?"

"You know where I'll be." He turned and strode away.

I closed the door, but didn't turn around; I stared at the dark green panel, as if I would find answers in it. I wasn't even sure what the questions were.

"Ah, old friends," Pär said.

I turned around, expecting to see him grinning at me, but his expression was dead serious.

"He'll be dangerous as an enemy," Pär said. "Better if you could somehow stay friends."

I shook my head. "It's too late for that."

23

THE Wasteland was hot and dry. Unlike the other nature rooms, the Wasteland had no seasons, no weather changes. I stood just inside the ground entrance, dizzy from the heat and blinking against the glare reflecting from the sand and white rock. The designer of this room had been brilliant—looking in any direction from any location, the desert appeared to continue without end, or at least for many kilometers, stretching to the vague suggestion of distant dunes.

Formally named the Desert Conservatory, the Wasteland was the largest of the nature rooms, and also the least frequented; but Nikos had always liked it. He would spend hours there when he needed to think, or needed to escape from the pressures of the captaincy. When we were young, fifteen or sixteen, he had brought me there and tried to explain why he loved it so much. I hadn't understood at the time, but over the years I came to appreciate his fascination for the place, although I never could shake my own unease, and avoided it like nearly everyone else did.

I scanned the Wasteland, searching the shadows of cacti and rocks, taking in everything several times before I finally spotted Nikos sitting with his back against a large boulder, gazing into the distance.

A dull ache worked its way through my chest as I thought about all the years we'd known each other, everything we'd been through. I walked toward him slowly, surprisingly apprehensive; I didn't relish any more intimate conversations. When I was a few meters away, I stopped and waited in silence.

"You never did like it here," Nikos said without looking at me.

"No."

"That always surprised me. It was one of the few ways you were like everyone else on this ship." He finally turned and looked up at me. "I don't think you understand what's going on aboard this ship."

"Maybe not, but you don't either."

"What's that supposed to mean?"

"Just what I said. I'm not sure anybody really does."

He nodded, resigned. "Except maybe the bishop."

"No, not even the bishop. He probably thinks he does, but he knows less than he imagines. I would guess that's how it is with most of us."

Nikos stared out across the bleached sand, the scattered cacti and rock. "Walk with me a while, Bartolomeo."

We walked together across the hot sand, an arm's length apart. I'd already lost my orientation, and when I looked around, I found I could not locate the entrance I'd used; I was struck by the irrational fear that I might never be able to find my way out of there. Or that Nikos would murder me. My body could remain undiscovered for decades.

"We've been friends a lot of years, Bartolomeo."

"*Were* friends," I corrected him.

"No more?"

"I don't think so, Nikos."

He stopped, turned, and looked at me, his expression steady. If he'd been drinking recently, I couldn't tell. Everything about him seemed sober and firm.

"We've both made mistakes. Out of fear, or mistrust.

Or perhaps even simple misunderstanding. Whatever the reasons. But is the damage to our friendship irreparable?"

I'd thought so, but suddenly I was unsure. Watching him, listening to him, I was unable to detect any dissembling. He seemed sincere. Nikos could be deceptive and manipulative, but I always thought I could see through him. I'd missed it before, although looking back on it, I realized the signs had been there—I just hadn't recognized them; maybe because I hadn't wanted to. Now, though, I saw nothing but a sincere effort at reconciliation.

"I don't know," I finally said.

"Honest enough. I don't know either. But I'm prepared to make the effort, if you are."

"Because you're desperate, and you need my help?"

"No, although both those things are true. It's possible, maybe even likely, that I'm going to lose everything in the coming weeks. But if I go down, I'd rather not go alone."

"You want to drag me down with you."

"No, that's not what I meant."

"I know," I said. "But you're not alone. You have Aiyana."

"Yes, and that's a comfort. But it's not enough."

"I'll have to think about it," I told him.

He nodded. "Do that, Bartolomeo." He paused. "Now, let's talk about who we want on the team."

24

I stepped into the dark, silent transport hold and came to a halt, searching through the shadows. When I saw the bulky forms of the shuttles, my chest tightened, cutting off my breath. Almost a year, but the memory of that day was still vivid, and carried with it everything that had happened since—five masked and armored men coming for me with electronic shackles; the days of waiting for a trial that never occurred, then the months of isolation and deathly tedium; the fear that I would go out of my mind; my release, and the end of a lifelong friendship with Nikos; the awe and wonder of an alien starship; and finally this: preparing to lead an exploration of that ship with all of its dangers and wonderful possibilities.

My life would have been so different if the insurrection had been successful. *Everything* about it would have been different. I would not be here, I reminded myself; I would be on Antioch. I might be dead by now, killed by some strange and deadly organism or toxin, or an accident caused by unforeseeable dangers. Or I might be sitting on the bank of a river, watching the water flowing past filled with alien aquatic life, basking in the heat of the sun.

I turned and looked at the hold doors, which were now

closed and lifeless. I would never forget the sight of the harvesters rising into view, that silent and terrible nuclear fire slowly swirling, hypnotizing me. My world coming to an end. Or so it seemed at the time. It was only changing, but I hadn't understood that.

Across the hold, the shuttles were nearly lost in the darkness, camouflaged by shadow. The tiny firefly lights far above me provided just enough light to illuminate the floor. I walked toward the largest of the shuttles, my footsteps echoing dully.

I had asked for complete authority over the expedition, and was granted most of it. First, I'd decided the trips in the maintenance module were inefficient. Instead, I would take eleven other people on one of the shuttles, with enough supplies and support for several weeks, and we'd park the shuttle right beside the alien starship. With twelve people, we could form three teams of four, or four of three, depending on which seemed more effective. We would stay there and make regular trips, sharing information and insights, intuitions and assessments. We'd learn how to work together, we'd acquire a feel for the ship, and the exploration would be our only focus.

That's what I hoped for. I didn't really know if it would work that way, but it made more sense to me than the haphazard, directionless excursions that had been undertaken in the weeks since the alien ship had been discovered.

I stopped in front of the shuttle, tried to look into its darkened interior, but I couldn't see a thing. Twelve of us, plus the pilots and a med-tech. It was a good team, for the most part. A couple of people I was apprehensive about: Eric Casterman, the bishop's man; and Aiyana, which showed how much Nikos trusted me—as much as I trusted him, apparently. But there were also good, experienced people like Sherry Winton, Trace Youngman, and Leona Frip, who had all spent a lot of time in the alien ship. William Rogers and a man called Starlin, neither of whom had spent time on the ship, but who were by all accounts both competent and diligent. Rita Hollings, who Costino said was the best "fixer" on the *Argonos*—she could repair or jury-rig almost anything. Also part of the team were Maria Vegas, Toller's apprentice, and Margita Cardenas—Cardenas was my biggest surprise, and the best. And finally, Pär. I had to fight for him, but I won.

I put my hand against the shuttle hull. It was cold and hard, but not as cold as it would be out there in deep space. In a few hours the preparations would begin—not just provisioning the shuttle, but modifying it. One of the cargo bays would be converted to a combination air lock/ decontamination chamber. Sleeping cots and food preparation equipment would be installed. We would need a large monitor to follow the teams, and a wide variety of equipment and tools, testing and measurement instruments. The list went on. Four days. Maybe five.

"Hey."

The voice startled me. I couldn't see anyone, couldn't hear anything. Then Francis stepped silently out of the shadows.

I hardly recognized him. He had grown, and was taller and lankier now. His hair was long and ragged.

"Hello, Francis."

"Hm," was all he said at first. He twisted his head and neck and I heard a soft cracking sound. "I want to go with you," he said.

"Go with me? Where?"

"To the alien starship."

I almost laughed, but I realized he was serious. "The team's already been selected."

"Change it," he said. "Or just add me. I want to see it. Take me with you."

"I can't, Francis. Besides, you're too young."

"I am not. I'm older than you think. I'm older than I am."

I suspected there was a lot of truth to that statement. But I couldn't do what he wanted.

"I'm sorry, Francis."

"I thought you were different," he said. "You're all the same."

"Francis . . ."

He turned and, just as quickly and silently as he had appeared, retreated into the shadows behind the shuttle.

I felt bad, as if I had made some mistake, or misunderstood something. I almost called after him, but held back. There was something about Francis that moved me, and I wished I knew how to make things better between us. But I felt stupid, and had no idea what to do.

Footsteps broke into my thoughts. I turned, and saw Father Veronica standing just inside the hold, scanning the darkness.

"Bartolomeo?"

"I'm here."

"Where? I can't see you."

I stepped away from the shuttle. She saw me and started across the metal floor, her steps loud and echoing.

"Pär told me you would probably be here." She smiled, and seemed genuinely pleased to see me. "So it's true, you've been released." Her smiled faded. "I'm sorry I never could visit again. You asked me to let it go, but of course I couldn't. For a while I tried to convince Bishop Soldano or the captain that you should be allowed visitors, but it was futile. I finally stopped trying after two or three months. But I thought of you often."

"Did you pray for me?"

"Not the way you might think." I thought she was going to explain, but she didn't.

"I tried to see you as soon as I was released," I told her.

"Yes, Father George told me."

"He said you were gone, and that no one knew where you were."

She nodded. I waited for an explanation, but it soon became obvious she was not going to give me one.

"He seems to think the alien ship has been delivered to us by Satan," I added.

I expected her to laugh, or at least smile, but instead she sighed. "There's something about that ship, Bartolomeo, something . . ."

"Evil?" I suggested.

"Not exactly. Malign, perhaps."

"I'm not sure I understand the difference."

"Perhaps malign is the wrong word. 'Dangerous' might be better. Lethal. But without intent. I don't know, I can't explain what it is I feel, but it's something substantial." She glanced at the shuttle. "Is this the one you'll be taking?"

"Yes." I hesitated. "I wish you were going with us."

"I wanted to," she said. "Despite my reservations about that ship. Bishop Soldano told me that Eric Casterman would be going as the Church's representative, and I asked if I could replace him. The bishop refused." She paused. "Perhaps it's better this way."

"Why?"

"I don't know. Maybe it is, that's all."

I wanted to know what she was thinking, but apparently she wasn't going to tell me.

"How soon are you going?" she said.

"Four days. Maybe five. I don't think there's any rush."

"Let me know when everything is ready, and I'll come by and bless the ship."

"And will you pray for our success?"

"Someday we'll have to talk about that."

"Talk about what?"

"Prayer. Most people have the wrong idea about it."

"And what's that?"

"That prayer is to ask for things. To make requests of God."

"It's not? Then what is it?"

She shook her head. "Some other time, Bartolomeo. It's a serious subject, and not to be dealt with lightly."

"All right, some other time."

"Do let me know when you're prepared to leave."

"I will."

She turned, and I watched her walk away, feeling as always an aching sense of loss. Pathetic.

25

GHOSTLY blue light and a black surface that seemed to draw in that light and swallow it: that was the alien ship from two, three kilometers away as we slowly approached. Already the ship was blotting out much of our field of vision, cutting off the stars like a rent in the universe.

Nikos was right. The alien vessel was enormous, and it seemed we were being deliberately sucked into it. I also felt a hint of what Father George and Father Veronica had suggested—the sense of some malign quality to the ship, though it appeared dead and harmless.

I was in the front cabin with the pilot, watching the alien starship grow and spread all around us, appearing to extinguish the stars in all directions until there was nothing to be seen but the black mass coming at us. I felt lost in all that darkness, and I had the strong urge to retreat from the pilot's cabin, find a window looking back at the stars. For a moment I had to close my eyes, overwhelmed.

"Jesus," I whispered, opening my eyes once again to that dark immensity.

"Don't take His name in vain," the pilot said to me.

I turned to her, but there was no indication that she'd

been joking. "Sorry," I said. She shrugged, not looking at me, keeping her gaze on the ship ahead of us and the instrument panels. I wondered how many of his own "agents" the bishop had managed to include on this expedition.

We passed near one of the bright blue navigation lights, a space buoy hovering untethered. More blue lights in the distance helped provide a sense of perspective that threatened to disappear as we neared the black vessel. We passed another blue beacon, then another, until there were no more to be seen. Then, directly ahead of us, I made out an oval of dim white lights on the black surface, and some of the surface features became indistinctly visible—half-pods, shallow depressions, a series of raised ridges, long thin projections.

"The white lights mark the entrance," the pilot said. She slowed the shuttle's progress, and eventually brought us to a halt seventy-five meters from the alien vessel; then she turned the shuttle around so the bow faced away from the ship, and the stars came into view once again. She had orders to leave if anything serious went wrong and she thought the shuttle and those aboard it were at risk, even if it meant leaving people behind on the alien ship.

I regarded the dense, crystalline ocean of stars, unable to pick out the *Argonos* from among them. Although I could no longer see it, I could *feel* the alien ship behind me, could feel it drawing all of us toward it, both physically and psychologically. My skin buzzed with fear and anticipation.

O N C E outside, Trace Youngman took the lead, pushing off the shuttle; he drifted across the seventy-five meters and landed gently on all fours just outside the circle of lights. We would use suit jets to get back to the shuttle, since it was smaller and easier to miss, but this was the easiest and presumably safest way to reach the ship.

"Don't kick with too much force," Youngman reminded me, his voice clear and sharp inside my helmet. "And you'll be surprised at the number of projections that will serve as handholds." Youngman and Winton were taking me on a reconnaissance excursion, to give me a feel for the alien ship before we officially resumed exploration with the new teams.

Like most of the inhabitants of the *Argonos*, at least those in the upper levels, I'd made a number of excursions outside the ship, but I was thankful for the reminder. I flexed my knees slightly, then straightened them and floated off. I was overcautious, perhaps, and it took me much longer to reach the alien ship, but I landed only a few meters away from Youngman, hardly feeling my touchdown. Almost immediately I had a grip on a smooth-cornered cube projecting from the ship's hull, and anchored myself.

Then I made my first mistake: I looked "up" along the ship's hull. The hull rose vertically to the sky above me like the metal face of an insurmountable cliff. Suddenly I lost my orientation, and the stars seemed to shift, lurching into slow, slow motion; with no gravity, I suddenly felt that if I didn't hang onto the ship I would fall away from it, hurtle helplessly into the cold night of space. I scrambled desperately for a second handhold, while my legs were flailing about of their own volition, my feet searching for some purchase.

"Relax," Youngman said. "I warned you about this. This ship is huge, and the way it sucks light away . . . Stop struggling and don't look at anything except the surface directly in front of you."

My left hand found another projection, and I did just as Youngman told me—stared at the hull in front of me, and stopped the kicking of my legs. Another minute or two, and my breathing had returned to normal.

"You okay?" Youngman asked.

I nodded. "Yes." My mouth was dry, but I did feel fairly calm. "I'm fine." As a test, I worked my way across the dozen or so meters to Youngman's side, without trouble.

Within minutes Winton had joined us. We gathered together inside the lights, around a rectangular panel larger than I had expected—about ten meters long and eight or nine wide. Youngman popped open a smaller panel above it, twisted something inside, and the large panel slid open.

He went in first, swinging himself into the ship, and saying, "Wait here for a minute." A few moments later, the interior of the air lock brightened slightly, and Youngman said, "Come on through."

The air lock would have been large enough for all twelve members of the team; it was illuminated with a ghostly light from two portable lanterns that had been mounted to the air lock walls with adhesive pads. Every passage and room in the alien ship had to be illuminated.

When Youngman wheeled the outer door shut, cutting off the night and the stars and sealing us inside, I felt a brief shiver of panic. Then the inner door slid open, as large as the outer one, and we moved through dim light growing dimmer until Youngman switched on the next lantern. Even then the passage—far larger than any passage on the *Argonos*—remained dark: the lanterns cast faint gray light like the *Argonos* lights at night.

"Raise the brightness," Winton said. "He's here to see what it looks like."

Youngman looked at me. "They're on reserve mode, to prolong battery life. But I can boost them."

"No," I said. "This is fine." The truth was I liked it better that way. I was afraid the wonder and mystery would be dispelled by brighter light.

We weren't very far inside when we entered the spherical chamber I'd seen in Winton's video. Nylon straps were webbed across the opening through which Santiago had fallen to his death. I drifted over to it, anchored myself, then put one hand through a gap in the webbing. As my hand inched forward, I expected to feel the faint tug of gravity giving it new weight. I felt nothing, and aimed my hand torch through the webbing, playing the beam along the length of the room. It was a long way down.

"I thought there was gravity in here," I said.

"There is," Youngman replied.

I reached my hand and arm farther into the room, but still felt nothing. I released the hand torch and it hung in the air by my fingers, drifting slightly but otherwise not moving, and certainly not falling.

"What the hell . . . ?" Winton said.

"How far in does it start?"

"It starts right inside the doorway," Youngman answered. By then he was beside me, and thrust his own hand and arm through the webbing. "I don't understand." He grabbed my hand torch, then gently tossed it toward the far end of the room. It drifted steadily, but never picked up speed, and when it eventually struck the far wall or floor, where Santiago's body had lain, it bounced off at an angle and headed back to us, though far more slowly now.

"I don't like this," Youngman said. "I don't like this one bit."

Winton joined us, and, as if to confirm things for herself, inserted her own arm through the webbing, all the way to her shoulder. "What the hell is going on?" she said.

We hovered together around the opening.

"Ideas?" I said.

No one offered any at first, then Youngman said, "Maybe after Santiago fell in, it triggered something, and the gravity got turned off."

"Except the gravity was still there for days," Winton pointed out. "Hell, I think it was there the last time I came in here. That was three weeks ago, but still . . ." She shook her head. "I suppose it's possible this ship isn't so dead after all."

"What?" I said. "There are aliens still alive somewhere, and they've switched it off?"

"I don't know. You have a better idea?"

"No."

No one spoke, no one offered any answers. Distressed, we moved on.

N O W I saw first-hand what Nikos had tried to explain to me—that there was no evidence of human hand or mind to be seen. We pulled ourselves along corridors far higher and narrower than those on the *Argonos*; or far shorter and wider from the alternate perspective. We entered rooms and cabins and chambers unfathomable in design and purpose—devoid of machinery or tools or instruments or furniture, devoid of objects altogether.

There were recognizable doorways, like those of the air lock, with mechanisms workable by human hands encased in pressure suit gloves, but our hands did not fit well around or into those mechanisms, and the necessary actions were often awkward and unnatural.

We saw no signs or labels or other kinds of markings anywhere, nothing with letters, characters, ideographs, nothing to convey a message or notice or identification or warning. If there were any, they were unrecognizable as such, like an alien Braille.

Alien. That's what that ship was, there was no doubt.

We came to a long, wide room or corridor that corkscrewed several hundred meters deeper into the ship. This was the site of the second and third casualties. The walls were ridged with silver-blue metal ribs that glinted in the lantern light. These ridges were sharper than surgical blades, and when a woman named Zellie Askan pulled herself into the room she brushed against the walls and the fine edges sliced open her pressure suit. Not knowing what had happened, Michael Singer rushed to help her, and contact with the ridges sliced open his suit as well. The cuts in the suits were so numerous, and so long and deep, that repairs were impossible. Within minutes, they both were dead.

Passage through the corkscrew was relatively safe now. A taut cable ran the length of the corridor right down the center. We attached short safety lines from our suits to the cable—the lines didn't allow enough freedom for us to make contact with the surrounding walls—then pulled ourselves along the cable to the far end.

The rooms and passages in the alien starship were so *empty*. Barren. It was certainly possible that furniture, appliances, instruments, or other accouterments of daily life had at one time been mounted on the walls, connected to power grids, and could be so again. Perhaps not, perhaps they never had been. Who could say?

I thought about the rooms and cabins on the *Argonos*, different areas of the ship serving different functions, and I could hardly imagine any of them ever appearing quite so empty without aggressive efforts to strip them bare. Why would we ever want to do that? Why would *anyone* want to do that?

In the end I was left with a terrible sense of disappointment. I had expected wonders, indecipherable devices, marvelous instruments and tools whose purpose could not be divined, enigmatic chambers filled with artifacts so perplexing yet awe-inspiring, they would leave the mind reeling, overcome by amazement. But the utter emptiness seemed to dispel the wonder that might otherwise have existed.

Near the end of my "tour," Youngman pointed to the doorway where Goran Durra was killed. After working out the mechanism for the door—a thick, metal panel that slid back into the wall to create an opening—Durra started through the doorway. The metal panel slammed shut on Durra, crushing him. There was no suit rupture, but by the time he was freed and rushed back to the *Argonos,* he had died of extensive internal bleeding. Now, even though I knew the panel was secure, I pulled myself quickly through the doorway, my stomach tight.

Finally we came to a wide, cylindrical room with coppery walls, entering at what appeared to be the "bottom."

"This is as far as we've explored," Youngman said. "Sinclair died here."

"What happened?"

"We don't know."

"You don't know."

"She was on a team with two others," Youngman explained. "They'd just worked out the entrance to this room, but they'd been inside this ship for hours at that point, so they decided to hold off, return to the module, then come back later. The other two left first. They hadn't gone far when they realized Sinclair wasn't with them. They called to her, but she didn't respond. When they backtracked, they found her drifting in this room. She was dead. No call, no signal . . . not a sound."

"Cause of death?"

"Unknown."

"Autopsy?"

"They did one. Couldn't find a thing. She just died. That's when they decided to suspend exploration for a while."

"Aren't you afraid to be here?" I asked.

Youngman shook his head. Winton said, "Not really. That's why *we're* here with you and not someone else." She smiled at me. "Are *you* afraid?"

I looked around that coppery, cylindrical room, at what appeared to be another hatch or door at the far end, and thought about the prospect of resuming the exploration of this enormous and mysterious vessel. I tried not to think about the now zero g room or the bishop's clandestine excursion to this vessel.

"No," I finally replied. "I'm not afraid."

There seemed to be nothing else to say. We started back.

L ATER that evening, Cardenas came to my makeshift cabin. I was on my pallet, reviewing the notes I'd made from repeated viewings of the previous excursion recordings. I didn't expect any new insight or revelation, but it was something to do.

"Sorry if I'm disturbing you," she said. "I need to speak to you, privately."

A churning began in my stomach. I had no idea what she would say, but I figured it couldn't be good. "Close the door."

She shut the door and held herself against the wall, facing me. I'd always admired Cardenas, partly because she was a member of the crew—I admired everyone in the crew, to an extent, because they were so much their own people, staying outside of all the social and political machinations on the *Argonos*—but also because of the way she represented them on the Executive Council. Like Geller, she always argued for what was best for the ship as a whole, not for herself or for any one faction. Although I would never have said we were friends, she was one of the few people who I believed did not actively dislike me—that was worth a lot.

"All right," I said. "Give me the bad news."

"Oh, I don't know that it's *bad*, exactly. Weird. Three things, and you should know about them. Nikos ordered me not to speak of one, and he doesn't know I'm aware of the other; I don't think *he's* even aware of the third. But I won't keep them secret any longer. Not when we're about to start explorations tomorrow." She cocked her head. "Whether you choose to tell the others, I leave to you. It probably doesn't matter. But *you* should know, since you're in charge."

"I'm glad *someone* thinks so."

She smiled, but only briefly. "This first thing is mostly just a mystery, maybe some physical phenomenon that we don't recognize, but it could have some significance we can't yet determine. We also can't do anything about it, but it's worth being aware of." She shrugged uncomfortably. "We maintain a steady three-thousand kilometer distance between the *Argonos* and the alien ship. The problem is this: every couple of days we have to retreat a bit, because the *Argonos* drifts closer to the ship." Another shrug. "Well, we drift closer to it, or it drifts closer to us, or we're drifting together, it doesn't matter which."

"Frame of reference," I said.

"Yes. However you chose to view it, every two days we have to make a several-minute burn of some of the attitude jets to pull back to three thousand kilometers."

That was weird, all right. And disturbing.

"What's the mass of the alien ship?" I asked.

"We've already run that, and it doesn't work. That damned ship is huge, dense in some sections, and it's got significant mass, but not enough to account for this, not at three thousand kilometers."

Cardenas may have thought it was just a mystery, but I didn't like it.

"Any ideas?"

"No. We still don't pick up anything from the ship except a hint of ambient heat, which isn't much higher than its surroundings. No one's been able to suggest an explanation."

"That's encouraging." I shook my head. "What about the shuttle? We'll drift into the ship as well, won't we?

She nodded. "Probably. A couple of choices. We can set down on the ship's hull, anchor the shuttle with a few cables. Since there's no rotation, and there will be a tiny bit of natural gravity, it wouldn't take much to secure us. The cargo hold has all the necessary equipment."

"Thinking ahead."

She gave me a quick shrug. "Just wanted to be prepared. The other choice is to tell the pilots that the mass of the ship is enough to cause a small attraction, and let them use the shuttle engines regularly to keep us parked."

I nodded. "Preference?"

"Land on the ship and anchor to the hull. If that ship *is* dangerous, being seventy-five meters away won't make much difference."

"I agree. We'll make a final decision tomorrow." I sighed. "Okay, what else?"

Cardenas hesitated a long time before answering, which only increased my anxiety.

"Did you ever wonder how it was we found this ship?"

Sure, I had wondered—a dark mental creature of doubt had gnawed away at my thoughts, although I had always managed to suppress it for a time. I hadn't wanted to think about it too much. I knew something was wrong.

"Just coincidence," I tried. "On our way out from Antioch, it was just there, near our flight path. Coincidence. Luck."

Cardenas made a kind of snorting noise. "This ship, this alien vessel, is nowhere near *anything*. You take all the possible flight paths we could have charted out from Antioch's system, and just by chance we choose the one that takes us right to this starship."

"Were we on a flight path to make a jump to the bishop's next star?"

She shook her head. "The bishop hadn't made a selection yet. He doesn't usually make one immediately, but he'd never hold off that long. Either Captain Costa somehow convinced him to postpone his selection, or the bishop and the captain worked together on this. I don't know how it played out between them."

"Tell me."

"A few hours after you entered the chamber on Antioch, the transmitter at the original landing site sent off a long, highly directional signal burst. It stayed on long enough for Communications to chart its path. Didn't seem to be directed at anything in particular—the nearest star in its path was hundreds of light-years away. Working backwards in time, it still would have been a couple thousand years ago before anything would have been much closer."

"So Nikos got curious."

"Apparently. He set course to follow the signal path, and we stayed under conventional propulsion all those months until we picked up the alien ship. Even so, we almost missed it; we nearly went right on by. The only reason we didn't is because the captain had all the ship sensors on full alert, *looking*."

"So you think the signal was directed at the alien ship."

"What do *you* think, Bartolomeo?"

"And Nikos doesn't know you know about this?"

"No. He ordered the people in Communications not to speak of it to anyone. When he set our course, he gave no explanation, just gave the orders to the navigators."

"Then how did you learn about it?"

She hesitated. "The crew obeys most of the captain's orders, but not in certain matters. We have open communication among ourselves. We keep no secrets from one another."

"Any ideas about the signal?" I asked. I had a couple myself, but they were only partially formed, and I wanted to hear what Cardenas thought.

"We talked about it. The crew. A number of suggestions, but most extremely unlikely. Two primary possibilities, we concluded." She held up a finger. "One, it was a signal to the alien starship that the chamber had been discovered. Or breached."

"But you said the signal wasn't sent until several hours after we'd entered. Why the delay?"

Cardenas smiled. "We worked that out. Long enough
for Antioch to rotate and bring the transmitter into a position
where it could send the signal to the correct location."

I nodded. "Second possibility."

She held up another finger. "The signal was meant to
lead us here."

"A trap."

"Of sorts. Except there's no one left alive on the ship.
The trap, if that's what it was, can't be sprung."

"That's what we think. Maybe it's what we're supposed
to think."

Cardenas shrugged. "Haven't seen any signs of life yet."

"There's always tomorrow," I said. "You said there
were three things."

"Yes. The third bothers me the most. It's the bishop."

My gut tightened still further. "Go ahead."

"Not sure what to tell you. It's been three weeks now
since exploration of the alien ship was suspended. During
that time, the bishop has made three excursions of his own,
three trips here with a shuttle and a crew. I'm fairly certain
Nikos doesn't know about the trips, and the bishop probably
thinks no one does—he managed to override all the security
alarms, took circuitous flight paths, arranged for the bridge
to shut down sensors and detection equipment until the shuttle was far from the *Argonos,* that kind of thing. Very
thorough."

"Not quite thorough enough, apparently."

Cardenas gave me a hard smile. "People usually under-
estimate the crew."

"Nikos knows about one trip."

She nodded, still smiling. "And I guess I underesti-
mate Nikos."

"What was the bishop doing?"

"Don't know. But we think he brought something back
to the *Argonos* on his second trip." She shook her head.
"No idea what."

That *was* distressing. And I wondered if it had anything
to do with the fact that there was no longer any gravity in
the room that had killed Santiago.

"Any suggestions?" I asked. "A plan of action?"

"Not really. The crew's looking, but it's unlikely they'll find anything. The bishop is too smart, and the *Argonos* is too big. You want a plan? We keep a close eye on the bishop. Wait, and watch our backs."

26

THE next day we secured the shuttle to the alien ship's hull, after extensive and contentious discussion with the pilots, Nikos, and the bishop—we argued that extra stability for the shuttle was necessary since we might be there for weeks—but only after working out a way for the pilots to perform a quick-release and takeoff. Rita Hollings set up a system of boosters and relays throughout that part of the alien ship already explored, so video and sound would be transmitted from the suit helmets to the shuttle with minimal loss of signal quality. We could have someone monitoring the exploration teams at all times.

As a precaution, we continued to use two remotes, although they slowed our progress considerably and were too crude to be much real help. We sent them first into each new passage or cabin, but aside from acting as a decoy that could spring any traps awaiting us, and providing preliminary images, they were practically useless. In addition, each of us had a hand stunner secured to our pressure suits, although none of us expected to use them.

I would like to say that the following days were filled with awe and excitement, with marvels and wonders, astonishing discoveries. If they were, the marvels went unrecognized.

Mysteries we *did* find, and they were many. But I learned that something can be *too* mysterious, *too* alien—so mysterious or alien as to approach being meaningless:

—Two connected rooms crisscrossed by metal rods; we had to laboriously climb through them each time we went in or out of the ship until we found a curving passage that bypassed them. We couldn't even guess at the purpose or function of the rooms or the rods.

—More bare and empty cabins with walls so featureless, the rooms appeared to be incomplete.

—Mazes of interlocking tunnels that doubled back on themselves and led nowhere.

—A series of dead ends—high, narrow corridors ten to twenty meters in length that simply ended at solid, featureless walls.

—And finally, a large spherical room we dubbed the Greenhouse. Ninety meters across, the inner walls consisted of hundreds of hexagonal facets of clear material like steelglass; with the hand torches and lanterns we could see through the facets to another layer about a meter behind the glass, this one consisting of smooth unmarked metal. There was only one entrance to the room. Did we really think it served as a greenhouse? No. What would have been a light source? Where would plants be mounted? As with everything else we'd seen, we had no idea what the Greenhouse's function was.

But there was one major plus during those early days: there were no deaths, and there were no injuries. We made steady, though slow, progress farther and farther into the alien starship, and there was a growing sense of accomplishment, and a belief that better things were to come.

TWO and a half weeks after we'd arrived, the team of Starlin, Cardenas, and Winton explored a room with blistered walls—metal covered with crusted, discolored, irregularly shaped bubbles. They spent some time studying and probing the blistered metal, speculating on whether the discoloration and blistering were intentional, or were symptoms of neglect and abandonment. Then the team drifted toward a wall adjacent to the one through which they'd entered, and approached a second door.

Instead of sending in one of the remotes, Starlin got careless. Perhaps because they were at the end of their shift and tired, the door seemed to be in the "ceiling" of the room, and it had been weeks since we'd encountered any portion of the alien ship that had gravity—nothing since the room where Santiago had died. The door was quite large, wide and tall enough to accommodate three or four people at once; when Starlin turned a handle on the wall beside it—a rectangular bar that moved easily with the slightest pressure—the door slid smoothly open, disappearing into the thick wall.

Starlin swung himself "up" toward the opening, holding out one of the lanterns. As the lantern and his hand moved through the doorway, followed by one of his legs, the gravity kicked in. He didn't have a good grip on the lantern and it was pulled out of his hand; it shot off like a jet beacon. Starlin, too, was pulled into the next room, but he had one hand and arm outside, his hand still gripped around the bar, and one leg hooked on the doorway. He let out a cry, but managed to hang on, half in the next room, half out.

"Help me!" His helmeted head was still in the blister-walled room, but his grip seemed to be weakening.

It's uncertain just what happened next. Starlin was never unsure, and neither were most of the rest of us, but the seeds of doubt are still there even now.

Sherry Winton pushed off the wall and floated across the room toward him, moving quickly. Starlin wasn't looking at her, and his helmet camera was directed down at the door bar; Winton's own video was too jerky, shifting around, missing much of the action of her hands and arms; and Cardenas's view was blocked by Winton's body. Winton crashed into Starlin, and he lost his grip. Winton claimed that in her panic to save Starlin, she misjudged her speed and direction and accidentally struck him, then

scrambled to catch herself. Starlin said she intentionally
crashed into him, then deliberately pried his gloved fingers
from the door bar.

With his primary hold gone, Starlin began to slide farther
into the next room, his fingers scratching frantically for
something to hang onto. Then Winton's leg kicked out—
accidental, she swore; deliberate again, Starlin accused—
knocking Starlin's leg through the doorway. Starlin's slide
accelerated.

But as he went through the opening, he managed to get
both hands onto the door frame, with just enough grip to
stop his fall.

He hung there, and I remember watching on the shuttle
monitor—by that time Aiyana, who had been posted on the
monitor, had alerted us to what was happening—and feeling
that time was stretching out interminably; an aching fear
drove through me, fear that he couldn't hold on. But it
was probably no more than twenty or thirty seconds before
Cardenas was at the doorway, anchoring herself to the door
bar with the security cable attached to her suit, and reaching
out to Starlin.

By that time Winton was settled, and began to help.
Starlin, of course, later argued that Winton no longer had
a choice; her opportunity was gone, and she had to help in
order to cover herself. Whatever the reason, Winton worked
with Cardenas to pull Starlin up through the doorway and
out of the other room.

As soon as he was free of the other room's gravity,
Starlin lunged at Winton. They struggled, although the suits
made fighting awkward and difficult. Cardenas tried to sepa-
rate them, but her own actions were clumsy, and everyone
was losing control. Cardenas kept her head, though, quickly
unhooked her security cable from the door bar, then turned
the bar back to its original position. The door slid out from
the wall and sealed shut just moments before Starlin and
Winton both struck it; if it hadn't shut, they both would
have gone through the doorway and plunged to their deaths.
As we were later to learn, the room was like the one Santi-

ago had died in: the gravity was twice Earth normal, and
the fall would have been more than thirty meters.

B Y the time they got back to the shuttle, Starlin was
still furious, and Winton continued to vigorously deny
any harmful intent. Both were confined to their compart-
ments while the rest of us talked to Cardenas and reviewed
the recordings. Cardenas couldn't make a judgment. Much
of her view had been blocked; everything had happened so
quickly, and she'd been focused on Starlin, not on Winton.

"I can't be sure," she said. "I really can't." There was
a long hesitation. "But I will admit that my impression at
the time, and I want to emphasize that it wasn't a *strong*
impression by any means, was that . . . was that Winton
tried to push him through the opening."

No one said anything for a long time. Finally Maria
Vegas said, "But why?"

I don't think the lack of an answer changed anyone's
mind about what had happened. We watched the recordings
again, all three frames of reference. Still inconclusive. But
like Cardenas, I, too, had the *impression* that Sherry Winton
had tried to push Starlin into the next room, to his probable
death. I knew others felt the same way, and Cardenas's
words had charged the air. More silence, no one knowing
quite what to say, where to start. But I knew what needed
to be done.

"They both have to go back to the *Argonos*," I finally
said.

There was no argument.

27

NOR was there any argument from the Executive Committee back on the *Argonos*. But they strongly suggested we *all* return to the ship for a few days, even a couple of weeks. The bishop declared that we needed a break from the alien starship, from the hard work of suiting up every other day and moving about in zero g, from being cooped up together for so long. Nikos, too, said he thought it would be a good idea. I told them I would discuss it with the others, and we would let them know. In the meantime, they would select two replacements.

I called everyone except Starlin and Winton into the main cabin and told them what the Executive Committee had suggested. I included Taggart—the med-tech—and the two pilots because our decision would affect them as well.

"I want to know two things from each of you," I said. "First, do you want to continue as a member of this team? If your answer is no, you can go back to the *Argonos* with Starlin and Winton, and no one will think less of you. This has been hard on all of us, and there's no reason to think it's going to get any easier. As I said before we came here, I don't want anyone on this team who isn't willing." I looked out at all those who had been on the shuttle with

me all this time. "If you need to think about it, just say
so. Take a few hours if necessary."

"What's the second question?" Aiyana asked.

"If you *do* want to remain a part of this team," I continued, "do you think we should go back to the *Argonos* for
a time, get away from the alien ship? So, let's start with
the first question."

As I'd expected and hoped, not a single person wanted to
withdraw from the team. We moved to the second question.

"You're in charge of this . . . mission," William Rogers
said. "I'd like to hear what you think about it."

I looked at the others, saw some nodding, and no signs
of objection. From the expressions on most of their faces,
I had the feeling that at least some of them were beginning
to respect me.

"I *don't* think we should leave now," I said. "I believe
it would be a mistake. We've developed a feel for the alien
ship. It may not be much, and we may not understand one
damn thing about it yet, but we know it as much as anyone
can at this point. Yes, we need to be more careful, remind
ourselves of what can happen, what can go wrong. Starlin's
a perfect reminder of that. But if we go back to the *Argonos*,
we risk losing that feel, however intangible it is. If that
happens, we're more likely to make mistakes when we come
back. There *will* come a time when we'll need to stop, when
we will have been here too long. But I don't think we're
anywhere near that point."

Casterman spoke up. "I must disagree," he said. "In
part because I represent the Church, and I should argue the
bishop's position, but also because I personally agree with
it." He paused, and sniffed. I couldn't help wondering what
it was he was sniffing at. "I believe we will be *more* prone
to mistakes if we don't take a break from the daily excursions into the alien ship. We're tired, we're despairing—"

"Speak for yourself," Pär interrupted. "I'm tired, but
I'm not even close to despair."

Casterman nodded. "Fair enough. But we *are* tired, and
at times tired of each other. A break from all this would

allow us a fresh start. We would come back with renewed enthusiasm.''

"No, I think Bartolomeo's right," Cardenas said. "Eventually we will need that kind of a break, but taking one now . . . It would be an implicit admission of failure, or defeat.''

"Not at all," Casterman responded. "Just a recognition of the difficulties, of the stresses involved."

"You can say that all you want," Cardenas argued, "but I know that's how it would feel. Inside." She pointed to her stomach. "Where it counts."

We took a vote. Casterman and Aiyana were the only ones who voted against staying.

"We stay right here, then," I said. Then, to the two dissenters, "Do you want to go back to the *Argonos*? If you need the time away from here, we'll adjust the schedule around it until you feel you can return. We won't replace you.''

Casterman surprised me. He shook his head, smiling. "No. We're in this together. I can't speak for Aiyana, but I'll stay.''

Aiyana hesitated, then nodded. "I will, too."

We were decided.

I had Casterman and Aiyana with me when I contacted the *Argonos* so that they could assure the Executive Committee that I wasn't making the decisions on my own. We spent half an hour discussing our decision to stay with the alien ship, and another on the logistics of getting Starlin and Winton back to the *Argonos*—we didn't want to send them back together, so two maintenance modules would be sent and, at least for the time being, Starlin and Winton would have a security officer with them at all times. No one wanted to talk about a long-term solution, so it was ignored; everyone, I'm sure, was hoping any animosity between them would eventually disappear once they were back on board the *Argonos*.

Finally we got to the two replacements. Everyone on the

Executive Committee turned to Bishop Soldano, so it was
obvious who had made the final decision. The bishop looked
at us, and a half-smile worked onto his face.

"We thought you would stay," he said. "So the first
replacement will be Dr. Glienna Sommerwild. Do any of
you know her?"

Pär grunted. "I know her. She's a head twister."

The bishop nodded. "Yes, she's a psychologist. We
think her presence would be a good precaution, and she's
quite willing."

I turned to Pär. "Any objection to her?"

He shook his head. "If we've got to have one, it might
as well be her." Then he smiled. "Nothing *I* do will surprise her."

"All right," I said. "Who's the other replacement?"

The bishop hesitated, but the smile was still there. "Father Veronica."

I avoided looking at Pär, and glanced at Casterman. His
face was set hard, as if he was straining to keep any expression from appearing. I wondered if he thought the choice
of Father Veronica a criticism of him by the bishop.

"Father Veronica," I repeated. I felt stupid, unable to
say anything else.

"Yes," said the bishop. "Even though she would be a
second representative of the Church, I did not think you
would object. We've discussed her once before. She's expressed a strong interest in joining the team."

As always, I did not trust his motives. "No, I don't have
any objections. She'll make a good addition."

We spent some more time discussing details, including
new equipment and supplies we needed. When we cut the
communication, Casterman left without a word, and I
thought to myself that we were going to have trouble
with him.

TWO days later, Father Veronica and Dr. Sommerwild
     arrived. Frip and Cardenas helped them out of their
pressure suits, and then we had a round of introductions. I

stayed in the rear corner of the main cabin, watching and waiting. Dr. Sommerwild came over to me and we shook hands. She was a small woman, with graying hair and skin that was beginning to wrinkle. I was surprised that the Executive Committee would have chosen someone of that age, but her handshake was strong, and her movements indicated she was in good shape, and comfortable in zero gravity.

"Do you remember me, Bartolomeo?" Her voice was gravelly, yet somehow comforting, and it did sound familiar. But I couldn't place it, or her face.

"I'm not sure," I said. "Should I?"

She shrugged. "If you don't, you'd make a good demonstration for the concept of repression." She smiled then, and with that smile the years came away and the memories washed over me. I couldn't muster a response; I felt a little shaky.

"Dr. G.?"

She nodded, still smiling. "That's me."

"I'd always assumed the G was the first letter of your last name. Wrong all that time. What is it . . . Glenna?"

"Glienna. Now you know my big secret." Her smile slowly gave way to a more thoughtful expression. "It has been many years, Bartolomeo."

Oh yes, a lot of years. When I was ten or eleven, someone in authority, perhaps even one of my invisible, unnamed parents, decided I might not be psychologically healthy, and that I could benefit from some counseling or therapy. Of course I wasn't psychologically healthy. I'd been born a freak, abandoned by my parents, raised by committee, taunted and harassed by other children, and shunned by adults. I've *never* been psychologically healthy, and I never will be. I feel a sense of accomplishment because I have managed to achieve a certain level of functionality.

Someone thought Dr. G. could help me. It's very possible that she did. We met once or twice a week for almost a year; usually for an hour or so, other times for an entire morning or afternoon, wandering through different parts of the ship, talking part of the time, but often not talking at all. Sometimes I looked forward to our meetings with so much anticipation I couldn't sleep; but just as often I felt only dread. Who knows? I might have been much worse off than I am today if not for her.

"For years," she said, interrupting my thoughts, "I couldn't decide whether you were one of my successes, or one of my failures."

"What did you finally decide?" I asked her.

"That you were neither." She paused. "Over time I have come to understand that I have much less impact on my patients than I'd once believed. Oh, I can help, provide some guidance for those who truly want to be helped, for those who have some understanding of their difficulties and are ready, who are trying to change. For those people, who would probably find their own way eventually, I might be able to speed up the process, make it a bit easier. But if the patient doesn't want to get better, to change in some way, I can't do a thing for them. Nothing." She paused again. "It seems so simple, and so obvious in some ways, but when you are trained intensely for this work, you end up with an inflated sense of your own importance, your effectiveness. You, Bartolomeo, were going to be what you are, with or without me. And look what you've achieved: adviser to the captain of the *Argonos*, and now leader of an expedition exploring an alien starship."

"You forget 'despised by thousands,'" I said.

She tipped her head slightly to one side. "I have heard rumors to the effect that that's changing."

"Only rumors," I said.

She hesitated, looking directly at me, then said, "I suspect not."

Father Veronica joined us then. She took my hand in hers. "Hello, Bartolomeo."

"Father." I felt suddenly awkward.

"I'm here after all," she said.

"I'm going to go settle in," Dr. G. said. "I understand I will have a compartment all of two meters square."

"Closer to two and a half," I told her.

"Luxury. Well, until later, then."

She left, and Father Veronica watched her go. Then she

turned back to me and said, "Renewing old acquaintances, I see. Glienna said you'd known each other a long time ago."

I nodded. "When I was a child. Did she tell you *how* we knew each other?"

"No."

"I was a patient."

"I wondered."

I left it at that. I didn't feel like going through it all again. "So the bishop changed his mind," I said.

"I was persuasive. I heard there would be a need for two replacements, and I insisted. After some hesitation, he acquiesced."

"That worries me."

"You distrust him that much?"

"Yes. And with good cause."

She sighed, but whether it was because she thought I was being unfair, or because she thought I was right, I couldn't tell. But then she smiled gently. "I'm looking forward to this, Bartolomeo. Truly."

"I'm glad you're here, Father."

"Please, Bartolomeo. We're friends. Call me Veronica."

"All right," I said.

"We start tomorrow?" she asked.

"Probably. Or the next day. We've got some work to do first."

"Then I'll follow Glienna's example, and settle in."

I watched her move awkwardly across the main cabin, and realized I didn't know whether or not I was glad she was here.

28

I knew I needed to make changes to the teams; I did not want both new people together, even if it would be with Cardenas. So I started over, and not a single team remained the same. I shifted Pär to a team with Casterman and Maria Vegas, and I assigned Father Veronica to my own along with Leona Frip. I put Dr. G. with Rogers and Cardenas, leaving Hollings, Aiyana, and Youngman for the final team. Pär smirked at me when I announced the new arrangements, but I decided I could live with that.

The next day, we began again.

AT the end of Father Veronica's first shift inside the alien starship, which had been more of a "tour" to familiarize her with the ship than a real exploration, I asked her what her impressions were.

"It *is* such a strange place. I understand now what people mean when they say it seems so alien. I understand how people can be so certain that this ship was not built by or for human beings. And yet, there is also something quite wonderful about it, because it is so different." She paused.

"But I can see how that feeling might change over time, when nothing means anything."

"Do you still sense that malign quality to the ship?"

"No, not really."

"What do you sense, then? Anything?"

She nodded. "Indifference."

O VER the next several days, our rate of progress increased. We were learning patterns, the way doors and hatches opened, recognizing dead ends before wasting too much time on them. The only negative occurrence was a report from the *Argonos*. Nikos opened the communication alone one day, and spoke to me in private.

"Winton's disappeared." He looked tired, the dark areas beneath his eyes more pronounced.

"What the hell does 'disappeared' mean?"

"What do you think?" His words were slightly slurred, but I couldn't tell if it was from alcohol or exhaustion.

"All right, tell me what happened."

"We don't *know* what happened. She was supposed to report to the central med clinic for more tests, but never showed. The security escort posted outside her cabin eventually overrode her door locks, but she wasn't anywhere in her rooms. She just disappeared."

"I suppose the security escort swears he or she never left the door unattended."

"That's absolutely correct. He says he never left his post, and the escort on before him says the same thing. She's just gone."

"It's probably nothing, but I'd warn Starlin," I said.

"I already have. He's not worried. I got the impression he welcomed a confrontation with her."

I leaned back in my seat, thinking about what, if anything, this meant for us.

"What do you expect me to do from here?"

"Nothing. I just thought you should know. It's one more complication in this whole mess." He paused. "Are you going to tell anyone there?"

"What's to tell? As you said yourself, we have no idea what happened. Until we know more, all it would do is set off useless speculation, and maybe start some people worrying. We don't need that."

I watched him shrug and nod. "How is it going there?" he asked.

"Everything's fine. Nothing exciting, but nothing bad, either."

"How long will you stick with it, Bartolomeo? You're learning nothing, you're finding nothing. How long?"

"A lot longer than this, Nikos. Why do you care? Isn't finding this ship what you wanted?"

"What do you mean by that?"

I shook my head. "Nothing. Thanks for letting me know about Winton."

We spoke for a few more minutes about official matters, and ended the linkup. I sat in the pilot cabin, thinking and worrying. Winton's disappearance *did* disturb me. But as I'd said to Nikos, there was nothing I could do about it from here. I tried to forget about it.

F IVE days after Father Veronica and Dr. G. joined us, we found something remarkable. Actually, what was remarkable was not the object itself, but the fact that we found it, when we had found nothing like it in all the weeks we'd explored the alien starship.

My team was in a large room broken up by metal girders so that our lanterns cast long and harsh shadows in all directions. Each of us had gone off to explore different parts of the room, but none of us had yet seen anything of interest.

I was crawling through a triangular opening where three of the girders intersected, when Father Veronica said, "I've found something."

Leona Frip and I joined her where two pairs of girders were fused together as they entered the wall. She had spotted a box wedged into the junction, and she pointed to it as we approached. Then she reached into the junction, gently took hold of the box, and pulled it out.

The box was half a meter long and twenty or twenty-five centimeters high and deep. It was made of dark, reddish polished wood, the top inlaid with tiny bits of colored stone—dark blue pieces irregularly shaped but placed in a swirl pattern. Leaflike shapes were carved into the two ends. There were no clasps or visible hinges, but the fine separation of the lid was visible.

"Do we try to open it?" Father Veronica asked.

That was a good question. We hung there, drifting slightly, looking at each other.

"Remember Pandora," Leona said. No one laughed.

"It's just a box," said Father Veronica.

I think we all knew we were going to open it, just as we all knew the logical and cautious approach would have been to bring in a remote and try to open it from a distance.

"I'll do it," Leona said.

She reached for the box, but before her gloved fingers touched it, Father Veronica raised the lid. The lid came free—no hinges, nothing physically holding it in place—and nothing happened. Father Veronica angled the box so that lantern light fully illuminated the interior. Inside were delicate balls of dust, or disintegrated matter. Nothing recognizable.

The underside of the lid appeared to be painted, and the images looked vaguely like white clouds against a deep blue sky, but they could have been anything.

No one spoke. When I looked at Father Veronica, who still held the box in her hands, I thought her eyes had grown moist.

"What's wrong?" I asked.

She just shook her head.

"Father?" Leona put her hand on Father Veronica's arm.

"This was once somebody's box," she finally said, her voice little more than a cracked whisper. "Human or alien, this was something *personal*, I'm sure of it. It meant something to someone. And that person is gone, long gone, and there is no one left to remember what this box was, or what it meant. Or why it was placed here.''

I thought it an odd sentiment from someone who believed in life after death. The owner of the box was physically long gone, but in Father Veronica's belief system his (or her or its) soul was still with us, alive, somehow, presumably with the memories and feelings about that box intact. But it's also possible there was something to her feelings that I did not comprehend.

Father Veronica carefully closed the box, then put it back where she'd found it, gently wedging it into place so it would not drift away.

EXCITEMENT gradually returned. Or perhaps it's more accurate to say that the kind of true excitement we'd been expecting was only now manifesting for the first time since we started exploring the alien starship. Much of it came from the increased speed of our progress, and from the other new places we found: another spherical chamber like the Greenhouse, but this time with facets made of a reflective material that repeatedly refracted light and images throughout it; long, clear tubes leading through a tank of some kind of liquid, lantern light revealing bits of slowly moving matter in the fluid; and a long corridor illuminated by rows of faint green phosphorescence. There were still no revelations, no mysteries solved, no understanding of the function of anything, but we all sensed a growing complexity, or variety—something different.

Most tantalizing of all, as insignificant as it might have seemed on the surface, was the discovery of the box. Although we never touched it again, it was always there in our minds, and I am sure I was not the only person who detoured to look at it as we moved through that room. It was an artifact, something that was not an integral part of the alien ship. More than that was the feeling, unspoken but felt by most of us, that it had been made by human hands.

29

I was alone in the galley, eating hot soup and working a
stereograph puzzle when Rogers stuck his head through
the doorway.

"Bartolomeo? You're going to want to see what's on
the monitor." Then, after a slight pause: "We're all going
to want to see this."

I sensed the excitement in his voice and pushed the puzzle aside, letting it fall apart as it drifted across the room.
"On my way," I said.

I fought to stay calm, trying not to expect too much.
We were all too keyed up, too ready to find something of
importance; I was afraid of disappointment, and not only
my own.

By the time I got out to the main cabin, the others were
gathering around the large monitor. I took a quick mental
census, and no one seemed to be missing. Two or three
people were drifting free, but most were sitting, strapped
into chairs or wall cushions.

On the screen was a suited figure viewed from behind;
captions in the upper left indicated we were watching from
Aiyana's camera, which meant we were seeing either Rita
Hollings or Trace Youngman. The figure was standing up-

right in the center of a long corridor. From the figure's size, I guessed we were watching Hollings; she was next to a lantern which had been mounted on the wall at chest height. Aiyana was too close for us to see Hollings' feet, nor could we see a ceiling; beyond, the walls seemed to curve out of sight even before the light faded.

Cardenas was at the cabin console, controlling the sound and video; she glanced up at me, nodded, then turned back to the console.

"I think we're all here now," she said. "Rita, you want to give us a quick rundown on what you've found? We're on Aiyana's camera here."

Hollings turned to Aiyana, and seemed to be facing *us*. Now I could make out her face inside the clear steelglass helmet.

"I don't know how much you can see back there, but this looks an awful lot like one of the corridors on the *Argonos*. One big difference is, the ceiling here's a *lot* higher." She looked up and Aiyana did the same, our view angling upward so we could see the ceiling far above Hollings' head. "I'd guess six or seven meters, easy," she said. Both heads tilted back down and Hollings smiled. "But here's the great thing."

She crouched, then jumped. Up she went, then immediately came back down. She was grinning.

"We'll have to get a precise reading, but it feels damn close to a normal one g. I feel like I'm walking along in the *Argonos*."

The picture on the screen shifted to Youngman's viewpoint. He was just back of the corridor doorway—which was at least twice the size of those on the *Argonos*—one hand on the frame; from the way the video moved around, it was obvious he was still weightless. He was far enough from Aiyana and Hollings that we could now see their booted feet planted solidly on the corridor floor.

"You two have had enough of the fun," Youngman said. "It's my turn."

I don't know why, but I was overcome by a rush of panic, and I wanted to yell out STOP! I was suddenly afraid that it was a trap, that as soon as he was inside the corridor, the doorway would seal shut behind him and something terrible would happen to them all.

Youngman carefully pulled himself into the corridor, the gravity settling him firmly to the floor.

Nothing happened.

"Yeah," he said. "This feels great." He started walking toward the others.

"How far down the corridor have you gone?" I asked.

"This is it," Hollings said. "Once we realized what we had here, Margita told us to wait until everyone was there to watch. Can't see much, except to know it goes a long way. It curves, so our line of sight gets cut off."

I looked up at the clock. "You've got a couple of hours," I said. "Take it slow, but see if you can find out how far it goes."

"Thanks, Captain," Hollings said.

"I'm not the captain," I quickly replied. "Not yet."

A few people laughed, and I hoped everyone thought of it as a joke. Especially Aiyana.

THE corridor curved gently to the right and continued unchanged for half a kilometer. The walls were smooth and unbroken, but set in the ceiling high overhead were regularly spaced depressions lined with strips of a milky blue material that might have been lights, although they now gave off no illumination.

The team had only three lanterns with them, so they couldn't mount any to illuminate the corridor. That would be the first task of the next team in. Instead, they carried the lanterns to light their way, leaving darkness behind them as they went.

They reached the end of the passage before their shift was over, but didn't find much else. At the end of the corridor was a single door. I ordered them to leave it untouched and return to the shuttle. Surprisingly, there were no objections. I think they were more tired than they let on; probably from the extra effort of moving in full gravity, and the comedown from an adrenaline high. Even *I* felt tired, and all I had done was watch them. Hollings mounted one lantern at the end of the corridor, leaving it on to provide a beacon for the next team; then they all headed back.

But despite everyone's exhaustion, I sensed once again a renewed energy and excitement. Gravity, and this time suitable for human beings. Coincidence? None of us thought so.

30

LEONA Frip would not suit up.

We were up early for the first shift, long before most of the others. It was quiet in the shuttle; Father Veronica, Leona Frip, and I ate quick-heated meals for breakfast; De-anna, one of the pilots, joined us in the galley, drinking coffee. Dr. G. was scheduled to take the first watch on the monitor, so she, too, was up, and pulled herself into the galley still half-asleep.

We didn't talk much, but there was still an air of excite-ment. The presence of Earth normal gravity on the alien ship continued to imbue us with a sense of anticipation. We'd abandoned use of the remotes—awkward and practi-cally useless in zero g, they were even more useless in full gravity. Two more days and all we'd found were another half dozen empty rooms and passages, but gravity was pres-ent in all of them. Most of us felt certain that we were moving toward something important, some significant dis-covery or revelation.

But when Father Veronica and I headed for the doorway, Leona Frip remained strapped into her seat. I didn't notice at first. I heard Father Veronica say, "Leona, it's time," but even then I only hesitated for a moment, then kept on going.

"Leona." Father Veronica's voice sounded more urgent. "Leona, is something wrong?"

That stopped me. I turned around and came back into the galley. Father Veronica had one hand on Leona's shoulder, and was bent over her in concern. Leona was staring straight ahead, at nothing and nobody, one hand wrapped around her empty coffee packet, the other resting in her lap. Deanna and Dr. G. hadn't moved, but they were both looking at her.

"Leona?" Father Veronica gently shook her. "Leona?"

She did not respond. I pulled myself around till I was directly in her line of sight, then crouched so that my face was on the same level as hers. Her eyes were open, hardly blinking; her facial muscles appeared relaxed. She seemed very much at ease.

"Leona," I said. "Our shift is beginning. We need to suit up, get started. All right?"

Still no response. I knew she hadn't suddenly gone deaf, mute, and blind, but I was also fairly certain that nothing was registering. Leona Frip had very effectively blocked all of us out of her perception. I looked around at the others, who were looking at me as if I had some answers. I didn't even have the questions.

"Dr. G.," I said.

She nodded and moved to Leona's side. Father Veronica backed away. Dr. G. didn't say anything for a long time, just watched Leona's passive face.

"Leona," she finally said, "can you hear me?"

By this time I don't think any of us expected a response, and there wasn't one. For the first time, I noticed that Leona's eyes were a pale, grayish green, and there were a couple of darker flecks in her left eye. Her cheeks were slightly flushed, but I had the impression that it was her normal state. She wore small gold loops in her ears; from each of the loops dangled a string of tiny, beautiful green beads. I felt suddenly guilty, because I realized I had never looked this closely at her before, had never paid enough attention to her as a person, even though she had been a part of my team for weeks.

Dr. G. touched her very gently on the arm—"Leona . . ."—then her hand—"Leona . . ."—and finally her cheek—"Leona . . ."—speaking her name softly with each contact. There was still no response.

The psychologist looked at each of us, then motioned with her head toward the doorway. We headed out of the galley, and Dr. G. followed us after telling Leona she would be right back. Once we were all outside, Dr. G. closed the door.

"I want to get some things from Taggart, and then I want to examine her alone. We *could* take her to her compartment, but I would rather not try to move her yet. I'm almost certain she wouldn't go on her own, and I don't want to force anything unless we have to."

"What do you think is wrong with her?" I asked.

Dr. G. shook her head. "Just let me examine her first. Then we'll talk."

AFTER notifying everyone else about what had happened, we remained in the main cabin for the next hour while Dr. G. was with Leona. More people got up and joined us, since they were unable to go into the galley to eat. Everyone spoke in low voices, and most of them deliberately avoided mentioning Leona's name. But not Father Veronica. We talked together near the monitor and console, drinking tea from the main cabin's beverage dispenser.

"I feel so badly for her," she said.

"For whom?" I asked. "Leona or Dr. G.?"

"Leona. I can't imagine what must be going on inside her to get to this point."

"Until this morning she seemed all right to me. Even this morning, for that matter. She joked with me about fighting to see who would get to shower first."

Father Veronica shook her head. "That doesn't mean anything. Except that she was good at hiding what she really felt. Or good at denying it."

"I suppose." I, too, felt concern and sympathy for

Leona, but to be candid, I was just as worried about the effect this would have on our mission. The Executive Council was going to react badly to this incident, and I was afraid of what they would do.

Pär emerged from the rear of the shuttle, hair still wet from the shower, got coffee from the dispenser, and came over to us.

"A hot shower in the morning usually picks up my spirits," he said, "but it doesn't seem to have worked today." He drank some of his coffee and grimaced. "And this muck isn't any help, either."

"Pär's a coffee connoisseur," I explained.

Father Veronica smiled and nodded. "So I understand. I don't drink it myself, but I have been told by a reliable source that the coffee he makes is remarkable."

"Thank you," Pär said. Then: "Nothing new, I take it."

I shook my head.

"This is going to be trouble," he said.

"What about Leona?" Father Veronica asked. "Forget about trouble, what about what she's going through? Don't you have some concern, some compassion for her?"

"Yes," Pär replied. "But I can't do anything for her. Maybe it's insensitive, but I'm thinking about consequences, which I *might* be able to do something about."

Relief washed over me, because I felt much the same way, but it was Pär who took the brunt of Father Veronica's disapproval.

Dr. G. came out of the galley then, but only long enough to talk briefly to Taggart, who followed her back inside.

"That does not bode well," Pär said.

"**S**HE'S catatonic," Dr. G. reported an hour later when she emerged from the galley with Taggart. Leona was not with them.

By now everyone was awake and waiting in the main cabin. Someone—Aiyana, I think—asked, "What exactly does that mean?"

"I can't tell you 'exactly,' " the psychologist replied. "I

assume you've all been told what happened with Leona earlier this morning. She hasn't changed. She's non-responsive to external stimuli, but it's not physiological. She hasn't gone blind or deaf. Her pupils react normally to changes in light, for example. We really need to conduct more extensive tests, including a check for pain responses and the like, but Mr. Taggart and I both agree that we can't do it properly here. We're also concerned about her reactions to any kind of invasive examination, and would prefer we were back on the *Argonos* where we have better equipment and support before undertaking anything like that."

She paused, trying to formulate her thoughts. "Essentially, Leona's conscious mind appears to have cut itself off from the outside world. I don't pretend to fully understand it. I've only seen one other case first-hand. Most of what I know about catatonia comes from clinical descriptions in old texts and case histories. Usually a traumatic event is the proximate cause of a catatonic state. But that doesn't appear to be the case here."

"*Now* what do we do?" I eventually asked aloud, the question I'd been silently asking myself for an hour.

"She's got to go back to the *Argonos*," Dr. G. declared.

T**WO** hours later we were all gathered again in the main cabin, watching the monitor. On the screen, seated around the conference table, were all the members of the Executive Council (except Cardenas and Aiyana, of course, who were with us on the shuttle). Dr. G. had explained Leona's condition in some detail, and requested that one of the modules be dispatched as soon as possible to take her back to the *Argonos*.

"I would like to return with her," Dr. G. said. "I want to stay with her."

"That will be arranged easily enough," Nikos said. "But we don't need to dispatch anything. You should all return."

Before I had a chance to protest, the bishop leaned toward the camera and said, "I concur with Captain Costa. I believe we all sense the mission is getting out of control."

He held up a hand. "No one is to blame. I commend you all for your efforts, but enough is enough. . . ."

I jumped in before anyone else could say anything. "You aren't seriously suggesting we abandon this mission. You *can't* be."

The bishop leaned back and looked at us with hooded eyes. "And why not?"

"I don't think the bishop is suggesting abandonment," Toller quietly said. "Not permanent." He turned to the bishop. "At least, I hope not." He turned back to us. "An extended sabbatical, perhaps. A few weeks. Time enough for everyone to rest, to get away from the pressures and frustrations, to take a fresh approach." He sighed. "There have been other developments of which you are not aware, Bartolomeo."

"What developments?"

Nikos explained. "Barry Sorrel's wife and daughter have both developed the same . . . symptoms as Barry. Extreme lassitude. Loss of appetite. Avoidance of social interaction, even among themselves."

Pär moved forward. "Are you trying to say this . . . this psychological 'malaise' . . . is contagious? Even worse, you seem to be implying that it's caused by something from the alien starship. That's just crazy."

"Is it?" said the bishop. "It could have been something that survived decontamination. That's why we've placed everyone affected in medical isolation."

"What about the rest of us?" asked Rogers. "Why aren't we *all* losing our minds?"

The bishop shrugged. "Different susceptibilities, different immune systems, different levels of exposure, different eye color for all I know. I don't have to explain it. Just add them all together." He held up his closed fist and uncurled a finger as he counted off each name. "Barry Sorrel. His wife. His daughter. Sherry Winton. Nazia Abouti." With that he held up his thumb, then raised his other hand, fist closed, and continued to list the names. "Starlin. Now Leona Frip." He paused, holding up six fingers and a thumb. "That's too many."

"That's too many, all right," I said. "Nazia Abouti doesn't fit the pattern, and with her you assume an extended incubation period besides. You're also making assumptions about Sherry Winton that can't be confirmed—it may all have been an accident, just as she claimed. And how can you add Starlin? All he did was get understandably angry about what he perceived was a deliberate attack that nearly killed him."

"*Perceived* is the significant word," the bishop said. "If he imagined it, then perhaps some psychological deterioration was occurring."

"If he was imagining it," Pär put in with a sneer, "then it *was* an accident, and you can't say Sherry Winton was affected. You can't count them both, for Christ's sake."

"Yes we can," the bishop replied.

He didn't explain, so Nikos did. "Winton and Starlin have both disappeared. There have been reports of confrontations, fighting, ship damage. The two of them appear to be stalking each other through the ship."

I shook my head. "I don't care about any of that. No, I do care, but there are other considerations. We've reached an area in the alien ship with Earth-normal gravity. That's significant. Long passages, rooms, all with gravity. We have no idea how much more is like this. And we've found things. Like the box." I paused, reluctant to say aloud what I had thought for some time. "None of us has said it, but I know that many of us believe that box was made by human hands." I let that sit. In the edges of my sight I could see some slow nodding of heads.

"We're close to something important," I continued. "We all feel it. There is evidence that human beings have been on this ship. Maybe not anymore, but at one time. We can't stop now." I started to say more, but stopped myself. I didn't really need any more arguments. It was there, simple and clear and compelling. If they were not persuaded, nothing more I could say would help. "We can't stop now," I repeated.

Surprisingly, it was Casterman who spoke. "I believe Bartolomeo is right, Eminence."

"You believe he's right," the bishop said.

"Yes. Unless you are here, I don't think you can understand what is happening. You have to feel it. There's something in that ship, Eminence. I don't know how long it will
take us to find it, but it's there."

"Perhaps we don't want to find it." The bishop leaned
forward again. "Perhaps what is in that ship . . . is Evil."

Casterman shook his head, but said no more.

"I will add my voice to theirs," Dr. G. said. Another
surprise. "There is a change in the spirits of these people,
and it is still here despite what has happened with Leona.
You asked me to become a part of this mission so I could
observe, assess, recommend. Well, I recommend we be allowed to continue. I think it would be devastating to all of
us, as well as to many others on the *Argonos*, to suspend
the exploration now, permanently or otherwise. In fact, although I want to accompany Leona back to the *Argonos*,
and stay with her for a few days, eventually I will want to
rejoin this group of people. I'll want to rejoin this mission
as soon as I can."

"And if there *is* some contagion?" Nikos asked.

Dr. G. frowned. "How likely is that, Captain? Not very,
I think, and it's a risk I believe we are all prepared to take."

"Is there anyone who doesn't want to stay there?" Nikos
asked. "Is there anyone there who thinks exploration should
be suspended, if only for a short time?"

The only response was a number of shaking heads.

"Aiyana?"

She, too, shook her head. "I'm with them. We should
stay. We should keep going. Something's going to happen
soon."

Nikos sighed. "That's what I'm afraid of."

After more argument, the Executive Council voted. The
vote was close, but we won. We would stay here and continue exploring.

I did not like what I saw in the bishop's face, however.
There was no real acceptance in his expression. Rather, I
detected a smoldering anger, and a disturbing sense that he

was merely biding his time. I realized that I feared the bishop more than the dangers of the alien ship. I thought again of the bishop's three excursions, wondering what he had found and what he planned. Wait, and watch our backs, Cardenas had said. I was afraid that wouldn't be enough.

31

TWO days later, the second-shift team was in a small, low-ceilinged room, preparing to try another door. Pär was on point, and his video was displayed on the shuttle monitor. He stood in front of a narrow door with a simple wheel mechanism set into the wall beside it. "It can't be this easy," he said.

He took hold of the wheel with both hands, turned it, and the door slid open. A shower of ice crystals poured out of the opening; the picture frosted over, and Pär yelled, "Shit!"

A harsh expulsion of breath. The monitor was grayed out. Rita Hollings fumbled with the console, switched over to Casterman's camera. Pär was sitting on the floor, his helmet covered with ice crystals. More crystals were on his suit, the floor, the wall beside him.

"Shit," he said again. "I can't see a damn thing!"

"Are you all right?" Maria Vegas asked. Presumably she was somewhere behind Casterman.

Pär nodded. With his gloved hand he brushed crystals from his helmet until he had most of it cleared. Vegas came around Casterman and helped Pär to his feet.

"Thanks," he said. Then: "What the hell was that?"

"Must you curse so much?" Casterman asked.

Pär turned to him. "Yes, I must." Then, to those of us watching, he asked, "Whose camera we on?"

"Casterman's," I said.

"Then switch over to Maria's so I don't have to keep looking at him." He turned to face Maria Vegas.

Hollings turned and looked questioningly at me. I saw I would have to make another change in the teams. I shrugged and nodded, and she switched over. Pär now appeared to be looking out at us.

"Okay," I said. "What happened?"

"I don't know. All these ice crystals came flying out, startled me, and I fell on my ass."

"Anyone got any brilliant ideas about it?"

Rogers was beside me, and he nodded. "I would guess that it was pressurized atmosphere."

THE three of them moved into the next room. Now we were on Pär's camera. The cabin looked a lot like the air lock in the outer hull. In the wall directly opposite the door through which they'd entered was an identical door. Next to it was an identical wheel, and when Pär looked back at the open door, we could see another wheel on the inside beside it.

Rogers spoke up. "I'm fairly certain you won't be able to open the next door before sealing this one. This has to be another air lock. But before you try it, I suggest someone go back and seal off the previous door as well. The chances are good that there is air beyond the next door, and we don't want to lose it. The air lock *should* take care of that, but we don't know how old this ship is, or how long it's been abandoned, and I don't think we should count on the air lock door being secure. So I suggest we seal another door as a backup, and hope for the best."

"Okay," said Maria Vegas. "Makes sense, and it shouldn't take too long."

"I'll do it," Casterman said.

While Casterman was gone, there wasn't much talking.

Maria and Pär explored the air lock. The walls had hooks and handles and panels that opened to reveal empty cabinets or lockers with more hooks.

"Someday," Pär said, "we're going to open one of these cabinet doors and something will actually be inside." He laughed to himself. "And it will probably lunge out and kill us."

Casterman finally returned. "I went back two doors," he said, "and sealed them both. We're ready."

He then turned the inner wheel of the open doorway, and the door slid shut. They were sealed inside the air lock.

"Who wants to open the door this time?" Pär asked. "Who wants to fall on their ass?"

"I will," Maria Vegas said. Then, looking at Pär: "I'm not afraid."

She approached the wheel, but stood well to the side of the door.

"That's hardly fair," Pär said. "You should be standing right in front of it, like I was."

Maria didn't bother to answer him. She took hold of the wheel with both hands, and turned it. The door slid open.

Not surprisingly, a shower of ice crystals seemed to pour in through the door. What *was* surprising, although we should have expected it, was that the shower kept coming. It blossomed, became a rushing cloud that filled the room, frosting over everyone and everything, including the cameras.

"Damn!" Pär exclaimed.

Cardenas switched from camera to camera, but we couldn't see a thing through any of them.

"Sound off," I said.

"I'm okay," Maria said. "I'm not moving."

"Yeah, I'm fine, too," Pär added.

Nothing else for a few moments. The quiet was a barely audible hiss, disconcerting.

"Casterman?"

Another few moments of that quiet, then, "Oh . . . yes . . . I'm sorry, I'm all right. I was just . . . overwhelmed for a minute."

We still couldn't see anything. "Get your visors clear,"
I said, "then try to get the cameras clear."

"Aye, aye," Pär said.

But something odd was happening. The image on the
monitor—from Casterman's camera—was already trans-
forming. The frosty gray congealed into discrete droplets,
leaving tiny areas of clearing around them. Then the droplets began to stretch and run, sliding downward. Finally I
realized what was happening: the ice crystals were melting,
then dripping down the camera lenses.

"It's melting," Maria said.

We had a spotted, distorted image for a while, even after
Maria went over and tried to wipe Casterman's camera lens
clear. The suit gloves weren't much good at wiping away
liquids.

"It's not only pressurized," said Rogers. "It's heated.
Should have realized." He was excited, watching and thinking about what was happening in there.

When visors and cameras were relatively clear, the three
of them prepared to go through the now open doorway,
Maria in the lead. As they approached the door, she stopped.

"Wait . . . wait a minute."

We were still with Casterman's camera, in the rear. He
and Pär stopped behind Maria and waited. She was just a
step from the doorway, looking through it.

"What is it?" I asked.

"Light, I think." She switched off the lantern she was
carrying.

I turned to Cardenas, but she was already switching to
Maria's camera. The image darkened with the change, but
it soon became clear that it wasn't completely dark beyond
the doorway, though the light from the lanterns behind
Maria made recognizing that difficult. There was a dim,
bluish illumination, so faint that it was impossible to gauge
the shape or dimensions of the space.

"Turn off all the lanterns," Maria said.

Two more were switched off, then Casterman or Pär
walked over to the one they had mounted on the air lock
wall and switched it off.

The blue illumination was more distinct now, although
it was still terribly faint. There was a vague sense of shadow
or form farther in. A feeling of deep blue smoke or mist,
or even suspended water. It's difficult to describe. The combination of illumination and atmosphere, perhaps, gave everything an appearance so different from what we had all
been seeing on the alien ship that it seemed almost solid,
more substantial.

"I'm going in," Maria said.

She turned on her hand torch and aimed the beam down
at the floor on the other side of the doorway. As she stepped
through the opening, the deep blue light brightened perceptibly. Maria stopped. She turned off the hand torch.

The light was still dim, but it was bright enough now to
generally make out the shape and extent of the room. It
was circular and quite large, twenty-five or thirty meters
across. The walls appeared to be fairly smooth; the floor,
too, was smooth for several meters; then it sank with a
series of circular steps to a flat circular section in the center
of the room about ten or twelve meters across.

I felt a hand on my shoulder. I turned to see Father
Veronica, not looking at me but gazing at the monitor with
fear and wonder.

"Bartolomeo," she whispered.

"I know," I said. I knew what she was thinking. The
room resembled the central chamber of the star-shaped
building on Antioch. There were differences, of course—
there were no banks of instruments circling the central section, for example—but the resemblance was close enough
to trigger those memories.

"It's not the same," I said. "It's just a circular room."
I think I was trying to convince myself as much as reassure
Father Veronica. It wasn't easy.

Maria finally resumed her progress. She began a circuit
of the room, staying close to the wall; Cardenas ran through
the cameras to confirm that Pär and Casterman had also
entered the room, and were following Maria. No one spoke
much, because there wasn't much to talk about. A third of
the way around the room they came across a door with a

simple metal handle; two-thirds of the way around was another door exactly like the first.

When the circuit was complete, they walked in toward the steps. "Let me take them first," Maria said. "You two wait until I'm on the lower floor. And if it opens up . . . well, just don't leave me here."

She started down the steps. She took them slowly, pausing on each one for a few moments before taking the next.

"How does it feel?" Rogers asked when she had gone down four, and had three to go.

"What do you mean?"

"The height of the steps. Are they comfortable to walk down? Do they feel like a natural height?"

"I hadn't noticed. So I guess they *do* feel pretty natural. Normal steps."

She continued. When she was on the last step, she crouched, set her lantern on the floor, and slid it out toward the center. Nothing happened.

"It's one of those traps that doesn't activate until it detects a living creature," Pär said.

"You come down and try it, then," Maria replied. "You'll be safe enough." She waited a few moments longer, then stepped onto the floor.

Still nothing. She took a few more cautious steps, then finally walked with normal strides to the center and picked up the lantern. "It's just a floor," she said.

Then she tilted her head back and looked up at the ceiling. The central section was stepped up in the same way the floor was stepped down, and the blue light was so dim that we couldn't make out any detail. Maria turned on her hand torch and swept the beam across the ceiling. It was covered with faceted glass, or at least what appeared to be glass.

By this time her teammates had joined her, and Casterman said, "Maybe that's the source of the light."

That didn't seem likely—the blue glow seemed too diffuse to be coming from a single source like that, and before Maria had aimed the torch beam at the ceiling, it hadn't

seemed to be glowing or emitting any illumination. But I
didn't have a better idea, so I kept silent.

"There's not much here," Pär said. "I'd say it's time
to try one of the other two doors."

"No," I said. "It's time for the three of you to come
back to the shuttle."

"Not a chance!" Pär threw up his hands in disbelief.
"We're in new territory here," he continued. "Heat and
air, light, who knows what else. Everything's changed.
We've got to keep going."

"Yes," I replied, "everything's changed. That's why
you've got to come back now. You're almost at the end of
your shift, anyway. We've got to be even more careful now
with how we proceed. Before we go any further, I want to
get some air samples to analyze, measure the temperature
and pressure in here, see if we can determine the light
source, anything else. We need to take it slowly."

"I'm with Pär," Maria put in. "I want to keep going.
At least let us go through one of the other doors and see
what's beyond it."

"No," I insisted. "If there isn't anything of interest, it
won't matter anyway. And if there is, you won't want to
come back before doing a thorough examination."

"Just an hour," Pär tried.

"Time is not the issue."

Casterman finally spoke. "Bartolomeo is right," he said.
"We should go back now."

There was a silence that went on so long I was beginning
to fear defiance from Pär and Maria. If that happened, we
were going to have serious problems. *Don't do this to me*,
I silently said to Pär. *Don't do this to all of us.*

"All right," Pär finally said. "Let's head back." Then,
after a slight hesitation, he added, "You're no damn fun,
Bartolomeo."

T W E L V E hours later we had air samples headed back
to the *Argonos* for analysis, and we had some preliminary findings of our own. The air pressure was slightly

higher than Earth normal, but nothing that would be harmful to us. The temperature was surprisingly warm—-26 degrees Celsius; 79 degrees Fahrenheit. But we still couldn't determine the light source.

Another two days, and we had the stunning news—the air was breathable for human beings.

32

WE did not, however, take off our helmets in that room to breathe the air. The lab analysis did not pick up any obvious toxins, but there were tiny, unidentifiable particulates in the samples, some organic; it wasn't worth the risk.

We could deny it no longer—this region of the alien ship was almost certainly built or adapted for human habitation. Proper gravity, atmosphere, temperature. Far too much for coincidence. At the same time, we still did not doubt that the starship itself was alien, and had been constructed by alien "hands." The driving question now—one we feared would never be answered—was how this section had come to be built this way. When, by whom, and to what purpose? None of us had any ideas.

I was inside the alien ship with Hollings and Cardenas. As I stepped into the circular chamber with its diffuse blue light, I was again reminded of the circular room on Antioch, gateway to nightmare. I struggled to dispel the resurgent tremors of memory, the fleeting but horrifying images of metal hooks and gleaming bones.

Cardenas and Hollings both took a circuitous route down

the steps, across the lower level, then back up the steps again. I stayed on the upper level, followed the perimeter to the left, and met them at the first door. No one had yet gone through it.

The mechanism seemed straightforward—a metal handle in the door itself long enough to be gripped with two hands. I tried pulling up; then, when it wouldn't budge, I pushed down. It moved a quarter turn and stopped.

I had been expecting an automated movement since nearly every other door in the ship worked that way, but there was nothing.

"Try pulling it open," Hollings suggested.

I did. The door swung slowly, haltingly toward me, as if its hinges had become rusted stuck; although it sounded faint and distant, I could just hear a muted squealing with each scraping movement, which surprised me until I remembered we were now in an atmosphere, where sound would propagate. Light angled out of the new opening, a brighter yellowish light cutting through the blue. I kept tugging at the door, jerking it until it was completely open; a high, wide shaft of light sliced across the circular room, spreading and diffusing as it reached down to the lower level, up the steps and washed across the opposite wall. Beyond the door was a short passage that angled off to the right.

The light frightened me. For weeks we had been exploring what appeared to be a dead, abandoned alien starship. No signs of life, no signs of machinery still functioning. Nothing. Then we reached a section with Earth-normal gravity. Soon after that we had pressurized atmosphere; more than that, it was being maintained, somehow, at a habitable temperature; then some strange, blue light; and finally this— full, day-like illumination. Too much.

I looked at my companions and noticed that all three of us, consciously or not, had moved out of the path of the light and were well back into the shadows.

"I don't like this," I whispered.

"I don't either," Cardenas replied.

"Why are you whispering?" Hollings asked, although she, too, whispered.

"Sound carries," Cardenas answered. "Didn't you hear that when Bartolomeo was pulling the door open?"

"I wasn't sure what it was. I forgot about sound. You think our voices would carry through the helmets?"

"Probably not," I said, "but I'm not taking any chances."

"You think somebody, or something, is in there?" Hollings asked.

"It's not too damn likely," Cardenas said, "but I'm with Bartolomeo on this. We can't take chances." She unstrapped her hand stunner and gripped it. "Didn't think I'd ever need this. Still hope we don't."

I backed farther away from the door, still keeping to shadow but gaining a greater view into the short passage. Nothing moved, nor were there shadows of any kind. Now I could see that the wall was off-white streaked with soot, or paint the color of soot. Down low on the wall, near the floor, was a raised brown smear. The first real signs of imperfection we'd seen.

"I'll go in," I eventually said. "Both of you stay out here until I clear it."

Neither protested. This was no time for phony heroics.

I set the lantern on the floor beside me. I wasn't going to carry my stunner, either; I wanted both hands free. I stepped into the swath of light.

The sounds of my companions' breathing seemed terribly loud, and I was struck by the irrational fear that they would drown out any warning sounds. I hesitated, then stepped through the doorway.

I stopped for a few moments when I was completely inside, waiting, then continued. As I passed the streaks on the walls, I looked more closely at them, but couldn't determine whether they were soot or burn marks or simply paint. I knelt beside the brown smear—which, frankly, looked like dried excrement—but again, it was impossible to know what it was.

The passage took a 90-degree angle to the right, then opened out into a large room or wide passage, but I had no idea yet *how* large. Once again I hesitated, keeping back so

that I could not be seen, which also meant that I could not
see much either.

I took a step into the short, angled section of passage
and stopped. In the far left corner—the only corner I could
see, and which was ten or twelve meters away—was a pile
of torn and rumpled cloth. In the wall nearby was a darker
area that might have been an opening or doorway; my angle
was too severe to tell.

Two more steps, and I was around the corner, fully inside
the room.

A wild, flailing dark form lunged at me. It struck me at
chest height, knocking me off my feet and onto my back
with a jolt; my head slammed against the floor. Darkness
covered my helmet and I cried out, some sound without
words. I tried to grab the thing on top of me. I couldn't
see what it was. It squirmed and fought at my arms and
hands, pounded at my suit without much effect. I tried rolling to the side and a slice of light came through for a
moment. I thought I heard a faint cry or screech; the pounding shifted to my helmet, jarring my head. The darkness
over my helmet shifted away for a second, but all I saw
were jerking flashes of what seemed to be limbs and claws
and fur before the darkness returned.

"Cardenas!" I yelled. "Hollings!"

The creature was long and heavy, and I couldn't get a
grip on it, couldn't roll it off of me. I felt like an insect
stuck on my back with a weight holding me down, my legs
fluttering helplessly above me.

"It's a woman!" Cardenas's voice cut through her harsh
breathing—she'd been running. "Help me, Rita."

The darkness and the weight both lifted from me. I
wasn't sure what was happening. My helmet was clear, but
my vision wasn't right—silver glitter drifted in front of my
eyes, and everything else was blurry. I tried to sit up, saw
a tangle of pressure suits, long, whipping hair, layers of
fabric, naked feet and hands, but everything began to spin
around me and I lay back down.

"God damn it, she's . . . strong!" Hollings hissed between ragged breaths.

I thought I could hear Cardenas grunting; in the middle of it she managed to ask me if I was all right.

"I think so," I said. I closed my eyes, but the spinning only increased. "If I don't puke all over myself." Eyes open again, I tried to focus on the ceiling above me. There was another dark smear almost directly overhead, and I concentrated on it, keeping my head and body still. The smear functioned as an anchor, and my vision slowly stabilized; I tried to ignore the movement in the corner of my sight—Cardenas and Hollings struggling with the woman.

As my vision settled down, so did the struggle, and Hollings's cursing slowed to a trickle.

I finally managed to sit up, shifting around so I could lean back against the wall. Cardenas and Hollings had their arms wrapped around the woman, who was in turn wrapped in layers of cloaks or robes, and all three of them were on their knees, like one big tangled knot. The woman's hair was gray and long and stringy, and her head was bent so I couldn't see her face. For the moment, at least, she was resting.

"Who's on the monitor?" I asked. "Is anyone watching this?"

"We're all here," said Casterman. "We're on your camera, Bartolomeo. Pär and Maria are already suiting up. They should be in the ship in a matter of minutes. We figure an hour to reach you if they push it."

"Taggart, are you there?"

"Yes."

"I want you to go with them. We're probably going to have to sedate her to get her out of here."

"On my way."

"One more thing, in case you've forgotten. We'll need a suit for her."

There was a long pause, then Casterman said, "We *hadn't* thought of it. I guess we didn't think about bringing her out."

"We're not going to leave her in here."

"No. Okay, we'll send a suit with them."

The woman quieted down and kept her head bowed so

her face couldn't be seen. I was still shaky, and my heart-beat hadn't slowed much; my throat burned with each breath.

I looked around the room, which was nearly twenty meters long. In the far right corner, on the floor, was a thick pad piled high with blankets, clothes, some metal bowls, a box, scraps of paper, and other things too lost in folds of material to identify. In the other far corner was another, smaller pile of clothes. Beside the pile was a tall cubicle with a round canister set in the floor. In the middle of the wall between the two piles was an open doorway leading into a long corridor.

"What next?" Cardenas finally asked.

"I wish we could talk to her," I said. "Maybe if she heard a human voice . . . Maybe I should just take off my helmet and risk it. *She's* been breathing this air, and she's still alive."

"You *can* talk to her, Bartolomeo." It was Rogers. "We forget because we never need it, but there's an external speaker you can activate. It'll also activate a mike so you can hear her."

I *had* forgotten. The speaker was small, built into the helmet collar. I fumbled around until I found the stud that activated it. I started to get to my feet, but still feeling a little dizzy, I worked my way toward the others on my hands and knees. The woman still wasn't moving. Not wanting to frighten her any further, I stopped before I got too close.

"Can you understand me?" I said.

The old woman went crazy again. She screeched and lunged forward, and I could see her face now—lined and gaunt—and her maddened eyes glared deep into my own. She lunged again, then sprang straight upward, breaking free of Cardenas and Hollings. I didn't have time to brace myself before she struck, again knocking me over.

"Stop!" I said, trying to hold onto her. "We don't mean you any harm."

The old woman didn't stay on me. She scrambled to her feet just as Cardenas and Hollings got to theirs, then she

ran past me, hit the wall, rebounded and swung around the
corner and down the short passage toward the circular room.

"Damn," Hollings said.

"She can't really hurt us much—" Cardenas began.

"Speak for yourself," I broke in.

"Sorry. You know what I mean. But I'm afraid we're
going to have to hurt her to bring her back to the shuttle."

"Shit, maybe we should just leave her here," Hollings
said.

I was fairly certain she was kidding. The two of them
helped me to my feet. All that remained of the vertigo was
a vague sense of imbalance, but it wasn't too bad.

"Let's go find her," I said.

THAT turned out to be more difficult than I would
have thought. When we entered the circular room, she
was nowhere in sight. I checked behind the door, but she
wasn't there. We crossed the room (I still felt uneasy descending the steps to the lower, center level, and was relieved when we climbed back up), then entered the air lock.

"Where the hell did she go?" Hollings said. "Not out
of the air lock."

"No," Cardenas agreed. "First, I'm certain the other
door wouldn't open unless this one was sealed first, and we
would have noticed the air rushing out even if it did."

"Then where? There *is* nowhere else."

"The other door," I said. "In the blue room. The door
we haven't opened yet."

Back into the circular room, following the wall to the
right this time until we reached the door. This one, too, had
a long metal handle. But after we pushed the handle down
a quarter turn, we could not get the door to open. We tried
it with two of us on the handle, Hollings pushing off the
wall with one leg, her boot planted firmly against it right
next to the door. Finally it budged, but with far more resistance than the other door. With the external mike activated,
I could hear the loud squealing it made with each pull.

After we'd managed to get it open a few centimeters, it

wouldn't go any further. Bright light slashed through the opening, but we couldn't see very far beyond the door— just enough to see that there was a similar passage.

"She's strong," Cardenas said, "but not that strong." She shook her head. "She couldn't have opened this door."

Cardenas was right, unless the door had been easy to open at first and the old woman had jammed something into it after she'd gone through. We all agreed it was unlikely.

"Then where is she?" Hollings asked.

Father Veronica spoke over the open channel. "There are cabinets in the air lock," she said. "For suits or something. From what I remember, some of them might have been big enough to hide in."

We headed back to the air lock. When we were all inside, we sealed the door; we weren't going to give her anyplace to go.

The old woman was in the second cabinet we checked. She came flying out at us, screeching again, but this time we were prepared. She was still strong and wild, but there were three of us and it wasn't long before we subdued her. I held her from behind, pinning her arms to her side, my hands gripping one another tightly; my artificial arms would not tire, although my shoulders eventually would.

"We mean you no harm," I said softly. "Do you understand me?"

Her only response was a pained, high keening, which gradually faded and she let her head hang, as though she was unconscious. As before, she had ceased to struggle.

"*Habla español?*" I tried next. I didn't speak Spanish very well, but it wouldn't take much if the old woman did. Still no response.

"We've got to get her out of here before the others arrive," Cardenas reminded me. "So they can use the air lock to come through." She went to the door and opened it.

Hollings picked up the old woman's legs, bending the knees, and we carried her into the circular room. Cardenas came through behind us, then spun the wheel and sealed the door shut.

"*Français?*" Cardenas tried. "*Nihongo?*"

Nothing. The old woman hung in my arms like a newly dead corpse, tangled filthy hair covering her face. I thought she'd passed out, or fallen asleep. But then she began to softly weep. The sound was so quiet, almost a whimper, I doubted Cardenas and Hollings could hear her. My heart aching for her, I held the woman tightly to me, and we waited in silence for Taggart and the others to arrive.

33

WE sedated the old woman before putting her into a pressure suit. Her soft crying, although it had ceased long before, still resonated in me. I held her while Cardenas pulled away the layers of fabric, exposing her shoulder. Taggart put the gun against it and pulled the trigger. It took a couple of minutes to take effect, but eventually she slumped in my arms and I laid her gently on the floor.

At rest, she looked even older than I'd thought, and I wondered if she'd ever undergone re-gen treatments. She was quite tall but extremely thin, what we could see of her. Her skin was deeply lined, and there were several dark brown spots on the backs of her wrinkled hands. Her mouth hung slightly open, revealing portions of stained teeth.

Taggart pulled away the layers of clothing and made a cursory examination of the old woman; he was clumsy in his suit, but remarkably gentle. The one peculiar thing he found was a tattoo. The initials S.C. were tattooed in dark blue on the inside of her left bicep. He nodded when he was done, and wrapped the cloaks around her once more.

"She appears to be okay. I don't know how healthy, and she's clearly undernourished, if not malnourished. But her pulse is surprisingly strong, and the heart sounds are good.

Lungs seem to be clear, although her breathing is a little shallow." He paused for a moment. "She needs medical attention, but I don't believe she's in immediate danger."

"We can move her, then."

"Right."

"Then let's do it," Pär said.

We did. We bundled her into the extra pressure suit, and carried her back to the shuttle.

THERE seemed to be too many decisions to make, too many things to be done, and none of them could wait. We put the old woman through decontamination, but weren't sure what to do after that—leave her in the pressure suit, or take her out and risk exposing us to whatever she might be carrying? We also had to recognize that there was a risk to *her* from *us*.

In the end, we left her in the decontamination chamber. Taggart put on a body suit, gloves, and mask, then went back into the chamber with a mat and blankets and a body suit for the woman. He eased her out of the pressure suit, cleaned her up (she'd soiled herself by then), put the body suit on her, secured her to the mat, then hooked up pressurized IV drips, including one to keep her sedated. Then he bagged up her clothes and blew them out the garbage lock, shoved his own body suit, gloves, and mask into the burn box, and returned to the main cabin.

"The sooner we get her back to the *Argonos*, the better," he said.

"We'll get a linkup right now and have them come and pick her up."

"It would be better," Taggart said, "to bring her back ourselves. Easier on her if we don't have to move her until we're back on the *Argonos*. We can have a team ready to take her to the med center."

"I thought you said she wasn't in any danger."

"I don't *think* she is, but I can't know that for sure. I don't understand. Why is this a problem?"

Others had gathered around us by now, but they were going to let us hash it out.

"Because there might be other people in the ship, that's why it's a problem. We need to get another team inside right away."

"Can't it wait a couple of days?" Taggart asked.

"No," I said. "Even one day might make a difference to someone inside there." I paused. "I'm even more afraid that if we go back to the *Argonos,* the Executive Council will prevent us from returning. I don't want to take that chance."

"It doesn't have to wait," put in Youngman. "We send a team in right now. The team can stay on the ship until the shuttle gets back. Or two teams would be even better. One can rest while the other keeps searching. We can live in the suits that long. It'll be uncomfortable, but we can do it."

I looked around at the others who were listening, and saw a nodding of heads. I nodded myself.

"I like it," I said.

Ten minutes later, after we had gathered everyone in the main cabin, I had nine volunteers to stay in the alien ship while the shuttle took the old woman back to the *Argonos*; ten, including me. That was everyone. We would all stay.

"I don't like it," Nikos said over the linkup. "If something goes wrong, there's no way to get to you."

"Come on, Nikos. The shuttle can be back thirty-five, forty hours after it leaves. We won't be on our own that long."

"Long enough. It's not worth the risk."

"Of course it is," I said. "There might be other people in there," I reminded him.

"If there are, and if they're still alive, they'll keep for another two days. Who knows how long they've been on that ship? If the woman is any indication, it's probably been years."

The conversation was pointless. "We're staying," I said.

"Not on my approval. I'll convene the Executive Council, and we'll discuss it."

"Don't bother, Nikos, there's no time. The others are already suiting up and checking suit provisions. I've got to join them."

"Are you deliberately defying me, Bartolomeo?"

I sighed. "If that's how you want to characterize it, Nikos. There's no Executive Council Order. You want to give a Captain's Order and force us to disobey it, that's your choice. I'd advise against it."

I was glad we had the video link, because I wanted him to see my face, I wanted him to understand my determination. He gazed at me, hardly even blinking. He finally shook his head.

"You're such a bastard sometimes, Bartolomeo. You damn well better hope this isn't the wrong decision."

"No matter what happens, it isn't the wrong decision."

Nikos snorted. "You think not? Things are never that simple, Bartolomeo. You should know that better than most." He paused, then leaned back in his chair. "Go, Bartolomeo. Go before they leave you behind." With that, he disconnected the linkup, and the screen went gray.

I T was something to see: all ten of us in pressure suits drifting in a long, irregular, ragged column, moving from room to room, along corridors and through vast, mysterious chambers in a slow-motion dance of shadow and light from the lanterns as the first person to pass each one turned it on, and the last person to go by turned it off. I was on point, and occasionally I stopped and turned around to watch the others moving toward me. I felt wonder, and even pride.

We didn't talk much on our way in—a few words now and again, and only when necessary: to direct the opening of a hatch or door, to check that another hatch was closed—tasks of that nature. But it was not a quiet from fear or tension; it came, I believe, from calm assurance and a sense of unity.

Three hours into the ship we reached the area of gravity, and the drifting dance changed, steadied to a silent march through more regular shifting of the shadows. When we entered the circular chamber, we unloaded the equipment and supplies we'd brought with us—extra air, replacement food and water—then formed three teams. After we worked together to get the second door open, one team took that corridor, and the rest of us cautiously entered the room in which we'd found the old woman. Pär, Father Veronica, and I stayed in the room and more thoroughly searched through the old woman's belongings, while the third team went through the open doorway at the far end and explored the area beyond.

We found little in the old woman's room. The open cubicle we'd seen the first time, and which we hadn't been able to examine, housed a functioning toilet; above it was a basin with running water—presumably both hot and cold, since there were two different buttons, each of which produced a flow of water when pressed.

In the right corner was a covered pad which must have served as a sleeping mat, two or three torn and filthy blankets, and several pieces of clothing as worn and dirty as the blankets—a pair of trousers, something that might have been a skirt, a couple of shirts. No underclothing.

There were four metal bowls crusted with bits of dried matter. Food, probably. Scraps of colored paper, a pair of rubber sandals. An oxidized metal bracelet inside a wooden box.

Father Veronica discovered a wall panel above the sleeping mat that opened to reveal a small cubbyhole filled with a jumble of objects. She carefully removed them one at a time, handing each to me after she had inspected it, while I in turn handed each to Pär.

The first was a large, deep blue stone about the size of my thumb. The blue had depth, and embedded in it were opalescent swirls that seemed to undulate within the dark color around them. I held the stone a long time, mesmerized, before I finally broke out of my trance and handed it to Pär.

Next came a pair of earrings with pale yellow beads and

tiny silver butterflies. After that was a small, red-bound book not much larger than my hand; inside, all of the pages were blank except for a single ink drawing of an eye on the final page. Then there was a pink, egg-shaped candle that had never been used. Also, a thin flexible tube with a cap, but nothing to identify it; when I uncapped it and gently squeezed the tube, a dark blue substance oozed from it.

The last thing Father Veronica removed from the cubbyhole was a cracked and curling photograph of a middle-aged woman with her arm around the shoulders of a much younger woman. The photograph appeared to have been taken at sea; an expanse of blue-green water stretched behind them, meeting a paler blue sky fluffed with bright white clouds. I couldn't tell if they were standing on the deck of a boat, on a pier, or on a spit of land extending into the water from shore.

"She looks like the old woman," Pär said. All three of us were huddled around the picture, staring at it.

"Which one?" Father Veronica asked.

She was right. They *both* looked like younger versions of the old woman. It could have been a photograph of the old woman and her daughter, or the old woman and her mother. Or neither.

"We can show it to her," Father Veronica said. "Maybe it will help." She carefully placed the photograph into one of her suit pockets.

We returned the rest of the objects to the cubbyhole and moved on.

T H E results of our initial explorations were interesting, but unremarkable. The team exploring behind the stuck door discovered only an empty room shaped much like the old woman's, and from there a passage that terminated at a blank wall. The other team had more luck, but not much more excitement. They found a functioning wall unit in the corridor beyond the old woman's room that produced water and what appeared to be food. That corridor, in turn, led to a cluster of empty rooms lined with benches or sleeping platforms; each room in the cluster had another door, but the team had been unable to open any of them.

When we'd been inside the ship for fifteen hours, I ordered all activities to cease. We needed rest, and a break from the disappointment of not finding any other survivors.

I T felt like the dead of night. We were in the circular room, and most of us, at my insistence, were trying to sleep—I looked around at suited forms propped against the walls, lying face-up on the floor; Youngman was wedged in a doorway. Sleeping in the suits was difficult until exhaustion took over.

I sat on the top step, facing the center of the lower level. My eyes were barely open, and I thought I might fall asleep in that position. Night. Arbitrary, but even the diffuse blue light seemed dimmer than usual, although I am sure it was my imagination.

Movement brought me fully awake, but it was only Casterman getting up from his knees in the air lock, where he had been praying. He stepped over Youngman's sleeping form in the doorway and came back into the room. For a few moments he stood motionless; then he opened one of his suit pockets, dug around in it, and pulled something out. In the dim light I couldn't see what it was, and I wasn't much interested.

Casterman resumed walking, headed toward the center of the room. He descended the steps, took a few more paces, then stopped. He was not quite in the center of the lower level.

"Bartolomeo," he said.

I looked at him, waiting, but he didn't say anything more.

"Try to get some sleep," I eventually said.

"I've been trying to pray. But I'm not making a connection. The link is broken."

I didn't like the sound of his voice, or what he was

saying. It sounded a little bit crazy. I pushed myself up to my feet.

"Eric . . ."

"You've never called me that," he said. "Always Casterman." He shook his head. "It doesn't matter. None of it does. I've made a different connection."

He took two more steps and stopped, standing directly in the center of the room. He looked at me, and I thought I could see him smile. He knelt and felt around on the floor with his free hand. It seemed he found what he was searching for, and pressed his fingers into the floor.

Suddenly a bright silver light came on in the ceiling directly above him, bathing him in a radiant glow that cut through the dim blue fluorescence and made it all seem even that much darker around him. Now I could see what he held in his hand, could see light reflecting from the shiny metal blade of a large, long knife. He brought himself erect, staring up at the light.

I thought he would try to use the knife on me, and I was afraid; I took a step toward him, anyway. But before I could take another, Casterman popped the seal of his helmet with his left hand, pried the helmet off, and tossed it aside. He was definitely smiling, a soft and gentle smile. Then he brought the knife up, tipped his head back, and drew the knife swiftly and deeply across his throat, crying out in surprise and pain.

I rushed forward as he fell, blood already spurting from his neck, splattering his face and suit. He hit the floor hard and heavy, and I sprawled on my hands and knees beside him, slipping in the blood.

"Help me!" I shouted, although I have no idea what I thought anyone could do.

Blood was everywhere. His body convulsed. I could see the arterial pulsing, a tiny fountain shining in the light from above. I covered the fountain with my gloved fingers, knowing it was hopeless.

My helmet filled with a babble of voices, but I tuned it all out; in the periphery of my vision there was chaotic activity, people scrambling all around the room.

"Eric," I said, forgetting he couldn't hear me.

The smile was gone, but his face was suffused with peace. He continued to shake and jerk under me. I knew he was dying, and he was dying quickly. Casterman himself knew he was dying, and he seemed to welcome it.

The flow of blood had slowed, but didn't cease; it was finding new pathways around my gloves, which could not seal the gaping wound.

Then there were people all around me, hands pressing pieces of fabric and rubber patches into the blood. It was all so pointless, I wanted to knock the hands and arms away; but I kept my own hands on his neck, although I knew that was just as pointless.

I felt a hand on my shoulder, and turned to see Father Veronica kneeling beside me. She didn't say anything, didn't do anything but look at me and squeeze my shoulder.

I turned back to Casterman. His mouth opened, lips and jaw moving silently; I'm sure he was trying to speak. A rolling shudder worked its way through him; then something happened to his eyes—they locked hard on something far beyond me. They stayed that way for several long moments, then shifted away, life leaving them, and he went still.

The light from above continued to shine.

PART THREE

Ship of Fools

34

I was one of eight pallbearers at Casterman's funeral. The Mass was to be given by the bishop, with Father Veronica assisting. The cathedral was packed, every pew full and several rows of people standing in the back. Like Midnight Mass on Christmas Eve, or Easter Mass.

We carried the casket down the central aisle; it was large and heavy, burnished copper decorated with folds of rich black cloth and garlands of white ag-room flowers. The scent from the flowers was heavy and cloying. The casket had always seemed a strange part of the ritual to me, but as I gripped one of the handles I thought I understood it a little more. It was one of half a dozen reusable caskets of different sizes. After the funeral, Casterman's body would be removed from the casket, interred in a much smaller, cramped metal canister, then expulsed from the ship into deep space. Cremation had become more common in recent years as the supply of canisters dwindled and the material to manufacture replacements became more difficult to obtain, but the Church still frowned on it, particularly for its own.

We carried the casket to the front of the cathedral, up

two steps, and set it on the catafalque. Then we walked over to the pew on the side that had been reserved for us.

Nikos was one of the other pallbearers; he sat beside me, then leaned into my shoulder and whispered.

"You still think staying was the right decision?"

I didn't answer. I had not stopped asking that question of myself since I knelt beside Casterman with his blood and life flowing all around me. I did not need Nikos to ask me the same damn question.

Bishop Soldano stood at the pulpit and spoke, his voice little more than a drone. I didn't listen to him. I hardly even saw him. What I saw much more vividly were Casterman's eyes and mouth, both open to me, yet beyond help or understanding.

"Sorry," Nikos said quietly. "That wasn't fair."

I still didn't respond. I wasn't sure where I stood with Nikos; I wasn't even sure I knew where I *wanted* to stand with him. We'd managed an uneasy truce of sorts since our talk in the Wasteland, but I couldn't say that we had made any progress restoring our old relationship. Maybe that was just as well.

I looked at Father Veronica standing motionless behind the bishop, her expression steady and unblinking and ultimately impossible to decipher. I found no comfort in it.

Nikos put his hand on my shoulder, a surprising gesture for him. "It'll be all right."

I didn't look at him. I stared forward, wondering if I could stand to remain through the entire Mass.

"**S HE** can't see us," Taggart said.

"No kidding. Her eyes are closed," I pointed out to him.

He sighed. "Even if they weren't, she still couldn't see us."

I was looking at the old woman through a large observation window of one-way glass. There were also three concealed cameras in the room, and their images were displayed on monitors above the window. The old woman was sleep-

ing on a bed in one of the med center rooms, curled in a
fetal position, mouth slightly open.

"She always sleeps like that," Taggart said. "As if she's
holding herself together."

The old woman had been aboard the *Argonos* for five
days now. She was still hooked up to IVs, and monitoring
strips were taped across her forehead and arms. Every time
she'd been given solid food, she'd refused to eat. On the
other hand, she drank all the juices offered to her, and
appeared to plead for more.

"She whimpers when she sleeps," Taggart added.
"Sometimes she cries out. When she's awake she speaks
gibberish. She doesn't appear to understand a word we say
to her."

"Are you sure it's not just another language?"

"Of course we're not sure. We've tried as many languages as we can find speakers on this ship, which isn't
that many, to be honest. Some languages have been lost
over the centuries. Toller's been dredging up old texts in
any language he can find, and he reads a few lines to her
to see if we get some reaction. So far . . . nothing." Taggart
shrugged. "Whatever she's speaking doesn't *sound* like another language to anyone who's heard her."

"Maybe it's *alien* language," I suggested half seriously.

"Yes, and maybe it's just gibberish. Think about it.
She's been through extreme deprivations—social, nutri-
tional, psychological, maybe even sensory. And for an unknown period of time. Years, most likely. I would guess
that would turn most people's minds into mush."

"That's what you think has happened to her?" I asked.

"That's what I think. Severe psychological trauma. You
should talk to Dr. G. about it. That's her area of expertise."

I don't know why I was giving Taggart such a hard time
about his evaluation of the old woman. I agreed with his
assessment, but I hoped that, given time, the woman would
become more secure and comfortable here on the *Argonos*,
her mind would come back to her, and we might actually
begin to communicate. I told Taggart as much, but he didn't
respond, and I realized he was annoyed with me.

"Physically, how is she doing?" I asked.

"All right. Getting better slowly. Remarkably strong heart. She was terribly undernourished, but her lytes showed she wasn't too badly *mal*nourished, if you see the distinction."

"I do. That glop she was living on must have been well-formulated."

Taggart nodded.

"I'll check in with you once a day or so. You'll let me know if there are any major changes?"

"I will."

I started to leave, and had just opened the door when Taggart said, "Bartolomeo?"

"Yes?"

"I don't think she's ever going to get better. Mentally. I don't think she's ever going to recover from what she's been through."

I took another glance at the woman, who was still holding herself tightly, and I remembered the way she'd wept as I held her. "Let's hope you're wrong."

35

THE dwarf and I roamed one of the lowest levels of the ship, quietly drunk. Pär smiled crookedly and cast furtive, sidelong glances at me; my limp had become more pronounced and almost out of control—occasionally I crashed against the corridor wall, cursing, and rebounded, losing my balance. The motorized exoskeleton caused the problem, exaggerating each slight misstep or drunken shift of balance.

We had spent two hours in Pär's room drinking the harsh and bitter liquor he claimed was Scotch whiskey. I was trying, unsuccessfully, to blot out the recurring images of Casterman's blood splattering away from his face and neck and across my helmet, his eyes so calm and peaceful as if leaving his life behind was a great relief. Pär was trying to help us both forget.

I stopped, put a hand against the metal corridor wall to steady myself, and glanced down at the dwarf.

"Never again," I said to him.

Pär just laughed.

"How much farther?" I asked.

"Not much," Pär replied.

"Stop grinning."

Pär's smile widened, and he turned away and started off again along the corridor. I followed.

WE dropped one more level, and everything seemed to change: the air was muggy and stagnant, and stank of overcooked ersatz meat; the corridor walls were streaked with soot and paint; a thumping bass beat seemed to come from all directions, or no direction. Farther on, a wide doorway on the left opened into a bistro where a trio of mad-rock musicians played to a dozen tables of diners and drinkers. The atonal squeals hurt my ears as we hurried past.

We were no longer alone in the corridor; we passed people who appeared to be even drunker than we were, as well as a few who looked as if they hadn't touched alcohol in years—men and women with tight lips and frowns and furrowed brows, in stark and simple clothing.

Finally Pär led the way down a short side passage and activated a door panel. Out from the doorway rolled a quiet cloud of voices and music and lights. Pär waved me inside, then followed and closed the door behind us.

I stood just inside a large room with half a dozen chairs and settees. Light came from two hovering globes that drifted in spiral patterns about the room just beneath the ceiling. The voices stopped with our entrance, but a quiet ether jazz played in the background.

There were five or six men and at least as many women in the room, but I could not refrain from staring at one woman in the corner, seemingly shy, and in appearance amazingly like Father Veronica, if Father Veronica were to wear a blouse and trousers instead of cassock and collar.

The dwarf grinned. "Remind you of someone?"

"No," I answered, too sharply and too quickly.

Pär's grin widened; then he clapped his hands. "Drinks everyone!"

I could do nothing except stare at the woman in the corner staring back at me.

* * *

AN hour later I walked side by side along a dark corridor with the woman, whose name was Moira. So much about her reminded me of Father Veronica, even up close: her build, the pale and almost translucent quality of the skin on her arms, the shape of her eyes, and the thin but somehow sensuous lips. Even the way the left side of her mouth turned up when she smiled. I began to wonder if she was Father Veronica's twin.

But I noticed differences as well: the gold-flecked green of her eyes in contrast to the dark brown of Father Veronica's; the narrow nostrils; and especially the voice. When Moira spoke, her deep, coarse voice drove all uncertainty away, and I knew she was not Father Veronica in disguise. I wanted desperately for her not to speak at all.

Suddenly the woman stopped, swung around, put her hands behind my neck and pulled my face to hers, kissing me deeply. I didn't respond immediately, taken aback and tasting smoke and alcohol on her lips and tongue, tastes I hadn't expected, for I had forgotten for a moment who she was. Or who she wasn't.

But then, overcome, I *did* respond, and kissed her deeply in return, wrapping my arms around her and pulling her tight against me.

Then her hands were at my belt, unbuckling it and pulling at trouser buttons.

"Not here," I said, closing my fingers around hers, stopping her movements. "We might be seen."

The woman nodded, grinning. She worked one hand free and plunged it inside my pants, grabbing me. I have to admit I was already aroused.

"My, my," she said, "*that's* not artificial."

"No," I insisted. "I can't . . . not here . . . not . . ."

She released me, but then she took my hand in hers and led me farther along the corridor. "No sense of adventure," she said, and once again I wished she just wouldn't speak.

Another two minutes and she opened the door to a small, dimly lit cabin, closed the door behind us after we entered.

She kept my hand in hers and led me to the wall bed, which was rumpled and unmade. There was a faint smell of old sweat and a hint of stale perfume; on the shelf beside the bed was a worn brown Bible.

"Now to where we left off," she said.

"Don't say anything more," I told her, trying to keep the pleading out of my voice. "Just silence."

Thinking she understood, but not understanding at all, the woman smiled and nodded, and pulled me onto the bed beside her.

I had spent my life on the *Argonos* watching men and women fall in love, or at least make the claims of love for one another; watching pursuits and resistances both real and pretended, and other related behaviors that were often ridiculous, petty, cruel, and only occasionally touching. I had long before decided that falling in love was pointless at best. But falling in love with a priest was even worse, so absurd I could hardly believe it was happening to me. More than that, having sex with a woman because she looked like the priest I had fallen in love with was simply pathetic.

When I saw Father Veronica the next day, my skin flushed; I could feel the heat rising up along my neck, and I wanted to walk away. We were in a small chapel off to one side of the cathedral. She smiled uncertainly at me.

"What is it, Bartolomeo?"

"Nothing." My response seemed inadequate, so I added, "I think I might be ill." Which was true in more ways than one.

She nodded, as if that were to be expected. "It was awful, watching him die like that," she said.

"And being so completely helpless."

"You tried, Bartolomeo. You reacted more quickly than anyone, and you did everything you could."

"Yes and no. Maybe Nikos was right, we shouldn't have stayed. Maybe if we hadn't . . ."

"Don't, Bartolomeo. Going that way accomplishes nothing. Nothing unusual happened while we were in there. If he hadn't done it then, he would have done it some other time. I am certain of that."

I knew that intellectually, but in my gut I didn't yet believe it, and I wasn't sure I ever would. It helped to hear it, nonetheless.

"How well did you know him?" I asked.

"I'd known him most of my adult life, worked with him in the Church. But to be truthful, in important ways I did not know him well at all." She paused, and sighed. "I'm ashamed to admit I didn't like him."

"Why are you ashamed?"

She gave me a rueful smile. "It wasn't very generous. To dislike him."

"No one's perfect."

She almost laughed then. "Certainly not the priests." She paused again, became serious. "Eric was mean-spirited and unpleasant, and although he claimed he wanted to become a priest, he would never have been approved. He knew he was disliked by most people, and that must have been difficult to live with."

I knew what that was like, and I wondered if I was as mean-spirited and unpleasant as Casterman had been. I didn't think so, but how could I know? I also believed that I had changed over the last year, so that even if I had been that way once, I hoped I had become less so.

"Did he ever strike you as being suicidal?" I asked.

She hesitated before replying. "As I said, in some ways I didn't know him very well. Does it matter?"

"I'm just trying to understand what happened."

"You think you can?"

"Probably not. But I have to try. I'm in charge of this . . . expedition, mission, whatever you want to call it. What happens is *my* responsibility."

"You take too much on yourself."

"Someone has to."

"No, Bartolomeo. That's part of why Christ died on the Cross. He takes on what we can't."

I really didn't want to start down that road. There were

times when I relished discussing theology with her, because although we disagreed on most things, she was thoughtful and reasoned and often insightful. But this was not one of those times. I think she sensed my feelings, because she let it go and moved on to another subject.

"How is the old woman doing?" she asked.

"Still alive. She's undernourished, a little dehydrated, very weak, but the physicians think she'll survive."

"It's incredible. Has she been able to speak?"

"Not really." I related the conversation I'd had with Taggart.

"So we may never know what happened to her," she said. "One more mystery held by that alien ship. Full of mysteries, and no answers."

"We've only explored a small portion of it so far."

" 'So far?' Do you plan to go back?"

I was surprised by her question. "Of course."

"After everything that has happened?"

"Yes. After everything that has happened. We may have to rethink our approach, be more careful . . . I don't know. But yes, we continue."

She looked at me with concern. "I wonder how many other people feel the same way."

That hadn't occurred to me. "You?" I asked.

She shook her head. "I won't go back into that ship, Bartolomeo. I don't think any of us should."

"Have you come to believe the ship is evil?"

"No. Just dangerous. Perhaps willfully so."

I couldn't really argue with her. "Maybe," I said, "but it's still the most remarkable discovery ever made in the history of the *Argonos*. We can't leave it behind."

She hesitated for a minute, then breathed deeply. "You had best prepare your arguments, Bartolomeo."

I cocked my head at her. "What do you know that I don't?"

"Bishop Soldano is going to propose we set course for another star system and leave the alien starship behind. Before we have any more casualties."

"Formally? Before the Executive Council?"

She nodded.

I didn't respond. There was no point in making any of my arguments to Father Veronica; she was not one of the people I would need to convince. I had to think about the council members; I had to think about the case I would make.

"Thanks for the warning," I finally said.

She smiled sadly at me. "I think you'll need it."

36

"**TAKE** me there," the bishop demanded. "Into the belly of the beast."

I led the way into the alien starship, the bishop surprisingly graceful in his pressure suit, completely at home in zero g. I wondered how much of this the bishop had already seen. We worked our way slowly but steadily through the explored cabins and passages, the bishop taking it all in, asking few questions. He had insisted there be no record of our excursion, but even so we hardly spoke.

I pointed out the cabin where Santiago had plummeted to his death; we pulled ourselves through the corkscrew passage that had killed Askan and Singer; I opened the door to the second room with gravity that had almost killed Starlin, and let the bishop look down into that long drop. We paused a long time gazing into the strangely lit depths of the huge spherical chamber pocked with its thousands of reflecting facets; the bishop seemed lost in thought, perhaps thinking, as I often did, that there was something significant to that chamber. We crawled along the tubes of glass, surrounded by the dark, mysterious fluid. Finally, after more than two hours, we reached the point where Earth-normal gravity began, and started walking. We went through the air lock leading into the pressurized section, then stopped in the circular chamber where Casterman had cut his own throat.

We stood silent and still for a long time, the bishop's breathing steady, calm, showing no distress. I kept thinking of Father Veronica's warning about the bishop, and wondered if he had made this excursion to gather more evidence to bolster his proposal to abandon this ship.

"Why here?" the bishop asked.

"Why not?"

He turned to me. "Are you trying to be funny? Or clever?"

"No."

"It's a valid question. You don't think he just arbitrarily, *randomly*, removed his helmet and slashed his own throat, oblivious to his surroundings?"

"I have no idea."

"No, you don't. Well. Perhaps there's something in the air." With that the bishop quickly removed his own helmet and took a deep breath.

"Stop!" I said. "What are you doing?"

He said something, but I couldn't make out a word. The com systems are built into the helmets, and he was holding his down below his waist—too far away to pick up anything more than a faint tickle of speech. I turned on my exterior speaker and microphone. "What are you doing?"

"Take it off," he said. "Join me."

"Not a chance. Put yours back on, Bishop. The air could be lethal."

"Are you afraid?" the bishop asked.

"Yes."

"That's honest. You needn't be. After all, the old woman is still alive."

"Yes, and she's lost her mind."

The bishop took another deep breath, closing his eyes. He held it for a long time, then slowly let it out. Eventually he opened his eyes, looked at me, then reattached his helmet.

"I wanted to know what evil smells like," he said.

"Evil."

He nodded.

"I didn't think you believed in evil."

The bishop looked confused. "Why do you say that, Bartolomeo?"

"You don't believe in God."

He hesitated for a moment, taken by surprise, I think. "Of course I believe in God."

"Why 'of course'?"

"I'm the bishop. I'm the head of the Church."

I shrugged. "Nevertheless."

He stared at me without speaking. The sound of breathing—his and mine both—seemed loud in my helmet. Then he turned away and walked past me, through the open doorway into the next chamber. I followed.

We entered the room where the old woman had been found. Everything was undisturbed—in the back corner was the sleeping mat and the pile of filthy blankets, littered with scraps of paper and the metal bowls smeared with the remains of old, dried food; in the other corner were stacks of mismatched, ragged items of clothing set aside for disposal. The bishop walked over to the cubicle next to the clothes, and looked down into the opening of the cylinder that had served as a toilet.

"Looks uncomfortable," he said.

"I doubt it was designed for human use," I said. "Certainly not designed *by* humans."

He made something of a snorting noise, but didn't comment further. After a brief glance at the clothes, he knelt beside the blankets and poked through them with his gloved hand. He picked up one of the larger scraps of paper, pressed it flat.

"She wasn't much of an artist," the bishop said dismissively.

He dropped the scrap and stood. "Show me where she was getting food."

"Out in the next corridor."

I led the way through the door at the far end of the room and into the long, wide passage. About ten steps into it, I stopped and gestured at an opening in the wall about chest-high.

"You set one of the bowls on that platform," I said, "then press one of those two squares." The squares were colored indentations in the wall next to the opening—one green, one red. "Red, and the bowl fills with water. Green, with a thick mixture of awful-looking stuff that's food. There are two tubes above where the bowl sits."

"And this still works?"

"Yes. We tried it. Water and food have both been analyzed in the labs, and there doesn't seem to be anything toxic in either, although no one has put it to the test. And the food is surprisingly nutritious. You'd get sick of the same thing all the time, I'm sure, but the lab techs say you could live on it forever."

The bishop was silent for a long time; then he turned to me and I could see a faint smile. "This would be *my* idea of Hell," he said. "It's no wonder the poor woman lost her mind."

We continued along the corridor in silence. When we reached the cluster of rooms, we went through each of them, but the bishop had no more questions or comments. Back in the corridor, he studied the strips of nacreous blue light that illuminated it.

Finally he spoke again. "Let us assume, purely for the sake of this discussion, that I *don't* believe in God. That does not preclude my believing in evil. This ship is evil."

"You really believe that?"

"Oh yes. Have you forgotten what has happened on this ship?"

"Accidents."

"So many?"

"This is an alien starship. Everything about it is alien. We don't understand it, we don't know anything about it. Accidents are inevitable."

"And how is Casterman an accident?" he asked.

"He's not. But I don't need 'evil' to account for a man killing himself. It's infrequent, but not unknown."

"He was a cleric," the bishop said. "His faith was important to him. Suicide is a mortal sin."

"For those who believe."

"Yes, and Brother Casterman believed."

"Did he? He didn't act like a man of faith."

The bishop nodded in acknowledgment. "He was a weak man in many ways. And yes, what you suspect is true: he was with the team to be my eyes and ears. So he was capable of deceit. But he believed, Bartolomeo. Suicide would have been unthinkable to him."

"A mortal sin, you say, but you held a Mass for him."

"Circumstances," the bishop said. "I believe that, in a way, he did not kill himself. Something else did it to him."

I shook my head, realizing we could go back and forth like this for hours, getting nowhere.

"And what about the others?" he added.

"What others?" Although I knew what he meant.

"Barry Sorrel. Sherry Winton. Starlin. Sorrel's wife and daughter. Nazia Abouti. I can't remember all the names. How do you account for them?"

"I don't."

"Exactly."

But what the hell did "exactly" mean? I didn't want to talk about it anymore. I was as disturbed by what had happened to people as the bishop was; probably *more* than he was. I didn't pretend to understand it; I couldn't even offer a reasonable explanation. But I knew that to attribute to the alien ship an abstract concept such as Evil, to somehow infuse this dead, inanimate object with that quality and blame our own psychological and emotional failings on it, was absurd. At the same time, I recognized that it was also absurd to deny that something extraordinary was occurring among those who had explored the ship, and that its effects were often devastating.

"What *does* it smell like?" I asked.

"What?"

"Evil."

He gave me that faint smile again. "Like unwashed flesh and bodily wastes."

With that, he started back along the corridor, and I followed.

37

"**W**E cannot continue in this way," the bishop declared, his gaze slowly sweeping the long table and the twenty-four other people who sat around it. Instead of an Executive Council meeting, the bishop had requested a session of the full Planning Committee. It was a gamble. The rules were different, the dynamics uncertain—no one could count on committee member votes. Although the Executive Council could override any vote or action taken by the Planning Committee as a whole (the Executive Council formed a third of the Planning Committee, but acted independently as well), they would need seven votes out of eight to do so.

I was sitting with Maria Vegas and Dr. G. in chairs set back from the table. We were there primarily to answer questions, but it was also understood that we could participate in any aspect of the discussion, as long as we did not abuse that privilege. The eight Executive Council members sat together at one end of the table, Nikos at the head. Then there was a gap the size of an empty seat on each side, and the other members of the Planning Committee occupied the remainder of the table.

"The exploration of the alien starship must end now," the bishop continued. "Before there are further casualties."

No one objected to his argument, but no one spoke out to support it, either. Caution all around. When it became clear that even the bishop was not going to take it any further unless pushed, I spoke up.

"The bishop says we cannot continue this way. I would agree with that much. But I would also argue that we can't abandon the alien ship. There are two reasons. First, there is the possibility of other human survivors like the old woman. I find it incredible to believe that on that entire ship, with large sections habitable for human beings, there was only one person aboard. If there are others on board that ship right now, and we abandon them, we are responsible for their deaths."

Again there was no response, as if everyone was content to let me and the bishop argue the issue between us—possibly they were afraid of the responsibility for any decisions. But I could feel the tension gradually increasing throughout the room as people sensed the building confrontation.

"Before I respond to your point," the bishop said, "what is the second reason?"

"The alien starship is far too important to be left behind. There has never been anything like it. It's the greatest discovery the *Argonos* has ever made, and possibly the greatest discovery *anyone* has ever made in human history. Its potential value is unlimited. We have no way of knowing what we might find."

The bishop sighed heavily. "Not everyone would agree with your characterization of 'greatness.' But that aside, we do know what we *have* found. Evil. Death. And one tortured soul. There is nothing to suggest we will ever find anything more than that." He shrugged. "And that is my response to *both* of your points."

"There is *plenty* to suggest we will find more than that," I said. "The alien starship is so large, it holds months, if not years, of exploration. That's daunting, perhaps, but it's also exhilarating. Leave it all behind? If we abandon it now, the odds are—if you will excuse the expression—astronomical against its ever being found again."

The bishop smiled slyly, without looking directly at me. "Oh, it will be found again. It *wants* to be found."

"What do you mean by that?" asked Costino.

But the bishop only shook his head and would not reply. I knew what he meant, but I wasn't going to explain it either.

Silence hung in the room. I waited, hoping someone else would venture into the discussion—preferably taking my side, of course. If the debate remained between the bishop and me, I knew I would lose.

I could sense Maria and Dr. G. shifting in their seats beside me, but neither spoke up. Just as well, I thought. I needed support from outside sources. But I needed *something*.

The bishop was leaning back in his chair with a sense of satisfaction, and I had just decided I couldn't wait any longer, when Alexandra Malfi, the chair of the Planning Committee, spoke.

"We should carefully consider what Bartolomeo has said. For both of his reasons, but primarily the possibility of other survivors. He is right about one thing. If there *are* any, and we abandon that ship, we are abandoning *them*. If they die, we are responsible."

"But if we leave, we would never know either way," Costino said.

"Does that make it okay? That we wouldn't know if we'd left anyone to die?"

"That's not what I meant," Costino said defensively.

"Then what did you mean?"

"I was just pointing out that there is no way for us to know. We could spend the rest of our lives searching for survivors that don't exist. When do we stop?"

Toller spoke up. "We certainly don't stop right after finding *one* survivor. *That* makes no sense at all."

"Perhaps it's like Schrödinger's Cat," the bishop said with an amused expression. "As long as we don't look for them, as long as we don't explore any more of the alien ship, then there's no one really there. Or if they *are* there, they are neither dead nor alive. Finding them could be the worst thing for them.''

''What the hell are you talking about?'' asked a man named Wexler. ''What's Schrödinger's Cat?''

Cardenas answered, shaking her head. ''The bishop misunderstands it, either deliberately or through ignorance. I won't speculate on which.'' The bishop's expression hardened. ''It's an ancient, theoretical paradox suggested by quantum theory,'' she added. ''First, it's theoretical, as I said, and probably has no actual application in the physical world. Second, it's completely irrelevant to the discussion. It has absolutely *nothing* to do with whether or not there are any more people on that ship, and nothing to do with whether they are alive or dead.''

I was afraid someone was going to ask her to explain it, anyway, but thankfully no one did. The bishop leaned forward as if to say something, then thought better of it. He settled back in his chair, eyelids lowered, his expression not at all softened.

''Let's get back to it.'' This was said by Renata Tyler, a dark-haired woman blind in one eye from a wild bird attack in one of the nature rooms when she was a child. ''While I have sympathy with Bartolomeo and others concerning the possibility of survivors, there are some important considerations. Even if we assume there *are* other survivors, and I suspect that's actually unlikely, how much are we willing to pay to search for them? Look at the cost so far.'' She looked down at her hand screen. ''Six dead, and another ten or twelve with severe psychological problems. All to save one woman who has lost her mind and may never recover. At that rate, we'll have half the population of the *Argonos* dead or deranged in another year, and we'll have rescued a few dozen traumatized men and women who will need to be cared for the rest of their lives.''

A few people laughed, but most realized Renata was essentially serious. I could feel Maria getting angry beside me, could sense her trying to keep her anger under control. She stood and spoke, her voice tight but steady.

"We also might find a section with a hundred survivors tomorrow, if we go back in. We have to take that into consideration as well."

The dynamics in the room shifted, and several people started talking at once. Suddenly everyone wanted in.

I sat silently in my chair for the next hour as the discussion and arguments swirled back and forth and all around. For a long time it didn't seem that any one point of view was dominant, but during the last part of that hour I began to sense a subtle coalescing of opinion—most people *wanted* to stay and continue searching for more survivors; but the majority of those who wanted to stay also felt the risks and dangers were too great, and the possible benefits did not outweigh the probable costs.

I had to get back into the discussion before it was too late. I'd been hoping it wouldn't come to this, but I'd known it probably would. I stood and waited for the talking to subside as the committee members turned to look at me.

"I have a proposal to make," I finally said. There must have been something in my voice because I could sense a palpable intensifying of their attention.

As I stood there preparing to speak, I wondered at how much had changed in the last year. Before, these same people would have been listening to me, but only to gauge what Nikos was thinking and planning, to assess the political currents and to aid their own ambitions. Now, I felt certain that many of them were listening to me with a genuine interest in what I had to say. It was different for me, too. My proposal was coming from *me*, from what I believed, and not simply to achieve some subtle (or even unsubtle) manipulation of people and actions.

"A full-scale, comprehensive exploration of the alien starship *is* beyond our capabilities," I began. "We do not have the time, or the human and physical resources necessary to do it properly. But I will reiterate what I passionately believe—that the alien starship is too important to abandon. I've already explained why, and more than once."

I paused, looking around the room. "There is also the question of more survivors. But that, too, is problematic.

Even if we could agree that it was worthwhile to spend
more time searching, it is clear that we can't agree on how
to decide when we have done enough.''

"We have already done enough," the bishop interjected.

"So you've said," I replied. "But there is no universal
agreement about that."

"Give us your damn proposal," Costino demanded.

"All right," I said. "We leave, but we take the alien
ship with us."

That set them off. For five minutes the meeting room
was a demented, disorganized chorus of voices. Finally
Nikos stood, and held up his hands until the babble faded.

"There will be plenty of time for . . . discussion," he
said. "Later. For now, let's hear from Bartolomeo, let him
explain what it is he's suggesting."

I nodded my thanks. "Just what I said. We take the
alien ship with us." I paused for a moment, organizing my
thoughts. "I don't know how, but I'm fairly certain it *can*
be done. We would ask the experts—Cardenas and her
crew, I'd say. Tether it to us with cables, maybe. The details
aren't important at the moment—"

"The details are always important," someone interrupted.

"They *will* be important, but not right now. For the
moment, let's assume it can be done. The question becomes,
To what purpose?"

"As I said, we don't have the resources for a thorough-
going exploration of the alien starship. But it needs to be
done. It *must* done, or too much will be lost. What we do,
then, is take it with us so someone else, someone who does
have the time and resources, can do it properly." I paused
again, looking around at everyone. "We need to redis-
cover civilization."

I was surprised by the restraint, by the rapt attention.
There was some squirming, and I could sense the struggle
within a few people to refrain from throwing questions at
me.

I sensed Nikos's excitement and anticipation. Cardenas
was nodding to herself, both waiting for me to continue

and, I knew, trying to work out the logistics of taking the alien ship with us. And Bishop Soldano steamed silently, his half-closed eyes radiating something close to hatred.

"There are worlds out there," I said, gesturing expansively with my right hand, "worlds we haven't seen in centuries, if ever. Worlds with millions, billions of people, huge thriving cities of advanced civilization, powered by wonders of technology, and with the resources to explore the alien starship in a way we never can. All we need to do is find one of those worlds."

"Yes," the bishop said, nodding and smiling. "That should be an easy task."

Someone snickered, but choked it off quickly. No one was really sure where this was going to end.

"No," I said, "it won't be easy. But there must be a way. There must be records somewhere in this ship. The *Argonos* must have visited worlds or systems like that in the past. If nothing else, it had to have been built in orbit around one those worlds, if not Earth itself."

Before the bishop could interrupt, I turned to him and held up a hand. "I know what Bishop Soldano claims—that the *Argonos* has *always* existed. Presumably created outside of time in some way and disconnected from Earth." I shook my head. "But none of us really believes that. I'm fairly certain the bishop himself doesn't believe it."

The bishop surged up from his chair. "You!" he roared. "I have had enough from you! Now you presume to tell me, tell all of us, what *I* believe. I will not have it!"

I'd gone too far. His arms trembled, his hands gripped the edge of the table; his skin was flushed and sweating. I had to do something.

I bowed my head once, then said, "I apologize, Bishop. I was out of line—" I hesitated, not sure what else to say. Saying too much could be just as bad as saying too little. "I apologize." I left it at that.

He remained standing a long time, glaring at me. Neither of us had good options. He could walk out of the meeting, but that would be dangerous for him; he needed to know what occurred, he needed to see and hear it; he needed to be there to try to influence the outcome. As for me, I could do no more than I had. And I still had to complete my presentation. I wasn't backing down now, and I couldn't afford to appear as if I had any hesitations. The bishop would leap on any sign of weakness.

The silence and the tension stretched out until at last the bishop breathed deeply once and nodded. "All right, Bartolomeo." He slowly lowered himself back into his chair. "I will accept your apology. But that doesn't mean I accept your absurd notions, your ridiculous proposal."

Okay, I thought. Standoff. I turned to Toller. "August. You're the ship historian. You know our records. What do they tell us about what I'm looking for?"

The old man slowly shook his head. "They are incomplete. Or rather, they are complete only for the last two hundred seventy-three years. That is when they began. We have nothing before that."

"Two hundred seventy-three years?" I repeated. "That's all?"

Toller nodded.

"Why? The *Argonos* has been around much longer than that. It's understood. According to the bishop, it's been around forever."

"Something happened," Toller said.

"What?"

Toller shrugged. "A plague that went through the *Argonos*. Most of you have heard about it. In itself it should not have caused such . . . devastation. But people got scared, and many went mad. That time came be to be called the Repudiation."

I'd heard the name, a few stories, but I'd never been sure it was more than a myth. No one seemed to care much about it; it had occurred so long ago. I'd imagined mobs of diseased people tearing through the corridors of the *Argonos*, burning everything they could find, destroying machinery, defacing walls, screaming at everyone they saw.

"Before it had run its course, the plague killed almost a third of the population of the *Argonos*. The Church was blamed by some. God by others. The ship, captain, and crew by still others. The Church managed to protect itself, but several factions of scared and maddened people took over the *Argonos* for a short time. Only a few weeks, but long enough to disable much of the ship's infrastructure, and purge the ship's logs and navigational records. When the crew regained control of the *Argonos*, most functions were restored, but the logs and other records were never recovered."

He leaned on his cane and adjusted his position. "Before that, there was no official ship History. The only official records were the ship's logs." He sighed heavily, shaking his head. "But they were *all* destroyed. Which is why the History was begun, to provide an alternate record should anything like that occur again."

Someone spoke up, asking the question I was about to ask myself. "Couldn't the ship History be destroyed as easily as the ship's logs?"

Toller smiled. "There are too many copies made, distributed and hidden throughout the ship, in various formats. Even I don't know how many, or who has them. Some would always survive."

"But there is nothing in these that can help us," I said.

Toller shook his head. "That's not quite true. There is an Appendix to the History, recorded summaries of what the early historians remembered or had been told about the decades and centuries that preceded the beginning of the official History. It makes for fascinating reading, particularly the discussions of the Repudiation and the years leading up to it, but by its nature the Appendix is fragmentary, anecdotal, sketchy in parts. There are, however, several references to just what you want, Bartolomeo. Star systems with populated worlds, interplanetary transportation, political and social networks. But when we encountered those systems, those worlds, we never stayed long. We were looking for isolated outposts, colonial settlements, lost missions. More importantly, there is no navigational data in the Appendix. There are planetary and system names, but no locational coordinates. The historians are not navigators. Only the ship's logs would have the information needed to locate any of those worlds.''

I closed my eyes, thinking. ''And the ship's logs were *all* destroyed?'' I asked. I opened my eyes and turned to Cardenas for confirmation. She nodded.

''Toller is correct. They were all destroyed.''

''But we still have the star charts, right?'' I wasn't giving up. ''We don't navigate blindly, the charts still exist with all the coordinates.''

''But no names,'' Cardenas said. ''All named references were deleted except Earth's. We've gone back to Earth, many years ago, and there was nothing there. We have names without coordinates, and coordinates without names.'' She paused and sighed. ''The Repudiators did a very thorough job. Navigators have worked with Toller and previous historians, trying to match the names and references in the History to what we have in charts . . .'' She shook her head. ''We've never been able to do it.''

I looked around the room. The bishop had a content, almost smug look on his face. ''There must be records somewhere on this ship that weren't destroyed,'' I said. ''No one can be that thorough. There are always dissidents who will hide copies, who will smuggle information away. They must be out there somewhere.''

''Probably,'' Nikos replied. ''But also probably lost, forgotten, damaged, accidentally destroyed.''

I surveyed the room again. ''Give us time to find them,'' I said. ''We'll send a plea throughout the ship, to the downsiders as well as the upper levels. Just give us time.''

''Why?'' Bishop Soldano rose slowly to his feet. ''So more people can die? Even if we could find complete records somewhere, that doesn't make your proposal any less absurd. I said it earlier—that starship is evil. Even if we could take it with us, which I very much doubt is even possible, and even if we could find a world filled with a billion people and all their wonderful tools and resources, taking that ship to them would only increase the harm it can cause, would only spread its evil. Would only magnify the death and destruction." He paused for effect. "We cannot do it. We *must* not."

I turned to Cardenas. "Can we do it?"

She nodded. "I think so. Your idea of tethering it to us with cables is probably not too practical. Acceleration is one thing, but trying to stop without its ramming us from behind would be more difficult. But I think we could manufacture a docking mechanism that would be workable." She shrugged. "If the Planning Committee wants me to, I can talk to the engineers and work out the feasibility."

I nodded. "That's all I ask for now," I said. "Time to search for logs or historical records that point us to a place to go, and time for Cardenas to explore the feasibility of taking the alien ship with us." I paused, thinking about whether or not I should suggest that, with or without the alien ship, it would be good for us to end our isolated wanderings, connect with real civilization again, but I thought it might actually scare some of them off. "That's all," I repeated. "No commitment to a course of action, just the time to explore the alternatives."

No one else said anything more. When we finally took the vote, it wasn't as close as I'd expected. The Planning Committee gave us the time.

38

I was taken aback when I saw Father Veronica the next day. A dark, despairing air surrounded her, the darkness haunting her eyes, even the way she carried herself. I had never seen this side of her, never suspected it existed. She was seated on the top step leading to the apse, leaning against the pulpit at which she'd spoken during Casterman's funeral Mass. As I approached she tried to smile, but the effort was weak and unsuccessful.

"What's wrong?"

She rose to her feet, her hands trembling slightly. "I am overcome by a sense of despair . . . and I can't tell you why. Two or three times a year, it happens. Usually I disappear for a few days, go into isolation until it passes. Bishop Soldano is aware of what happens, although he doesn't understand it. He accommodates me. I would be gone today, but we'd agreed to meet. Too much is happening now anyway. I can't disappear this time."

I nodded, remembering. "You were gone when I was released from prison. Father George said no one knew where you were."

She looked up into the darkness of the upper vaulting as if searching for solace she knew she wouldn't find. "Today,

this place makes my mood even more foul." She turned
back to me. "We'll go to my quarters," she said. "And
you can tell me what happened in the Planning Committee."

Her quarters were located two levels below the cathedral.
The outer two rooms were for church duties—meeting with
people, informal confessions, prayer; the interior rooms
were her private quarters.

Father Veronica directed me to sit in one of two chairs
partially facing each other, a small table between them. I
did; then she withdrew to the interior rooms. The room I
was in was small and dark and comfortable. On one wall
was a bookshelf constructed of real wood and filled with
bound volumes, most of which appeared to be quite old.
Another wall was draped with a dark tapestry picturing
the Creation.

She returned a few minutes later with a cup and a carafe
filled with coffee. She sat in the other chair and poured
coffee for me. I drank some and looked at her in surprise.

"Good, isn't it?" she said.

I nodded. "How?"

"Your friend Pär was kind enough to provide me with
a small supply."

I would have expected her to smile at some point in this
brief conversation about the coffee, at least with her eyes,
but she didn't, and I began to truly appreciate the depth of
her despair.

"Do you want me to leave?" I asked. "Leave you
alone?"

She shook her head. "I want to hear about the Planning
Committee session."

I related to her in some detail what had occurred, including my own assessments of the dynamics, the tensions, and
the uncertainties. When I had finished, she appeared to be
even more distressed.

"What is it?" I asked.

"You really want to take that ship with us?"

"Yes. You understand why, don't you?"

She nodded. "Yes. It's perfectly rational. But I'm still
uncomfortable with the idea. I would prefer to leave it be-

hind, and never see it again." She sighed heavily. "There's something else." But she didn't go on.

"What?"

"I don't know, Bartolomeo. I don't know if I should say anything. I'm not sure I have the right to say anything."

"You can say anything you want to me."

"It has nothing to do with you, Bartolomeo. It's me, and the Church."

She didn't say or do anything for a minute; then she abruptly stood and went into the other room, sealing the door behind her.

I assumed she wanted me to stay, but how could I be sure? If she'd wanted me to leave, she would presumably have asked me to do so. How could I know what she wanted?

I stayed. The room was quiet, a hushed silence that seemed to have substance. I drank my coffee, poured myself a second cup. I got up and walked over to the bookcase, studied the ancient volumes: *Vetera Analecta*. No author. *Meditations*, by Marcus Aurelius Antoninus. *Summa Theologica*, by Saint Thomas Aquinas. *Black Commentaries*, by Straphe. *Confessions*, by Saint Augustine. Books in French and Spanish, a couple of other languages I didn't recognize. Even alphabets that were unfamiliar. None of the names meant anything to me. I was tempted to pull one off the shelf and open it, but I didn't know what Father Veronica's reaction would be if she were to return and see me with one of the books in my hands. Were they holy texts not to be touched by unbelievers?

I returned to my seat, drank more coffee. As time passed, I grew increasingly uncomfortable, afraid I had misunderstood and was expected to leave. Twice I got to my feet, intending to leave, but both times I sat again to wait a while longer.

I was about to get up for the third time, when the door slid open and Father Veronica walked back into the room. She did not sit down, but stood in front of the tapestry.

"The bishop never mentioned the Church's own histori-

cal records." It was more statement than question, but I
knew she expected a response from me.

I hesitated, sensing the implications of what she'd just
said. "No," I replied.

She nodded slowly, as though still thinking, still trying
to decide something. "They are quite extensive," she said.
"And detailed. They go back hundreds of years . . ." Her
voice trailed off.

"How detailed?" I asked. I could feel my heart rate
increasing.

"They include much that would have been in the
ship's logs."

"Including star coordinates."

"Yes."

He had said nothing. The bishop had sat there as we
discussed trying to find lost or damaged records, any surviving remnants, and had said nothing about the Church's own
substantial and *intact* records.

"Nothing would be as simple as you might imagine,"
Father Veronica said. She finally sat again in the chair,
glancing at the books, then back at me. "There is no in-
dexing of any kind. And they are *very* extensive. I have
read little of them. The bishop is probably most familiar
with them, but even he has read only a small portion. Trying
to find very specific information, which is what you want,
would be extremely difficult."

I hesitated, watching her. My thoughts were jumping
frantically, barely under control. "Are you willing to tell
the Executive Council about the records? I know this must
be hard for you, and it's a bad time, *you're* having a hard
time—"

"If necessary," she said, cutting me off and closing her
eyes for a moment. "But could you not tell the council
about them yourself?"

"Sure. But you don't understand the dynamics. With the
bishop there fighting me all the way, everything would be
changed. It's not so much that they wouldn't believe me
concerning the records' existence; but the bishop would
have a good chance of convincing them that the records are

unimportant, would not be useful, and would in fact not have the kind of information you say they have." I paused. "If *you* tell the council, he won't be able to do that."

She hesitated a long time. "I'll talk to them, Bartolomeo."

"Thank you, Veronica."

"It's the right thing to do." She stood. "Let me know when you want me to talk to them. But until then, I need to be alone."

Now I knew it was time to leave. I rose to my feet and did.

39

I went to Nikos. Time for further reconciliation. I was going to need all the support I could muster from now on, and he represented my best opportunity. And I hoped there was still something salvageable between us, a remnant of friendship, mutual respect. Something.

I found him in the command salon, the canopy retracted, the stars and the eternal night sky engulfing him. He was relaxed and at ease in the command chair, more so than I had seen in months, if not years; he appeared rested, no longer haunted.

"What is it?" I asked. "What's happened to the strain and tension? You look almost . . ."

"Peaceful?"

"Yes."

He nodded and sighed. "I don't feel like the captain anymore, Bartolomeo. Surprisingly, that's a *good* thing." He smiled gently. "It's as if no one is in charge, and who would want to be? Circumstances are in charge. I wonder now why I was so caught up in it, in holding on to this position. If people wanted me out, I should have let them depose me." He shrugged, the smile fading. "But I didn't know anything else. It was my life. It was all I had." He paused for a few moments, then said, "I don't need it anymore."

We were both silent for a time. I tried to find the tiny occlusion that marked the alien ship, but couldn't locate it.

"Then what do you think of my plan?" I asked.

"Oh, it's a good plan, Bartolomeo. Alien ship or not, it would be beneficial for the *Argonos* to contact civilization once again, good for all of us. We've been out here far too long." He looked at me and frowned. "But I'm not hopeful of finding any records that will show us the way."

"Be hopeful," I said. "They exist."

"How can you be so sure?"

I grinned and told him what Father Veronica had revealed to me.

"So the bishop was holding out on us," Nikos said when I had finished. "I'm surprised she told you about it. I would have thought that it was some kind of Church secret." He fingered the chair controls and the canopy began closing over us; the salon grew darker until the canopy was completely sealed and the only illumination came from glowing colored lights on the command chair. I could barely tell that he was looking at me. "I assume you have something in mind," he said.

"Call an Executive Council session."

"And?"

"Father Veronica and I will be there, and she'll repeat what she told me. We demand that the bishop grant us access to the church records."

"And if he refuses? The Church has a certain degree of autonomy on this ship. He could legally refuse, and we could not force his hand."

"He won't refuse. Right now, that would be politically disastrous for him. He'd lose most of the support he has on the Planning Committee, even the Executive Council."

Nikos pulled slowly at his beard, an old habit I had once found reassuring.

"I believe you're right. That's what we'll do." He sighed heavily. "We could have been a formidable combination, Bartolomeo. We *were* at one time."

"We can still work together, Nikos."

"Yes, and we will. But it can never be the same as it once was, and that's a sad thing."

He was right, and I had no response.

W H E N Father Veronica and I walked into the council session, the bishop leaned forward in his chair, face tight, and said, "What is this?"

"I asked them both here," Nikos replied. "They have information that is useful to us." He gestured at us to sit, and we did.

"What kind of information?"

"Patience, Bishop." Nikos looked around the table. "We're all here, yes? Then let's start." He turned to Cardenas. "Margita, do you have answers from your engineers yet?"

Before she could reply, the bishop interrupted. "If this concerns Bartolomeo's demented proposal, we should be meeting with the full Planning Committee."

Nikos waved a hand in dismissal. "No formal action will be taken here, Bishop. We won't be voting on anything. We're simply gathering information that will be presented to the full committee." He tipped his head toward the bishop and his tone hardened. "Besides, Bishop, I think that before we're through here, you will be glad it's just the council."

The silence was tight with tension, with the bishop's struggle to maintain his composure. Nikos finally turned back to Cardenas and said, "Margita?"

She nodded once. "A simple answer, though not a simple task. Yes, we can do it. We can construct a docking mechanism, build one half onto the bow of the *Argonos*, the other centrally located on the hull of the alien starship— we put the ship right on our nose. Acceleration will be slower, but the drives can handle the extra mass. The docking mechanism will be somewhat simplified by the fact that we need no communication, no passage between the two ships, no cabling, no air locks. Everything on the exterior. It will take some time, but we can do it.''

''That's what we wanted to hear,'' Nikos said. ''No, let me correct that. That's what we *expected* to hear. I have more faith in the ship's crew than in almost anything else. Thank you, Margita.'' He glanced down at the table as if reminding himself of something, then looked up at Father Veronica. ''Now, for the second thing we need. Father Veronica. Tell us about . . . the Church's historical records.''

''NO!'' Bishop Soldano rose to his feet, slamming his hands on the table.

''Let her speak,'' Nikos said.

''Don't do this, Veronica.''

Father Veronica appeared unhappy, yet determined. ''It's too late, Eminence.''

''It is a betrayal of the Church!''

''No. It is upholding the Church's principles. God's principles.''

The bishop sat down heavily and closed his eyes for a moment. ''You are making a serious mistake, Veronica.''

''Perhaps, Eminence. But I make it with good conscience.''

The bishop had no response to this except to stare at me with that same malevolence he'd directed at me the day before; eventually he sank back, still shaking with rage. Father Veronica regarded him, then looked away.

''Father?'' Nikos said quietly.

''Yes. Sorry.''

She then proceeded to describe the Church's historical records to the Executive Council. She spoke at length, without interruption; as she spoke, the bishop sat rigid, his eyes hardly blinking.

When she was done, Father Veronica was obviously still conflicted. She slowly rose to her feet.

''I'm sure the bishop can answer any questions you may have. He is more familiar with the records than I am.'' She hesitated for a moment, then said, ''I'm sorry, but I must leave.''

"Certainly," Nikos said. "Thank you for speaking with us."

Father Veronica nodded once, then left. I wanted to follow her, and talk to her, but I couldn't leave now. There was more to come in the session, and if Nikos had his way we would immediately convene the Planning Committee. I sat in silence at the foot of the table and waited.

Most of the council members were stunned, but Toller was excited. "I always suspected," he said in an awed whisper. "Bernard, you've kept this from me all these years."

The bishop glared at Toller. "In public, you call me Bishop or Eminence."

Toller nodded, but could not keep the smile from his face. "My apologies, Bishop." He breathed deeply once. "Those records must be wonderful. I can't imagine what it will be like to see them, to start reading through them—"

"Don't get carried away, Historian." The bishop leaned forward and stared at Nikos. "I can refuse access. I *will* refuse access."

"Can he do that?" Costino asked.

"Yes," said Nikos. "Legally." He turned to the bishop. "You can, Bishop. But in the current climate, I don't think refusal would be wise."

We all waited for the bishop to speak; I looked down at his hands lying flat on the table, and I thought I could see one trembling slightly. When he finally spoke, his voice was tight and controlled.

"Access will be strictly limited."

"Understood," said Nikos.

"Toller and his apprentice only. No one else. They will have access only under strict supervision, and they will not be allowed to remove any materials from the Church archives. The records are sacred texts. We will not risk loss or damage."

Toller nodded. "Of course, of course, that's quite acceptable."

"Good," Nikos said. "With these two issues resolved, I propose we call an immediate meeting of the full Planning

Committee, present this information, and discuss our alternatives.''

His motion was seconded and passed, with the bishop abstaining. Nikos was about to close the meeting when the bishop spoke up.

''You say that the two issues are resolved. But that is not necessarily true. What if nothing is found in our records? What if that information, the location of some speculative advanced culture or society, doesn't exist?'' He leaned forward again. ''What if it isn't there?''

''I don't think that's a very likely outcome,'' Nikos said. ''Is it, Bishop?''

The bishop didn't answer.

THREE hours later, the full Planning Committee came to order. Nikos, Cardenas, and I made our presentation. There was surprisingly little discussion, and the vote was overwhelming. Toller and Maria Vegas would begin their search through the Church records, and the engineers would immediately begin preparations to construct the docking mechanism—we were leaving, and we would take the alien ship with us.

40

I wanted to apologize to Father Veronica for putting her into a difficult position with the bishop. I also wanted to know how she was holding up.

As I entered the cathedral, I caught a glimpse of her leaving, stepping through a doorway on the right, behind the apse. I was going to call out to her but I stopped, my mouth silently open, when I saw all the long, narrow metal columns in front of me—several mounted in the floor, others hanging from the ceiling at various heights. I'd never seen them before, and had no idea what they were.

I hurried the length of the cathedral, staring at the columns; as I neared them, I realized they were longer and larger than I'd realized. I climbed the half dozen steps to the first of them, and saw they held long glass tubes that I guessed to be light sources. Still puzzled, I turned away from the lights and went through the doorway on the right.

I was in a long, gently curving corridor, dimly lit and gray. I thought I could hear footsteps in the distance. Again I stopped myself from calling out; instead, I followed the sounds.

Closed doors lined the right wall, but I passed them all. I heard a door hiss shut far away, then nothing. Two minutes later the corridor ended at a suit locker, which in turn led to an air lock; panel lights warned that there was some-one suiting up inside—Father Veronica was leaving the ship.

I waited until the panel lights indicated the air lock had cycled and she was outside (I didn't have a choice; the doors had automatically locked and didn't unlock until she was gone), then entered the locker. I donned a suit, waited impatiently for it to size itself to me, then started the cycling process. Fifteen minutes later I, too, was outside the ship, drifting free.

I didn't see her anywhere. The ship's hull spread out around me in all directions, a dark and jagged metallic plain. Yet it was not as dark as the alien ship, and tiny shafts of light leaked out of view ports in the distance so that I did not feel lost or isolated or abandoned, as I sometimes felt on that other vessel. But I did not see Father Veronica, although I turned slowly in a full circle. No signs of move-ment anywhere.

A brief flash caught my eye; I looked up, and saw her moving far out from the ship. The flash had been one of her suit's small jets. I crouched, then kicked hard, launching myself from the ship, angled away from Father Veronica.

My momentum carried me quickly away from the *Argonos*, and soon I was passing her, about fifty or sixty meters distant. Her outward motion had stopped, and her suit's attitude jets were briefly firing again, orienting her so that she was now directly facing the ship.

Somehow I had made it past without her seeing me. I hit my own suit's jets and brought myself quickly to a stop. A couple of minor adjustments and I, too, was facing the ship. We both drifted in the dark, surrounded by stars, the ship in front of us. I watched her, wondering what she was doing out here.

It started so slowly that I was barely aware of it at first— a diffuse flicker of color on the *Argonos* hull. I was watch-ing Father Veronica, and only dimly sensed it in the periph-ery of my vision. I almost ignored it. Then I realized something unusual was occurring and I turned to look at the growing bloom of color. Just as I did, it silently, almost blindingly exploded to life.

Christ on the Cross.

The enormous stained glass window at the head of the cathedral, which had always been too dull, indistinct, and chaotic to reveal any concrete images, now blazed in the depths of space, burning in the side of the *Argonos*. The Church's beacon to the stars.

The Crucifixion.

A crimson sky blazing as if the air itself was on fire.

Against that flaming sky, the Cross, the wood so dark it was almost black, stained with sweat and blood.

Jesus hanging from the dark wood, metal spikes driven through wrists and ankles. He stared not upward but out at the universe, at whoever looked at Him. At me.

Blood on His forehead, His chest, His ankles and wrists. His mouth open in His suffering.

The images seemed both three-dimensional and somehow alive. I thought I sensed movement—the twitching of a thigh muscle; the strained and ragged shudder in His chest; beads of sweat inching along His jaw; the tremor of His cracked and bleeding lips. I knew I had to be imagining it, but it seemed so real. I began to feel hot and sweaty inside my pressure suit.

Terrible and beautiful . . .

I realized I'd been holding my breath, and I finally let it out. My breathing was deep and ragged for a time, as His must have been. My heart ached for Him, for His suffering.

What was happening to me?

I wanted to turn away from Him, but I couldn't. His image seemed to be growing, becoming even more vibrant and alive. I felt lightheaded, dizzy. Finally, unable to turn away, I managed to close my eyes.

For a few moments a cool relief washed through me and I felt almost in control again. I kept my eyes closed, although I could still sense the bright colors through my eyelids, and breathed slowly, deeply.

But when I opened my eyes again, His image overwhelmed me once more. I was being drawn into Him,

toward the scorched wood, the crimson blazing skies behind
Him, toward His scourged flesh, drawn into His glowing
visage. . . . His eyes . . . His eyes . . . so deep and penetrat-
ing and . . . and what? Terrified? No, I realized. Tortured.
It was awful, and I felt I was being accused by those eyes.
But accused of what?

"Who's there?"

It was Father Veronica's voice, coming over the open
suit channel. I looked at her and saw she had turned toward
me. More than that, I was now much closer to her than I
had been—she was drifting away from the ship, or I was
drifting toward it. Or some of both.

"Who's there?" she said again. There was no fear in
her voice, but there was puzzlement.

The spell of the stained glass broke. "Bartolomeo," I
finally managed to say.

I used the jets to shift closer to her, and matched her
drift until we were only a few meters apart.

"You followed me."

"Yes," I said.

I expected her to ask me why, but she didn't. Her face
was visible through her clear helmet, but her expression
was indistinct. I could not even guess at what she was
thinking or feeling.

"I wanted to see it one last time," she said, turning back
to the blazing images.

"One *last* time?" I said.

"I'm sorry, I didn't mean it that way. Although it is
possible I never will see it like this again."

"I don't understand."

"We'll be closing with the alien ship soon. Presumably
we'll be docking with it." There was a long pause. "I will
not illuminate this image while we are joined with that other
ship. It would be blasphemous. Or at least indecent and
disrespectful."

"Have you changed your mind about the alien ship? Do
you now think it is evil?"

Father Veronica shook her head. "No. But the terrible
things that have happened in there . . ."

"Terrible things have happened on the *Argonos*."

"That's true. But they are *our* terrible things." She turned back to me. "I don't know if that distinction has any meaning to you, but it does to me."

"I'm not sure it does," I said. I glanced at the stained glass, then turned again to her, and finally asked her the question I had wanted to ask for a long time. "Either way, though, how is it that God lets these terrible things happen?"

She hesitated before answering. "That is a meaningless question," she eventually said.

"I don't understand. Isn't that the kind of question the bishop and priests try to answer all the time?"

"I have beliefs somewhat different from others in the Church."

"Having belief of any kind would be different from the bishop," I said.

I thought I could see her smile. "Oh, the bishop has beliefs," she said. "God just isn't one of them."

I was no longer surprised at her candor about the bishop. But I wondered if she would be equally so about herself.

"Tell me about your beliefs," I said to her.

I thought she was going to say that her beliefs were a private matter, and that she would not talk about them. But then I caught the slow exhalation of a sigh, and she began to speak.

"When I was a child, everything seemed fairly simple and straightforward. I believed in a benevolent, all-knowing and all-powerful God who watched over us at all times, who acted upon our lives, who answered the prayers of the faithful. If it sometimes seemed that he did not answer your prayers, it was because your prayers were selfish or self-serving, or you had done something, or *not* done something, that made you unworthy.

"I'll try not to be tedious with all the particulars, but from very early on, from the time I was six or seven years old, I wanted to be a priest. As soon as I could, I began my studies toward that goal. Bishop Soldano was Father

Bernard at that time, and I studied under him for many years.''

We drifted in silence for a time; I could see the bright reflection of the stained glass in her suit helmet, but I avoided looking directly at the images.

"He was ambitious even then," she went on, "though I only recognized it in retrospect. But I am fairly certain that his faith and belief were both strong and sincere during those years." There was another brief pause. "I don't know what happened to him later. It could have been something similar to what happened with me, but I don't think so."

This time the pause was much longer and I sensed her reliving that period in her life. I wondered if she looked back on it with fondness, regret, or a sense of loss.

"There came a time of grave doubts," she resumed. "I was in my early twenties, finally an adult, a grown woman, although I had not yet entered the priesthood. I was very close to taking my vows.

"There was no one thing that raised doubts within me, no one tragedy or horror. It was an accumulation of small, personal tragedies and miseries that I saw all around me, directly and indirectly, in all parts of the ship, in stories people told me, in the Church's historical records as well as my own observations of daily life. There were so many people, good people with deep and abiding faith, who nonetheless suffered terribly in their lives—physically or emotionally, or both. People whose prayers never seemed to be answered.

"The most distressing, and troubling, were the children. Young, innocent children who could not have sinned, who could not even know what sin was, and yet who lived protracted, agony-filled lives, or died horrible, painful deaths. There weren't many, but I couldn't understand it for even *one*. Why did these things happen?" She slowly shook her head. "I had no answers. None.

"I could not reconcile these things with my earlier conception of a benevolent, all-powerful God who listened to our prayers and who interceded in our lives. The priests would tell me that the suffering was a test, or a lesson for us to learn from. Or, alternatively, that God's ways were just too mysterious for us ever to understand, that applying any kind of logic or looking for rational reasons for why things happened was useless.''

She turned and looked directly at me. ''I could not accept any of those answers. I still can't. So I began to seriously doubt God's existence. Or, I told myself, if God *did* exist, if he *was* omniscient and omnipotent, could intercede in our lives and ease or end our suffering, but chose *not* to, or in fact chose to make us suffer . . . then I wanted nothing to do with such a God.''

She stopped again, still looking at me, but I couldn't read her expression. ''Father Bernard recognized my growing doubts, even though I had not overtly expressed them to him. Actually, they were more than just doubts. I was ready to quit my studies and abandon my plans to become a priest. Father Bernard asked me into his chambers and talked with me at length. He encouraged me to take some time for myself—away from the Church, away from my studies, away from my family and friends. He encouraged me to meditate upon my doubts, upon my faith. Like Jesus, I went into the desert.''

She paused, and it took me some time before I made the connection.

''The Wasteland?'' I said.

''Yes, the Wasteland. I spent ten days there, ten days in the desert. I packed food and water for two weeks, a sleeping pad, and nothing else. Not even a Bible.'' Again she paused as if reliving her desert retreat. When she resumed speaking, her voice had a distant but sure quality to it.

''After ten days, I had what I can only describe as a revelation. An unconventional revelation, some might even call it heretical, for it differs from the standard Church doctrine. Some people might put it off to a fevered mind addled by heat and thirst and semistarvation, hallucinations caused by days of isolation. But it was so crystal clear to me, everything finally falling into place, and it all made sense to me at last. It felt *right*, it felt *true*. Most importantly, the understanding, the feeling of rightness, stayed with me long after I'd left the Wasteland and returned to my quarters. It remains with me to this day."

I had to fight the urge to question her, to encourage her to speak.

"Free will," she eventually said. "That's what I finally understood. *True* free will."

She looked away from me, although not toward the stained glass. It was as if she was staring into the depths of space, into the depths of time.

"When God created human beings, He bestowed upon us the greatest gift besides His love. *Out of* His love. Two gifts, really, but so interconnected they are like one. First, the capacity to do *anything*, good or evil, wise or unwise, loving or hateful. And second, true free will to act upon that capacity.

"Those are God-like qualities. Not in power, but in choice. If He had created us in such a way that we could only do good, if we were incapable of acting badly, selfishly, causing pain or harm, then the notion of free will would be meaningless, would it not? Not only that, true free will precludes God's intervention in our lives. There is no real free will if God intercedes to protect us or save us from the consequences of our own or other people's actions and choices. We have to face those consequences ourselves. That is the price we pay for free will."

Father Veronica sighed heavily, and when she resumed there was an ache in her voice. "Can you imagine the sacrifice God has made to provide us with this gift? He knows we will not always make good choices, He knows we will cause ourselves and others terrible pain and grief. Can you imagine His own pain and grief, knowing that He *could* intercede, could change our lives and ease our suffering, but knowing also that to do so would be to take back the wonderful gift He has bestowed?

"For we can also love and comfort one another, we can *choose* good over evil, we can relish and appreciate life, we can revel in all the small, wonderful pleasures of being alive, we can love and be loved, and those things are all the greater because they *are* freely chosen. Because we are not puppets."

I had listened and reflected all this time without interrupting, and I finally questioned her.

"Does God know everything that will happen? Every choice we will make? All the future laid out before him?"

"No. He knows everything that is happening now, as time flows, He knows everything that has happened in the past, and He can make very accurate assessments, I am certain, of what any of us will choose to do. But, once again, our free will would not be *true* free will if He *knew* absolutely what every choice would be. When He created us, and gave us free will, He effectively canceled out His foreknowledge of the future."

I thought about that, and I could see that it made a kind of sense. But I still had more questions, and although I had in the past refrained from questioning Father Veronica about her beliefs, about her faith, this seemed, at last, the time for it.

"You mentioned prayer, earlier, and some time ago you said you would talk to me about it. What is it, if God will not answer? Worthless? A farce?"

"No, not worthless at all. Misunderstood. Misguided and misdirected. When I talk to people about prayer, I try to explain to them what I believe is its nature and use." She sighed. "Most don't listen, or they dismiss what I have to say, because they want the promise that conventional belief gives them—that if you ask for something in prayer, it may be given to you."

"Explain to me," I said. "*I* will listen."

"Yes, you will listen, Bartolomeo, even if you won't believe." She paused for a moment. "Prayer is a kind of communication with God. It is opening yourself to God's presence, to His Spirit, to His *essence*. And when you are truly open to Him, God's essence can provide comfort and understanding, and guidance. That is why some prayers *are* answered, in a way. Not because God has actively interceded in our lives, but because people have taken that comfort, and taken in the guidance and understanding that are there for us, and then they act, they live their lives and *view* their lives informed by that, in such a way as to essentially answer their own prayers.''

That, too, made a kind of sense, although I wasn't sure I completely understood what she was saying.

''And what about Him?'' I asked, gesturing at the crucified figure glowing in the side of the ship, that terrible and beautiful vision of light and life, and a death that held the promise of *new* life. Or so the Church claimed. ''Why?''

''God's own guilt,'' she said, but so quietly I wasn't certain I'd heard her correctly. I tried to understand what she meant, but she began to speak again as if she hadn't yet said anything, ignoring her own initial response.

''He was speaking to us. God. He sacrificed His Son, Himself. Became us. Died like us. And resurrected Himself to show us the way. One final, ultimate attempt to help us in our lives to make the right choices. And to show us He will forgive us when we don't.''

That I could understand somewhat, but I was more intrigued by her first response. ''What did you mean by 'God's own guilt'?''

''I'd hoped you hadn't heard me. I don't talk about that, certainly not with anyone in the Church.'' She hesitated, then went on. ''It's an idea I have about Jesus and the Crucifixion. I wouldn't call it a belief. Another subtext to the Crucifixion.'' I could hear her take a long, deep breath, then slowly release it. ''He created us. He gave us true free will. Therefore He is in some real way ultimately responsible for the suffering we inflict upon one another. He has His own guilt. And sacrificing His Son, Himself, was a way to help expiate that guilt.''

Suddenly the stained glass image before us went dark. Everything else remained—the stars, the faint lights scattered about the hull, Father Veronica's dim contours beside me.

''Someone's entered the cathedral,'' she said. ''The lights are set to go out when anyone enters. They're far too bright, and would cause optical damage.''

''Perhaps we should go in,'' I suggested.

She didn't immediately reply. "One more thing," she
eventually said.

There was something in her voice that caused my stomach to tighten, and I was suddenly afraid, although I didn't
know of what. I didn't say a thing, I just waited.

"I know how you feel about me, Bartolomeo. I'm not
naive, and I'm not oblivious." There was a slight pause.
"Unless I've completely misread you."

I knew she would not go on unless I replied.

"No, you haven't misread me."

"It's all right, Bartolomeo. I like you, and I admire you.
I take it as a great compliment. We both know nothing
could ever come of it . . ." Her voice trailed off, unsure.
"I just wanted you to know that *I* know."

There was a long and tense silence between us. I didn't
know what to say.

"I've distressed you," she said.

"No." We both knew I was lying.

"We should go in," she said.

"Yes," I replied.

We activated our suit jets and headed toward a ship that
now seemed dark and empty.

I was despondent. I kept telling myself it was absurd,
that I had never expected anything to "come of it," as
she put it. I'd always known the way it was.

So why did I now feel so bleak?

I knocked myself out with sleep tabs, and hoped I would
feel better when I woke.

41

THE *Argonos* closed with the alien ship. Four days of slow but steady approach, then we stopped several kilometers away and maintained that distance. We waited another two days to see if there would be any response from the alien ship, although no one, except perhaps the bishop, expected anything. There was nothing; it remained just as dead as it had always been.

Work began on the docking mechanism. There were two crews, one working on each vessel. Progress was slower on the alien ship, because the crews exercised extreme caution—when anything was burned into the ship's hull, or welded to it, initial roughwork was done by remotes; there were long delays between phases while we waited to make sure nothing untoward would happen. The work was tense and tedious, but there were no accidents, no injuries or deaths.

Toller and Maria Vegas began their search through the Church archives. No one else was allowed access to the archives, and they promised to immediately report any discoveries of interest. As the days passed, we heard nothing from them.

Life on the *Argonos* returned to normal routine. There was nothing for me to do. All further exploration of the

alien starship, though it could now be undertaken much
more easily, was suspended until the actual docking took
place.

I checked on the old woman, but she was still in shock,
unable to speak. Leona's condition, too, remained unchanged. Pär was occupied with a new coffee harvest. Nikos
had gone on retreat to one of the nature rooms with Aiyana.
I avoided Father Veronica.

Violating ship orders, I suited up and made the short trip
across to the alien ship. I worked my away along the hull
to the air lock entrance I had gone through so many times,
and which hadn't been used since I'd taken the bishop there.
After I turned the handle and the hatch slid open, I moved
across the entrance but did not go in. I drifted just outside,
contemplating the dark interior.

It seemed like a different place already, as if we had
already turned it over to the scientific teams of some advanced society in a star system we might never discover,
or might never reach. As if we had abandoned it.

I still felt a twinge of fear as I looked into the darkness;
an air of mystery, too, still emanated from it, vaguely threatening—I thought I could feel a subtle yet persistent force
tugging at me, pulling me inside. I nearly succumbed.

Were there other people alive in there, waiting for rescue? Unlikely, I thought, but it was possible. Yet I did not
dare propose further exploration, another "rescue mission."
I couldn't risk opinion turning against me; we could not
leave this ship behind.

F O R days I stayed away from the cathedral. I felt em-
barrassed and guilty. At the same time, I was afraid of
losing the friendship Father Veronica and I *did* have, and
the longer I avoided her, the more likely it seemed that
would happen.

On Sunday I went to early Mass, but there was no sign
of her. The bishop said Mass, with Father George assisting;
Father Archibald gave the sermon, but I didn't register a
word of it. At the midday Mass, it was the same. This time

I waited for everyone to leave, hoping to speak to Father George alone.

It was the bishop who remained. When everyone else had gone, he walked down the center aisle and sat two pews in front of me, body twisted around so he could face me as we talked.

"She's not here, Bartolomeo. She won't be for some time."

She had disappeared after all.

"Aren't you going to ask me why?"

"No," I said.

He nodded. "You know, then."

I shrugged.

"She's a complex woman," the bishop said. "A complex priest, for that matter. Sometimes she thinks too much."

"Better than not thinking enough," I said.

He smiled at that. "You're arrogant, Bartolomeo."

"And you're not?"

"Oh, I am. Very arrogant. I readily admit it. I try to account for it. I don't think you do."

I got up to leave.

"Don't go yet, Bartolomeo."

"Why not? We have nothing to talk about."

"Of course we do. Father Veronica."

I shook my head. "I have nothing to say to you about her."

The bishop chuckled. "So sensitive, Bartolomeo. One would almost think . . ." He let his voice trail off, as if expecting me to respond. I didn't.

"She will make a great bishop when the time comes," he said. "A better one than I."

"Why is that?"

"Because, as you pointed out some days ago, I do not believe in God. She does."

"If you don't believe, why are you so opposed to bringing the alien ship with us?"

"Because I do believe in Evil, which is what that ship

is." He paused. "We did not discover that ship by accident."

"I know that."

He raised an eyebrow. "Do you? Nikos told you?"

"No."

"It doesn't matter. Especially now. We have been led into this trap, and we're staying in it. We've had warnings, opportunities to escape, but now we're about to spring it shut on ourselves."

I shook my head, exasperated. "There is no *trap*, Bishop. There is only fear of the unknown, and paranoia."

He shrugged in resignation. "Nothing to be done, then."

"What if she doesn't want to be bishop?"

"Veronica? She'll have no choice." He smiled again. "But that's a long time away." He stood. "All right, Bartolomeo. Go. You're probably right, we have nothing to talk about. More in common than you realize, but it means nothing." He waved a hand at me in dismissal. "On your way."

42

PÄR and I watched the docking from the back of the amphitheater; most of the five hundred seats were occupied, and another two hundred people stood in the aisles or off to the side. Thirty or forty teens congregated in small groups, and some of the adults had brought their young children with them to watch.

The main screen showed the view from a camera on one of the maintenance modules which had gone out several hundred meters from the two ships, providing the best overall view of the entire procedure. In the corners were smaller screens showing video images from other cameras, all of them closer, including one set right next to the docking mechanism on the *Argonos* so that we could watch the alien ship coming slowly but inexorably toward us—I was glad that picture wasn't on the main screen.

"I sense an anticlimax approaching," said Pär.

I nodded. "Why is that?"

"It's not real. It might as well be a story film. We *know* it's real, but that's intellectual. It feels staged. For most of these people, *nothing* outside this ship is real."

All of the images stopped moving; only an occasional flicker of light gave evidence that the transmission hadn't frozen. The two ships maintained their distance, the docking mechanisms fewer than ten meters apart.

Guide cylinders emerged from the *Argonos* and tele-scoped toward the alien ship. Just before contact, they were positioned to enter corresponding shafts. The *Argonos* began to slowly move again.

We felt the brief, muted jolt. A caption flashed on the screen: DOCKING COMPLETE. Someone applauded, and another dozen or so joined in halfheartedly.

"What did I tell you?" Pär said. "These people have no idea what this means to them." He turned to me. "They have no idea it means the end of their way of life."

"What do you mean?"

"When we find human civilization again and take this alien ship there, the mission of the *Argonos* will be finished. No, not finished . . . that implies completion. This mission, whatever the hell it is, or was supposed to be, will *end*. We won't continue on afterward. We'll all leave this ship, and never set foot in it again."

I hadn't thought of that, but Pär was right. I reflected on it as we watched the people drifting out of the amphitheater. The screens went dead. Someone, probably one of the teen-agers, threw something at the main screen; red and brown splattered across the gray surface.

"It will be good for us," I said.

"I doubt the bishop would agree," Pär replied.

I nodded. If the bishop had considered these implications, it would help explain his opposition.

"None of this will matter, though, if we can't figure out where to go," I said. "I'm going to see Toller."

TOLLER hadn't been this happy in years.

I was not allowed into the archives. Instead, a cleric asked me to wait in an anteroom while she went to get Toller. The room was small, furnished only with two chairs; the walls were bare. I had the feeling it was rarely used.

When the cleric escorted Toller into the anteroom, the old man gave off an aura of contentment and well-being.

The cleric withdrew, the door sealing behind her. Toller clasped my shoulder, shaking his head with a smile.

"You should see the archives, Bartolomeo. They are incredible."

"Believe me, August, I'd like to see them."

"I know, it's crazy. Does anyone really think you'd steal or harm anything?"

"The bishop, apparently."

"The books, Bartolomeo . . . there are thousands of bound folios in the History. Beautiful workmanship, quality materials . . ."

"That's fine, August, but what about what's *written* in them?"

"That, too, is incredible. Not so much the prose itself, which is sometimes awkward and pedestrian, but the content . . . the detail and texture . . ."

I was becoming impatient. "What about what we're looking for?"

Toller shook his head. "Nothing yet, Bartolomeo. It's so slow-going. *All* of it is handwritten, none of it is recorded in any other media, so it's impossible to do a computer search. I've asked the bishop if we could scan the records into the computers, but he refused." He shrugged. "We can only push him so far."

I shouldn't have expected this to be easy; I was beginning to realize it could take weeks, or months, to find what we were looking for. I knew we didn't have that kind of time—people on the Planning Committee would grow impatient, support for my proposal would wane, and eventually the decision would be made to undock from the alien ship and resume our travels in the same manner we'd been traveling for decades.

"We're working our way back from the time of the Repudiation," Toller said.

"Why start there? Why not start at the beginning?"

He smiled. "You forget, Bartolomeo. The bishop claims there *is* no beginning. According to him, the Church's History goes back forever. We have no choice but to work backwards. What else should we do? Pick out volumes at random? Ask for one from three hundred and fifty years ago? Five hundred? Any other approach would be arbitrary. This is the best way. We won't miss anything.''

"Try to hurry it up, August. Skim the damn things.''

"We are, Bartolomeo. Maria and I are working in shifts, and most of our shifts overlap. We're not getting much sleep.'' He grinned. "But it's wonderful. It's difficult not to get caught up in the archives, not to get lost. . . . We *are* historians. But we're working through them as fast as we can.'' He sighed, frowned. "There may not be anything there, Bartolomeo.''

"It's there, August. Somewhere in all those beautiful folios of yours is the information we want.''

The cleric returned. "Mr. Aguilera?''

"Yes?''

"A call for you. From Mr. Taggart.''

"All right.'' I turned back to Toller. "Find it, August.''

He nodded. We left the anteroom through the same door, but Toller went down the connecting corridor to the right while the cleric led me off to the left and a communications station. Taggart's face was on the screen.

"Bartolomeo,'' he said, "I've been trying to find you for half an hour.'' His face was flushed. "You'll want to get up here. She's talking.''

"The old woman?''

"Yes. In English.''

"I'll be right there.''

43

BY the time I got to the med center, the woman had lapsed into incoherence. Dr. G. was with her. Nikos was already in the observation room with Taggart, and the three of us stood side by side, watching the two women through the one-way glass. The old woman lay on the bed, trembling slightly; Dr. G. was seated beside her, holding the woman's gnarled hand. The old woman whimpered through dry, cracked lips.

"It's all right, Sarah," Dr. G. said, her voice soft and comforting. "Nothing can hurt you here."

"Sarah?" I said to Taggart.

He nodded. "She said her name was Sarah."

I remembered the letters tattooed onto her arm—S.C. "Sarah what?"

Taggart shrugged. "She didn't say. Or couldn't. Dr. G. asked the same question, but she didn't seem to understand."

We watched the old woman, listening, but nothing changed. Nikos appeared rested and at ease, more so than he had in a long time. I wondered if he'd quit drinking.

After five minutes without change, Taggart nodded toward the glass. "It looks like we won't get any more for

a while. You can watch the recording of what you missed."
He shook his head. "It was something."

"What do you mean?"

"I'll let you see for yourself." Taggart crossed the room
to his console.

The old woman's eyes were closed now, but her hand
still gripped Dr. G.'s: a pale, shaking claw that would not
let go. Dr. G. adjusted her position, prepared to stay a while.
The woman's face seemed to relax.

A monitor came to life above the one-way glass. The
image jumped, then settled and the recording began to play.
Dr. G. was seated in the chair beside the bed, and appeared
to be dozing. The old woman lay on the bed with her eyes
open, staring up at the ceiling. The only sounds at first were
of breathing.

The old woman's eyes widened; then she sat upright and
croaked out, very distinctly, "Help me!" Her fingers clawed
at the blanket. "Help . . . ahhhh . . . ." Her voice trailed off.

Dr. G. had jerked awake at the woman's cry and now
rose. She stepped to the bed, cautious, as the woman turned
to look at her. "It's all right," Dr. G. said. "You're safe
here."

"Safe?"

"Yes, you're safe now. No one will hurt you." She
reached out to her patient, but the woman flinched and Dr.
G. pulled her hand back. "Safe."

The woman looked around the room, her head movements stilted. When her attention returned to Dr. G., she
stared at the psychologist for a long time, hardly blinking.

"You understand me?" Dr. G. asked.

The woman hesitated, then said, "Ye-e-esss . . ." Drawing it out.

"You didn't speak when we found you."

"Where . . . ?" the woman said. "Where am . . . ?"

"You're on the *Argonos*," Dr. G. answered.

"Ar . . . go . . . nos." Then: "What . . . Argonos?"

"It's a starship. We found you on board another ship."

The old woman closed her eyes and trembled. "Found,"
she whispered, her eyes still closed.

"My name's Glienna. What's yours?"

The woman hesitated for a long time, then finally opened her eyes and looked at Dr. G. "Sarah."

"Sarah." I saw Dr. G. glance at the woman's arm tattoo, thinking along the same lines I had. "Sarah what?"

But as Taggart had said, the woman didn't seem to understand the question.

"Sarah," she repeated. Then: "How . . ." She stopped, grimaced. "How . . . how long have I been . . . ?" She could not quite finish the question.

"We found you three weeks ago."

"Weeks?" As if she didn't understand the word.

"Twenty-one days."

"How . . . how long was . . . was I . . . how . . . other ship?"

"We don't know," Dr. G. said. "We have no idea."

"They . . . they rescued us," Sarah said, trembling again. "They rescued us, then . . . then . . . died. They died."

"Who rescued you, Sarah?"

Again, she either didn't understand the question, or ignored it. Instead, she shook her head slowly, making a faint, keening sound.

"We were on . . . Antioch," she eventually said. "Oh . . . God . . . all the . . . all the killing . . . the bodies, bodies hanging . . . we couldn't . . . couldn't couldn't couldn't get away, madmen . . . slaughtering us . . . slaughtering . . ." She was becoming more agitated, clawing again at the blanket. ". . . men monsters, they were men and women they were . . . madmen . . . madmen killing us. . . ."

She closed her eyes for a moment and when she opened them she looked up toward the ceiling. "They came . . . they came. Then they rescued us . . . who were left, who were . . . took us onto their ship and . . ." She paused. "I . . . they . . . they saved us."

"*Who* rescued you, Sarah?"

She made a sound like a strangled laugh. "They did. Then . . . then something happened . . . happened to them and they died, leaving us all alone."

"How many of you were there?" Dr. G. asked. "Are there others still alive on the ship?"

Sarah didn't answer. She held up her hand and studied it, turning it slowly. "I was . . . young, then." Her voice was soft, sad. "I'm old . . . old." Then she turned back to Dr. G., reached out with the hand she'd been studying, and gently touched Dr. G.'s hand. "I want to die now."

She lay back, closing her eyes once again. Dr. G. took Sarah's hand in her own, then sat on the bed next to her.

"No," she whispered. "You're safe now, Sarah, you're . . ."

"I want to die now," Sarah repeated.

Taggart stopped the video. "That's the last thing she said. She's opened her eyes a couple of times, sat up once crying out, but not another word. Dr. G. has tried talking to her, but she hasn't responded in a long time." He shrugged. "Hopefully there'll be more later."

Nikos looked at me. "Your thoughts, Bartolomeo."

"She was there. And it sounds like it happened a long time ago."

"Yes, but what about other survivors? Do you think there are others still alive?"

"You saw the same thing I did, Nikos. She couldn't answer. Or wouldn't. If I had to guess, I'd say no. I'd say she was it."

He nodded. "I have the same feeling." He turned to Taggart. "I think we should keep this to ourselves for now, until she talks some more. Until we have something more definite. Okay?"

"Whatever you say, Captain."

"Bartolomeo?"

"Absolutely."

"Taggart, you'll tell Dr. G.?"

Taggart nodded. "She'll understand. She won't want anyone bothering the old woman anyway."

"The next time she talks, you inform only Bartolomeo or me, understand?"

"I understand."

Nikos and I left the observation room together. As we

walked along the corridor, he said to me, "What else do you think, Bartolomeo?"

"Nothing, really. I don't see how it changes anything. Survivors or not, we can't leave that ship behind."

"Her story of being rescued might defuse the bishop's ranting about a malevolent ship out to kill us."

"But the probability of no survivors might also erode some of the more fragile support we have. I think it's too risky. I think we should do just what we're doing. Keep it quiet."

Nikos nodded. "Agreed, then. We keep this to ourselves."

44

THE face on my cabin's video screen was familiar, but I couldn't remember who she was. It was two o'clock in the morning, and I was still more than half asleep; pieces of a dream still floated through me—amorphous, phantom aliens drifting above me in a huge, spherical chamber while I hung onto a slippery metal ring for support; I was not wearing a pressure suit and I was holding my breath.

I rubbed at my eyes, switched on low light and the camera, and mumbled something incoherent even to me.

"I'm sorry about waking you," the woman said.

"I know you," I said, "but . . ."

"Catherine. Francis's sister."

It still took me a few moments, until I remembered talking to her in the ag room. I nodded. Then, realizing what time it was, I said, "Has something happened to him?"

"I don't know. I hope not. He asked me to contact you if he wasn't back in forty-eight hours. It's been almost that long, and he's not back."

"Back from where?" I had a sick feeling I knew what she was going to say.

"The alien ship."

I was completely awake now, though I still felt a buzzing through my limbs from being dragged out of deep sleep.

"You let him go?"

Catherine shook her head in disgust. "Come off it, Bartolomeo. You've met Francis. He decides to do something, who's going to stop him?"

She had a point, and I admitted as much. "So it's been two days since he went."

"Nearly. I just can't stop worrying about him. He's pretty self-sufficient, but it's been a long time."

"Try not to worry too much," I told her. "Forty-eight hours isn't really that long. He doesn't know the ship, and it would take a long time for him to make his way to the end of the explored areas, which is what I'd guess he would do. He's probably just working his way back now."

"How long are we supposed to wait?"

"I'm not going to wait," I assured her. "I'll suit up right now and get over there."

"I want to go with you."

I shook my head. "That would just slow me down. I know that damn ship inside and out. Or that part of it, anyway."

"What if something's happened to him? What if you need help?"

"Then I'll call for help. But I'll be able to get to him a lot faster on my own."

"Okay. Call me as soon as you know anything. Promise me that."

"I promise."

She gave me her com code. Her concern for Francis surprised me; the last time I'd talked to her I didn't get the impression they were very close. I was glad for Francis that she obviously *did* care so much for him.

"If anything's happened to him . . ."

"Don't worry," I said. "It doesn't do any good." It also wouldn't do any good to tell her not to worry, but I had to say it.

"Is it true, what we've heard?"

"What?" I had no idea what she was talking about.

"That we've actually docked with the alien ship, and that we're taking it with us?"

"Yes, it's true. Or mostly true. Nothing final has been decided yet."

"You people in charge of this ship are all crazy, you know that?"

"Why?"

"You figure it out, Bartolomeo. You're supposed to be so intelligent. But obviously you can't." She paused. "You're risking the lives of thousands of people. And for what? The trophy of an alien ship."

"It may be the greatest discovery mankind has ever made."

"It may be the *last* discovery the *Argonos* ever makes." She sighed heavily, resigned. "Just find my brother, Bartolomeo. Please."

"I will."

A N hour and a half later I was back at the air lock entrance to the alien starship. When the hatch slid open, I was not surprised to find the lamp on inside.

I pulled myself into the air lock and spoke over the open channel. "Francis? Are you in here? It's Bartolomeo."

No response. I didn't even hear breathing, but he could have closed the channel.

I didn't move for a long time, just hung there in the air lock, unwilling to close the hatch behind me so I could open the interior door and continue. I didn't understand why, but I did not want to have to do this; I did not want to work my way through all those rooms and passages. Maybe I was simply afraid of finding Francis dead in one of them. But it seemed more than that. Something like Father Veronica's nameless dread. All of my excitement and enthusiasm for exploring the alien ship was gone, replaced by disquiet and exhaustion. I wanted nothing more than to turn around, return to the *Argonos*, and go back to sleep.

But I couldn't. I finally turned the handle and watched the hatch close, cutting off the stars.

I worked my way quickly through the explored areas, following Francis's progress by the lights that were on in the rooms and corridors. Either he'd known the most direct route to the farthermost rooms, or he'd turned off the lights in the dead ends after he'd backtracked.

After a short time, I slowed a little. Not by choice, but because the dread returned and seemed to drag on my limbs, although I was still in zero gravity. Damn him. I moved slowly but steadily from room to room, passage to passage. As I continued, I periodically called out Francis's name, but never got a response. If not for the lights, I would have believed there was no one in the ship.

It took me two hours to reach the section with Earth-normal gravity and atmosphere. I was already sweating, and it got worse; in normal gravity, I was working harder just to move.

I found Francis in the circular blue-lit room. He was sitting on the steps holding his head in his hands; his pressure suit lay on the floor halfway across the room. He heard me come through the doorway and looked up.

The blue light was dim, but I could see the haunted look in his eyes. Something was terribly wrong. I wasn't sure he knew where he was.

"Francis." Then I realized he couldn't hear me and switched on the external speakers. "Francis, it's Bartolomeo."

He didn't respond. His expression didn't change.

"Francis, put your suit back on. We don't know what's in this air." I spoke gently, afraid to spook him.

His mouth turned up slightly and he said, "I'm still alive, aren't I?"

I started toward him. "Put it on, Francis."

"I needed air," he said.

"You've got air in the suit," I said.

"I needed air," he repeated.

I sat beside him. "What happened, Francis?"

He turned to me, his expression still haunted. "What are *you* doing here?"

"Looking for you. Your sister called me."

"Oh. It's been that long?"

"It has. Francis, what happened?"

He buried his head in his hands again. He mumbled something I couldn't understand.

"What did you say?"

He raised his head and without looking at me said, "Go see for yourself."

"Where?"

"Past the place you people got stuck. One of the doors just opened when I tried it. A couple more empty rooms, then an air lock." He breathed in deeply, then slowly exhaled. "Be careful. You lose air and heat and gravity all over again."

I was afraid to leave him alone, but I had to go see. Besides, I told myself, he'd been alone here for hours, and he was still alive.

"I'll be right back," I told him.

I stood waiting in the air lock, weightless and unsure, reluctant to work the bar in the wall which would open the door. What had Francis seen? I was afraid to find out.

I had a single lantern with me. After breathing deeply once, then again, I reached forward and grabbed the bar. I pulled and turned it, and the door slid open.

A short empty passage that angled to the right. I pulled myself into it, drifted along until I reached the angle. Ten meters farther on, the passage ended, opening up into darkness. I moved slowly forward and stopped at the opening.

I held up the lantern, but its dim light did not penetrate deeply into the darkness beyond. I had the sense of an immense room, but that was all. I maximized the lantern's brightness, and the light radiated somewhat farther, but only revealed that the room was even larger than I'd thought. Something like a strange, frozen mist seemed to swallow the light from the lantern.

I held the lantern out past the opening to confirm there was no gravity. The lantern remained weightless in my hand, but as an extra precaution I released it. It hung in the air before me, turning slightly. No gravity. I put my head into the room, looked around the opening, and saw only walls that extended beyond the reach of the lantern light; no floor or ceiling was yet visible. I took hold of the doorway and pulled myself into the room.

I hung there in front of the opening, searching the emptiness before and above and below me. Nothing happened, nothing changed. But I knew there was something out there. I breathed very deeply once, set my boot against the wall behind me, and kicked off into the gloom.

As I moved forward, a deep blue luminescence slowly bloomed, filling the open space as if my entrance had triggered it. The strange mist itself seemed to glow with the blue light, revealing this place at last. The room was enormous, a vast artificial cavern whose dimensions were still unclear. The light continued to grow, then stabilized, slightly brighter than the blue-lit room where Casterman had killed himself, and where Francis now waited for me. Like the *Argonos* corridors at night. As my eyes adjusted to the light, and as I continued to drift steadily across that huge cavern, I finally saw on the distant wall what Francis had seen.

Bodies. Human bodies. Men and women and children naked, blue and gray and dusted with ice crystals twinkling in the faint light, the bodies impaled on hooks like the skeletons of the dead infants back on Antioch.

Rows of them on the far wall, row after row both rising and descending until I could no longer see them in either direction. Thousands of mutilated corpses preserved in this cold dark chamber for who knew how many years, how many decades. Preserved for what purpose? Why would they let us discover this? Why *now*?

I drifted closer, paralyzed, unable to think, unable to stop myself, unable to look away. The bodies stared back at me with open, frozen eyes glittering with a false life. Drawing me to them.

Vicious metal spikes protruded from broken ribs and ragged flesh. Other wounds decorated their bodies, their faces: bloodless gashes, deep holes rimmed with scorched and blackened skin, blossoms of deep blue-black and purple, broken limbs and broken fingers with jagged bone visible in the open wounds, torn and shadowed sockets that had once held eyes.

Still closer, still paralyzed. I felt pulled to them by my own horror.

Finally, when I was no more than a few meters from the nearest body, I found I could move again. But it was too late; I could not stop my momentum. I fumbled for the suit jets, but couldn't locate the controls and drifted toward the corpse of a man with flesh more bruised than not and a broken jaw twisted unnaturally to the side.

I panicked. I kicked out, I flailed with my arms, desperate to get away. The corpse's hand seemed to reach for me and I kicked again, making contact with its leg and sending myself at last back across the metal cavern.

Terrified and disoriented, I tumbled slowly across the deep blue abyss, the endless wall of tortured bodies flipping in and out of my vision. I may not have believed in God, but in those interminable moments I believed in Hell.

I made contact, stopped tumbling, and scrabbled for purchase on the wall just above the opening through which I'd entered. Trembling, I managed to hold myself against it, facing the smooth dark metal. I closed my eyes and didn't move for a long time. I was sick and dizzy.

And then, against my will, I slowly turned around to again face the horror of those innumerable mutilated bodies. I stared, and did not turn away for a long, long time. It was as if I felt an obligation, to them and to myself, to witness this, and to sear their images into my mind so I would never forget.

I dragged myself back into the air lock, shaking violently, barely able to control my own hands. Somehow I managed to work the wheel and the door sealed shut. My breathing was way too fast and irregular and I tried to slow it, concentrate on each breath, control it . . . control it. . . .

I needed gravity. I pushed myself across the air lock,

worked the other door, then pulled myself into the short corridor and back into normal gravity. I sealed the air lock door, then lay down on the corridor floor and stared up at the ceiling.

My breath was still ragged and loud, and I was feeling hot again. A clammy sweat broke out all over my body in places that didn't normally perspire—forearms, thighs, knees, every inch of skin, it seemed. I understood why Francis had taken off his suit.

There was something wrong here, terribly wrong. I thought about what the old woman had implied, that this ship, the aliens on this ship, had rescued her and others from Antioch where they were being slaughtered. They may have rescued them, and they may have kept her alive, but the aliens had surely killed all these others.

What had happened here?

I had to get out. *We* had to get out.

I pushed myself to my feet and staggered back to the blue-lit room. Francis was where I'd left him. He looked at me as I came through the doorway.

"You saw?"

"I saw. Get your suit on. We're going back."

"Was it this bad on Antioch?"

"No," I said.

And that's when my stomach tightened and turned on itself. Antioch. *Antioch*. The old woman had said she'd been rescued from Antioch. How had she known that's what we had called that world? I knew then that this ship was no longer dead, if it ever had been.

"Get your suit on, Francis. *Now*."

He nodded. He stood and walked across the room and began to work himself into his suit. All of his movements were slow and deliberate, like an awakening somnambulist; too slow for me, but I was afraid to rush him, afraid to sound afraid. I was sure that we were being watched, and I did not want to let whatever was watching think there was any panic, any rush to get away. It was crazy, but that's what I was thinking: show no fear, and we might get out alive.

I opened the command channel link to the *Argonos*, tried calling Communications. Nothing. I wondered if all the translators Hollings had set up were still functioning. Maybe something was blocking the transmission.

My heart was pounding, I felt my pulse thumping in my throat. Breathe slowly, I told myself, slowly. . . . I couldn't afford to lose control here.

Francis had his suit on, but held his helmet at his side, looking at me.

"Come on," I said.

"They did it, didn't they?" he said.

Don't say any more, I wanted to tell him. But my throat was stuck, I couldn't speak, I couldn't swallow.

"These aliens. They did this, they killed all those people in there, and they killed all those people on Antioch."

"Yes," I managed to say. "Get your helmet on now. We have to go."

"We can't take this ship with us," he went on. "They'll kill us."

I grabbed the helmet from him and put it over his head. Finally he reached up and worked the neck seals. I turned off the external speakers. "Is the open channel activated, Francis?"

"Yeah."

"Let's go. Quickly now. But don't run. Don't act like you're scared."

"I understand," he replied. "I'm *not* scared."

He really wasn't, I could tell, but I didn't know if that was a good thing. Maybe in the short run. I nodded, and we started off.

We didn't talk. We moved at a steady pace, turning lamps off as we went, as if we needed to conserve their batteries for our next excursion. Light ahead of us, darkness behind.

Every ten minutes I tried to contact the *Argonos*, but always without success. I was on edge, expecting at any moment . . . something, I didn't know what. A horde of aliens pouring out of a hatchway. Barriers sliding across our path, cutting us off. Sharp, vicious hooks springing from the walls.

Nothing happened, and I couldn't understand why. We continued unimpeded, the alien ship still empty, silent, and dead.

Finally, when we were only fifteen minutes and a few rooms from the outer air lock, I got through to the *Argonos*. I had them patch me through to Taggart at the med center. He wasn't there. I finally got him in his quarters, as sleepy as I had been when Catherine called me.

"Bartolomeo, why are—?"

"Listen to me, Taggart, this is important. The old woman from the ship."

"Sarah, yeah."

"Sarah, nothing. You've got to get up there right now and secure her room. Do *not* let her out of that room, do you understand?"

"Dr. G.'s probably in there with her. She's set up a cot and sleeps in there. Wants to make her feel safe."

"The old woman is plenty safe, Taggart. She's dangerous. Get Dr. G. out of there, I don't care what you have to do, get her out of there and get that damn room secure."

"Where the hell are you, Bartolomeo?"

"I'm on my way back to the *Argonos*. I'm inside the alien ship."

"Did you find something—?"

"And get her sedated."

"I'll secure the room, but I won't sedate her without authorization from the captain or the Executive Council."

"Fine, damn it, but at least secure the room!"

"I will," he said, and broke the connection. Then I had Communications patch me through to Nikos.

"Crash session of the Executive Council, Nikos. *Now.*"

"Where are you, Bartolomeo? Why isn't there any video?"

I patched through the suit camera transmission to him. "How's that for video?"

"You're in the alien ship? Who's that with you?"

"Never mind who. I'm on my way out. Just get the damn session called!"

"What is it, Bartolomeo?"

"I've got no time. But we're in trouble, Nikos. Just call it. And call Taggart, authorize him to sedate the old woman. I'll be there as soon as I can get in."

"The old woman? What—?"

"Just do it."

I broke the connection. Ten minutes later, we emerged from the hull of the alien ship and drifted away from it. We fired our suit jets, and headed back to the *Argonos*. Nothing tried to stop us.

45

I did not get a warm reception in the council chambers. Most of the council members had obviously been awakened, and none were happy about it. Someone had brought in two pots of coffee, and they were already working on the second. Even Toller looked annoyed—unhappy, no doubt, at being called away from the Church archives. He was about to get more than just annoyed.

"A crash session, and we have to wait for *him*," the bishop said, waving toward me. "I know we have a serious problem."

I looked at Nikos. "You talk to Taggart?"

"Yes, I gave him the order. He should be taking care of it right now."

"Taking care of what?" Costino demanded.

I ignored him and sat at the foot of the table. "Yes, we have a serious problem. The alien ship. We've got to undock from it, and we've got to get out of here."

I expected a sarcastic remark from the bishop, but he didn't say a thing. No one else did either. There must have been something in my tone that warned them. They all waited intently for me to explain.

I told them then what I'd seen, what Francis had discovered. I had difficulty talking about it, but I gave them enough detail so they would appreciate the enormity of what was there, and the implications. My pulse had become rapid again, and I felt dizzy. Breathe deeply, I told myself, breathe; this was no time to collapse.

When I had finished, Cardenas stood.

"Unless there is going to be some insane vote in the next five minutes, I'm going to get us undocked from that ship. Any objections?"

There weren't any, and she hurried from the room.

Susanna Hingen was the first to speak. "Okay, okay . . . the obvious conclusion is the aliens killed all the people you saw on their ship. But their ship is dead now. No signs of life. That's what we keep hearing. Doesn't it seem likely that something happened to them, to the aliens, that they've died out, or abandoned ship, something like that?"

Before anyone had a chance to respond, Nikos said, "What about what the old woman said, Bartolomeo?"

"What old woman?" Geller asked.

"Sarah," I answered.

"Sarah?" snapped Costino. "Who the hell is Sarah?"

"The old woman from the alien ship?" asked the bishop. As always, he understood more than the others. Or more quickly.

I nodded. "Yes, the old woman from the ship."

"I assume she started talking," the bishop said, "and you did not feel it necessary to inform us."

"Jesus Christ!" Costino exclaimed. "What the hell is going on around here?"

"Please don't use His name in that manner." The bishop's tone was stern and unyielding.

"I'm sorry. But what *is* going on?"

"Yes," Nikos said, "the old woman started talking. But she didn't say much. Dr. G. was with her. The old woman seemed to be comfortable with Dr. G., and she finally came around a little, and started talking. In Standard English. She said her name was Sarah. It was all a little disjointed, but she seemed to be saying that someone had been killing people on Antioch. Not aliens, but other people. Madmen,

she said. She said the aliens rescued her and others from
the slaughter. She also said she was a young woman at the
time, so it must have happened years ago." He paused.
"She said something had happened to the aliens, and they'd
apparently died."

"Antioch is the problem," I said. "The old woman said
'Antioch.' She said she'd been rescued from Antioch." I
left it there, hoping they would truly understand.

The bishop did, of course. "*I* gave that world the name
of Antioch," he said quietly. "I refuse to believe those
living there all those years ago had given it exactly the
same name."

I watched the understanding work its way through the
other council members. Even Michel Tournier got it; but he
was confused.

"What are you saying? That the old woman is . . . what?
She's an alien?"

"She isn't human," I said.

"What? The aliens look just like us?"

"I don't know, Michel; I won't even pretend to know.
It could be anything. An alien . . . essence animating an
old woman's body they kept alive. Or some creature that
can take on the form of an old woman. I . . . don't . . .
know. And it doesn't matter. What matters is, she isn't
human." I paused. "And we've got to get her off this
ship."

"How?" the bishop asked.

"I told Taggart to get Dr. G. out and secure the room,
and Nikos gave him the order to sedate the old woman."

"Then what?" asked Geller. "After she's sedated."

"Then we give her a burial," I said. "We seal her in
one of the coffins and jettison her from the ship. Just like
we did to Casterman."

"She'll die," Toller said.

"Yes, she will."

"What if you're mistaken? What if she's just what she
says she is? A confused, traumatized old woman who heard
someone mention Antioch?"

"I'm not mistaken."

Nikos tapped at the table controls and the wall screen came to life. A few moments later it was filled with Taggart's face.

"Damn, I'm glad it's you," he said. "I've been trying to get through, but I was told you were in emergency session and couldn't be interrupted. I told Communications the survival of the ship was at stake, but they didn't believe me. I'm not sure I believe it myself."

"You get Dr. G. out?" I asked.

"Yeah, I got her out." Dr. G. moved into the picture behind Taggart, nodding toward us. "As soon as I got her out and secured the room, I started pumping in an aerosol sedative. The old woman woke up and went crazy. She's been trying to get out ever since." He shook his head. "Only she's not an old woman. I don't know what she is, but she's definitely not human."

Without warning, Taggart switched the video, changing the transmission to the video from a camera in the room. The old woman was clawing at the door with a hand now larger and darker with thick, crusted talons. She appeared to have shrunk in height but gained bulk, limbs now heavily muscled; yet, except for the one hand, she still maintained human form. The talons made slight gouges in the metal, but it appeared the door would remain secure.

Taggart's voice cut in, although the picture didn't change. "I'm pumping in the sedative at maximum rate, but I don't know how long it will take to put her under." The woman picked up the chair and slammed it against the door, again and again. Her strength was incredible. "It'll get her eventually," Taggart said. "I hope to God before she manages to break out." He paused and switched the picture back to himself. "When she's under, then what do we do?"

"I'm sending a security team right now," Nikos said. He was already tapping out commands on the table. "They'll have a coffin. When you're certain, *absolutely* certain that thing is sedated, we'll send the team in. They'll seal her up in the coffin and dispose of her. Just hold on until they get there."

"We'll be all right here," Taggart said.

Nikos broke the connection, then finished tapping out the orders.

"Why don't we just kill it?" Susanna interjected.

Nikos shook his head. "We don't know what it would take to kill that thing. We don't know what would happen if we tried. Poison defense? Energy feedback? Shit, anything is possible. We don't take chances. Clean as we can make it."

"Should we attack the ship?" Tournier asked.

Everyone turned to look at him incredulously.

"Once we get undocked," he added. "Shouldn't we attack?"

"Michel," Nikos said, "I've wanted to tell you this many times over the years, and I'm going to tell you now. Sometimes, you have the brains of a carrot. Once we get undocked, we get the hell out of here as fast we can, period. We are not going to complicate this mess by launching an attack. We just might be able to get away without much trouble if we do nothing at all." He punched in more commands. "Unless I hear any objections, I'm ordering Navigation to set course and Engineering to run the drive start-up sequence." He glanced up, then back down at the table console and resumed keying.

We waited to hear from Cardenas, or Taggart, or maybe even someone else who would be calling through with more bad news. Time stretched painfully with the silence and tension.

Finally the wall screen flickered, and Cardenas appeared. She looked haggard. She was in a darkened control room, mute-lighted instrument panels in the background.

"We can't undock," she said.

"Explain," Nikos demanded.

"The docking mechanism has become nonfunctional. It does not respond to commands. We've been trying every alternative routing, but there is no response. The whole thing has gone dead."

"Diagnostics?"

"Dead also. I've got a team suiting up right now to go

out and try to disengage manually. If they can't do that, they've got equipment to cut and burn us the hell off that damn ship."

"Wait," Nikos said. "Hold off on the burning. That's too risky."

"We have no choice, Captain."

Nikos slowly nodded. We all knew Cardenas was right.

"All right," Nikos said. "Keep us informed."

"I will."

The screen blanked out. The silence and tension returned.

After some time, the bishop turned toward me and said, "You." He paused for a moment, then went on. "You are responsible for this. You've doomed us all."

"Don't be so damned melodramatic," Nikos said. "We're not dead yet."

The bishop laughed. "You don't think so? What world are you living in, Captain?" His expression turned hard and bitter. "We are all dead men."

With that he got up and left the room.

No one would look at me. No one except Nikos, who almost imperceptibly shook his head as if to say, Don't worry about it. But I couldn't blame them. We had taken votes, but this had been *my* idea, and I had persuaded the Planning Committee to go along.

"What do we do now?" Costino asked.

"We wait," Nikos replied. "The bishop shouldn't have gone. Our job isn't done."

Costino started the pot of coffee around. There was no cup for me, and no one offered to find one or have one brought in.

No one had the heart for small talk. Costino obsessively rubbed his right thumb and forefinger together while staring down into his own lap. Susanna bounced a leg up and down. Tournier chewed on his lip. Toller, Nikos, and Geller tried unsuccessfully to appear calm.

Costino finally broke the silence. "I'll do it," he said. "I'll ask the question no one wants to ask. What do we do if we can't break free? *I* don't have any good ideas. I don't even have any bad ideas. But we'd better start working on it, because I have a strong suspicion we're going to need an answer."

"Not now," Nikos said.

"Why not?"

"Because we may not have to deal with that. And even if the problem *does* arise, we can't anticipate the circumstances. For now, we just wait."

"Brilliant leadership from our captain."

"You want to take over, Costino, I will step down right now in your favor."

Costino's only response was to slump in his chair and jam his chin into his fist.

"Quarreling isn't going to help," Geller said quietly.

"Fine," said Costino. "Why don't *you* be captain? Hell, I'll gladly support you."

"This isn't the time for leadership changes."

The room lapsed into silence again. A few minutes later we were shaken by a rolling vibration. It persisted for two full minutes, rattling the coffee cups, shaking the chairs and table. I wondered if this was what an earthquake felt like. Then the vibrations abruptly ceased.

Nikos had started keying the console when Cardenas's face appeared on the wall.

"The alien starship is coming alive, Captain. We don't know whether that was engines starting up, or some other internal machinery, or what."

"What about the docking mechanism?"

"The crew's out there now. They've just started working on it. Nothing yet."

"Maybe we should call them back."

"No, Captain. If anything, it's become more imperative we find a way to break free. I've given them orders to continue."

"All right."

Cardenas's face disappeared.

"Maybe my idea of attacking is not so crazy after all," Tournier said.

"It's still not a good idea," Toller responded.

"And why not?"

"We're still locked together with that ship, that's why not. We risk damaging the *Argonos*. Retaliation's also much easier since we're so close."

"Launch missiles at those areas of their ship farthest away from us."

"To what end, Michel?"

"Maybe it'll frighten them enough to let us go."

Toller just shook his head.

"How do we know that's such a bad idea?" Costino asked. He was rubbing his thumb and finger again.

"It may come to something like that," Nikos said. "But we're not close. We've got alternatives. Give Cardenas's crew a chance. They may get it done."

The waiting dragged on, with increasing tension. I wanted to leave, to get away from the hostility and fear being directed indirectly at me. I didn't know how long I could stand it.

An hour passed, maybe more. People began to talk a little, trying to fill the void, but the conversations were forced and awkward. No one talked to me. Nikos might have, but he was at the far end of the table, which made it impossible.

A faint jolt; then another. We all turned expectantly to the wall screen. It remained dormant. Maybe it was nothing.

No such luck. There was no image, but Cardenas's voice came through the speakers. She was breathing hard.

"I haven't got much time," she said. "I'm suited up and on my way out. We don't know what happened, some kind of massive energy feedback, an explosion of some kind, some . . . we just don't know. The crew's down. Telemetry tells us we've got three dead, the others badly injured and crashing hard. No one's responding to our calls. We're on our way out to bring them back in."

"I'm on my way," Nikos said. "What kind of support do you need?"

"Nothing," Cardenas answered. "Med teams are on their way. You don't need to come, Captain. By the time you get here—"

Nikos cut her off. "I'm on my way," he repeated. "Ship damage?"

"None. And we're still docked. Whatever happened didn't damage the docking mechanism, didn't damage a damn thing except our people. We'll have to try something else later. . . . Okay, that's it. We're going out now."

"I'll be there as fast as I can."

The sound cut out; Cardenas was gone.

"Okay, *Captain*." It was Costino, leaning forward against the table. "Maybe now we'll have to start thinking about other alternatives."

"You start thinking, Costino. You come up with any ideas, you just let me know." Nikos turned to me. "Bartolomeo. Make sure the old woman gets taken care of."

I nodded and stood. Nikos stood as well, then said, "I declare this meeting adjourned."

As we left the council chambers, Costino called after us. "The bishop was right! We are all dead men!"

46

"**MAYBE** we shouldn't jet her," Taggart said, watching the old woman through the one-way glass.

The woman was on the floor of the room, apparently unconscious. A security squad, five-strong with a metal coffin, a wheeled cart, and a portable welder, waited in the corridor outside, all of them armed and armored and masked. The sedative was still pumping invisibly into the room; we weren't taking any chances. What did it matter if we overdosed and killed her?

I couldn't look away from the old woman, the alien. Unconscious, she was having difficulty maintaining human form. She shuddered occasionally, and with each shudder it seemed a wave of aborted form-changing rolled through her—her skin shivered and glistened, turning dark and rough; the contours of her limbs expanded briefly, taking on bulk; and her facial features came apart: the flesh flowed and darkened and threatened to take some new form. But before it did, before anything could establish itself, everything coalesced and she looked like an old woman again.

"Why not?" I asked Taggart.

"Maybe we could use her as a hostage. Negotiate with the aliens. We give her back, they let us go."

"It's a lousy idea," I said. "Negotiate?" If Taggart couldn't figure out for himself why it was such an idiotic idea, I didn't feel like explaining. I was sick of explaining, especially since I seemed to be wrong as often as not.

We waited another half hour, then I opened the door to the corridor and signaled the squad leader. I'd better be right about the timing, I thought; this section of the med centers had been sealed off from the rest of the *Argonos*. If I was wrong and that thing wasn't unconscious, or if it suddenly revived, we would be trapped here with it.

Taggart and I watched through the one-way glass as the mangled door was pushed open and the security squad entered the room, carrying the coffin. They moved quickly to the old woman, set the coffin beside her, and opened it. Four of them lifted her—one on each limb—and laid her inside. Another change-wave rolled through her, startling the squad and causing two of them to draw out stone burners; when the human form restabilized, they quickly closed the coffin lid and sealed it with the welder.

I turned to the security camera in the corner, nodded, and said, "We're on our way."

Taggart and I met the squad out in the corridor; I took the lead, Taggart the rear. I couldn't help thinking that the squad wasn't any larger than the one that had come to arrest me. We moved quickly along the corridor, doors opening before us and closing behind us—a moving secure-zone, the path cleared for us to the nearest ejection tube. I kept looking back, but the coffin didn't change. *Don't wake up,* I silently chanted to myself, *don't wake up . . .*

At every door I called in the "clear" signal after looking back at the squad. The door would open, we'd move through, Taggart would call in his signal, the door would close. A half hour that seemed much longer.

Finally at the hull, I keyed open the ejection tube. The squad inserted the coffin, and I keyed the panel closed. Now was when a few more words were usually spoken, a private eulogy for the closest friends and relatives of the newly dead. No words this time. I didn't hesitate.

I activated the chamber, and we felt the faintest tremor

as the coffin was expelled. The viewing monitor came to life and we anxiously watched the gleaming silver vessel streak away from the *Argonos*, a tiny metal bullet hurled into the darkness of space.

The trajectory was away from both the *Argonos* and the alien vessel. I half expected some glowing energy beam to lance out from the other ship, capture the coffin, and draw it back into its interior. But nothing like that happened. The coffin continued to sail away from us unimpeded until, like every coffin ejected from the ship, it dwindled, dwindled, then finally disappeared altogether.

I caught up with Nikos and Cardenas in the chaos of the med center crisis ward. All of those still living were being attended to, and the three of us went down a passage for some privacy and quiet.

Five crew members were dead now, and two others probably wouldn't make it to the end of the day; the other four were stage five critical, and had a chance. The explosion, if that's what it was, had ruptured suits and helmets and sent them all careening away from the ship; two of the dead had only recently been located.

"The old woman?" Nikos asked me.

"Gone."

"At least that worked."

"We've got to try something else to break free of that ship," Cardenas said.

"Any ideas?"

She shrugged. "Send remotes to attach explosives. Damage to the *Argonos* is more than acceptable." She paused. "My guess is that won't work. Then maybe try firing explosives at the docking mechanism; that would cause us even more damage, but still acceptable. That may not work either. So then we set charges *inside* the *Argonos*. Blow off the forward sections of the ship." She shook her head. "I don't like that one bit, but we may have no choice. It should break us free, but it'll cripple us somewhat, and by that time who knows what kind of response we'll have pro-

voked." She paused. "We have no good options that I can
see. But I am more than open to suggestions."

"What about attacking their ship?" Nikos asked.

"I don't know. Riskier to the *Argonos* as a whole, I'd
think. A full-out battle with that ship? Not good odds for
us, but it may come to that. Or they may attack us first, so
there wouldn't be much of a decision. My own opinion,
attacking their ship would only be a last resort."

"Bartolomeo?"

"I can't argue with anything Margita's said."

Nikos was working through the options, and Cardenas
was waiting for orders. I was reflecting on all the mistakes
I'd made, and wondering if there was any way I could make
up for them; in despair, I knew there wasn't.

"As far as I'm concerned," Nikos said, "we are in a
state of war. I'm not going to the Executive Council for
approval of any of my decisions. Will that be a problem
with the crew?"

Cardenas shook her head. "Not at all, Captain. The ship
is yours."

He nodded. "The remotes first."

Cardenas nodded in return. "Right away, sir." She
turned and left the room.

Nikos looked at me with concern. "We're in deep trouble, Bartolomeo."

I searched desperately for Father Veronica. Queries went
out to everyone I knew, to every place I could think
of. No one had seen her for days. Then I finally thought to
try the place I should have remembered earlier, a place
where no queries would reach—the Wasteland.

The Wasteland was hot and dry, as always. Sand the
color of rust, boulders and stones bleached by an appari-
tional sun, and the palest blue- and rose-tinted sky; scraggly
trees, stunted purple cacti, dense low bushes of thorns; a
horizon that stretched into the rising waves of heat.

I closed the hatch over the metal stairs of one of the
ground entrances, then turned a complete circle, my gaze

sweeping across the shimmering expanse. The sun was far along its downward arc on my right. I saw no movement, heard nothing but a faint hiss of sand as a faint breeze eddied past my feet.

"Father Veronica!" I called. No response. I turned and called again. "Father Veronica!" Then twice more with the same results.

I felt certain she was here. I picked out a cluster of rocks in the distance, flanked by spindly brush, and walked toward it.

The place was disconcertingly quiet, especially after all the chaos and noise of the previous hours. The heat seemed to bake all sound out of the air so that I barely heard my own footsteps in the coarse sand. Within minutes I was sweating and thirsty.

When I reached the cluster of rocks, there was no sign of Father Veronica. A pipe with a spigot emerged from the ground. I opened it and eventually cold water trickled forth. I drank deeply, splashed water across my face and neck, then closed the spigot. A six-legged lizard scuttled out from the shade and stopped at my feet. Its thin, forked tongue flicked out and lapped at the spilled moisture already drying in the heat, then it scuttled back out of sight.

The largest rock wasn't more than two meters high, but it would offer a slightly better view. I climbed it and surveyed the surrounding desert. Far away were two groupings of rocks and cacti; a flash of white came from the larger grouping. I called out Father Veronica's name again, but there was still no answer. I climbed down and headed for them.

It took me half an hour to reach the two groupings; they hadn't seemed that far away. The larger consisted of several massive boulders interspersed with light purple spined cacti. Caught on the spines of a half-dead cactus was a scrap of white cloth; between two of the boulders was another water spigot, but nothing else.

"I'm here, Bartolomeo."

Her voice came from the smaller cluster of rocks, which was only a few meters away. She rose to her feet from the shelter of a large boulder, brushing sand and dust from her cassock. She looked tired and drawn, thinner somehow, but also very beautiful. My heart ached as I realized we had not spoken even once since the excursion outside the ship to view the illuminated stained glass.

I walked over to her. She'd made a small camp nestled in among the rocks—sleeping mat, canteen, and a large satchel presumably filled with food packets and personal items.

"Looking for me?" she said with a tired smile.

I nodded. "How long have you been here?"

"Six days."

"Things have changed. A lot has happened just in the last fifteen or twenty hours. You should know what's going on with the alien ship."

"I already know," she replied. "Bishop Soldano has kept me informed."

"He came out here?"

"No. I've got a private com unit with me. With all that's been happening, it would have been irresponsible to just disappear. I told Bishop Soldano I needed to get away, and told him to contact me if it became necessary." She shrugged. "I'm preparing to return in a couple of hours. I'll be needed."

"I'll stay and help," I told her.

She shook her head. "The preparation is mental, Bartolomeo. I'm not ready to offer either counsel or comfort to anyone right now, and I'll need to be."

"Doubts again?"

"Always doubts. They change, but they're always there." She paused. "But so there is no misunderstanding, the doubts are personal . . . not spiritual."

"What do you mean by personal doubts?"

"They're personal." She crossed her arms and held herself. The sun was setting, but it was not cooling off. "How bad is it, Bartolomeo?"

"I thought the bishop told you."

"He's not always reliable. He would exaggerate if he thought it would benefit him."

I shook my head. "I don't see how he could have exaggerated."

She took a few steps to the side and sat on a low, flat stone, half in shadow, half in sunlight. I sat beside her, all in sun, and looked at my shadow stretched out for several meters across the sand. Exhaustion suddenly threatened to overwhelm me, aided by the heat. I had not slept since being awakened by Catherine, and the day had been long. My eyes wanted to close, my body wanted to lie down on the warm sand.

"Sometimes," Father Veronica said, "when I come here and look out across the desert, I think that maybe this place actually *does* go on forever, that we've been told it doesn't, told that it's just a visual effect, because it would be too much for us to comprehend. Too much for our minds to accept. *I* could accept that, I think. I might even welcome it." She turned to look at me. "What do you think our chances are of breaking away from their ship?"

"Not very good. We're going to try several courses of action, each one more drastic than the one preceding. Maybe one of them will work. I would guess that none of them will. I have no particular evidence for that. Just a gut feeling."

She nodded slowly. "What will happen then?"

"I don't know. I think it's likely that we will attack their ship, although since we're docked to it the logistics will be difficult, and since we know nothing about it or its possible vulnerabilities, any plan of attack will be arbitrary. I don't hold out much hope for that, either."

"Attack before they attack us?"

"Probably. No one will want to wait."

"But they haven't taken any actual hostile actions yet, have they?"

"They won't let us go. Some people would characterize that as hostile by itself. And when we sent a crew out to manually disengage, there was an explosion of some kind that killed five and badly injured the others. That's hostile enough to me."

Father Veronica wasn't convinced, or was trying hard

not to be convinced. "Perhaps that was just an act of defense against what *they* interpreted as hostile action directed against them."

"Did the bishop tell you what I found in their ship?"

She turned her head away and nodded.

"I think their intentions are clear," I said.

"That must have been awful, Bartolomeo. Once was almost unbearable. I can't imagine what twice must have been like."

"A reminder that the first time was real," I told her. "A reminder I didn't want or need."

We sat in silence, our shadows lengthening as the sun continued to descend at our backs. Faint stars appeared in the darkening sky.

"I've never been here at night," I said.

"It's peaceful. And awe-inspiring. It makes me feel quite small, which is sometimes a good thing." She turned back to me. "If our attack on their ship fails, what will we do then?"

"Wait for them."

"Will we be able to defend ourselves?"

I just shrugged. We were far too deep into unknowns and uncertainties. "Maybe it won't come to that."

She nodded. "It's nice to think so." She sighed heavily. "I need to be alone now, Bartolomeo."

"All right." I felt stupid and selfish for staying as long as I had. I stood, looked down at her for a few moments. My heart was aching again. I wanted to say something more, but I had no idea what it should be. I turned away from her and left.

47

THE alien ship remained strangely quiescent except for a rolling vibration that started up every few hours, continued for two or three minutes, then ceased abruptly. No lights appeared anywhere on the hull, nothing emerged from the ship, nor were there any other signs of activity—no indications of a long dormant ship coming back to life. But we knew it was doing precisely that.

NIKOS, Cardenas, and I watched the launch of the remotes from the command salon. Close-up tracking was displayed on the monitors, but we preferred the direct view through the steelglass dome. Laden with explosives, two dozen remotes—looking very much like three-limbed, gleaming metal crustaceans—emerged behind us one at a time from the hull of the *Argonos*, then flew over the command salon, rockets flaring sporadically as they adjusted course.

"We probably need to have three or four get through," Cardenas said.

The trajectories and speeds were randomized; with their erratic flight paths above and around us, they appeared out of control, like crazed animals scattering in fear from a fast and powerful beast, but they all had the same destination—the docking mechanism.

"Only three or four?" Nikos asked, as if it would be too easy.

Cardenas just shook her head in response.

The remotes flew chaotically beyond us and indirectly toward the bow of the *Argonos*. One plunged toward the ship, and I thought it would crash into the hull. Just before impact it veered away and shot forward, accelerating toward the bow only a few meters above the ship's surface.

Suddenly even the chaos fell apart, as if the remotes had abruptly gone mad. They began to quiver and wobble, spinning and arcing away from both the *Argonos* and the alien ship.

Nikos slapped the command channel open. "Kirilen! What's going on?"

"Don't know, sir," a man's voice replied. "We've lost control of them. They're not responding to any commands."

The remotes continued to disperse, tumbling farther from the two ships, growing smaller and smaller. Mechanical diaspora.

"Are you still trying, Kirilen?" Nikos asked.

"Still trying. Still nothing, sir. We've lost them."

The remotes were gone from our view; tiny images still appeared on the monitors, but even those were shrinking rapidly.

"Kirilen."

"Nothing, sir."

A series of small, bright flashes sparked in the black sky above us.

"Explosives have detonated, sir," Kirilen announced. "All of them. They're all gone."

Nothing left. Nothing. The monitors showed nothing except two untouched starships.

Cardenas shrugged. "Yes, Captain, three or four. Zero didn't quite get it done."

THERE was still no activity from the alien ship. Over the next several hours, preparations were made to launch guided missiles at the docking mechanism, which included evacuating the three most forward levels.

Again, we observed the attack from the command salon, although this time, since the missiles would be launched from the opposite side of the *Argonos*, we watched on the monitors.

Nikos gave the order. The missiles were launched, blasting out from cylinders in the stern and initially heading away from the ship. Then they altered course, sweeping around and heading straight for our bow and the docking mechanism.

As with the remotes, the guidance systems failed long before the missiles reached their target. Attitude jets fired randomly, sending the missiles weaving in all directions. Three missed the ships entirely, but several actually struck the *Argonos*, although nowhere near the docking mechanism, and rebounded from the ship; fortunately, none of the warheads detonated.

The last missile, purely by accident I am certain, actually continued directly toward the bow of the *Argonos,* very near the docking mechanism.

"Detonate!" Nikos shouted over the command channel. "Detonate that warhead!"

Five seconds . . . No response.

"Detonate!"

Ten seconds.

"Nothing, sir."

The missile struck the ship at a shallow angle, but without detonating; it caromed away and joined the others, tumbling into space where they all quickly disappeared from sight and eventually could not be detected at all.

S T I L L , nothing from the alien ship. I thought about what Father Veronica had suggested in the Wasteland, and I could understand how an argument might be made that the aliens (or, I suppose, the alien ship's systems, in an automated response mode), were taking only defensive actions, and that their lack of any other overt action was an indication that they meant us no harm.

But I had seen all those bodies in their ship, the frozen and mutilated corpses, along with all those on Antioch, and I knew the aliens were responsible for them. I'd also seen that old woman who was clearly not an old woman, and I *knew*. I had made mistakes, and I had been wrong about any number of things, but I was not wrong about this. We might not understand what they were doing, or why they had not yet made an overt attack or attempt to board us, but I knew it was only a matter of time. They would come after us—in stealth or in a frontal attack, singly or in hordes. They would come.

I met with Cardenas and Nikos after the failure of the missiles. We went to a viewing room much like the command salon where we could sit and look out at the alien ship. Cardenas looked haggard—her face was drawn, the skin beneath her eyes puffy and dark. Nikos didn't look much better. I wondered how *I* looked.

"When was the last time you slept, Margita?" Nikos asked.

She shrugged. "Don't know, and it doesn't matter."

"It *does* matter. We need to remain alert. Take a one- or two-hour sleep tab whenever there's a lull. That's what I've been doing. You, too, Bartolomeo. Anything will help."

"Sure thing, Captain," Cardenas said. "Now let's talk about something important—what we do next."

Nikos sighed in resignation. "Fine, Margita. What *do* we do next? Blow off the forward levels of the *Argonos*, if I remember right."

"That's the plan." She gave a tired laugh. "Hopefully we won't be blowing off too much of the ship. I'm not surprised nothing's worked so far. They were able to detect explosives directed at them, and their technology to deal with them is obviously better than ours. But I don't see how they'll be able to stop this, because this time we'll set off explosives in *our* ship.''

Nikos gestured for her to continue. ''Just tell us what needs to be done.''

''As a precaution, we evacuate three more of the forward levels.''

''That'll mean personal cabins. They won't like that.''

''Too damn bad. And we can't give them time to take anything with them. Tell them it's only a precaution, and that their cabins will be intact afterward. It's probably true. Just get them out. Hell, if they don't want to get out, screw 'em, let them die.''

''Then what?''

''While that's happening, we place shaped charges on the interior walls of the hull, in a ring around the area of the docking mechanism. Two rings, actually. And we go an extra level deep. Make sure every hatch in the top few levels is sealed. We're going to rupture the hull, we're going to blow a big hole in it. If the docking mechanism remains intact, it won't matter, because we'll have blown off that section of the ship.'' She cocked her head at Nikos. ''The drives and engines are still ready, yes?''

''Yes.''

''Good. As soon as we break loose, we'll want to get out of here faster than hell. The crew and security soldiers will be at battle stations.''

''Battle stations,'' Nikos repeated with a shake of his head. ''I didn't believe we'd ever resort to that on this ship. Drills, theory, irregular practice runs on weapons . . . I wonder what the real thing will be like. I wonder how people will perform.''

''We're going to find out soon enough, Captain.''

SEVEN hours later, everything was ready. I joined Nikos, Cardenas, and a small operations team in the emergency bridge. The bridge was small and dark, the only lights coming from instrument panels and tiny, focused hazard lights. Kirilen manned the main controls. Small monitors displayed images of the area around the docking mechanism.

Nikos nodded, and Kirilen keyed in the codes to arm the charges. Red lights flashed in front of him, indicating they were armed. Nikos looked around the dark room once more. He turned back to Kirilen and nodded again.

Kirilen pressed the detonation switches and we all tensed, waiting for the shock to hit us. Seconds passed. Too many seconds. We felt nothing, not even the slightest jolt.

The red lights continued to flash. Kirilen pressed the switches again. Ten more seconds. Still nothing.

"Son of a bitch!" Nikos said. "What happened?"

"Nothing, sir. Nothing at all."

"Again, damn it!"

Kirilen punched the switches. Nothing. Nikos looked at Cardenas.

"I can't believe it," she whispered. "They *can't* have known. They *can't* have deactivated those charges inside our own ship. They *can't* . . ." Her voice trailed off. Her expression was blank, her gaze unfocused. Then she turned and stared at the still flashing red lights.

"Sir?" Kirilen asked, waiting for orders.

No one answered him.

"Margita?" Nikos said.

She blinked once, then finally looked up. She stared at him, her expression still unchanged. "I don't know, Captain."

She straightened, the sounds of her back cracking loud in the small room, then walked to the door and opened it, letting in a wide beam of dim corridor light. As she went through the door she stopped and turned back. "I'm going to take your earlier advice and get some sleep. If I come up with any other ideas, I'll let you know." She paused. "But I wouldn't count on it." Then she turned and walked out.

Nikos turned to me. "Bartolomeo?"

"Think the bishop still wants to be captain?" It was the only thing I could think to say.

It did get half a smile from him. ''Go get some sleep, Bartolomeo.''

''And you?''

''I will, too. I doubt anything will happen soon—they don't seem to be in any hurry—but I've got to set the watch.'' He looked at the flashing red arming lights. ''In twelve hours, Executive Council session. Assuming nothing's come up before then.''

''I'll be there.''

48

I slept for six hours, and could have slept six more. When I emerged from my quarters, I could feel the change—a stifling, acrid and electric bite to the air. Fear.

In the corridor not more than fifty meters from my quarters, an old woman lay facedown against the wall, arms cradling her head. I shuddered, fearing for a moment that the old woman from the alien ship had returned, teleporting herself from her coffin back into the *Argonos*. But the hair color was wrong, the clothes were different, and she was shorter than the alien had been.

The woman was murmuring to herself, punctuating indistinct words with tiny, quiet, barking sounds. As I passed her, she turned her head, exposing her face and staring at me. She looked familiar, but I couldn't place her.

"*Cantus astronomicus, domine astronomy . . .*"

She was chanting what seemed to be a mix of ersatz Latin and Standard. I knelt beside her.

"Can I help you?"

She stopped her chanting and closed her eyes. "No one can help me," she said, quite distinctly. "No one can help any of us. We're drowning in the whirlpool of the universe.'' She turned her face back to the wall and resumed her murmured chant.

I tried to check in with Nikos, but he was unavailable. There was no emergency, or at least no new one, so I didn't pursue it. Cardenas was also unreachable. When I tried to contact Pär, his com system answered, but there was no video.

"Pär, are you there? You all right?''

No answer. I broke the connection and headed for his rooms. On my way to the lower levels I passed through corridors so empty and quiet it seemed the *Argonos* was deserted, and others so crowded and noisy and panicky, I was afraid a riot was about to break out. Nothing was normal.

I found Pär reeling drunk, clutching a whiskey bottle. He could hardly keep his eyes open, and couldn't walk. He half rolled, half crawled across the floor after he let me in, then pulled himself up onto a chair.

"Tried calling you,'' he said. Surprisingly there was no slur to his words, but his voice was faint and hoarse. "No response. Calls denied. Couldn't remember override.''

"I was sleeping.''

He looked at me with one half-open eye. "How can you sleep?''

"Exhaustion. And timed sleep tabs.''

"Drank too much,'' he muttered, the eye closing. His head rolled back so that he would have been staring at the ceiling if his eyes had been open. "Hate being this drunk.''

I went into the bathroom and at the meds console punched up a mega-vites patch and a three-hour sleep patch.

"Your turn to sleep now,'' I told him when I came back.

I took the bottle out of his hand (it was empty, anyway), pressed the patches to his neck, and helped him to the bed. He didn't resist. Eyes still closed, he waved a hand at me, but said nothing.

"I'll be back later, Pär.'' I turned the lights down and left.

T H E cathedral was nearly full; a sense of fear and despair permeated the atmosphere. The bishop was speaking, but I didn't pay much attention—something about the arbitrary nature of God's mercy and the wages of sin. If anything, he was making those in the cathedral even more frightened.

I sat in the last pew in one of the side sections. There was a crackle in the nearest speaker so that the bishop seemed to spit and sputter as he spoke; then it cleared up, and his voice came through loud and resonant.

Nearly all the people around me appeared to be downsiders. Entire families huddled together. Younger children squirmed in their seats, and infants slept or fussed in their parents' arms. A few of the older children listened intently, their faces marked with confusion and concern, trying to understand what was happening to them. Most of the adults, however, seemed resigned. How many here were nonbelievers searching desperately for a new faith? How many were believers praying for a miracle? How many had simply given up all hope?

The bishop finished his speech or sermon or rant or whatever it was, and turned the pulpit over to Father Veronica. She stood for a minute or two in silence, looking out over the congregation. When she began to speak, her voice was steady and calm.

"We are all frightened," she began, "afraid of what may happen to us. It is nothing to be ashamed of. It is normal. It is *human*.

"There is a strange and mysterious ship out there, manned by strange and mysterious beings we have never seen. We are trying to escape from them, and it is likely they mean us harm. As much as anything, though, our fear comes from uncertainty: we do not know what will happen to us, or when. We do not know if we will be able to defend ourselves. We do not know."

She paused, her gaze again sweeping across everyone in the cathedral.

"I won't tell you *not* to be afraid," she resumed. "But I want to remind you of what we *do* know. Of what we know about ourselves, and what we know about what will happen to us.

"We are the children of God. It is very possible that those alien beings are *also* children of God. Perhaps they have lost their way. Perhaps they do not understand us, perhaps there is something critical they do not understand about themselves. Perhaps they do not understand what God wants from them. After all, sometimes *we* don't understand. Sometimes *we* lose our way.

"The most important thing to remember now is that no matter what happens to us, or when, in the end we will be with Him. Our souls will go on, in life eternal. Our suffering will end, our pain will end, and we will dwell forever with peace and joy and love in His Kingdom."

I sensed a change gradually manifesting itself in the people around me as she spoke. The fear eased—not completely, but perceptibly, little by little as a sense of peace gradually suffused the cathedral.

Father Veronica continued to speak. I don't remember much of what she said after that, but I will never forget the effect she had on those who were in the cathedral. She accomplished what the bishop had utterly failed at—she eased their fears, she calmed and comforted them, and she renewed their faith, both in God and in themselves.

I felt proud for her, and admired her more than ever. But I also felt increasingly uncomfortable and guilty. I still did not believe, although at that moment I wished I could, and I felt I did not belong in that place of worship with everyone else.

I rose to my feet and walked out of the cathedral.

S EVERAL hours later I returned to Pär's quarters. He was sober and freshly showered, his hair still damp, and he was drinking coffee.

"I'm ashamed," he said.

"There's nothing to be ashamed of," I told him.

He snorted. "When I heard, I thought to myself, 'What's the point of being sober? So I started drinking, and couldn't stop." He poured me a cup of coffee, refilled his own.

"I . . ." He sighed and gave me something like a smile. "I thought I was better than that."

"You're as good as any of us, Pär. And better than most. I slept, you drank, and hundreds of people have gone to the cathedral to find comfort in God."

"You've been there?"

"Just now. The bishop was useless, making people even more terrified. But Father Veronica managed to give them what they needed—comfort. Eased their fears. Gave them some peace."

Pär nodded thoughtfully. "I wish I could find comfort in faith," he said. "I used to think that religion was for the ignorant, but I've seen some intelligent people who have a sincere belief in God. Father Veronica's at the top of that list."

"So why is it she can't convince either one of us?" I asked.

He shook his head. "You and I will never believe, Bartolomeo."

"No," I agreed. "We won't."

I checked the wall clock. "Sorry, Pär, but I have to go. Nikos has called for a council session."

"Ah," he said. "Brilliant minds working together to solve all problems. I'm sure you'll figure out something to save our asses."

"Yeah. I'm sure we will."

Pär just shook his head again, and I left.

EVERYONE was there, and everyone was exhausted. Most also appeared to have already given up. Bishop Soldano stared at me with a barely controlled malice that made me distinctly uncomfortable.

"Everyone rested?" Nikos asked. "Good," he said without waiting for answers. "I'm open to ideas."

No one knew how to respond. Nikos had been so abrupt, and at the same time almost nonchalant.

"There's only one thing left to do," Michel Tournier said, his voice rising. "What I *tried* to suggest before. We attack them. Now. We have plenty of weapons, we're not defenseless. We have the Metzenbauer Field to protect us. It's so damned obvious, and I don't understand what we're waiting for.''

"It's not damned obvious," Toller said. "You really think an attack on their ship has any chance of success? After what happened with the remotes and the missiles?"

"We have to try," Tournier insisted. "What else can we do? Just wait for them to come and slaughter us?"

"No, we *don't* have to try," Toller said. "We haven't made any direct attack on them, and that may be the main reason they have not attacked *us*. We don't have any idea what they're thinking, or *how* they think. Attacking them may provoke just the kind of response you're most afraid of.''

"I'm willing to take that chance, and I would wager that most of the council—"

"It doesn't matter," Nikos broke in. "We've already tried it."

Faces turned quickly to him.

"What do you mean?" Costino asked.

"I decided not to wait. I have the authority. Margita and I carried out a full weapons attack on the alien ship."

Toller smiled wryly and nodded. "Successful, was it, Captain?"

"Missiles and rockets and bomb clusters all detonated long before they reached the alien ship. Lasers and radiants and vibrationals were deflected or absorbed without effect. We launched three full strikes, and not one thing got through."

"All those explosions?" Tournier said in disbelief. "I didn't hear or feel anything."

Costino sneered at him. "You understand the concept of a vacuum, Michel?"

Tournier just looked confused, but no one was going to explain it to him.

Nikos shrugged. "That is why I'm open to ideas. I don't have any more myself. I am hoping *someone* will."

"Pray," the bishop eventually said.

No one else said anything. Nikos stood and paced deliberately back and forth at the head of the table.

"I know it seems hopeless. It may *be* hopeless. But I will not give up. And *you* will not give up. We'll reconvene every twelve hours to talk about possibilities and impossibilities, sooner if someone comes up with anything. In between, *think*. No idea is too strange or ridiculous. An unworkable idea may inspire in someone else an idea that *will* work."

He stopped pacing, swept his gaze slowly around the room, letting it rest briefly on each of us. "I am the captain of this ship, and I will not give up." He paused. "Questions?" When no one spoke up, he said, "We'll meet again in twelve hours. I expect everyone to be here."

49

FOR the second time in less than a week, I was torn from a deep sleep, this time by a relentless pounding at the door. I lay in bed with my eyes closed, hoping the pounding would stop. It didn't.

I staggered in darkness from the back room, through the front, and opened the door. Fortunately it was still shipboard night and the corridor lights were dimmed, but I still had to blink against the light, trying to focus on the man who stood before me. He looked familiar. One of the church clerics, I thought.

"I have a message from Father Veronica," he said. He handed me a sealed tube.

I stared stupidly at the metal tube, then looked up. "Why?" I asked. "Why didn't she call?"

"I don't know. I was just asked to deliver it to you." He paused, then bowed his head slightly and said, "Good night." He turned and left.

I closed the door and felt my way to my reading chair, dropped into it, and turned on the wall lamp, low illumination. In the dim light I cracked open the tube and withdrew a single sheet of vellum. Handwritten in violet ink, the strokes long and beautiful, was a brief message:

Bartolomeo,

Please, meet me as soon as possible in the cathedral. It is urgent.

Veronica

I was suspicious. Why would she send a messenger rather than call me? Then I remembered that I had programmed my system to deny all calls except from Nikos or Cardenas. Maybe she *had* tried. I was still suspicious, though I could not have articulated why.

Suspicious or not, I could not ignore the message. I showered, dressed, and headed for the cathedral.

I had expected the cathedral to still be filled with people who had come for comfort, who would be afraid to leave, as if sanctuary in the church would somehow protect them from whatever horrors awaited at the hands (or other appendages) of the alien creatures biding their time. But I passed dozens of people camped in the surrounding corridors, and the massive cathedral doors were closed, posted with a sign.

CATHEDRAL CLOSED UNTIL 0600. MASS AT 0730, 1100, 1330, 1800.

I tried opening the doors, desperate eyes watching me, but the doors would not move.

"Help us," an old man pleaded.

I looked at him, not knowing what to say.

"No one can help us now," another man growled. "We're doomed. We're wasting our time out here." He gestured at me with his bearded chin. "It's people like him got us into this mess."

I remained silent, at a loss for a response.

"Forget it, Strekoll," said a woman seated at the younger man's feet. She cradled a three-year-old girl sleeping open-mouthed, thin curls plastered to her forehead with sweat. "We have nothing better to do."

I walked away from them. The other two regular entrances would be locked as well, so I'd have to find another way in. Seventy-five meters from the cathedral doors I turned down a short dead-end corridor, stopped in front of a door leading into the maintenance passages, and keyed in my security code. The door slid open, and I stepped into the narrow, dimly lit passage, the door sliding shut automatically behind me.

Pipe and cable networks lined the wall and ceiling, forcing me to bend over slightly as I walked through the patchwork of shadows and dusty shafts of light. At a fork I took the left turning, and some ways on reached a break on the left wall. I opened the door and stepped through it.

I entered the cathedral through the side wall, near the large main doors and the rear pews. Candles provided the only illumination, and the cathedral was awash in flickering warm shadows and wavering pockets of orange light. I was nearly at the midpoint of the cathedral's length. Just visible far to my left was the small stained-glass window of the galilee.

To my right, of course, was the enormous stained-glass Crucifixion towering above the apse, looming over the entire cathedral. Yet it held no power now, the colors flat and lifeless, dull reflections of candlelight; I could barely make out the actual images that had blazed with such immeasurable force into the darkness of deep space not many days earlier.

I remained just inside the cathedral, my back against the wall, listening and watching. I was still suspicious, especially since I saw no signs of Father Veronica. I saw no signs of *anyone*. Silence and candlelight; the air was warm and stuffy.

I considered calling her name, but was reluctant to reveal my presence. The longer I stood there in the warm and heavy silence, the more frightened I became. Frightened of what? I didn't know, which made it worse.

The doors to the galilee, a small, private chapel, were

usually closed. Today they stood open, so I decided to investigate. Keeping to the wall, I worked my way slowly and quietly along the length of the cathedral to the entrance of the galilee. I waited, listening intently, then stepped carefully through the doorway.

There was no one inside. More candles in dark-red glass containers wavering gently; padded kneelers, an empty cistern. The stained-glass window was taller by half than I, yet seemed tiny compared to the Crucifixion window. It depicted Mary holding the dead Jesus in her lap, her eyes and face filled with grief—as moving in its own, intimate way as the Crucifixion window was on its more cosmic scale. I understood why someone would want to come here and pray.

I left the galilee and started back toward the main cathedral, still keeping to the shadows along the wall. It was a long walk, and the tension was wearing on me. I even searched the darkness of the vaulting high above me, expecting something to come swooping down. By the time I returned to the maintenance door, I was sweating heavily and breathing hard, although I had hardly exerted myself.

I continued a bit farther until I reached the back pews. Then, deciding I had to bring things to a head one way or another, I stepped away from the wall.

"Father Veronica?" I called out quietly.

I thought I heard a slight rustling, but it stopped immediately and I couldn't be sure. I also began to feel a strange vibration in my chest and belly, a thrumming, queasy sensation.

"Father Veronica?" I called again. Then, louder: "Father Veronica!"

"I'm right here, Bartolomeo."

Her voice startled me, kicking up my heartbeat and stopping my breath. Her head and body rose to a sitting position on one of the pews just seven or eight meters away.

"I was sleeping," she said. She brushed her hair away from her eyes.

The fear and panic were replaced by an almost electric sense of relief spreading through me. It was a purging, or cleansing. I took a deep breath. She *was* here. She *had* sent the message to me.

"Do you feel that?" she asked.

I nodded. The thrumming was still there, deeper now and more persistent.

Was it the aliens? Were they here? Were they finally attacking?

The vibration strengthened, working its way down through my legs and up my neck.

"What is it?" Father Veronica asked. She pulled herself up to her feet and, like me, looked around the cathedral. There was nothing to see.

"I don't know," I said. "But it can't be good."

She turned back to me. "What are you doing here, Bartolomeo? The cathedral is supposed to be closed."

I stared at her, my fear returning. But before I could answer, the vibration stepped up again. The queasiness intensified, and I felt dizzy. I reached out to the back of the nearest pew for support, trying desperately to maintain my balance.

The cathedral was spinning all around me. Suddenly everything turned, and the gravity in the cathedral rotated 90 degrees. The floor had become a wall, the Crucifixion window the ceiling, and the galilee, so far away, was now the floor.

My feet dropped and pulled out from under me and I started to fall sideways. But I had one hand on the pew, and by instinct I managed to grab the pew with my other. A shower of candles and other objects fell and bounced past us, banging and shattering.

Above me, Father Veronica cried out as she lost her balance and began to fall toward me. Her hands and feet scrambled for a secure hold on the pews, and for a moment I thought she was going to be safe. One hand gripped the back of a pew, the other swung about for something to hold onto, and one shoe seemed to find support on another pew. I hung from the back of the last pew, looking up and watching her, unable to help, unable to do a thing.

Her foot slipped, and she was hanging by only one hand.

And it was a hand of flesh and blood, not artificial like my own which tightly gripped the dark wood above me.

"Bartolomeo," she whispered.

"Hold on," I said, wondering what I could do, how I could reach her. "Just . . ."

"I can't . . ."

Her fingers slipped from the wood, and she fell.

She struck another pew no more then a meter away, then bounced away from it and plummeted past me.

"VERONICA!"

I craned my head around between my arms and watched her plunge the entire length of the cathedral, cassock whipping about her body, hands and arms outstretched, long seconds of free fall until at last she fell through the open doors of the galilee and crashed into the stained glass window.

"VERONICA!" I cried out again. "VERONICA!"

I knew she couldn't hear me. I knew she couldn't respond. There was no way anyone could survive such a fall. I stared down at her small, crumpled body, my heart exploding. "VERONICA!!"

I looked away and stared at the floor in front of me. Tears tried to come, but I wouldn't let them. I hung there, and for a brief moment thought about letting go, but that innate, stubborn human drive to live would not allow me to release my grip.

I hung there a long time. If my hands and arms had been normal, I wouldn't have lasted. But they weren't normal, and although my shoulder began to ache, I had no real difficulty maintaining my grip on the pew. I had more trouble maintaining a grip on my emotions, which threatened to burst out of me in screams.

Time? I lost all sense of it. Did I hang there for an hour? Or was it only one minute? I remember looking down at her once, but I couldn't look again. If I didn't see her body, maybe it hadn't happened to her.

I swung and hooked one leg up onto the pew, then pulled myself up into it, using it like a ledge. For extra support, I grabbed onto a kneeler with one hand.

The vibration, now only a barely perceptible thrum, strengthened once again. I hung on tightly to the pew and kneeler, and the gravity rotated another 90 degrees. The cathedral ceiling was now the floor, the floor the ceiling; my legs swung out and I was hanging again.

More breaking glass, sliding and cracking sounds. I twisted my head around to look down at the galilee. I couldn't see her body any longer. Better that way, I thought.

The gravity shifted ninety degrees once more. My legs swung out, slamming my body across the back of a pew, legs trying to drop now toward the Crucifixion stained glass. I kept my grip.

I heard more sliding, looked up toward the galilee. Another shower of glass, bits of metal, stone, books with pages tearing and fluttering. No, I silently pleaded, please let the walls or something catch her, please, *please* don't let her . . .

The sliding continued, and Father Veronica's body tumbled out of the galilee and plummeted again.

I closed my eyes. I could not watch this, I would not watch it . . . but I felt the breeze as she hurtled past me, and heard the sickening crunch as she hit the Crucifixion stained glass.

At least this time she wouldn't have felt any pain, I thought. Even so, at that moment I came the closest to opening my hands, releasing my grip, and falling to her side. Instead, I pulled my legs up and over the pew and lay there, both arms wrapped around the padded kneeler, my eyes closed.

Again I lost all sense of time. I hardly knew who or where I was. Veronica . . . Veronica . . . I pleaded desperately for this to be some drug-induced dream or hallucination, but I knew I would not be waking up from this nightmare.

Everything inside me seemed to be coming apart. No matter how tightly I wrapped my arms around the kneeler, pressing myself against the cold floor, I thought that at any moment I was going to completely shatter, and the pieces of my body and spirit would rain down upon her.

How could I stand this? I wondered. How does anyone stand it?

Finally, after what seemed like days, the gravity shifted one final time, back to its original orientation, and the thrumming vibration disappeared completely. It didn't matter. Nothing mattered. Barely aware of my own existence, I hung onto the kneeler without moving until six o'clock arrived and Father George opened the doors of the cathedral.

50

I found Bishop Soldano in his private offices above the cathedral. The doors were open and I passed through several rooms until I reached the last, which had a full-wall viewing port. He stood at the steelglass window, gazing up and out at the alien ship.

"Come in, Bartolomeo."

I was already inside the room, but I was so sick at heart, and at the same time so enraged, that I couldn't speak. I couldn't move. I was shaking inside, and I wanted to launch myself at that huge figure and beat him to death. My artificial hands and arms, which just hours earlier had saved my life, could easily have ended his. A huge desk stood between us, and I gripped the dark wood to keep my hands and arms from shaking away from me.

"It was you," I finally managed to say.

He did not turn to look at me, but he slowly nodded. "She wasn't supposed to be there." His voice was hoarse and cracked. "No one should have been there. Only you. Only . . . you." I could see him swallow, his throat moving with difficulty. "Now I am truly damned."

"You expect me to feel pity for you?" I shouted at him.

I was afraid of losing all control. "Because you killed her instead of me?"

The bishop just shook his head. He finally turned to face me, and I nearly attacked him. I'm still not sure what stopped me. She did, probably. I imagined I heard her voice saying, *No, Bartolomeo. Please. That's not the answer. It won't change anything.* I didn't care if it didn't change anything. But I didn't attack. Instead, I closed my eyes so I wouldn't have to look at that inhuman monster.

I stood there with eyes closed, my hands on his desk, and listened to the rush of blood in my head. Suddenly I couldn't believe I was there, that Father Veronica was dead, that the bishop had killed her and had just admitted it to me. Because I wasn't sure I could stand it if it was true.

I opened my eyes and looked at him.

"It was from the alien ship," I finally said. "That device you took from it."

He looked surprised. "How did you know about that?"

"What the hell does it matter how I know?" I shouted at him.

He sighed, staring at me. "I didn't know what I was going to do with it," he said, "but I thought it would be useful. I didn't intend this. But then the idea came to me. An inspiration."

"Why?" I asked.

"I told you before. You are responsible for this. We are doomed. Those . . . creatures, those alien beings, whatever they are, eventually they are going to come after us. They are going to kill us, they are going to torture and slaughter us, and you are responsible."

Suddenly I was so exhausted I could hardly move. I didn't even have the energy to hate anymore. I dropped into a chair, laid my head back, and closed my eyes again. The bishop began to murmur to himself. He stopped for a moment; when he resumed speaking his voice was louder and more distinct, and he seemed to be quoting.

"But unto Leviathan thou gavest the seventh part, namely the moist; and hast kept him to be devoured of whom thou wilt, and when."

I opened my eyes and looked at him. He stood gazing with despair or fear or awe, or all three, at the dark and unmoving alien starship. He did not turn away from the ship, and he said no more.

"Is that from the Bible?" I asked.

He didn't move or speak for several moments; then he turned to me and said, "Peripherally. It's from 2 Esdras, which is part of the Apocrypha."

"Which is . . . ?"

"A group of religious writings that are considered important, but not an official part of either the Old Testament or the New. The issues surrounding the Apocrypha—which writings are a part of it, and which aren't, their relative importance, and so on—are complex, and were debated for centuries. Our own Church recognizes many books of the Apocrypha as deuterocanonical—they belong to a second level of the canon, although that is not to imply that they are of less importance than those books that are in the Old and New Testaments. Oddly enough, though, 2 Esdras is *not* one of them. In a way, it floats around in its own canonical Limbo." He smiled to himself, shaking his head. "Sorry, I don't intend to bore you. And it doesn't really matter." He sighed. "That verse has been going through my thoughts for days now."

"You see the alien ship as Leviathan?"

The bishop nodded. "The moist referenced the oceans of Earth, or at least that was the original interpretation. But the world view, or *universe* view, was much more limited then. Imagine *deep space* as the moist. The oceans of the universe." He paused. "I can imagine the second part of the verse as perhaps once mistranscribed, or misunderstood—maybe even out of fear. Change it ever so slightly, just a couple of words, and it becomes something very different." He closed his eyes, and quoted the changed verse. *"But unto Leviathan thou gavest the seventh part, namely the moist; and hast kept him to devour whom thou wilt, and when."* He paused again. "Now we have something that appears to describe our alien ship quite well."

I sat up, but remained in the chair. Exhaustion still overwhelmed me.

"That implies responsibility on God's part," I said. "That God for some reason now *wants* Leviathan to devour us. Or is it supposed to be just a metaphor?"

"No," the bishop said, his voice quiet but firm. "No metaphor. God *is* responsible. You are responsible, I am responsible, we are all responsible, and He is a jealous and angry God."

"But you don't believe in God."

"Maybe I do, now. And wish I didn't." He sounded lost and confused. "What if I've been wrong all these years? If I have been, then after this life I am truly damned."

I felt no sympathy for him whatsoever. "You're worthless."

"What do you want from me, Bartolomeo? You want to kill me? Here I am." He held out his arms, as though welcoming me. "I won't resist, I won't fight you. Kill me, Bartolomeo."

I just slowly shook my head.

"What do you *want*, Bartolomeo? What do you want from me?"

I had no answer for him. I didn't know what I wanted.

"You want confession? I've already confessed. You want me put away in a cell like the one you were locked up in all those months? Call the security forces, call your friend Captain Nikos Costa.

"You want justice?" He laughed. "No, you know better than to expect that, don't you?

"Or do you want contrition? I can't give you that, Bartolomeo. I feel remorse, but not for trying to kill you. Only for killing her by mistake. I *should* feel remorse for trying to kill you, but I don't. And if I am to have any chance at redemption, I will need to repent, to—"

"Redemption!" I shouted, rising up out of the chair. I was shaking again. "You're beyond redemption, you monstrous bastard!"

"No," he said quietly. "No one is beyond redemption."

"*You* are, Bishop," I said, pointing at him. "And deep down, in your cold and loveless heart, you know that."

"I am not loveless. I loved *her,* Bartolomeo." He looked at me. "No, not like that," he said. "Not the way you did. I loved her for her righteousness, for the faith she had that I lost so long ago."

"And you killed her."

He buried his face in his hands, and began to weep.

I could take no more. If I wasn't going to kill him, I would have to leave. *Now I am truly damned*, he had said. I finally walked away, hoping with all of my broken and darkened heart that, about this, the bishop was right.

51

I returned to the chamber of abandoned machines. Darkness and deep shadows and the smell of old lubricants—just what I needed. Although I hadn't taken even a sip of alcohol, I felt almost drunk, or otherwise drugged. With my hand torch on its dimmest, widest setting, I stumbled along among the useless machinery, trying to think of anything but Father Veronica. The deeper I went into the chamber, the harder it was to keep away the image of her broken body, the warmth of her smile, the memory of honey and cinnamon.

I climbed across a tangle of metal pipes and sat on a pile of cabled wire, gazing down into the open bay at the bishop's lifeless machine. Damn him and his machines. I switched off the hand torch and sat motionless in the dark. Don't think about her, I told myself. Don't think about her. So I concentrated on the alien ship, envisioned it suspended in the depths of space, surrounded by black night and silver stars, and tried to imagine a means of escape.

TWO or three hours later, Pär and Nikos found me there. I heard them calling my name, and I thought about

doing what Francis had done that time—scramble deep into
the ruined machinery where they would never find me—but
I didn't have the heart or energy for it. What was the point?
I sat and waited for them, watching the thin beams of light
arcing back and forth, up and down, listening to them calling my name over and over. Maybe they would just give up.

Half an hour later they came around a wrecked cylinder
and one of their torch beams sliced across my face and they
came to a stop.

"Damn!" Pär said. "Scared me." He laughed nervously.
"Why didn't you answer, Bartolomeo?"

Nikos just looked at me, waiting for a response.

"I didn't feel like it," I said.

"We've been searching for you for hours," Nikos said.
"I tried signaling you, but Pär said you had the system
disabled. He suggested we look for you here."

Pär shrugged. "I know your secrets, Bartolomeo. Some
of them, anyway."

"Why are you looking for me? I just want to be left
alone."

"The bishop told me what happened," Nikos said. "He
seemed to expect me to order his imprisonment, and was
surprised when I didn't. I thought that if you hadn't come
to me demanding he be imprisoned, then you didn't want
that. I figure you probably don't care any longer what happens to him. He's in his own private Hell, and you're content with that."

I managed half a laugh. "You're so damn sure about
what I'm thinking and feeling."

"No," Nikos said. "Just a guess."

Neither of them said anything for a long time. Their
hand torches were aimed at the floor, and their faces were
barely distinguishable in the dim light.

"I know you're hurting," Nikos said, "but we've got a
ship with several thousand people who are still alive, and
we have got to figure out a way to save them."

"Are you both insane?" I asked. "Why would you want
my advice? *My* suggestions? Every decision I've made
seems to have been the wrong one. I chose to join with Pär

and the downsiders in the failed insurrection, and spent seven months in a cell. You put me in charge of the alien ship exploration team, and we end up with a shape-changing alien creature on board the *Argonos*, people dead and gone mad, Casterman's suicide. Finally, when almost everyone is ready to abandon that damned ship, I convince you all to dock with it and take it with us. Now we're probably all going to die. One bad decision after another, and you want *my* advice?''

Pär grinned.

"What's so funny?"

"You are, Bartolomeo."

"Everything you've said is true," Nikos added, "but it's not that simple. Your choices, your decisions, were not necessarily the wrong choices. Sometimes, they were the *right* choices, the *moral* choices. They just didn't work out.''

"That's an understatement."

"I'm not just saying this to make you feel better," Nikos offered, "but docking with their ship probably didn't make any difference in the long run.''

"What do you mean?"

"Did Margita tell you how we would drift closer to the alien ship every few days?"

"Yes." It didn't matter now if he knew.

"I'd bet they were just feeling things out. They have technology we can hardly imagine, and I would guess that they could have sucked us right into their ship any time they wanted, and we wouldn't have been able to do a damn thing about it. I also believe that if we'd tried to leave them behind the way the bishop wanted, they would not have let us go. They would have drawn us in, or come after us, and we'd be right where we are now, more or less.''

"So I just made it easier for them."

"*We* made it easier for them, yes." Nikos paused. "We need your help, Bartolomeo.''

"What about the rest of the Executive Council? I thought you were going to meet every twelve hours and exchange ideas.''

"Come on, Bartolomeo, we both know how useful that's going to be. With the possible exception of Margita or Geller, no one's going to come up with a damn thing, and you know it. And they don't need some misguided brain-storming session to think; if either of them comes up with something, they'll let us know." He paused. "We need your help."

"What? The three of us are going to brainstorm? You and I and Pär, sitting in the darkness surrounded by derelict machinery, we're going to come up with a way to save everyone?"

"Maybe. This is as good a place as any."

I looked from one to another. Finally, I gestured for them to sit and said, "All right. Stay a while." I managed a brief, mirthless laugh. "What the hell. You want an idea? I already have an idea. I've been sitting here in the dark, surrounded by ruins, and an idea has occurred to me, an idea I don't trust because I don't trust anything I think anymore. So I'll tell you my idea, and *you* two can tell me whether I'm as crazy as everyone else."

They sat, and Nikos said, "Tell us, Bartolomeo."

I breathed deeply. "We go back to Antioch."

Neither of them said anything for a long time. They stared at me, they looked at each other, and they stared at me some more. "I don't understand," Nikos finally said. "How?"

"We take the shuttles."

That gave them something to think about for a minute. "There aren't enough to take everyone," Pär said.

I nodded. "I know. That's only the first of a whole lot of problems with this idea."

"What are some of the others?"

"The logistics alone are a serious problem. Fuel and food and water . . . How long do you think it would take for a shuttle to get back to Antioch?"

Nikos sighed. "I don't know, but a long time. Weeks, or months. Yeah, fuel's a problem. Initial acceleration . . . deceleration . . . descent and landing . . ." His eyes were unfocused as he was thinking. "The less used for accelera-

tion, the longer the trip . . . the more mass in people and
food and cargo, the more fuel we'd need. . . ." His voice
trailed off. "Yeah. But we can work all that out. We'll
know how many can go on the shuttles."

"And how many have to stay," I said.

"Yes, and how many have to stay."

"And that's another problem," I started, "how . . ."

". . . to decide who goes," Nikos finished. "I know.
But, like the logistics, it's something that can be done. Even
if we can only save a thousand, or several hundred, that's
better than nothing."

"The harvesters," Pär said.

We both looked at him.

"We've got three harvesters," he continued, "and their
holds are huge. They'd carry a lot of people and food and
equipment."

The harvesters. I shuddered inwardly, thinking about
them. Once again I saw them rising before me during the
failed insurrection, like fire monsters, nuclear versions of
the bishop's Leviathan.

"There's a big problem with the harvesters," Nikos said.
"Actually with the shuttles, too. And why not? There's a
big problem with every aspect of this idea."

"What problem?" Pär asked.

"Gravity," Nikos answered. "The harvesters and shuttles don't have any. I don't care how much room you've
got, you can't pack hundreds or thousands of people in
zero-g holds for weeks and months on end."

"Constant acceleration of half a g or so," Pär said.

"And then constant *deceleration*?" Nikos said. "Way
too much fuel needed for that. If we could convert the ship
drives and install them, maybe, but that's just impossible.
With conventional fuel . . ."

I started laughing.

"What?"

"It's grotesque," I said, "but the bishop's got part of
the answer. The gravity device he used to kill Father Veronica. He can make it work. We install it on one of the
harvesters, rotate people in and out so no one has to do the

whole trip stored like cargo in zero g. Put people in two of them, one with gravity, and use the third harvester for cargo, food, and equipment, anything that can be tied down.''

"Okay, that's just my point," Nikos said. "Any of these problems can be worked out."

"Of course," Pär added, "even with the harvesters and all the shuttles, it may still not be enough space to take everyone."

"I know, damn it," Nikos snapped. "We'll deal with that when we have to. We'll deal with every problem. At least this is a way out."

"Maybe," I said. "There's one thing we should do before we bother trying to resolve all the logistical problems."

"What's that?" Nikos asked.

Par was nodding. "Yes," he said. "We need to find out what the alien ship will do when a shuttle or harvester leaves the *Argonos*."

I looked at him. "You willing to make a test run with me?"

Pär nodded. "Let's do it now," he said.

W E went out in one of the harvesters. I wanted to take one of the shuttles, but Pär argued that a harvester, being so much larger, would be a better test; I couldn't argue. The pilot's cabin was a half-bubble of steelglass atop the forward end of the harvester. We sat behind the pilots, watching the expanse of stars in front of us and the receding ships behind us. Monitors placed throughout the cabin gave us a variety of views.

We had launched from the *Argonos* at low speed, accelerated slowly for ten minutes, then cut the engines, traveling in silence except for the pilots' periodic exchanges. We were moving at a constant velocity away from the two locked ships, which grew smaller and smaller on the monitors. All four of us waited for something from the alien ship—a missile launch, an energy beam, magnetic disruption pulses, some other unknown and unknowable weapon or force that would destroy us, disable us, or pull us back into the *Argonos* or the alien ship.

A half hour passed without incident. Forty-five minutes. An hour. The ships had disappeared from view, then even from the monitors, although instruments still registered their presence.

"How far do we go?" one of the pilots asked.

I looked at Pär. "Another hour?" I suggested.

"At least. We have to be sure. Or as sure as we can be."

When we were two hours out we tried another fifteen-minute acceleration, boosting our velocity. Then we continued for another hour. Nothing.

Finally we were satisfied, and I think surprised. We told the pilots to turn around and take us back.

"Take it slow going back, too," Pär said. "We don't need to go roaring in, calling even more attention to ourselves." Then he turned to me. "Think it'll be this easy?"

"It didn't feel that easy," I said. "The truth is, even if we manage to get away from the ships, the journey back to Antioch in these things is going to be miserable."

He nodded. "Yeah. You know what *won't* be easy? Going to the Planning Committee with this. And we have to have their support, we have to have them all with us. Without them, we won't be able to retrofit and ready the shuttles and harvesters, get several thousand people prepared to go, all of that. Everything that will have to be done efficiently and quickly. They've got to be with us."

"I don't understand," I said. "What's the problem? There's no other choice. This is our only chance. Why would it be difficult to convince them?"

"Because many of them have already given up all hope. They're so far gone, it will be tough to bring them back. A tiny shred of hope isn't going to do it. We'll have to convince them that there's a good chance of success."

What Pär said made sense. "You're right. So let's hope no one brings up this other minor matter."

"What's that?"

"Assuming we get away from the ships, what's to prevent the aliens from following us back to Antioch?"

"Well, let's hope no one mentions it." Pär laughed. "Besides, I don't know why you worry about that. Forget this test. You know what the chances are they'll actually let us all get away in the first place?"

"Then why are you going along with this?"

"You said it. This is the only option we've got. And if by some miracle we can get to Antioch, at least we'll have a chance. We stay on the *Argonos*, we have none." He nodded once. "None."

No one said anything more the rest of the way in.

52

THE Planning Committee was something to see: despair, emotional paralysis, dishevelment. Dementia and
absentia—I counted five empty seats. But all the Executive
Council members were there, even the bishop. He sat list-
lessly in his chair, eyes unfocused. I could barely look at
him without screaming. I wondered how many people in
the room knew what he had done.

Nikos and Cardenas had met for several hours with Costino, Rita Hollings, and two or three others to discuss details
and logistics—how long the trip would be, the fuel needs,
how many people could go with each of the shuttles, how
many in the harvesters, what it would take to equip and
retrofit the vehicles, and on and on. They didn't need to
have every specific answer, but Nikos wanted to be prepared
with estimates for the Planning Committee.

Nikos finally called the meeting to order.

"Everyone in this room knows the situation we are in.
But the reason this meeting has been called is that we have
a proposal. An idea, a plan for a way out."

"What?" someone asked. "The Casterman Method?
Mass suicide?"

Someone else gave a halfhearted laugh in response, but it quickly faded.

"We're going to Antioch," Nikos said, replying quickly. He wasn't going to let the meeting get out of control. "Not in the *Argonos*, but in shuttles and harvesters."

The questions began immediately, as well as the criticisms, and outright dismissal from a few people. Nikos explained in some detail what we planned to do, then he and Cardenas spent the next two hours answering questions, responding to complaints, passing a few on to Costino or Hollings. Pär was right; it was taking a lot to drag most of these people out of their despair; but by the end of the second hour I could see that the mood had changed. People were coming around, slowly but surely, and a subtle but palpable excitement was growing, a blossoming sense of hope. Then Bishop Soldano tried to destroy it.

The bishop pulled himself forward and rose to his feet, silencing the entire committee. I was surprised there was any life left in him; I was surprised that he'd been listening.

"I have one question," he said. "What's the point?"

He remained standing, watching the looks of puzzlement and confusion growing around him. He finally spoke again.

"They'll come and find us. They know where Antioch is, remember? They were responsible for what happened there. They'll know that's where we're headed. After all, they *led* us out here from Antioch."

Oh no, I thought to myself, watching the fear and panic reappear in faces all around the table, although they could not know what exactly they were afraid of, they could not yet understand what he was saying.

Bishop Soldano turned and looked directly at Nikos. "Tell them, *Captain*."

Nikos nodded. "Yes, that's true. And that's why there is a second component to this plan."

"Forget the damn second component," a man called out from the far end of the table. "What the hell does the bishop mean, 'they led us here'?"

Nikos looked askance at the bishop; he was probably

wishing he had locked him up after all. Then he looked out at the committee.

"When we were on Antioch, after the skeletons were discovered, a highly directional signal was transmitted from the landing site—perpendicular to the system's orbital plane, so we knew it wasn't meant for any of the other worlds or satellites. We couldn't locate anything it might be destined for—the nearest star in its vicinity was hundreds of light-years away." He hesitated. "When we left Antioch, it was decided that we would follow the direction of the signal. We ended up here." He turned to me and gave me a half-smile. "See, Bartolomeo? Everyone can make decisions that don't work out."

"Who decided?" someone else asked.

"Bishop Soldano and I decided."

Cardenas stood up. "It doesn't matter who decided," she said. "It doesn't matter how we ended up here. What matters now is how we get out of here. That's all we're discussing."

"But the bishop is right," Renata Tyler said. "There's no point in any of this if they'll just follow us to Antioch."

I stood, intending to argue just what Pär had said: that at least we would have a chance on Antioch. But Cardenas spoke first.

"Let Captain Costa finish, and you will understand." She sat back down, and so did I. I wondered what Nikos had in mind; we hadn't discussed any "second component."

"I will be staying with the *Argonos*," he said.

I sat there stunned, not yet understanding.

"The bishop has a point," Nikos resumed. "We can't leave the alien ship here, even if we can escape from it. It will find Antioch again, or some other world, some other starship. We can't let that happen. Margita Cardenas and I, along with three other crew members, will stay aboard the *Argonos* to direct it on a blind jump out of this galaxy. With luck, completely out of the universe."

This set off a lot of murmuring, questioning looks; I saw someone biting their knuckles, as if afraid for Nikos and the others. I wanted to object, but I was dazed, and couldn't think very clearly, couldn't think of a reason to object. What Nikos said made perfect sense, as much as I didn't like to admit it.

But Geller spoke. "Can't we just set the ship to do a blind jump automatically?"

Cardenas shook her head. "It has to be piloted into the discontinuity. Besides, if it doesn't go as expected, we want to be aboard to make a second jump if necessary. I don't like it, but there's no choice."

Everyone was quiet, letting it settle in. The bishop slowly rose to his feet again. "Then I, too, will be staying aboard the *Argonos*. I will speak with Father George, and ask him to be the new bishop. I will stay with the cathedral, with our archives."

Now he would be a martyr, I thought to myself. Let him.

"That's it," Nikos said, essentially ignoring the bishop. "If we are to have any chance at success, we need the complete support of this committee. There is way too much that will need to be done, and it needs to be done quickly."

The vote was unanimous, but I felt sick. I was losing nearly everyone who had meant anything to me. I considered offering to stay with Nikos and the others, but I recognized the urge for what it was—a fear of appearing to be a coward; a conceit.

"One more thing," Nikos said. "I want to nominate Duncan Geller to replace me as Captain."

Though Geller was surprised, he reacted as a fine future captain should—he accepted the nomination with grace and respect and sincere humility. His nomination was seconded by Cardenas. That vote, too, was unanimous.

That was the end of the meeting. A dozen smaller meetings would take place almost immediately. We adjourned. Preparations began.

53

I F nothing else, I told myself, this gave people hope;
it gave them something to do, which had to be better
than withdrawing frightened and paralyzed and despairing
into psychological cocoons, waiting in terror for death.

There was too much to do, and of course no one knew
how much time we had. Maybe we had all the time we
wanted, maybe we could have spent weeks retrofitting the
shuttles and harvesters, rebuilding them and outfitting them,
planning carefully until everyone and everything was accounted for, packed and loaded, everyone leisurely boarded
and settling themselves in for the long journey. Maybe the
aliens would come the next day, and we wouldn't have
a chance.

We tried to decide on the absolute minimum necessary
to make it to Antioch and survive once we got there; then
we set to work on that minimum. There were screwups and
tempers and accidents, shouting and crying and fistfights,
pouting and nervous breakdowns. But there was also laughter and tears of relief and companionship, stolen moments
of affection, and much cooperation.

Through it all, the work got done. With the bishop's
assistance, we installed the gravity generator in one of the

harvesters. Partitions were erected in the vehicles; sleeping bunks and benches were built into walls. Bathrooms and recyclers, water tanks. Storage lockers and food systems. Minimal amounts of packaged foods in each vessel, just enough for the voyage to Antioch; larger stores would be loaded into the cargo harvester.

Fuel was a problem. We would maximize all tanks, but the shuttles weren't designed for long-distance space travel. If there had been more time, perhaps we would have been able to build special tanks to store the fuel in the cargo harvester, build fueling systems so the shuttles could be refueled during the journey. There *wasn't* more time.

Even if there had been time, it wouldn't have been a good idea; we couldn't depend too much on what was loaded in the cargo harvester. It would be the last to leave the *Argonos*; what would happen if it was attacked by the aliens, destroyed or disabled? What would happen if there was some other kind of unforeseeable accident? Each vessel, each shuttle and harvester, needed to be self-sufficient, equipped to be capable of making the journey to Antioch and landing without aid from any of the others.

We'd be crammed into the vessels, without privacy, like the herd animals down in the lower levels, but amazingly we had the capacity to take everyone. However, there were people who couldn't go. Decisions were difficult to make, they were brutal, but there was no choice. Most of those in the downsiders' madhouse would have to stay. The same for a dozen people in the upper-level psychiatric wards. Of those in the ship's jail cells, the lesser offenders were released; the more violent remained imprisoned.

One of the most difficult decisions was what to do with those people who had begun to behave strangely after going into the alien ship: Barry Sorrel and his family, Leona Frip, Nazia Abouti. We didn't know what was wrong with them. Infected somehow? Possibly contagious? Perhaps they were in the early stages of becoming possessed by the spirits of alien beings. It was impossible to know. As hard as it was, amid the feelings of guilt at the price they were paying for all their efforts, in the end we knew we had no choice: they would have to remain.

Starlin and Winton might have presented another problem, but they were both still missing, apparently stalking each other throughout the *Argonos*. We stopped looking for them.

There were also people who *wouldn't* go: some upper-level residents afraid of losing the power and authority they had enjoyed all their lives; twenty-three families who belonged to a religious sect called the First Ship of Christ, who believed it was blasphemous to leave the *Argonos*; twenty or thirty people on the official ship census that could not be located; and some people who simply couldn't imagine life outside the ship.

I can hardly remember now everything that had to be done, everything that had to be accounted for. I *can't* remember everything. So much of what took place during that time has now become hazy, distorted by tension, anxiety, fear, and severe sleep deprivation.

But it got done, somehow, and soon it became clear that we would be ready to leave in less than twenty-four hours.

TOLLER came to see me down in the harvester bay, where I was helping load cargo. I sat with him on bundles of packaged foodstuffs that weren't slated to be loaded for several hours.

"I'm staying with the *Argonos*," he said. "I wanted you to know."

I wasn't expecting it, but it did not surprise me. "Why?"

"I'm not a martyr like the bishop. It's not that." He sighed and held up his cane. "I'm an old man, Bartolomeo. I'm one hundred and thirty-eight years old, and I've spent every one of those years on this ship. I've been ship historian for sixty-seven years." He set the tip of the cane between his shoes, rubbed the carved wooden handle. "I need to stay here. I need to know how everything ends for the *Argonos*. Finish its history, if possible."

"Finish its history? For whom?"

"I don't know. For me. Hopefully for others. I'll work until the last possible moment. I'll have a copy of the Histories in a burial capsule, and when I have written my final words I will add them to the others. I will seal the capsule, and launch it into space. With luck, a *great deal* of luck, someone will find it someday and learn something from it." He smiled gently. "The historian's eternal hope."

I thought I understood how he felt. "I guess I won't try to talk you out of it," I told him.

"Thank you. I don't have the energy for it."

"Have you told Geller yet?" I asked.

"No."

"You should. He'll be our captain. Or already is."

Toller nodded. "Yes. I will. And I'll suggest to him that he maintain the position of historian on Antioch. On the journey as well. It's more important than most people realize. Maria Vegas has been well-trained. She will make a fine historian."

"I'll lend my own support," I told him.

"Thank you, Bartolomeo." He leaned forward and with the help of his cane rose to his feet. "I'll return to the Church archives, now." He slowly shook his head. "They will be a great loss." His gaze became unfocused for a moment, then he looked at me. "Goodbye, Bartolomeo."

"Goodbye, August."

He limped across the bay, his thin figure surprisingly erect, then went through one of the passage doorways and was gone. I never saw him again.

THERE were only a few hours until the first shuttle was scheduled to leave. Nikos and I met in the command salon. The clear dome was two-thirds filled with stars and one-third with the deep black hulk of the alien ship looming over us. There was still so much to do, and we both felt slightly guilty taking time away from the preparations. But this would be our only opportunity, our *last* opportunity.

He had a bottle of Scotch and two glasses with him; he held up the bottle and offered me a drink.

"Just one," I said.

He nodded, and poured some for each of us. "This is my first drink in weeks," he said.

I'd wondered about that. The Scotch burned, but it burned cool and smooth going down.

"This is the last of the best," he said. "Why let it go to waste? I'll probably finish the bottle once we've pulled this off."

Pulled it off, I thought. I watched him, trying to guess whether or not he was frightened. *Not,* I decided. Or at least not much. He'd come to terms with it, and if I knew Nikos, which I did, he was ready with a way to end it quickly for himself. He and Cardenas and the others might have talked about it.

"It's been an eventful year," he said.

I smiled. "That's a word for it."

"You and I have had our differences."

"Long done with," I replied.

He nodded slowly, sipped at his drink. He looked up and out through the steelglass at the alien ship. "That could have been the most fantastic discovery in history. It *was* the most fantastic discovery. But it's turned into the most fantastic nightmare. It's done terrible things to most of us." He turned back to me. "I'm sorry about some things, Bartolomeo."

"So am I, Nikos."

I was afraid he was going to get specific. It would have been a bad idea. It was possible that the things he was sorry about were not what *I* thought he should be sorry about. And vice versa. We didn't need that now.

Isolated in the salon, we couldn't hear anything at all except our own breathing. We might have been the only people on the *Argonos*.

Nikos finished his drink. "After all these years," he said, "there really isn't much to say, is there?"

"No," I answered.

"Bartolomeo." Then he hesitated, unsure. "Bartolomeo, do you want to know who your parents are?"

"You know?"

"Yes."

"How long have you known?"

"Since I became captain."

I didn't have to think about it long. I felt surprisingly little curiosity. "No," I told him. "It's too late for that. They've been dead and buried in space to me all my life. Better they stay that way."

Nikos smiled. "I thought you would say something like that." The smile quickly faded. "Well, *I* have a strange request. It seems strange to me, anyway." He glanced into his empty glass. "Watch my wife for me, Bartolomeo. Make sure she's all right. She's . . . she won't ask for help, especially not from you."

"Aiyana doesn't like me."

"No." He looked up at me. "Will you do that for me, Bartolomeo?"

"Are you surprised she chose not to stay with you?"

He didn't answer immediately, but I could see the pain working into his features. "Maybe. A little. Should I not have been?"

"I don't know, Nikos. You know her far better than I do."

"Were *you* surprised?"

I wondered what answer he wanted to hear. Probably not the one I would give him. Maybe I should have lied, but I just couldn't.

"No," I said. "I wasn't surprised."

He nodded and turned his attention once again to the alien vessel. There were still no signs of activity on that sinister, black ship. Sometimes, looking at it, it was hard to believe what was happening.

"I have to go," I said. "There isn't much time. Final preparations . . ."

"I would have stayed with her," he said.

"I know." I felt pity for him, and wished there was

something I could do or say to ease his pain. But I knew there wasn't, or if there was, I had no idea what it could be.

"This won't be forgotten," I said. "What you and Margita and the others are doing. What you're doing for us, for—"

He shook his head, cutting me off. "Just get to Antioch alive, Bartolomeo. Make it worthwhile."

"We will, Nikos."

He turned back to me one final time and took a step forward. For a moment I thought he was going to embrace me. But we had never done anything like that in all the years we'd known each other, and I couldn't imagine it even now. Apparently he thought the same thing, for he did not come any closer.

"Goodbye, Bartolomeo."

"Goodbye, Nikos."

54

I stood with Pär at the side of the transport hold, watching the first shuttle slowly move along the track toward the open doors. Apparently someone had christened it the *Veronica*—her name was painted on the hull in large, bright red letters. I choked up watching the shuttle and those huge letters rumble past, feeling the vibrations deep in my bones. One of the pilots signaled down to us from the cockpit that everything was clear.

"What would she have thought of that?" Pär asked.

I couldn't answer immediately. I had to struggle against the despair just waiting to overwhelm me. "I don't know," I said. "Probably she would have smiled and shaken her head and said nothing."

The shuttle's speed picked up slightly as it approached the energy fields across the open doors. Its nose made contact, and a rippling, iridescent hole opened in the field; the launch mechanism cranked forward and the bow supports dropped away as the shuttle was propelled through the opening. The energy fields re-formed and returned to invisibility, and the shuttle was free of the ship.

It drifted away for a minute, then the attitude rockets burned for a few moments; the shuttle's orientation turned, then the engines fired and it accelerated away from both the *Argonos* and the alien ship. The acceleration was gentle, but soon the shuttle was gone from view.

I turned to the monitor screen in the bulkhead behind us, my heart racing. Ship cameras had picked up the shuttle, and followed it now as it moved toward the stern of the *Argonos*, angled away from the hull. The flames from the engines cut off, and I held my breath, waiting. . . . The shuttle continued on, velocity steady now, but with no other signs of life. No attack from the alien ship.

"Everything looks good," Pär said, sighing with relief.

"Yes. For now."

For now. When each shuttle or harvester was ten hours out from the *Argonos*, a number chosen almost arbitrarily at what we guessed would be a safe distance, it would hold until the others joined it. When we had all arrived and rendezvoused, we would change direction so we were headed for Antioch, then resume acceleration. This time acceleration would continue for some hours. Four and a half months later, if there were no disasters, we would reach Antioch.

I turned around and looked at the five other shuttles in the hold. Every one of them was loaded, packed, ready to go. There were another five shuttles in the second transport hold, and finally the three harvesters in their own bay.

I wanted to send them out two or three hours apart, but that would have been too time-consuming—for many reasons, not the least being the psychological stress on those desperate to leave. Instead, they would go an hour apart. Two more shuttles, then the first harvester; the other three shuttles in this hold, then the second harvester; the remaining five shuttles, then finally the last harvester, loaded only with cargo and manned by three pilots. Pär and I would be on the third harvester, the last to leave.

If anything unexpected happened, if the alien ship came alive and attacked either the *Argonos* or any of the shuttles or harvesters, the timetable would be abandoned, and everyone would launch immediately, one right after another, scattering in all directions. I prayed—to what or whom I had no idea—that it wouldn't come to that. At the same time, I could not really believe that we would be able to launch all those vessels without provoking a response from the alien ship.

I turned back to the monitor. The image of the shuttle was larger than I'd expected; but it had now cleared the stern of the *Argonos*, and was slowly shrinking as it pulled away. I checked the running clock in the lower right corner of the monitor. Nineteen minutes. I breathed in deeply, then slowly exhaled. An hour was going to be a long time.

T H E tension heightened three hours later when the first harvester launched. Sixteen hundred people, all at once. The first three shuttles were safely away, with no response from the alien ship, but the harvester was so much larger, and filled with so many people . . . Pär and I watched on the monitor as the massive cylinder dropped out of the side of the ship, topped by the bubble of the pilot's cabin. So large, and yet so small when compared to the *Argonos* and the alien ship. Maybe it *could* get away unmolested.

Attitude jets fired briefly, orienting the harvester, then the main engines came on, a ring of fire at the vessel's stern; they burned brightly and the harvester gradually gained velocity. After several minutes, the engines were shut down.

My heart was beating hard and fast, and I kept forgetting to breathe as we watched the harvester head away from us.

"How many more of these do we have to go through?" Pär asked. "How many more hours?"

"Too many," I replied.

"No shit," he said. "I'm not sure I can take it."

We watched for the entire hour, by which time the harvester was only an indistinct fleck on the monitor. Nothing had happened.

I turned and signaled to the pilot in Shuttle Four to prepare for launch.

*   *   *

WHEN the last of the shuttles in the first transport hold was gone, Pär and I headed for the harvester bay. Geller was in the second transport hold, and would oversee the rest of the shuttle launches from there.

The *Argonos* was so quiet it seemed dead. Soon, one way or another, it would be. I had walked through empty corridors before, particularly at night; I had walked for hours without seeing a soul. But the emptiness now as Pär and I walked through those same corridors was palpable.

"We tried this once before," Pär said. "Escaping from the *Argonos.*"

"Under very different circumstances. This time we're going to make it."

Pär nodded. "Yes, it seems so. And it worries me."

"What?"

"Why they're letting us go."

"The aliens?"

"Yes."

"I've thought about it, too. Sometimes I think it doesn't make sense to try to understand them. They're *alien.*"

"But you have some thoughts?"

"Yes," I said. "Maybe they don't realize the shuttles and harvesters won't return. Maybe they don't realize how many people are inside them. Maybe they *do* realize those things and don't care, because they figure we're all headed toward Antioch, and they believe they can follow any time they want." I paused, not wanting to say aloud my greatest fear. "And maybe they want us to think we're getting away so that our terror is all the greater when they come after us."

Pär smiled and nodded. "You *have* been thinking about it. I have, too, and I suspect the latter alternatives are closer to the truth."

"It doesn't really matter," I said. "It doesn't matter what they think, or what they plan to do. This is the only hope we've got."

*   *   *

THE harvester eased out of its berth and onto the launch
pad. Stars before us, and no hint of the alien ship,
although it would become visible as we emerged from the
bay. Pär and I sat in the cabin with the three pilots, strapped
into the reserve seats. In a little more than one hour, we
would be the last to leave.

I felt as if we were abandoning those who remained
behind. The fact that many of them chose to stay did little
to ease the sense of guilt; I tried not to think about them
too much.

Maxine Shalimar, Jimmy Lycos, and Amar Mubarak
were the three pilots. I knew them only slightly, but enough
to know they were good.

"Bartolomeo?" It was Nikos, his voice coming through
the cabin speakers.

"Yes, Captain."

He hesitated a moment, then said, *"I guess I am still
captain."*

"As long as the *Argonos* sails, you are its captain,"
Pär said.

"Thank you. Everything ready?"

"Yes."

"The harvester, Maxine?"

"She's ready, sir."

"Video?"

"Everything's clear so far," Amar said. "But we're still
inside. Once we get out, who knows?"

"All we can do," Nikos said. *"How soon to launch?"*

Maxine glanced down at her console. "Ten minutes until
the last shuttle leaves, then one hour after that for us."

"Once you lock down transmissions," Nikos said, *"you
are to unlock for nothing, understand? I know we've talked
about it, but I want it clear. Give them nothing to track. No
matter what happens to us, I don't want to hear a thing
from you."*

"We understand," I said. "Radio silence, all the way."

We would still receive the command channel transmissions, which would be dispersion-broadcast so there would be no way to track them to us, as well as video from three different cameras and from a tracking probe the *Argonos* would launch after we all were gone; the probe would maintain a constant distance from the ship as it accelerated toward the jump. But we would be unable to send anything to anyone. We would be mute. Another precaution that was probably pointless, but almost everything was impossible to be sure about; so we took every precaution we could.

"I hear anything, I'll cancel all transmissions from the Argonos." He paused. *"And if something goes wrong here, I don't want you turning around and heading back. I know there are only five of you, but you've got a hold full of equipment, food, and supplies that could mean the survival of several thousand people."*

Maxine smiled. "Don't worry, Captain. No matter what happens, we'll leave all of you here to rot."

"Thanks, Maxine."

"Five minutes until the shuttle goes," Amar said.

We sat in silence. I swiveled my seat around in a full circle, studying the dark interior of the harvester hold. We were leaving the *Argonos*, never to return. My home. Home for all of us. No longer.

"Captain, we've picked up something." It was Cardenas, on the command channel.

"What, Margita? From their ship?"

"Yes. Very subtle, Captain. A change in hull reflectivity. It's increased. I don't understand it, and I don't understand what it could mean."

"Anything else?"

"Not yet. But we'd better expect something. What's left to launch?"

"The last shuttle in a couple of minutes, then the cargo harvester in another hour." He paused. *"You think we should hold up on the shuttle?"*

"I don't know," Cardenas answered. *"Maybe they both should go immediately."*

"Bartolomeo?"

"Let's not make any drastic changes yet," I said. "Hold the shuttle for five minutes. If nothing changes, let it go."

"*Sounds good. I'm switching over to their channel.*"

Silence for a minute, then Nikos came back on.

"*They're holding. Anything, Margita?*"

"*Not yet.*"

Another five minutes of silence that stretched on and on, time dilating.

"*Off channel,*" Nikos said.

"Amar," Maxine said. "Bring the shuttle bay to monitor one."

We watched the shuttle slide out of the transport bay, drift away from the *Argonos* for a minute, then fire its attitude jets, slowly swinging around. The jets cut, then the main engines fired.

A strange, rolling vibration went through us, ending with a sudden jolt.

"*What the hell was that?*" Nikos shouted. "*Margita?*"

"*I don't know, Captain. We're not detecting . . . no, wait, something's coming off the alien ship . . . I don't know what . . .*"

I looked at monitor two. Amar had the alien ship on it, and we could see a sphere of silvery light take shape, detach, then eject from the ship's surface with an incredible speed, headed for the rear of the *Argonos*.

"*What is that, Margita?*"

There was no answer. Amar was switching images, trying to follow the sphere. It was headed for the shuttle. Seconds later, it struck the shuttle and burst in a shower of silver glitter.

The shuttle engines died. But the shuttle continued to move away from the two ships, although much more slowly than the other shuttles had, and there were no obvious signs of damage.

Crackling sounds, then someone's voice came over the command channel.

"*We're hit! We're hit!*" It was Masters, one of Shuttle Eleven's pilots, breaking radio silence.

"*Masters!*" Nikos barked. For a brief moment I thought

he was going to berate Masters for unlocking transmission, but he didn't. *"Damage or injuries?"*

"Don't know, Captain. Don't think so. There was no concussion . . . we could see it coming, but when it burst over us we felt nothing except a kind of tingling, and the engines died. All other systems are still functioning. And we're moving. Slow, but moving."

"Captain!" Cardenas again. *"Here comes another one!"*

On the monitor, the silvery sheen was once again forming a sphere on the hull of the alien ship. The sphere detached and ejected from the ship, directed again at the shuttle.

The cameras followed its trajectory more closely this time, knowing what to expect. One zoomed in on it, and we could see more details. The sphere seemed solid, or at least opaque, its surface a glistening silver, electricity-like filaments sparking across it.

It burst over the shuttle, just like the previous one had, doing no visible damage.

"Masters. Status."

There was no answer at first. A minute passed, then two. Finally a faint transmission came through.

"We lost everything," Masters said. *"Systems are back up, but only at three-quarters power."*

"Masters, try to refire the engines," I said. "If they start, tell everyone to hang on and blast out of here at six g's."

"Captain?"

"Bartolomeo's right. Do it!"

"Jimmy," Maxine said.

Jimmy nodded. He knew what she wanted. He tapped away at the console and the harvester launcher lurched toward the open bay doors. There were no energy fields here, just the vacuum of space waiting for us.

The engines came to life on the shuttle, bright orange flaring on monitor one.

"We're on!" Masters said.

The shuttle engines erupted, orange turning almost white and blue. The shuttle's speed increased, slowly at first, then faster and faster.

"Number three!" Cardenas shouted.

"Wait, Jimmy," Maxine said.

Another sphere was forming. Just before it reached full size, Maxine turned to Jimmy.

"Release!" Maxine ordered.

Jimmy triggered the launch pad release; there was a slight jolt, then we dropped through the open doors.

The sphere detached. We drifted out from the *Argonos*. The sphere shot away from the alien ship, again headed toward the shuttle. We weren't in its path, but we were much larger than the shuttle, and I knew what Maxine was thinking. And hoping.

"Ten-second burn on the engines, then shut them down. Shut down *everything*!"

We lurched with the sudden acceleration, but almost immediately it stopped. Then all the lights went out, and the cabin was on batteries. Even the monitors were down, but now we were outside the *Argonos* and we could see the sphere coming.

What Maxine hoped for occurred. The sphere changed course and headed for us. Ten seconds later, it struck.

Like Masters said, there was no concussion. Silver glitter penetrated the harvester, a shower moving through us, tingling like electricity. A few moments later, it all faded away.

"Power up, Jimmy."

Lights and life support came up first, the monitors came to life, then he refired the engines. The vibration as they came to life was incredibly comforting.

"Lock down transmissions and go!" Nikos ordered.

"Yes, Captain."

"Lock down now!"

"Good luck, Captain." Maxine nodded to Jimmy, and he locked down the transmission. "Kick them, Jimmy."

The seats locked into place, the vibration became a roar, and I was crushed back in my seat as we blasted away.

55

W E were massive, barely maneuverable, and we accelerated slowly, the engines roaring. Jimmy angled us away from the ship, but not much; the quickest way to put distance between us and the alien starship was running the length of the *Argonos*.

The shuttle was still accelerating, growing smaller on the monitor as it left the *Argonos* behind. From the pilot's cabin we could see its bright tail flaring, a tiny circle of fire against the black sky, like a comet blazing away.

As he'd promised, Nikos left the command channel open, and now his voice came over it.

"Engage drive engines," he said.

We were nearing the rear of the *Argonos*, the drive engines coming into view—black and red and massive, the metal surfaces pocked and streaked and scoured by the detritus of space. They began to glow and shudder.

"We're too damn close," Maxine said.

"Got it," Jimmy said.

The harvester was slow to respond, slow to change direction. The engines seemed to strain, becoming unbalanced under Jimmy's commands; the entire structure of the harvester appeared ready to give. But the *Argonos* began to fall away from us just as we were approaching the drive engines now building up their energies.

"Number four!" Cardenas called out. *"No, no, it's . . . something different this time, I don't know . . ."*

The alien ship was aglow, the silvery skin encasing it; everything seemed to be warping, distorting. Then suddenly a mass swelled up from the ship; it quickly differentiated into twenty or thirty spheres which burst forth like a star exploding.

"Shut it down, Jimmy! Everything, dammit!"

Jimmy's fingers danced across the console, cutting the engines and power. We were moving fairly quickly now.

"Full acceleration," ordered Nikos.

The spatial distortion from the *Argonos* drive engines reached us just before the first of the spheres. The harvester rolled and swayed, metal buckling. Nausea drove into my belly as I lost my sense of balance.

"Hang on," said Maxine. "Just hang on."

A sphere burst through us, followed a few seconds later by two more bursts. I felt electrified, and the sweat that broke out all over my skin seemed to burn, a frozen, charged, and invisible searing.

"Captain," Cardenas said, *"A dozen objects have just launched from the alien ship."*

"Bring up the Metzenbauer Field."

There was a long silence. We were flying mute and almost blind, the engines still down.

"Maxine?" Jimmy asked.

"Don't do anything," she said. "Let them think we're dead."

We still had plenty of speed, though, and the two ships were receding from us; even faster now, I realized, because the *Argonos* was accelerating, though with the combined mass of the two ships they would be gaining velocity slowly at first. I swiveled my seat around, but we were at an odd angle, and I could only see parts of the *Argonos* and the alien ship.

"I'll be damned," Cardenas said. *"The Field stopped all of them, whatever they were."*

"Jump coordinates set?" Nikos asked.

"They're locked in, Captain. Nothing's changed."

"How long until we've got the velocity?"

"Checking now."

A long, tense silence. *"We can do it in thirty-seven minutes if we maintain full acceleration."*

"Do it, then."

"Captain." Someone else's voice. One of the crew?

"Yes, Kirilen."

"I think they're bringing up their own drive engines. We're picking up massive field distortions from the far side of their hull. Not the same kind we produce, but it could be their drives."

No response from Nikos. Cardenas finally said, *"Shit,"* in a voice little more than a whisper.

"What is it?" Pär asked.

Jimmy shook his head. "If they get their drive engines up, and if they're on the far side, they can counteract the acceleration of the *Argonos*. They might be able to prevent the *Argonos* from gaining enough velocity to make the jump. Or delay it long enough to attack in some other way. Something."

"Amar," Maxine asked, "how are the batteries?"

"Full reserve," she said. "We've got hours."

"Okay, bring the monitors back up."

In addition to the bad angle, the two ships were getting smaller and smaller so we could hardly make anything out. The monitors came up, and Amar brought in the transmissions from the *Argonos*. The harvester's cameras, even at full magnification, didn't show much more than we could see with our own eyes, but the *Argonos* cameras were still transmitting clear signals.

The alien ship looked dead again, although the view was slightly obscured now by the Metzenbauer Field. But the *Argonos* was definitely alive, the drive engines ablaze with blue and white fire, surrounded by a corona of distortion.

"The trailing probe was launched," Amar said quietly, as if we had to be careful even with the transmission locked out. Maybe we needed to be; what did we know?

We looked at the monitor screen dedicated to the trailing

probe's video transmissions—we had a perfect view of the two ships, filling the monitor. The probe was trailing the *Argonos*, but far off to the side, so the images weren't washed out by the drive engines.

"*Anything yet, Kirilen?*" Nikos, again.

"*No, sir. The field distortions persist, but there seems to be no acceleration, no thrust of any kind in any direction. Maybe it's not a drive.*"

I could hear Nikos sigh over the channel. "*It may not be a drive,*" he said, "*but it's got to be something.*"

"*Twenty-nine minutes,*" Cardenas said.

Silence for a minute, maybe two. Maybe even longer. Time was distending, becoming impossible to gauge. There was nothing to do, nothing to say. But the *Argonos* engines continued to burn.

"*Captain.*" It was Cardenas. "*Do you see that?*"

No immediate response, then, "*Yes. What . . . ?*"

"Look at that," Pär whispered, pointing at the monitor.

"Amar, bring that over to monitor one."

The video from the probe was switched over to the largest monitor, and now we could better see what was happening. There seemed to be a fracture forming in the alien ship, the gap flaring with a pale blue light. Then another fracture appeared on the other side so they were flanking the *Argonos*.

A booming sound came over the command channel, but no voices. Then Kirilen's voice, panicky. "*Something's coming out . . . !*"

Then we could see it, a dark, curling extension emerging from the alien ship. It appeared to be a massive cable of some kind, extending, lengthening; then it whipped around like the tentacle of a monstrous ocean beast. There was a brilliant flash as it penetrated the Metzenbauer Field and wrapped itself across the hull of the *Argonos*, another *boom* sounding, this one louder and more violent.

Alarms blared over the command channel.

"*The Field's down!*" Kirilen shouted. "*And we've got hull breaches!*"

There was another *boom* like the first; then a second

cable or tentacle emerged from the other crack in the alien ship, whipping through space before it struck the *Argonos* and wrapped itself across the hull, overlapping the first.

Leviathan, I thought, wondering if the bishop was watching this, if he knew what was happening. If he did, I'm sure he was convinced that damnation was coming for him.

"More hull breaches, Captain."

"Shut off the alarms, damn it! And how are the engines?"

The alarms ceased abruptly. Then another came on for a moment before it, too, was shut down.

"Engines are fine," Cardenas reported. *"The Field is down and won't come back up, but the engines are completely undisturbed. We're still accelerating."*

Two more *booms* sounded, and two more of the cables emerged from the alien ship, slamming across the *Argonos* hull. No alarms sounded this time, but Kirilen announced there were more hull breaches.

"Time?" Nikos asked.

"Fifteen minutes," Cardenas replied.

The *Argonos* now looked like prey in the clutches of its predator. There were no more booming sounds, no more cables. There was no change at all for longer than I could stand.

"Captain?" It was the bishop.

"Get off this channel, Bernard. We don't have time for this."

"We have all the time in the universe, Captain. Don't you understand what's happening to us? Don't you understand . . . ?"

He was cut off in midsentence. *"Thank God he's not here in the bridge,"* Nikos said.

"We've got movement," Kirilen broke in.

"What the hell do you mean, movement?"

"Inside the ship. I'm trying to pick up something on video. It's in several areas, near the hull breaches."

"You sure it's not our own people?"

"No, I'm not sure, but there shouldn't be anyone near those areas."

A tense quiet followed. More seconds, then minutes stretching out. It was agonizing being unable to do anything, unable to help.

"Damn, most of the security cameras are dead around there, probably damaged during the breaches."

"That's all right," Nikos said. *"Just keep trying."*

"I am . . . wait. Here. Here's something. The light's not good, though . . ." His voice trailed away, and there was more quiet.

"My God," Kirilen whispered. *"Look at that thing . . ."*

I looked from one monitor to another, just as the others were doing, but we had no interior shots. Whatever video Kirilen had picked up wasn't being transmitted.

"What do you think happened?" Nikos asked. His voice remained calm.

"Boarded through the cable," Cardenas answered.

"How close is the nearest hull breach to us?"

"Let me see . . ." Kirilen said, his voice still shaky. *"Seven levels and eight sectors. I can't get any video at that breach, but sensors are picking up some kind of movement there."*

"Engines?" Nikos asked again.

"No change, Captain. Acceleration steady."

"Time?"

"Nine minutes."

"Good, then it doesn't matter, whatever they are. There's no way they can reach us in time to stop the jump."

"But, Captain. Look at it!"

I squirmed in my chair, both wishing I could see what Kirilen was talking about, and glad I couldn't. Glad we couldn't really know what they would soon be facing.

"It doesn't matter," Nikos repeated. *"Besides, we've prepared, haven't we?"*

There was a slight pause, before Kirilen spoke again. *"Sorry, Captain."* The panic was gone, and he sounded composed.

On monitor one, nothing had changed. The two ships were locked together, and the drive engines continued to burn fiercely. But other than that, there was no movement on either ship.

We watched and waited in silence. Those on the *Argonos* were silent as well, except for Cardenas calling out the time every two minutes. Finally, it was time.

"One minute," she said.

"Coordinates locked in?"

"Locked in."

"Start jump sequence."

"Jump sequence started."

"Good luck, everyone," Nikos said. *"Lock down transmissions."*

"Locking down."

The command channel went dead. So did all the video transmissions we'd been receiving except for the one from the probe, which remained on monitor one. We all stared at it, waiting. Waiting.

I had never seen a jump from outside the ship, of course. None of us had. None of us knew what to expect.

The universe opened up and turned itself inside out.

A ring of distortion formed around the *Argonos*. Space seemed to twist; even the shape of the two ships appeared to bend and flow, as if becoming unstable. Starlight curved around the ring so that the stars became like liquid mercury, elongated arcs that slowly spiraled. The starlight stretched out, took on an almost reddish hue in places, blue in others.

As the ring grew, it separated from the two ships, like a hole opening. In the gap between the ring and the ships was . . . nothing.

Black. A deep black that was darker than night. No stars. An abyss. A true void. Discontinuity.

The curved starlight began to spin faster now, a whirlpool of colors bending and stretching with a ghostly sheen.

The harvester shuddered slightly, and I felt a queasiness rolling through my belly again.

"What is that?"

"I think we've been caught by the space distortions," Maxine said.

"We're decelerating," Jimmy announced.

The ring continued to grow, the vortex of starlight swirling still faster now.

"I'm not sure," Jimmy said, "but I think it might be pulling us in."

"We're too far," Maxine said. "It'll be over long before we reach them."

"Are you sure?"

"Of course I'm not sure."

"Then let's start up the engines!"

"Let it go, Jimmy."

I looked away from the monitor and out of the cabin. Maxine was right, I decided. Everything looked close on the monitor, but now I could barely make out the growing, swirling ring far behind us. I turned back to the monitor to watch.

A cocoon of glistening white energy had begun to form around the *Argonos*. As the shimmering strands of light spun around the ship, they flowed forward and began to enclose the alien ship as well.

Suddenly the black cables were released from the *Argonos* and began to writhe, whipping and slamming against the *Argonos*, both ships shuddering with the violence.

"They're going to tear the *Argonos* apart!" Amar cried out.

"They're trying to break free," Pär said.

I think he was right. But it was too late for that. The cocoon grew and swelled, filaments spinning, engulfing both ships, and soon we lost sight of everything within it.

The cocoon and the two ships moved through the swirling rim of the discontinuity, into the blackness. All the light from the energy cocoon was sucked away, and suddenly there was nothing but the black void surrounded by the vortex of twisted starlight.

The swirling of the vortex slowed, the starlight untwisting. Then it all collapsed in on itself, and the black night sky of space, spangled with the cold shining light of stars, returned to normal.

They were gone.

56

THERE isn't much more to write, now. We are nearing Antioch, less than two weeks away. Most of us have survived.

We lost the last shuttle, the one piloted by Virgil Masters. I thought it meant we'd lost our new captain, but Geller had gone with the previous shuttle. We don't know what happened to the last one. After the *Argonos* had made the jump, we tried to contact them, but without success. We continue to try, broadcasting a transmission every hour, but after all these weeks no one holds out much hope anymore. It's possible the shuttle is out there, intact and functional, headed for Antioch just as we are, and will one day arrive and join us. Possible.

Over the course of the three days following the jump, with the aid of navigational beacons and regular communications, all of the other vessels—shuttles and harvesters alike—were able to rendezvous, forming a space caravan which has stayed together now for nearly four months. We travel at a constant velocity, a static string of vehicles, and sometimes we have to take it on faith that we are actually making progress, getting closer to our destination.

Faith.

Four months is a long time under these conditions. Too long. Arguments and squabbles and screaming matches are too numerous to count. Actual fights erupt with regularity, and some have become quite violent; three people have been killed. Several others have died in accidents, two more apparently of old age. A number have died from illness, including fifty-three on Shuttle Six when an epidemic of a still unidentified disease broke out and swept through the passengers; but, as I've said, most of us have survived.

Pär and I, along with Maxine, Jimmy, and Amar, periodically rotated out of the harvester and onto other vessels during the first few weeks, to give us a break from the confined pilot cabin, which is the only habitable zone on the harvester. But I soon discovered I prefer the solitude of the harvester, and I have not left it in three months.

I am still blamed by most people for what happened. No one says anything to me, but it is obvious from the furtive glances, the sour expressions, the abrupt silence whenever I approach, the deliberate avoidance of my company. I can't disagree with their feelings; even if Nikos was right, that docking to the alien ship didn't make any difference, hardly anyone sees it that way. That I was able to come up with the means of escape does little to diminish the sense of resentment and hostility that emanates from nearly everyone.

Sometimes it becomes almost too much for me to bear. At those times I wish that I had stayed with Nikos and the others on the *Argonos*, no matter what happened to them. I imagine that I would have felt a sense of accomplishment that seems elusive to me now.

PÄR is one of the few people who does not seem to hold it all against me, and he has stayed on the harvester with me these last three months. His presence is a comfort. And there are small pleasures that come with his friendship—he loaded onto the harvester, in an easily accessible location, his entire store of coffee beans. He has carefully, although generously, rationed them during the voyage, sharing with whoever is stationed on the harvester. His supply will last, he says, at least a few weeks after landfall. He has also told me that he stored a large number of pre-germinated coffee-plant seeds, determined to start another plantation once we reach Antioch.

He has become a great friend, and I feel I would be lost without him.

FRANCIS, too, has become a friend, along with his sister, Catherine. They jet over to the harvester to visit for two or three days at a time. Francis seems much older than his age, as if whatever remained of his childhood had been taken from him. He almost never smiles.

I think often of Father Veronica. It would be nice to believe that her spirit, her *soul*, lives on and is somehow with us yet: watching over us, guiding us in whatever way she can. I want to believe this.

I don't. I still do not believe—not in an afterlife, not in heaven and hell, and I do not believe in the existence of God.

And yet . . . and yet she *is* still with me in a strange and mysterious way—through my memories of her, through my imagination. I talk to her, I imagine what her replies would be, and I talk further with her. I have long, internal conversations, discussions and even arguments; they sometimes bring me comfort, ease my grief, my guilt. She would probably say I was praying, and perhaps I am.

WHEN I was in the shuttle bay all those months ago, standing at Pär's side as we prepared to mutiny and leave the *Argonos*, I had believed we were about to begin a new life. It didn't happen then, but we are about to now.

Despite everything, I have great hopes for the future. Life is difficult for all of us now, but that will change when we make landfall on Antioch. We will have other difficulties, to be certain, hardships and trying times, but it will be different. Now, we can do nothing about our circumstances. There, on Antioch, we will have the opportunity to work together to overcome our hardships, to share and cooperate as a real community and build a new life on a new world.

Perhaps we will fail. Perhaps we will be unable to overcome our differences, our selfishness, the resentments and anger of our previous lives on the *Argonos*. But it is also possible that we will succeed. I find myself surprisingly optimistic and hopeful. This, too, may be part of Father Veronica's legacy.

THIS personal history is nearly done. I have taken a cue from August Toller, and have prepared one of the space-burial coffins. I'll keep the original document with us, but I will put two copies in different formats inside the coffin, seal it, and launch it into space before we reach Antioch. Perhaps some day it will be found. Perhaps some day *we* will be found.

And so I end this record with hope and anticipation. An old life ends. A new life begins.

Life. That, at least, is something I believe in.

PRAISE FOR THE NOVELS OF
Richard Paul Russo

Ship of Fools

"By deftly fusing two familiar themes—the self-sufficient starship that has lost its way and first contact with a mysterious alien object—Russo has carved out a sizable narrative space for his philosophical and spiritual concerns. He is not afraid to take on the question of evil in a divinely ordered universe . . . This is an ambitious novel of ideas that generates considerable suspense while respecting its sources, its characters, and most important, the reader." —*The New York Times*

"Space opera was never quite like this tale. Anyone who was enthralled by the aliens from the movie *Alien* will love Richard Paul Russo's latest masterpiece, *Ship of Fools*. The title is appropriate. The author creates a shocker of an ending that no one could have predicted, probably not even the author when he was drafting the novel. Even the day-to-day details of life on the spaceship seem fascinating as readers are simply hooked by a wonderful plot that would make a powerful movie." —*Midwest Book Review*

"The author of *Carlucci's Edge* explores the timelessness of space travel and its effects on the human consciousness while simultaneously telling a tale of high adventure and personal drama in the far future. A good choice for most sf collections." —*Library Journal*

"An intensely riveting tale that evokes primordial feelings of xenophobia. Richard Paul Russo freely uses misdirection, keeping the reader slightly off-kilter and setting the stage for confrontations on several levels. His bleak portrayal of life aboard ship is unsettling with its gritty realism." —*Romantic Times*

continued . . .

Carlucci's Heart

"Might well be Russo's breakthrough novel . . . This new effort surpasses anything he has done before . . . A lot more realistic than most near future SF, as well as being just plain better written than most of it."

—*Science Fiction Chronicle*

"A winner. It's set in the same run-down San Francisco as *Carlucci's Edge*, marked by the same empathetic characterization, and—perhaps because the weirder side of the cultural milieu is less prominent here—enough more convincing for me to call it potential award material."

—*Analog*

"A tough, down and dirty story that will appeal to fans of police novels as well as science fiction fans . . . An excellent piece of writing."

—*Dead Trees Review*

"Russo skillfully blends high-tech concepts and hard-boiled prose in a novel that will keep you turning pages late into the night. Carlucci is a Chandleresque hero . . . This is classic crime fiction as well as classic speculative fiction, and a thorough pleasure to read."

—*Contra Costa Times*